HORIZONS PAST

Bill Stephens'
Other Books

Novels

Vámonos!
Woke Up This Morning
(July 2013)

Short fiction

Life or Death
(August 2013)

Nonfiction

Losing the Lard: Permanent Weight Loss
(July 2013)

HORIZONS PAST

A NOVEL
BY
Bill Stephens

Published by Franklin Scribes Publishers. Franklin Scribes is a register trademark of Franklin Scribes Publishers.

Franklin Scribes books may be purchased in bulk for educational, business, fundraising, or sales promotion. For information please email: SpecialMarkets@franklinscribes.com

Publisher's Note: Horizons Past is a work of fiction. References to events, establishments, organizations, locals, and real people living or deceased are intended merely to equip the fiction with a sense of authenticity and shadings of local color. They are used fictitiously. All other names, characters, places, and all dialogue and incidents portrayed in this book are the product of my imagination.

Trade Paperback Edition

Shout Out to Author:
stephens.billy@att. Net

Summary: Horizons Past examines the possibility of two people with opposite lifestyles developing a lasting relationship, when all they have in common is a shared goal – to escape who they are. Guilt, "Hollywood," and a hurricane all collide, keeping the resolution just out of reach until the reclusive poet and movie star learn – letting go of each other is even harder than letting go of the past

ISBN 978-0-9886433-5-2 (softcover)

Note on Kindle Format us ASIN: B003GSLY0I

Printed in the United States of America

Dedicated to
Mustang Island.

Chapter 1: Mustang Island, 1999

State Park Ranger Jeffrey Randall slowed his Bronco and stopped before turning onto what was left of Fish Pass Road. Lottie looked at him. "It's something we really have to do, right?" Jeffrey nodded agreement, but said nothing.

He had driven the twelve miles of Texas Park Road 361 between Mustang Island State Park and Port Aransas several times daily in the seven weeks since the hurricane. His days were now totally dedicated to rebuilding the park's infrastructure, but each day after his shift, he drove into town to help friends with their efforts to rebuild and to regain their normal lives.

There were temporary repairs to the road, but potholes and washed out sections of pavement remained, which still caused him to bounce and weave through a series of small detours. Progress was slow on this trip out from Port Aransas, but neither he nor Lottie were anxious to reach their destination.

Since the hurricane, Jeffrey had become numbed to the destruction: the brown landscape killed by salt water standing for weeks; the dunes, flattened and spread over the island like Silly Putty. The watermark still prominent above the second floor of the highrise beach condos; their windows and doors now open holes staring blankly at the contents flushed through them by the storm surge and strewn about their once well kept grounds. The beach houses that had vanished still got to him, though. Until now he hadn't allowed himself to look at one particular cluster of three broken, leaning pilings standing like giant hat pins stuck in a sandy pincushion, a monument to the missing home that was their destination today.

Jeffrey downshifted and swung onto the ruts that were now the road. The Bronco bumped and lurched along the road until it finally cleared what was left of the dunes and hit the beach. He turned north and drove along the hardpan left by today's ebbing tide. The beach was surprisingly clean, and they both looked out on the Gulf of Mexico, rocking under a calm breeze. Jeffrey drew in a deep breath of salt air and held it before exhaling. "Out there I could almost forget all the misery behind us."

Lottie nodded acknowledgment, but not agreement. "I wonder if we'll ever forget." She picked up a red leather book from the seat between them and silently mouthed the title, *Horizons Passed*, by Christopher Maven. She reached down to adjust the ice bucket at her feet that held a bunch of mixed flowers and a champagne bottle. "I'll try not to get emotional, but I can't promise... "

Jeffrey smiled at her through eyes already glistening but said nothing. He stopped abreast of the three pilings, and they both sat in the Bronco for a while before Jeffrey said, "It's time we did this." He stepped from the truck, walked to Lottie's door, and offered his hand to help her out. She still clutched the book, and Jeffrey lifted the ice bucket from the floorboard and reached back for two plastic cups that rolled on the floor beside it. They walked toward the pilings and stood silently for an extended time, finally moving to the water's edge. Lottie handed him the book, removed her sandals, and took the flowers. She waded into the surf to her knees and gently placed the flowers in the water and stood as they drifted seaward on the tide.

Jeffrey handed her the book when she returned to shore. With the late afternoon sun behind them they gazed out to where an almost cloudless sky met the water. When she opened the book Lottie choked with emotion, but composed herself and read:

Horizons past were filled with dread
That barrier bisecting earth and sky
That stifled all escape.
Then you appeared and filled the void
With touch, and smile, and sacred scent,

And with your eyes you cast a light And woke my soul
To dream To love To Soar
Beyond horizons passed.

Jeffrey loosed the cork on the champagne. The sound of it exploding from the bottle was startling in the quiet; abrupt and urgent as it flew away toward the bisecting barrier. He handed one of the two cups to Lottie and filled each with champagne. They touched their cups, turned toward the horizon, and Jeffrey said, "To Chris."

Lottie added, as a single tear made its way down her cheek, "To the man we both loved."

Chapter 2

Christopher Maven flailed off the couch just before dawn and lay on the floor with fear creeping through his pores as sweat. He sagged as the terror slowly ebbed, and he saw beside him the empty wine bottle that had put him to sleep on the couch the night before and launched his re-visitation of the dream. He sat on the edge of the couch, gathering himself, and finally staggered to his desk. He picked up a desk calendar, tore off the "September 30, 1999" page, crumpled it, and dropped it into the wastebasket.

He had struggled beyond memory with his demons, endlessly repressing them, driving them deeper into those subconscious pools where they could repose with no compulsion to re-form. But vulnerability opened like an old wound when sleep dissolved his defenses. The scene, always the same, always a vivid scroll slowly unwinding through his psyche, projecting images of that part of his life he had tried for a lifetime to escape.

The rest of the predawn he sat at the desk, head in hands. Now, he stood looking up at the bedroom loft, and the demons of the night returned again. He moved to the desk, picked up a notebook, stuffing it into a beach bag along with a bottle of water. He wrapped a towel around his nakedness and headed out the door to the deck.

He stood for a moment on the deck of his beach house wearing only the modesty towel. At age sixty he felt good about his dark tan and youthful muscle tone that made others think him younger, even with his mane of silver hair. The horizon to the east was tousled and ragged with clouds slathered in first light and trimmed in orange hues. "Red sky in morning, sailors take warning, " he mumbled, staring for some time, first to the left and then to the right. The Texas beach stretched seamless and uninhabited in both directions.

Dunes shouldered the beach comfortably while dead calm left the surf clear to the sand. Fall's first norther had swept the beach free of seaweed and clutter the day before, but weakened by the effort, stalled and now retreated from the onslaught of the building cumulus. The cool air was still and clear enough to see into tomorrow.

This makes it worthwhile, he thought. He drew in a deep breath of air filled with the watermelon smell of sea trout schooling in the surf.

With hot summer days and tourists gone, the natural order of things returned as if from migration. Silence, except for an occasional seagull and the far distant hum of tires on the highway, was magnified in the fall air.

"A wake-up call for my soul," he said aloud.

Moving down the dune-bridge, he stepped onto the beach and walked toward the water, pausing at a raised shoal of sand above the beach, which, the day before, was packed by the surf and now stood dry above the nighttime high tide. He nodded, smiled, and wrote for less than a minute in a small notebook. Closing it, he looked again at the building clouds, shrugged, and retreated into the house.

Still bothered by the previous night, he felt he needed a distraction from the restlessness that stirred in him like an invisible insect buzzing around his head. He looked back at the water and thought, fishing! I need purification by fishing! He gathered his beach bag, fishing rods, sand-spike rod holders, bait bucket, cast net, umbrella, and chair. He headed back over the dune bridge. His passion for fishing often went underappreciated, like anything too familiar, but now the thought of battling "the big one" loosed a bedspring of excitement in his stomach.

Trish Lowe opened her Omni Hotel penthouse curtains, casting her eyes skyward at the roiling overcast and said, "Not a chance!" The sky, mottled and turbulent with dark clouds, made today's outdoor scenes impossible. The four weeks of filming since arriving in Corpus Christi, Texas, were blessed with great weather, and yesterday's cloudless sky provided a productive backdrop for movie making, but forget it today. There would be no way to match the sky in the continuing scene.

At the room desk she wrote a note asking the director to shoot around her today. After dressing in her jogging clothes, she grabbed her beach tote bag, her favorite book of poetry, and her room key. The cell phone on the nightstand caught her attention, but shaking her head she said, "Not today."

She left her suite and stopped by the concierge desk. "Ramon, give this note to my driver when he arrives, please." She handed him a tip and hurried through the lobby to the hotel parking lot.

The candy-apple red Sebring convertible flashed across the John F. Kennedy Causeway Bridge, top down, and the cool salt air breathed new life into her jaded soul. Her ponytail fluttered behind her baseball cap and her large sunglasses masked her face, completing her disguise. She slowed at the Padre Island red light, and turned left on Texas Park Road 361 toward Port Aransas.

Mustang Island State Park had been her sanctuary since shortly after her arrival on location in Corpus Christi to begin shooting her latest movie, but today she needed complete solitude. She drove past the entrance and did not turn toward the beach until Fish Pass Road. The convertible slowed, laboring through the loose beach sand at the pavement's end. It shuddered, bucked twice, and stuck. She slammed the accelerator to the floor, and the tires spun, spraying sand skyward, burying the back tires to the axle.

"Shit!" she shouted to a vacant beach. "I wanted to jog, but not back to town." As she fumbled in her beach bag, she remembered leaving her cell phone at the hotel to prevent unwanted disturbances "Damn." Her voice echoed again.

She stood in the car seat looking for help closer than the state park. Heat waves now shimmered from the sand, and the clouds drifted over like puffs of meringue, offering shade but promising showers. In the far distance she could see a beach umbrella and chair and behind that, a house above the dunes.

"Can do." She raised the convertible top, stepped from the car, and locked it. She checked her jogging gear one more time and set off at a lively cadence toward her deliverance.

Christopher Maven jolted from his sleep under the umbrella when something hit the sand behind him, and he jumped again when a female voice panted, "Wow! I think I'm gonna die. I can't jog another step. How far is it from Fish Pass Road to here?"

He didn't answer.

"Hello? Look, I'm stuck in the sand down at Fish Pass. It looked like about a mile up here, but it took forever." She still spoke to the back of his beach chair.

"Distances are a little deceiving when the air is this clear." The answer came from the chair.

"Ten more steps, and you would be giving me mouth-to-mouth right now."

"I think I'm sorry I missed that part."

Her head snapped up from her knees, and she considered the silver hair sticking above the canvas beach-lounging chair before answering, "Actually, I hope you'll help me pull my car out, or at least let me use your phone."

"Can't help you." There was agitation in the voice.

"Why not? I'm willing to pay."

"No car."

"You don't have a car? How do you get around?"

"Not that it's your concern, but I have a bicycle for emergencies."

"A bicycle? Well, could you phone for help?"

"No phone."

"No phone? Is there any way you can help me? Like I said, I'm willing to pay." She was beginning to get a little upset.

"Afraid I can't help you. Sorry." The statement sounded final.

"But... but why? I mean, I need help. Can't you understand that?" She was moving on the offensive.

"No clothes," he replied.

"No clothes?" she sputtered. "For God's sake, man, you don't have to dress for the occasion!"

"No clothes now." he said with emphasis.

"You're naked?"

"You've got it. I wasn't expecting company." He added, "I never expect company."

"Let's see if I'm right. I did a forced march just to find a nude man on a public beach with no telephone and no car?"

"Like I said. I didn't invite you."

She could see his arm make an emphatic gesture. She sat quietly in the sand for a time wondering what to do and thinking about her bad luck to run into this complete asshole.

"You still there?" His voice was a little more conciliatory.

"Yes."

After a slight pause he said, "Well, if you'll avert your eyes, I'll get up and do the best I can with this towel here. I guess I'll have to help just to get you to leave."

She thought about the millions of men dying to show her theirs if she showed them hers, but here was this grumpy old bastard telling her not to peek. "Okay, I promise I won't peek." She broke into laughter in spite of herself.

Christopher stood, turned to get the towel, and saw a stunning body sitting on the sand swathed in robin's egg blue Spandex, and black hair in a ponytail pulled through the back of a ball cap, but, as promised, no eyes. He quickly did a Turkish bath towel-wrap. "Sorry about your problem. I don't see many people around here, and any I do always want something." He started to walk away, then turned. "Why don't you sit under the umbrella while I go inside and get dressed?"

As she looked up, the sun produced a halo effect silhouetting his face and bushy silver hair. Her experienced eye gave high marks to his physique, but judging by his face and hair, he looked to be much older than she. I wonder what's under that towel, she thought. Then she waited for the inevitable exclamation, "You're Trish Lowe!" When it didn't come, she asked, "You catching a late vacation or just a cold?"

"No, I live here," he said with no apology.

She swung back to look at the beach house and wide-eyed, blurted out, "What on earth do you do out here?"

"You're sitting on it." He pointed to the sand.

"No, I'm sitting on what I do." She looked for a response to her joke, but there was none.

He just pointed at the sand.

For the first time since she collapsed, she looked down and saw writing, lines like poetry scratched into the sand:

> *The wind is changing.*
> *Will I hold fast?*
> *Or drift past the horizon*
> *Like dunes and clouds?*

She was sitting on the "S" in "clouds." "I'm sorry," she said.

"I wasn't looking when I flopped."

"No problem. It's just part of the test." Christopher adjusted his towel for security.

"The test?"

"Sometimes a verse or poem needs validation, so I pick a place and write it in the sand. If it makes it through the night, I know it deserves a shot at immortality." He traced a line in the sand with his toe.

"Why wouldn't it make it through the night?"

"Tide, wind, rain, even tire tracks... and, of course, people."

"People like me?"

He thought for a few seconds before replying, "No... I don't think people like you." He shook his head in disagreement.

"This one made the cut?" she pointed at the sand.

"Yup!" He was beginning to enjoy the conversation.

"What if it hadn't?"

"I would forget it." He thought for a second and added, "or if I really liked it, I might try again."

"That sounds like cheating."

"It might not be smart trusting everything to the unknown." He looked away and dug his toe into the word "horizon" as he replied. "Look, I'll go in and put something on. I'll be right back."

Trish turned and regarded the water for the first time. The surf, normally opaque from the sand, today lay blue to the edge. Tiny swells undulated and rippled to the beach. She breathed in the pungent smell of salt air and exhaled gradually. The lines on three fishing poles spiked in the sand swagged into the surf. A flock of gulls circled over a spot directly out from them. Several swooped, hitting the water before rising again with a small fish for a paycheck.

A gossamer mantle floated through her soul seining away all the debris. This was it! Sanctuary. Paradise with a naked sand-poet thrown in for good measure. Anonymity. Freedom from the constant grind of stardom.

The longest fishing rod began to quiver, then bow, and flex. "Why is that fishing pole jumping around?" she asked.

Christopher wheeled around and with the first glimpse of the rod, bolted toward the water, holding his towel and shouting, "We have a fish! Come on!"

Trish took up the chase as if her director had just shouted, "Action!"

When he yanked up the rod, rearing back to set the hook, the towel that had valiantly held fast, relaxed and drifted to the sand at his feet. "Whoops!" he shouted, but there was little he could do to repair the situation, with the fish trying to steal his fishing tackle.

She stopped a few feet behind him and chortled, "Why don't you slip into something more comfortable?"

"Here!" He handed the rod behind him without turning around. "Grab this!"

"What? I've never caught a fish."

"Just grab it and start cranking." He shook the rod at her.

When she took the rod, the force of the fish caught her off balance and pulled her forward, and she let out a combination squeal and whoop straight from a horror movie. She almost lost her grip on the rod but recovered, found the reel, and began furiously cranking.

Christopher, with his towel problems repaired, shouted, "Easy! Easy! Rod tip up! Hold your rod tip up! Now crank! Don't horse it around, you'll lose the fish."

"Easy? This thing's killing me here! Take the rod before I lose it!" Her voice escalated an octave of excitement.

"Nope, it's all yours. You're doing fine," he said. Just then the fish made a heroic run for freedom, and the reel drag screamed as it slipped.

"WHOOOAH! Steady, big fellow." She held the rod without cranking to get a breath.

"Keep cranking. If you're resting, she's resting. Rod tip up!"

"I think we both need a rest here." Her voice still registered high-pitched excitement. As she cranked, the fish began tiring, and after about five minutes it broke the surface twenty feet in front of her. She shrieked, "AHHHHH!" dropped the rod and retreated, stamping her feet in excitement. Chris grabbed the line and pulled the fish into the shallow surf.

"Look at him! He's huge! Jesus, what a rush! What is it?" she asked as he grabbed the fish and held it up, still clutching the towel with the other hand.

"Red fish. A nice one."

"A nice one? It's a whale? How big is it?" She continued bouncing.

"At least ten pounds, I'd say." Chris held the fish up to better examine it.

"What do we do with it?" She started laughing with glee.

"That's up to you. We can eat it, or turn it loose," he explained.

"Are they good to eat?" She bent over to look more closely.

"Wonderful. One of my favorites," he said.

"Let's eat it! No! Turn it loose! No! Oh, I don't know what to do!"

"If you've never caught a fish before, it might be a nice gesture to give back your first fish. An offering of kindness and respect to all the other fish, so to speak. Besides, I caught another one earlier and it's already cleaned and in the refrigerator."

"Great! Turn it loose." She stepped back in anticipation.

"No, you turn it loose." He motioned with his head to come closer.

"I've never touched one of those things." She backed away.

"Okay, come here," he said.

The "director" prevailed, and she moved into action, stepping beside him and squatting in the surf, $150 sneakers, and all. "Show me what to do."

He removed the hook, lowered the fish back into the water, being mindful of his towel, and explained, "Put your hands under her and just cradle her gently."

She obeyed without flinching and he removed his hands.

"How do you know it's a 'her'?"

"The big ones usually are female. Feel right here." He stooped and moved her hand back a little. "Feel that? She's full of eggs, thousands of them."

She didn't reply, but thought, what a wonderful feeling. Not at all slimy. I am squatting here cradling life.

"What now?" she asked her mentor.

"Move her back and forth and get the water moving through her gills until she swims out of your hands." He stepped back and admired the picture of this beautiful woman toiling over the fish to revive and release it. He saw the tail began undulating, and the fish swim slowly out of her hands and into deeper water.

"God, that was better than catching her." Trish stood to get a last glimpse before the fish disappeared.

Just as the red fish swam away, the clouds that had formed up to deliver their promise peppered the surf with drops, and the clean scent of ozone-laced rain filled the air. Christopher surveyed the rain and declared, "That's a real frog strangler. Better get inside. Lower the umbrella, and then take my beach bag inside. I'll get the rest."

They scurried over the beach as the rain and wind increased in intensity. He reeled in fishing lines, grabbed the bait bucket, bait net, sand-spike rod holders, and turned toward the house. He saw the wind towing Trish down the beach clutching the umbrella's pole. The squall's wind filled the umbrella, and she looked like a first time skydiver wrestling with the harness of her chute.

Holding the fishing gear and his towel as best as he could, Chris ran past her, stopped in front of the umbrella using his back as a bulwark, and shouted, "We need to turn it into the wind." Together they rotated 180 degrees until the wind helped close the umbrella. "Turn the crank!"

The umbrella obliged and collapsed as Trish cranked, but the crown-point caught his towel and dragged it down to his knees. The wind, as if cheated by the umbrella, grabbed the towel and sailed it over her head and into the sand dunes.

There it is again, she thought surveying his darkly tanned backside. He was a decent looking older sand-poet with hands full of fishing gear and his silver mane quaking in the wind and rain. Oh, what a day this is, she chortled, dropped the umbrella and beach bag, and collapsed to her knees laughing. She recovered enough to say, "Maybe we should be introduced since I'm seeing more of you these days."

"I'm sorry, but I can't shake hands right now," he replied. "But my name is Chris."

"Well, Chris, my name is Trish." She broke down laughing again. Recovering her composure, she added, "Seriously, Chris?"

"Yes?"

"Your place, or mine?" she said through peals of laughter.

Chris had grabbed a towel drying on the deck railing before she came over the dune bridge. "Come on up. I'll clean up and get dressed, and fix us some lunch. You can use the bath if you like."

Trish had time to look around while she toweled her wet hair. The dune bridge and deck were actually on the second floor of the house. Piling supported the A-frame portion of the house above the dunes, and the space beneath its floor was enclosed like a garage or large storage room. The main floor was one room sectioned into a well-equipped kitchen, a living room/ study with a fireplace, and a bathroom. Upstairs must be the sleeping loft, she thought. It was open to the room below and seemed to have a beach view through a triangular window at the house's apex.

On closer inspection, she saw that the house was unpretentious, but that her host wanted for very little. A computer occupied part of the desk. A television with a VCR, a library of videos, and an impressive stereo system rounded out the entertainment package. Full bookcases covered the walls, and a large, expensive looking painting of huge sequoia trees hung above the fireplace mantel. At the base of the trees was a nude reclining female bathed in sunlight. She remembered seeing a similar painting in California. The room was fairly well ordered, but not compulsive.

Trish moved to the videos, running her finger along the titles, and stopped with a jerk on the cover of a movie called "She." Removing it, she walked to the desk. A copy of the poetry book, *Lost Above the Far Below* by Christopher Maven, lay near the computer — the same book she had in her beach tote. A sand- poet would have a few poetry books, she mused.

God, what a devilish day this is, Chris thought while drying after a quick shower, and it isn't over yet! The stuck car would require a hike back with boards and shovel, then digging, then pushing and probably more of the same. "I hate life transfusions," he growled to himself. Strangers always left him restless and confused and often loosed the demons that had hounded him into sanctuary. And what about that ridiculous towel? He grimaced into the mirror. Christ, that girl must think I'm a freakish pervert. But then Trish Lowe seemed a little different — not at all like the assholes he thought movie stars to be. Actually, she was not like most other people.

She sat at the small dining table near the kitchen, reading a book as he stepped from the bathroom still barefoot, but wearing an old pair of blue jean cutoffs and a white T-shirt. His hair returned to its original mane with no hair dryer, or hairbrush for that matter. She glanced up from the book and smiled. "Well!

We finally meet, face to face."

"I'm sorry about everything out there. You know." He gestured toward the beach. "I'm not a very social person. And that towel... I mean, I'm not a pervert either."

She smiled to ease his apparent discomfort. "I hope you don't mind me borrowing your book. It's my favorite. It's helped me through some rough places in my life." She held the book out to him.

"Is it helping you through today?" He asked, taking the book.

"Actually, this is one of the better days in recent memory."

"Except for having to see a lot more of me than you cared to."

"We are about even, I think." She said holding up the video of *She*.

She was her first movie and Hollywood's fifth remake of H. Rider Haggard's novel. The title was the only similarity between the book and the movie. The critics dubbed it,

"A monolithic piece of trash!" Hollywood tired of She being an ice princess, and had set the movie in the jungle somewhere "in a distant land." It was a Tarzan knock-off tale of a white girl raised by a tribe of natives who held her as a deity dropped from heaven. She and the natives did fine until a group of explorers found her and kidnapped her, taking her back to civilization. A litany of tragedies saw her degenerate into an exploited topless dancer performing under the stage name, "She," whose native talent and raw emotions abounded. She mesmerized her audiences. But all was not lost as She escaped, and through a series of action scenes that included diving from a cruise ship on which she was an entertainer, She escaped back to the pristine life and sanctuary of the jungle.

Through all this drivel, one thing captivated the critics and later Christopher Maven. Trish Lowe, a new star, somehow built dramatic equity into hackneyed lines while wearing less than Tarzan. Her beauty was breathtaking, and as one critic said, "My God, that girl could dance!"

Chris stood motionless clearing his throat several times. He shuffled his feet and finally said in a muffled voice, "I guess you got me there."

"This piece of fluff is a little out of place beside *Cannery Row* and *Anna Karenina*." She pointed to the shelf of videos.

"Well, it had its moments," he replied.

"Still, you've seen a lot more of me than I have of you."

"Not really." He looked at the poetry book in his hand.

Chapter 3

Leah Armour, Trish's personal manager, picked up her room phone on the second ring, but before she could get it to her ear, "Where in the godamn hell is Trish?" blasted from the receiver. She struggled to gather her thoughts. "Oh, hi, Danielle, I was just going to call you. With the bad weather and all, I was unsure where you'd be shooting."

"Trish can't just crawl into a limo and ride until it gets to our location? Anyway, cut the crap, Leah, it's obvious you don't know where she is, either." Film director Danielle Stokes' voice pierced like a fire alarm.

"What do you mean, I don't know where she is... "

"Like I said, Leah, you're doing a miserable job covering Trish's ass. I've got a note from her asking me to 'shoot around her.' Shoot around her, my ass! I might shoot *her*. The weather partially screwed today, and now Trish totally messed it up. This is going to cost me about fifty grand. For nothing! I need to know what's going on."

"Danielle, I think you're over reacting here. I mean, she probably just had a couple of things to do. She'll show up soon."

"She doesn't have 'a couple of things' to do today. She's got one thing to do! Make this goddamn movie!" Danielle paused to get a breath. "I'm calling Rod when I hang up and tell him he better catch up on his lawyer's retainer because he's going to need him if this happens again."

"For God's sake, don't get Rod involved in this. You know how those two can get. Just give me a little time to sort this thing out. I'll call you back later." The thought of Rod Blitzer, Trish's agent, coming to town made her pupils dilate. She had seen the two of them go at each other too many times. "Danielle? You there?" There was no answer.

Leah Armour knew the signs. Trish Lowe was the third client for whom she had worked as a personal manager. Leah's previous two Hollywood stars had proved to be Roman candles glowing brightly before self-destructing. But Trish was the real thing. Trish was worth saving, even if Rod Blitzer sometimes seemed bent on destroying Leah's charge.

Blitzer, wanting to capitalize on her current popularity, had pushed Trish into six years of end-to-end movie shoots in far-away places. The obligatory firestorm publicity tours from each film overlaid each current shooting. Rod's smile broadened as his fifteen-percent fees mounted, but the grind left Trish exhausted, generally unhappy, and often depressed. At age twenty-nine, Trish's potential for a self-abusive lifestyle hovered over her like Los Angeles smog. The ego boost of being adored by half the free world's men had disappeared long ago, and her last significant other and her Malibu Beach house sanctuary were distant memories of paradise lost to the endless grind of movie making.

Even before the Texas shoot began, Leah knew Trish needed a diversion. It wasn't Malibu, but the Texas beach was only thirty minutes away, and Leah was told of a state park on Mustang Island.

"You understand what I'm trying to do here?" Leah asked Park Ranger Jeffrey Randall.

"Yes'm. You want me to ride herd on Trish Lowe, the movie actress, right?"

"Well, that's one way to say it, I guess, but mostly I want you to make sure she can come here on her own and know she won't be disturbed. Can you do that?" Leah asked.

"How much will I have to pay you?" Ranger Jeffrey smiled and adjusted his sunglasses.

"Actually, I was thinking I would pay you."

"The Great State of Texas pays me so handsomely, it'll be a pleasure to see Miss Lowe is safe as in the arms of Jesus here in Mustang Island State Park." Ranger Jeffrey tipped his regulation western hat.

"You realize if anyone hears about this, your park will be a mob scene, right?"

"Then this will be our little secret, won't it?" Ranger Jeffrey leaned forward and whispered.

When Leah completed the Mustang Island Park arrangements, she anticipated with pleasure loading the movie star into her convertible, driving her to the beach hideaway, and basking in the excitement and pleasure it gave her friend and employer.

Until today, Leah Armour had felt good about Trish's demeanor on this picture. Their last picture was a trial by fire, with Trish showing violent mood swings triggered by the inane story line of yet another puff piece called Passing Fantasy. They barely made it through with cast and crew relationships intact, but Trish did seem to enjoy the love scenes with the co-star.

With five hours of daylight left, Leah wrestled with what to do. A police report on a missing Trish Lowe and the CBS, ABC and NBC News jets would flock to Corpus Christi International along with all the "talking head" cable networks.

Leah phoned Mustang Island State Park. "Jeffrey, you know where Trish is?"

"I haven't seen her, Miss Armour," Ranger Jeffrey replied. "Why, what's up?"

"We're trying to reach her, but we're not sure where she is."

"You think there's a problem?"

"Don't even think about it, Jeffrey, but could you check around for me?"

Three cigarettes later, Jeffrey called Leah back, "Miss Armour, she's not in the park, that's for sure. But the ranger in the entrance booth thought he saw her red convertible roar past, headed toward Port Aransas about nine o'clock this morning."

"No one has seen her since then?"

"No, Ma'am. I'm off duty now. You want me to look for her in Port Aransas?"

"That would be great," Leah replied, "but no need to talk about this, right?"

Ranger Jeffrey turned onto Park Road 361 and drove the speed limit for the thirteen miles into Port Aransas. The red convertible would be a beacon in the small fishing village, but no such luck. Heading back out Alister Street, he turned onto Beach Street and drove to the water, down the beach to the next access road, back to the highway, and continued zigzagging back and forth between highway and beach toward the state park. He again headed toward the water at Fish Pass Road, where he found the vacant convertible axle-deep in the sand at the end of the pavement. He radioed back to the park and ordered the tow truck to retrieve the car and haul it back to the park for safekeeping, and set out to look for Trish.

Chapter 4

An awkward silence hung in the beach house air. Chris pointed to Trish's jogging clothes. "You might be more comfortable in something beside soggy Spandex. I think I have something that could fit you,"

"Chris, I'm gonna worry about you if you have a closet full of women's clothes." Trish crossed her arms and looked down her nose.

"I guess that would seem a little different. They're actually not mine, but they might fit you." Chris returned her smile.

"You been holding out on me? You have a girl friend out here in the boonies?"

"Not really." He turned to look for the promised clothes before his expression gave him away. Rummaging through the clothes in the storage closet, he found a smallish pair of cutoffs and a blouse. Trish accepted them with appreciation and went to the bathroom to change. "Use anything in there you need," he offered. Apparently, she needed a shower and hair dryer by the sound of it. He hoped there was a clean towel.

He busied himself with lunch, first lighting the butane grill on the deck and then gathering the ingredients for a salad from the refrigerator. The red fish filets of that morning's catch were basted in tarragon butter, salt and peppered, and placed on the grill after the flame was adjusted. Returning to the kitchen, he hand broke the romaine lettuce, sliced tomatoes and avocados, and placed two French rolls in the toaster oven to warm.

He came through the deck door with a platter of grilled fish as Trish emerged from the bathroom. Her efforts paid big dividends, and the sight of her jarred him to a halt. He stared at her perfect shape, her perfect tan, her black hair groomed into a ponytail, and the benign aura of innocence radiating through her eyes and smile. *God, what's happening here? What am I doing?* He thought.

"Better?" She made a small curtsey

"Sorry. I guess I was staring." He continued to the kitchen.

"I'm really hungry," Trish said. "All the excitement this morning gave me an appetite, and the smell of that grilled fish is killing me."

Chris set the fish, the salad, and hot crusty French rolls on the table. He poured white wine into their glasses. "This little French Sancerre should go well with the fish."

Her expression turned to astonishment as she surveyed the meal. The aroma of tarragon butter wafted from the fish as Trish picked up her fork. "Excuse me if I don't talk for the next few minutes."

Chris watched, amused at her obvious pleasure. She continued eating , and he poured a second glass of wine. Trish looked up long enough to say, "You're different."

"Because I can cook?"

"No, I mean about me. You knew who I was all along, and you didn't... go crazy. I mean, get silly about it."

"You didn't look dangerous. Besides, being naked got me a little off balance. Normally, I'm not so hospitable." He finally took his first bite of food.

"Really? That's surprising." Smile lines appeared at the corners of her eyes.

"I'm a certified recluse." He lifted his glass in a salute.

"Who certifies recluses in these parts? The county? The Great State of Texas?" She laughed, and the smile lines appeared again.

"The people, I guess. If they see less of you than they think they should, you are certified as a recluse — or worse."

"Well, Chris the Recluse, you really are different. Delightful, actually." She looked at her host across the small table with a predatory glint in her eyes. She felt comfortable, maybe even drawn to this older man. "How long have you lived here?" she asked.

"A long time." He looked out the window to avoid eye contact as his guilt tumbled back through time, as it always did with questions about his former life.

She wanted to know what he'd been like at her age, thirty something years ago, but asked instead, "What did you do before that?"

"I lived in a lot of places and did a lot of things I've tried to forget." He again avoided eye contact that might be a window into what lurked inside.

The wine, the laughter, the meal, the day, and the man all made Trish feel cozy. Warm and protected. Safe. She recovered from her reverie enough to feel herself blushing. "Ah... well, Chris the Recluse, what do we do now?"

"You've got a car stuck in the sand. People are probably worried about you," he said.

"My car! Damn, I forgot all about it." she said, "Can we get it out?"

"It'll take some digging."

"Should we drive into town and get a tow truck?"

"No car, remember?"

"No car! Right." Her brow furrowed. "Here we go again. How do you live out here in the middle of nowhere with no phone and no transportation?"

"A friend helps me with my mail and supplies... things I need."

"This must be a really good friend. You don't want for much here." She gestured around the room.

"I guess I'm lucky that way. Actually, most of this was here. A friend of mine drank himself to death, and left his place to me." Chris moved uneasily.

"What a sad thing." Her eyes showed concern. "Living here in this wonderful spot and not enjoying it. How sad."

"Oh, he enjoyed it all right. He just enjoyed it a little too much."

"Maybe that's even sadder." She brightened and added, "Like I say, Chris the Recluse, what do we do now?" She knew the answer before she asked. It would not be long before they loosed the hounds on her.

"Two choices. We could hike down to the car with boards and shovels and dig it out "

"Or?"

"There'll be a Coast Guard helicopter patrolling every morning. We flag it down, and they take you back to town." He stared at the floor, seeming uneasy over the suggestion of her sleeping over.

Maybe I might make it until tomorrow morning, she thought. She looked at his averted eyes and uneasy demeanor and thought; I wonder how Woody Allen would write this? Before she answered, she heard footsteps vibrating the dune walkway, and glanced out the front door to see Ranger Jeffrey walking up from the beach, his Stetson set purposefully above his dark tinted aviator's glasses. He was tall and just missed being in good shape with a slight bulge above the big buckle of his holster belt. His uniform trousers were pressed into a razor crease that wrinkled only slightly at the intersection with his cowboy boots that somehow escaped collecting any sand from the beach.

"The cavalry is here," Chris said just as Jeffrey stepped onto the deck.

"Chris?" Jeffrey called as he approached the door.

"Come on in, Jeff."

In the time it took Jeffrey's eyes to adjust to the dimness, Trish stood and moved into the living area. "Boy, am I glad to see you, Miss Lowe! I was sure hoping I'd find you here. I saw your car, and I tracked you this way."

"It's good to see you, Jeffrey." Trish smiled as she greeted him. "I guess I got in a little trouble here today."

"Yes'm, there's a surefire storm brewing with Ms. Leah. She called about an hour'n-a-half ago a might bit worried about you." Ranger Jeffrey removed his hat as he spoke. "You want me to radio back and have them call Ms. Leah and tell her you're all right?"

"That's not necessary, Jeffrey, but can you help us get the car out so I can get back to town?" she asked.

"Oh, no worry there, they've towed it back to the park by now." He smiled with pride. "Probably washed it too."

Trish turned to Chris and said, "Well, Chris the Recluse, it looks like the curtain comes down on one of life's little dramas. You were a lifesaver today for many reasons."

"Sorry I wasn't more help to you." He shrugged. "You two know each other?"

Trish responded first. "Jeffrey has been a great deal of help to me during the filming."

"The filming?" Chris looked puzzled.

"Oh, that's right, you're 'Chris the Recluse,' you wouldn't know we're shooting a movie over in Corpus."

"Chris doesn't read newspapers," Jeffrey said.

Chris mumbled, "There was something on television, now that you remind me."

An embarrassed silence broke when Trish said, "Well, I guess it's time." She hugged her host, kissed his cheek, grabbed her beach tote that was bulging with her wet clothes, and walked out the door. When she reached the dune walkway, she turned and asked Ranger Jeffrey to wait, ran back into the house, and kissed Chris on the lips, startling him enough that he rocked back on his heels and had to grab the doorjamb to keep from falling.

When they reached mid-span of the dune walkway, Jeffrey turned and with a big smile and thumbs up shouted, "See you soon, Chris... The Recluse," and he and Trish disappeared over the dunes.

Jeffrey said nothing as they drove down the beach, since Trish seemed deep in thought. Turning onto Fish Pass Road, he finally said, "You were pretty lucky today. You coulda' had a long hike."

"Yeah, Chris helped a lot."

"That's where you got lucky!" Jeffrey replied.

"How's that?" She turned with a questioning look.

"You got inside his house. Few have had that honor since he moved in there years ago."

The Bronco had turned onto the highway and gained speed before Trish asked, "So you know Chris well?"

"Yes'em, I do his errands for him," he said. "He pays me for it, but I'd do it for nothing just to get to talk to him. He's different."

"What's his last name?"

"He didn't tell you? It's Maven," Jeffrey answered.

"Chris... topher... Maven?" She sat silently for a while. " 'Sand poetry?' I just spent the day with Christopher Maven and didn't know it? The bastard didn't even tell me. Shit! How on earth did Christopher Maven end up living on a deserted beach in the middle of nowhere?"

Jeffrey explained a guy named Osborn Holmes who was anything but a recluse had owned the house up until about eight or ten years ago. Osborn gave huge beach parties open to anyone who wanted to party until they dropped. Jeffrey added, "If you believe the Osborn Holmes legend, he was the original party animal. But he got sick and somehow Chris ended up taking care of him. Osborn died and left Chris the house."

"And Chris has just lived on the beach since. Like a hermit?"

"Yes'm, old Chris is really different that way," Jeffrey said without looking at her.

"God, that is *really* different." She sat in contemplation. "But yet... how many times have I wanted to run away and hide?"

They rode for a while before Trish turned to Jeffrey. "Jeff, are you married?"

"Sorta." He shrugged by way of explanation.

"Sorta?" Trish looked puzzled. "How can you be 'sorta' married?"

"Connie, my wife, and I have our good times and our bad. We're having a bad time right now, and she moved home to her folks in San Antonio." Jeffrey looked away from Trish.

"How much does a Park Ranger make these days? If you don't mind saying."

"About 35K, with some extra shifts." He gave a little snort at what he knew to be a paltry sum.

"Would another 10K help you and Connie have a better time?"

"It sounds interesting. Why would you pay me 10K?"

"For doing some things and not doing others. For instance, you must forget everything that happened today. Never mention Christopher to Leah, and for God's sake, never mention to another human being that Trish Lowe spent time in Christopher's place."

Leah Armour gritted her teeth and was reaching for the phone to call Danielle about a missing Trish Lowe, when it rang. She grabbed it from the cradle in mid-ring, "Speak to me!"

"Ms. Leah, it's Jeffrey. You don't need to worry."

"Thank God, you found Trish?"

"No ma'am, not exactly, but I found where she was. She had a few drinks at Pelican's Landing, and the bartender said she left about thirty minutes ago saying she needed to get back to town. She'll be there pretty quick," Jeffrey assured her.

"What a relief! You sure she's coming back here?"

"Ma'am, I really don't think you need to worry."

Leah reluctantly put the phone in its cradle.

Trish waved again to Ranger Jeffrey and the state park crew from her top-down convertible as she turned onto the exit road. She was taken by the serenity of the park's wetlands. The air was cool, and the sun was low on the horizon, silhouetting the spartina grass and the statue-like wading birds staring into their reflections on the mirrored surface of the bay flats. The air was heavy with the musty marsh smell of creation, and Trish took in a deep satisfied breath. If there were only a way to bottle this quietude, she thought. When things got too hectic, I could open a jar and pour the calm over me like a healing balm.

Her mind drifted back to the day she'd just spent with Christopher Maven – an enjoyable day like none in recent memory. Certainly since Rick. Her hand rubbed her brow involuntarily at remembering Rick Gooden, M.D. They had met on the set of her fourth movie, a medical thriller about body organs harvested from kidnap victims held in comatose states by criminal doctors. Dr. Gooden carried the reputation as the leading organ transplant surgeon in California and was hired as technical advisor for the surgery scenes.

At forty, he was almost twice Trish's age and carried the self-assured bearing that his medical acclaim afforded. Handsome enough to be in movies himself, he caught Trish's eye on his first visit to the set. Their relationship blossomed to the point that Trish felt they might spend their lives together. But the tabloids and gossip columnists somehow caught scent of the relationship and built it into headline coverage.

Trish had known that this new world the doctor found himself in made him uncomfortable. She'd tried all the celebrity tricks to keep their lives private, but the tabloids still blasted out headlines of her every move, as if someone were trying to disrupt their relationship.

"Trish's Doc Dates Nurse," the headline and photos still burned in her memory. She knew it was just tabloid bullshit, but Rick's fury at the lie lasted for days. Then, "Doc is Up to No-Good," blasted from the cover of *The National Investigator* along with a picture of Rick with a nurse, both in scrubs. "Jesus Christ, Trish, we're in scrubs on the way to the operating room for crying out loud. What are these idiots talking about?" Rick was pissed off beyond consolation.

The media smelled blood and circled the couple for the kill. "Doc Drops Trish," was a tabloid self-fulfilling prophecy. Trish knew what was coming when Rick sat her down to talk, "I just can't function professionally with all this media bullshit going on. Our lives are just too different."

The bone-aching hurt of Rick's loss sent her to her only stint on a psychiatrist's couch. Little by little she recovered, but the emotional scar left her restless and uneasy about Hollywood life, and a day like today made her yearn for something more satisfying.

She had made her way up South Padre Island Drive and down Bayshore Drive to downtown Corpus Christi in the calm of her reverie. Turning into the hotel parking lot brought her back to the present. Trish said aloud, "Welcome back to the real world."

Chapter 5: Marin County, 1966

"They did what?" District Attorney Romney Anderson of the County of Marin, California, rocked forward in his overstuffed executive chair so violently that he found himself standing. Assistant District Attorney Sid Blevins jumped back, fearing a physical attack, but recovered enough to answer, "The Army's Judge Adjutant General's Office remanded the case to us to handle under state criminal law."

"For Christ's sake, didn't it happen on Fort Baker property? They still own the Marin Headlands, don't they? I mean, the bastard was trespassing on government property, right?" DA Anderson's stubby arms flailed about for emphasis.

Blevins flinched again. "They say it's a civilian matter and no concern of theirs."

DA Anderson, who was on the last year of his four-year term after election in 1962, moved to his office window of the Frank Lloyd Wright - designed Marin County Civic Center and looked down Civic Center Drive toward Lagoon Park. The park was already filled with hippies attending a rock concert billed as the "Marin Love In." He asked rhetorically, "How in God's name did this bunch of social trash get permission to use the Lagoon Park for their sex and drug orgy? It looks like every hippie in San Francisco and Sausalito is there."

Blevins moved to the window, looked over Anderson's shoulder, and saw young girls dressed in long flimsy dresses, some with flower wreaths in their hair, hugging every longhaired boy in sight. Rock music blared from speakers powerful enough at half volume to knock Jericho's walls down. Many of the kids sat silently stoned. Between each song, others chanted endlessly about giving love a chance.

Anderson frowned and pointed out the window. "I'm sick to death of this "flower power," hippie bullshit. The whole thing flies in the face of our cultural values. It's anarchy!"

"At least they're not violent." Blevins had to step back to avoid an elbow as Anderson wheeled to face him.

" Not violent? Trust me! They will be before it's all over! They represent the beginning of the end of our society!" Anderson moved back to his chair and sat in silent contemplation. "I have one year to get re-elected" He was thinking aloud. "Cleaning up this Hippie mess might just be the way to get it done." He looked up at Sid Blevins, "Swear out a warrant for "Murder One" on this guy, Marvin Christofferson."

"Murder One?" Blevins said in disbelief. "Isn't that a little stiff? Not to mention hard to prove?"

"Hell no, it isn't! There's no question he did it. We only have to prove motive."

"That's what I mean." Blevins flinched again and added, "There is one complication with the case though."

"What complication?"

"Lesa Tolivar was carrying a child in the third trimester."

Anderson leaped from his chair ecstatic. "Even better. Swear out a warrant for two counts of "Murder One.""

The assistant DA picked up his briefcase as if to leave, then turned back. "You know he'll plead 'not guilty.' You'll bargain that down to 'Reckless Endangerment', or 'Manslaughter', and that'll be probated. That's if we can even get a conviction, which I doubt."

"We'll make an example out of this guy," Anderson said. "We'll jerk him around so badly every hippie in Marin County will be packing back to San Francisco. Drive the damn hippies out of Marin and I'll be re-elected in a landslide."

"But... " Blevins began.

"No buts about it! Just get this guy arrested! Today!" Anderson plopped back in his chair looking like he had just hit the Lotto, and Blevins turned on his heel and stalked from the room

The fog had retreated back out to sea, and the sun shown brightly on a cloudless morning. Sid Blevins viewed the remnants of the previous day's Love In as he drove toward Marin General Hospital. The warrants for the arrest of Marvin Christofferson were in his briefcase. He shook is head in disbelief at the number of kids ragged out by a long sleepless night, overindulging on alcohol and marijuana, and dulled by sensory overload. They lounged about the streets trying to collect themselves sufficiently to make the trek back to San Francisco's Haight Asbury District. Some held up destination signs in the hope of hitching a ride.

The paddy wagon with its two officers was already stationed at the front door of the hospital when Blevins parked his car at the No Parking curb. The three walked to the Psychiatric Ward, and, after a short discussion with the administration office, Blevins signed the release form for police custody of Marvin Christofferson, while the two officers looked on with little interest. The attendant behind the desk stamped the documents, handed a copy to an orderly, and returned to his paper shuffling. The orderly took the three of them down the hall past a row of doors with only small, covered viewing portals, from which issued both subdued moans and howls of desperation. They passed through a door into a recreation room where patients moved about in drugged stupors. The room's appearance, intended to be bright and cheerful, became instead an institutional burlesque of anything that might lift a patient's spirits. The orderly looked around the room and said, "He's usually in here, but I don't see him."

"Maybe he went back to his room," Blevins said.

The four set off farther down the hall where the doors had double locks and windows reinforced with imbedded wire. The orderly looked through the window of Christofferson's room, and, not seeing him, said, "The door to his john is closed. Maybe he's in there."

The orderly tried his key, but the door was unlocked. The three went in, and the orderly checked the bathroom and found clouds of steam rising from behind the shower curtain. "Hurry up, Christofferson. There are some people here to see you." The orderly stepped outside the bathroom to wait.

Chapter 6

Lottie Langton busied herself wiping down the bar of her open air "Backyard Bar and Grill" in preparation for the evening's business. The Backyard had a central octagonal bar with a palm frond "palapa" roof shielding it from the day's intermittent showers, but the openness and the wind was a problem for lightweight napkins and swizzle sticks.

The Backyard, the main watering hole for both locals and the lucky tourists who stumbled in, was adjacent to the Port Aransas Harbor on Mustang Island where gleaming sport fishing cabin cruisers and sailboats rocked and strained at their moorings. At night the harbor lights, the reflections from other restaurants, and bars lining the harbor and the distant lighthouse on Lydia Ann Channel provided a backdrop that said, "It's happening here!"

Lottie already had cleaned the umbrella tables and set out the salt, pepper, and sugar shakers. She refilled the charcoal grill with new briquettes in anticipation of the demand for shrimp, chicken and beef kebabs that night.

After restocking the condiment trays, filling the straw and napkin holders on the bar, and weighting them with shot glasses, she turned to the beer box, which the last night's business had emptied. It was not her favorite job, but she doubled over the side of the beer box, head, shoulders, and hidden hands, groping into the bowels to clean it. Her butt threatened a jail break as it strained against her short shorts.

Jeffrey walked up to the bar and said, "Lottie Langton, why I'd recognize that face anyplace. I want to remember you just this way forever."

"Very funny, Jeffrey!" Her voice echoed out of the beer box. Her cleaning continued unabated, so Ranger Jeffrey sat on a bar stool immediately opposite her posterior to fully appreciate the view. Shortly after, she emerged from the box, wiping perspiration from her brow with her forearms and removing her rubber gloves. She was one of those rare island women who, after thirty-nine years, remained unblemished by sun, salt air, controlled substances, and the rigors of island nightlife. Her slightly tanned complexion served to accent her poodle cut, blond hair surrounding a beautiful face from which beamed vivid blue eyes and a smile of perfect white teeth.

"You're running a little bit late today." He leered.

"No, Jeffrey, you're a little bit early." She leaned against the beer box to catch her breath from bending over.

"I've done my good deed for the day, so I dropped by for my reward," he said smiling.

"And what might that be?"

"How about your pledge of undyin' love followed by wild Latin sex while shouting, 'Olé!'"

"You're married, Jeffrey, remember? What's your second choice?" Her manner was tolerant.

"Actually, it might be time to launch into the relationship of unbridled lust we're always talking about."

"You're always talking about!"

"How about a beer, then?" he said with resignation. She rolled a long neck in a napkin before opening and setting it on the bar. "Anyway, my marriage is more like the measles than matrimony." He looked down at his beer bottle before taking his first long pull on it.

"I suspect Connie might have even stronger feelings on that subject. So what was the good deed you're so proud of?" She pulled a roll of coins from the cash bag.

"I rescued that person I can't talk about from the clutches of old Chris." He chortled in anticipation of her reaction.

"What? Trish Lowe was in Chris's house? Chris the recluse?" She wheeled around, showering the nickels she was dumping into the register over the floor.

"SHHHHH! You know you can't say that name out loud!" Jeffrey beamed at his "gotcha!"

"Nobody gets into Chris' house! I mean, what was she doing there? I thought you guarded her down at the park?" Her eyes narrowed to slits.

"For some reason she decided to launch out on her own, and she got stuck in the sand at the end of Fish Pass Road. When I found her car, I followed her tracks down toward Chris' and there she was chowin' down on grilled red fish, swilling white wine, and purrin' like a kitten."

"Chris fed her?" she shouted, making a threatening gesture. "He cooked for her?"

"It was the hospitable thing to do, right?" Jeffrey was having too much fun.

She slammed a roll of quarters on the edge of the cash drawer so hard it left a mark. "The son-of-a-bitch never cooked for me!"

Somehow Trish avoided cast, crew, and autograph hounds in the lobby and halls of the Omni upon her return. Ranger Jeffrey had warned that Leah was urgently looking for her, so the note from Leah on the bed was not a surprise. Moving to the desk chair she read the note which detailed Danielle's reaction to Trish's absence and the threat to call Rod. She slumped, her elbows on the desk, feeling the noose of responsibility tightening around her again.

The cell phone caller list showed four calls from Danielle, five from Leah, and one from Rod. "Oh, my God." She said aloud as she stared blankly at the phone, trying to put together a response and damage control plan. The room phone on the desk rang, startling her enough to drop the cell phone. The phone rang three times before she drew in a breath, bracing for the caller's verbal blast, she said, "Yeah?"

"Hi. Pumpkin, it sounds like I called at a bad time." Her dad's voice on the phone was a tonic for the soul.

"Hi, Pop!" Her excitement sparked through the phone line. "You conldn't have called at a better time."

"You don't sound that great. Is everything all right?" She could always rely on his concern, the harbor against any storm that threatened. Years of searching had not produced another rock like her dad, someone to wrap her in a cocoon of tenderness and honesty when she felt vulnerable and afraid.

"Oh yeah, everything's great. It's just good to hear your voice." She almost whispered her answer.

"You sound pretty low. Is the picture goingokay?"

"The picture's going fine, Pop." Trish squirmed a little on the edge of the bed, changed hands with the phone, and thought of the trouble she was in and everything still in front of her before the end of the filming.

"Is this one better than the last one? What was the name, "Passing Flatulence"?

"Fantasy, Pop. 'Passing Fantasy'." She grinned into the phone.

"I just remember it stunk up the theater." She could picture him smiling as he said it.

"Don't hold back, Pop, just tell me what you really thought of the movie." Needling each other never grew old and always brought her back to reality. There was no man more meaningful in her life than her dad.. No man who simply accepted her for the person she really was, and loved her for it.

"Oh, and that square-faced guy? The one with the shaggy blond hair, you know, he was always rubbing on you. I didn't like him at all. I think his name is Pitts or something."

"Brad Pitt, Pop. He's okay. A pretty hot guy, actually."

"Course you were great as usual, but even you couldn't save that stinker." He paused briefly and added. "All seriousness aside, you don't sound like your cheerful self."

"Maybe I'm a little tired." Constant sixteen-hour filming days had toughened her, but she felt herself fraying around the edges.

"Tired, or weary?"

"You're amazing. You're right, of course. I'm pretty much weary of everything I do. I know I'm luckier than I'll ever deserve to be, and I know I ought to be deliriously happy."

"How long has it been since you got a little?" His chuckle rippled over the phone.

"DAD!! Be serious here!" A brief smile flickered across her face until she realized she couldn't remember the last time she had sex.

"I'm being serious. I don't care how many movies you make, or how much money, or how famous you are, that's no assurance of happiness. You gotta love someone or something more than yourself to be happy. I vote for someone, because if you get lucky, he'll love you the same way."

"Trust me, finding that someone is not as easy as it sounds. I can't seem to find somebody like you." Her eyes glistened with emotion.

"Pumpkin, I think you deserve somebody better'n me." His appreciation of his daughter's compliment was apparent in his voice.

Trish always put off asking about her mom, because she knew the answer. But now it was time. She sighed as she asked, "How's Mom?"

There was a pause as her father considered the question. "She has her good days and her bad. But she's definitely slipping."

"Could I talk to her?" Trish screwed up her face in the anticipation of a boxer hoping the next punch wouldn't land.

"You can try, but I can't promise anything. Hang on a minute, I'll try to get her on the phone." Trish heard the receiver rattle onto the table and sounds of her dad calling for her mother.

In a moment she heard, "Who? Who did you say it was?" Her mom was some distance from the phone, still.

"Martha, it's Trish. You remember Trish, your daughter, right? Trish wants to say hello." Her father's voice could be heard clearly in the background. The receiver clattered as someone picked it up.

After a pause a very tentative voice said, "Hel... Hello?"

Trish said, "Hi, Mom, it's Trish."

"Who?"

"Trish, your daughter. I just wanted to tell you I love you, Mom."

"Trish... I had a daughter named Trish once."

"That's me, Mom, I'm Trish your daughter."

After a pause Trish heard in the background, "There's someone on here who says she's my daughter, maybe you should talk to her." Trish had difficulty maintaining her composure during the pause as her dad took back the phone receiver.

"Sorry, Pumpkin, this just isn't a good day, I'm afraid."

"I feel so helpless. I have all the money in the world, and it doesn't matter. There's nothing it can do to make Mom better."

"I'm afraid that's true."

"Could we move her into a hospital or full-time care facility? Better still, move her to my Malibu house. She could enjoy the weather and walk on the beach."

"She gets very upset in unfamiliar places, I'm afraid. Just taking her to the doctor makes her frantic." Trish could hear resignation in her dad's voice.

"Dad, at least let me get 'round-the-clock help for you. An Alzheimer special care person or registered nurse. Somebody to help you out."

"Pumpkin, we do just fine. I'll admit sometimes it's hard, but having strangers in the house would make Martha uncomfortable. She's becoming suspicious, almost paranoid. She accused me of stealing her jewelry the other day." Her dad chuckled.

"I'm sorry I'm not there to help out, but when this picture is finished I promise I'll help you and Mom get through this." Trish lowered her head and facial contortions almost gave way to sobbing before she could continue. "I love you, Dad."

"I love you too, Pumpkin. Now get your chin up off your chest, and get out there, and make good decisions." Trish remembered her dad preceding her every teenage date with his mantra, "Have fun, but make good decisions."

Good decisions, she thought, who decides what's good? I made a "good decision" this morning and had a wonderful day. Met a really interesting guy. Now everyone is on my case, and I have to feel bad. The cell phone broke her reverie. The Caller ID showed that Leah was on the line. She sighed and answered, "I guess Danielle is a little upset."

"Little upset? Try ballistic! Where the hell were you today?" Leah's voice was more that a little agitated.

"Jesus, Leah, you gonna bust my chops before Danielle has a go at me?"

Chapter 7

Chris sat at his desk, pen in hand, notebook at the ready, not writing. The day's events crowded out his concentration. Trish Lowe seemed pervasive even in her absence. Just before sundown he wrote for several minutes; then walked to the beach with the notebook. He searched for a likely place and wrote in the surf-packed sand:

The void of loss seems timeless.
Your memory sifts through the fingers of my soul
Like dry beach sand drifting away on the wind.
Can even perfect wine refill a bottomless cup?

He was not hungry after their late lunch, and weariness sent him to bed shortly after dark. This was the first night of demonless sleep in weeks, and Chris sank lower and lower into the shapeless realm of silence and calm.

A thunderclap hinged him at the waist, and he awoke sitting and glanced around confused. Another cold front had pushed its way into the coastal night, engaging in mortal combat the warm moist air from the south. The electrical smell of ozone's negative ions was the fallout of a thunder cannonade. Lightning flared across the sky. Wind rocked the house, and rain pelted the roof gently at first, then in torrents. He descended the loft stairs and walked onto the deck, standing protected by the overhang and surveyed the night. The gods are angry, he thought. Spray from the surf crested the dunes to become part of the torrent. Lightning struck the water and ignited the whole scene in incandescent blues and greens. In the eerie light he saw the beach awash in surf — rain shivering and crackling in the reflection of the electric sky. He shuddered and went back inside.

At the kitchen counter he poured himself a shot of Don Sergio Tequila and downed it. Simultaneously, a power outage plunged him into darkness and the self-doubt of cause and effect.

Sitting at the bar, he lit a candle and concentrated on the mesmerizing flame as a distraction. Finally, he tossed down another tequila shot and waited for its impact. A moth appeared from the darkness and engaged in a dance with the flame. Hesitant at first, it swooped and flitted at the fringes. Gaining more confidence, it flew closer to the flame, drawn by its radiance, until it poised in flight, ready to attain the flame's full glory, and Chris reached and snuffed the candle between his fingers.

Moving to the couch, he lay for a time disturbed and sleepless before the rhythmic rain and the tequila lulled him to sleep.

The morning dawned gloriously. Gulls circled in a blue, cloudless sky, and the surf, murky from the night's storm, undulated in tamed submission. The beach glistened pristine and inviting. Four porpoise circled a school of whiting, which, with great reluctance, paid their breakfast tab.

Chris stumbled, sleep-weary, onto the deck just as the sun reached half-mast in the east. He felt rested for the first time in weeks, but not at rest. A hollowness opened inside him, a void dug by recollection.

In the past, the loss of a poem, wrenched from the grasp of immortality by the elements, had sent him into a pall of depression. It had taken him days to recover the loss of meaningful passages. But this morning's toll seemed less important. He felt a strange sense of replenishment, even anticipation.

Beach walkers are discouraged by a storm, but he went back in and put on his cutoffs anyway. He didnot want a repeat of yesterday's towel problem. "A swim might be the thing," he thought aloud. The crisp air sent him jogging into the water until he was waist deep; he fell forward into smooth strokes powering him past the surf into the swells beyond. He swam south until the entrance to Fish Pass Road came into sight and pulled up to tread water when he saw the hood of Ranger Jeffrey's Bronco nose into the sand at the end of the road. It lurched through the loose sand and onto the surf hardpan and turned north.

An unscheduled visit, thought Chris, and he swam to shore. The passenger-side window was down when he reached the Bronco, and Chris heard Jeff say, "It seems Chris the Recluse made quite an impression on Trish Lowe, considering I'm the one who rescued her. Hop in. I've been running all over town buying stuff Miss Lowe wanted you to have, and I'm making a delivery."

"I'm all wet and sandy... mess up your car." Chris pointed to the seat.

"Then open this one first," Jeff said. After digging around in the back seat, Jeffrey handed Chris a sack from what looked like a very pricey boutique.

"What's this stuff?" Chris asked skeptically, refusing the sack at first.

"Here, open it!" Jeffrey stuffed the box into Chris' hand.

Chris took the box from the sack and unwrapped it. It contained a beach towel with snaps down one edge designed to double as a wraparound. A note attached said, "Chris the Recluse, I thought this might come in handy. Thanks, Trish."

"Dry off and get in. There's a bunch of other stuff," Jeff announced.

"I really don't want a bunch of stuff from her. I just let her in the house. I didn't help her at all." Chris was backing away from the Bronco.

"Chris, quit being an asshole and just get in the car!" Jeffrey's voice carried enough authority for Chris to oblige him.

Jeff stopped the Bronco when they reached the dune walkway and, opening the hatch door, pointed at two ice chests, a bag of groceries, and an Omni Hotel valet service wrap containing the shorts and shirt Trish had borrowed the day before. "Man, I don't know what you did yesterday, but it sure worked. Miss Lowe said be sure you got this."

A note monogrammed "TL" read, "Chris, it's my turn to cook. How about tonight?" Trish. P.S. Since you didn't dig my car out yesterday, how about digging a hole for a clambake?"

Jeff opened one of the ice chests. Two enormous lobsters swam in ice and salt water beside a sack of steamer clams. He said, "These bastards are big enough to put a saddle on."

Chris stared at the two cautious lobsters swimming in the ice chest and said, "This is crazy. I'm not going to have a clambake with a stranger."

Jeff continued unloading Chris's booty and grinned as he got back into his Bronco, "Have a great adventure with your new friend... Chris the Recluse!" The Bronco started to move away, then it stopped suddenly and backed up. Jeffrey held a cell phone out the window toward Chris. "I almost forgot this. Ms. Trish wanted you to have it. I think she wants to keep tabs on you."

"I haven't used a phone in years, and I'm not going to start now."

Chris held his palm out in rejection. Jeffrey hesitated a moment, but knew it was useless. He smiled at Chris and drove away.

Chris considered the two Igloo ice chests sitting on the sand and opened the lid of one. The doomed lobsters went into defensive mode, claws open and ready to do battle. When nothing threatened them, they seemed to return to their contemplation of how the clear vistas of the cold Atlantic waters had muddled into an opaque white cloud. Unlike the irrationally happy clams in their burlap bag, the lobsters knew something was up. Chris opened the lid of the second ice chest and saw it contained an assortment of dairy products and produce.

He walked around the white ice chests as if they were turds dropped from albino plastic elephants. The lobsters fell back into their defensive posture when he nudged the Igloo with his toe. There is a clear and present danger here, he thought. The overt act of friendship on this woman's part was a Trojan horse in the guise of a friendly clam bake, and somewhere just out of sight was a huge Igloo cooler with his name on it, and the resurrection of everything he had tried for years to forget. "Nothing good can come of this," he said aloud as he picked up the sack of groceries and the valet package and started over the dunes.

The two ice chests were magnetic. He sat at his desk, and his eyes drifted out the deck door to them. From the kitchen, the beached ice chests again. Even from the loft, the ice chests tugged at him. Finally, leaning on the deck railing staring at the two ice chests still sitting on the beach, he thought, "Oh, what the hell!" Picking up a shovel he returned to the beach and dug at the edge of the surf. He lowered the lobster chest into the hole so that the surf just lapped salt water into it. "That should hold you until this evening," he advised the lobsters and clams.

At the base of the dunes he dug another hole, and then walked the beach collecting driftwood. He gathered dried seaweed, soaked it in the surf, and piled it next to the driftwood. After surveying his work for a minute, he picked up the second ice chest and carried it into the kitchen.

Chapter 8

"Thanks for picking me up a little early," Trish said to the limo driver as she slid her carry-on bag out of the seat. The sun was just peeking over the horizon as she opened her trailer door and went inside to steel herself against the inevitable confrontation with Danielle about yesterday's no-show. She changed out of her street clothes and into her robe, and sat in her makeup chair, staring blankly into the mirror as she thought back to her meeting with Chris the day before. She grinned at the thought of seeing him again at her clambake that night.

Her cell phone rang at about the time she expected Danielle's summons, but Caller ID showed it was Rod, her agent, on the line. She physically slumped at the thought of talking to Rod about yesterday. "Hey, Rod, you're certainly up early this morning."

"Always looking after my client's best interests; you know that, right?" Rod's voice didn't carry the accusatory tone she'd expected.

"That's comforting to know, Rod."

"So, we had a little problem yesterday, I hear." Rod's voice still lacked any admonition.

"Actually, I had a great day for the first time in my recollection." She was becoming defensive.

"I guess Danielle's day was not that great, since she's offering to sue us if you no-show again." His manner was too calm for his message. "But I managed to save your ass on this one."

"I don't think my ass needs saving with Danielle. She's my friend, remember?" Trish was becoming suspicious of Rod's intent.

"We got lucky yesterday. Right after I talked to Danielle, I got a call about a cancellation on Leno's, so I got the studio's permission for you to fill the slot tonight and promo "Passing Fantasy." And get this. They even kicked in a budget supplement for Danielle."

"Absolutely not!" Trish shouted into her cell phone. "I'm not going to Los Angeles today!" She thought about throwing the cell phone against her dressing trailer wall.

After a pause, Rod replied, "Come off your high horse, Babe, this is a win for everybody. Besides, the studio plane is leaving Los Angeles even as we speak to pick you up. You'll be back in Burbank by 2:00 this afternoon, do your bit on Jay Leno's show, and we'll have you back there in time for cast call tomorrow."

"I'm not going to be on Jay Leno's show or any other show, for that matter." Her voice elevated as she spoke. "I have plans for tonight."

"Babe, you know "Passing Fantasy" needs all the help it can get. Let's face it. It's a bomb!"

"That's not my fault. You got me into that piece of shit, anyway. You go on the `The Tonight Show' and tell the nation how good that disaster is!"

"Let's not go over all that again. This is an amazing piece of luck. How often does somebody get sick and leave a slot open? One of your 'girl next door' bits could breathe new life into the box office. Babe, we need this. You know that as much as I do," Rod pleaded.

"I'm shooting a movie here, remember?"

"That didn't seem to bother you yesterday. Have we got a little hanky-panky planned down there for tonight?"

"Rod, you're pond scum."

"That's right, Babe, but I'm your pond scum," he laughed. "Now, I've talked to Danielle, and she's cooled off after hearing about the budget supplement. She can shoot around you this afternoon. Be at the airport at 11:45, okay?" Rod paused with his fingers crossed, and then a crash on the other end of the line ended the conversation. He smiled and hung up.

A little after one o'clock the studio hospitality aide escorted Trish to the waiting helicopter at Van Nuys Airport where she was whisked away to a landing pad at the Hollywood studio, and then ushered her into a waiting limo for the trip to Burbank. She yanked up the car phone and dialed the number of the phone she'd had delivered to Chris.

"The cellular number you dialed is currently unavailable," said a recorded voice on the phone.

"Shit!" she shouted, slamming down the receiver. The driver turned to survey the damage.

Each time she re-dialed the number another expletive followed along with more phone abuse. She pointed, and the escort popped the cork on the iced bottle of Krug Crystal Champagne and poured without a word.

Emerging from prep and makeup into the Green Room at NBC, she kept calling Chris' number, pacing and sipping on the Martini she ordered from the bar on arrival. When the assistant stage director came for her, she told her, "Screw Jay Leno and this whole rotten show!"

The assistant stage director was unflappable. She said, "Miss Lowe, we're so lucky to have you here tonight. The whole world is waiting for you. Shall we go?"

"The only place I want to go is back to Texas."

"Oh, do you live in Texas, Miss Lowe?"

"No, I don't live in Texas!" Trish Lowe shouted. "We're shoot.... You know, that's not a bad idea."

"Well, we should be moving on, don't you think, Miss Lowe?" The assistant stage manager smiled and offered an arm to steady Trish as they headed down the chute to the stage and the waiting audience.

"And here she is – everybody's sweetheart – Trish Lowe!" The "applause" sign was redundant as pandemonium broke out. Wives scowled as their husbands leaped up shouting and whistling. Some younger guys loosed testosterone grunts and dog pound barks. Leno tried to restore order, but failing, joined in with a few grunts of his own. Trish was beaming ear to ear, laughing, acknowledging the adoration.

"Wow!" she exclaimed, settling onto the couch seat nearest Leno. "Frisky group here tonight!" The plain, form-fitting sapphire dress she wore was tasteful, and the long slit in the skirt was less of a fashion statement than a gratuitous gesture for the entertainment of the men.

"You guys didn't get this worked up over the chimpanzees!" Leno addressed the audience. More cat calls, grunts and barks.

"I'm down to following chimpanzee acts?" Trish laughed as she turned to the audience.

"Actually, folks, Trish flew all the way from Texas where she's filming on location just to be here with us tonight. We weren't sure she'd make the show," Leno said.

Generous applause again.

Trish crossed her legs and the dress slit fell open sparking another rustle of animal imitations from the men. She glanced down and in mock modesty repaired the problem. Leno looked away gallantly, shielding his eyes.

"So Trish, how are things down in the Lone Star State?" Leno asked.

"We just started shooting, but it's going well," she said, adding, "It's always a pleasure to work with Danielle Stokes."

"Danielle Stokes, let's see, was she the director of your last film?" Leno asked.

"Actually, "Passing Fantasy" was directed by Erik Burns."
"Passing Fantasy? How did they come up with that name?"

"I play Fantasy Hill, a very plain girl whose life is so drab she becomes caught up in her daydreams and begins losing contact with reality."

"How long did it take in makeup to make you look plain?" Leno asked.

The audience giggled.

"The plain part didn't take that long, but after Brad Pitt brings out the best in Fantasy and she blossoms into a beauty, makeup took a lot longer. That was kind of hard on my ego."

"We have a film clip. How about setting this up for us?" Leno asked.

"This is where Fantasy is trying to decide if Brad Pitt is real or just imagined."

The thirty-second clip ended in a big embrace and kiss between Trish and Pitt, and the audience broke out into their menagerie sounds again.

"He looks real enough to me," Leno said.

"Yeah, he's real, okay!" Trish laughed.

"Speaking of real, any improvements in the love life department, since we saw you last?"

"What love life?" The audience hooted in disbelief.

"Things can't be that bad for Trish Lowe, right?"

"Actually I met a pretty interesting man in Texas." She smiled. The audience aahed again.

"How interesting?"

"Pretty interesting!"

Leno looked at the camera. "Okay, guys, we'd better pick up the pace or we're going to miss our chance with Trish. This sounds serious! How about a name?"

"No name." She smiled.

After more banter, Trish excused herself and was back into the limo headed for the helicopter. On the plane back to Corpus Christi, she tried calling Chris several more times before collapsing into a sleep that lasted until the plane touched down well after midnight.

Chapter 9

The sun approached the dunes' horizon when Chris saw a car approaching on the beach. He continued punching up the coals of driftwood fire in the clambake hole and sorting out the condiments and side dishes pre-prepped in anticipation of the shore dinner. Both ice chests rested within easy reach, and a wine bucket nestled in the sand next to them, holding the Le Montrachet from Trish's provisions. Checkered napkins, tin plates and wine glasses, courtesy of "TL," decorated a blanket on the sand upwind of the fire.

As the car came closer, Chris saw it was Jeff's Bronco. "Now this is a recluse's layout if I've ever seen one." Jeff grinned from the Bronco window as he pulled next to the clambake.

"I'm glad you're here, you can sub in. Keep that girl company, especially since you got me into this boondoggle in the first place." Chris kicked the sand for poise.

"Well, I guess I could sub in, but it will have to be for Ms. Trish."

"What's up?" Chris glanced up under lowered eyebrows.

"She had to go to Los Angeles to be on the 'The Tonight Show.' Said to tell you how sorry she was." Jeff shrugged out the car window.

Chris looked up from the sand with no visible reaction. "You like lobster?"

Jeff thought a minute. "Don't believe I've ever had the pleasure."

"It's time you did. Unless you've got a better offer." Chris held a lobster up for Jeff's inspection. The lobster, experiencing height fright, began flailing its claws and flipping is tail.

"Evil looking bastards, aren't they?" Jeff replied, "So, Chris...?"

"Yeah?"

"If I stay, promise you'll be gentle with me?"

Chris and Jeffrey finished loading the clambake hole, first with one-third of the wet seaweed, then the lobsters, more seaweed, then the clams, more seaweed, and, at last, the pot of butter. Chris opened the first bottle of the Le Montrachet and poured two glasses, offering one to Jeffrey. They settled into their beach chairs facing out to the water that was sparkling and blazing in the reflection of the sun's curtain call.

A single pelican drifted along about fifty yards off shore, when it suddenly folded its wings and hurtled head first into the water, surfacing with a whiting in its beak. "Those damn birds look like a train wreck when they feed. It's not a pretty sight," Jeffrey said.

"But skimming over the water so low their wing tips dip into the surface, they're poetic," Chris replied. "What must pelicans feel when they soar and skim and dive in complete freedom?"

"Well, I reckon they feel like they're just doing their job, and trying not to break their necks in the process." Jeffrey shifted uncomfortably as he spoke, knowing he must be missing something in the life of the pelican. He had completely overlooked the "poetic" part. "We almost lost the brown pelican to DDT in farm run-off." Jeffrey tried to regain some poise. "It made their egg shells too thin, and the hatch rate dropped to almost nothing. I did some of the water sampling at the state park that eventually got DDT banned."

"Good work, Jeffrey, but I afraid it's all for naught." Chris took a swig from his wine glass.

"How's that?"

"Mankind refuses to accept its role here on earth," Chris said. "We try to forestall the inevitable."

"The inevitable?" Jeff squirmed a little again wondering if he was now going to learn what he had missed about pelicans.

"We constantly yammer about 'man destroying the world!' What a crock! The world has withstood every possible epoch in the past and come out just fine, thank you. Ice ages, floods, meteor impacts, global warming, volcanic eruptions that changed climate, catastrophic earthquakes, and the world keeps on spinning in greased grooves." Chris picked up a stick and began doodling in the sand.

"Yeah, but mankind is disturbing the ecological balance, right?" Jeff said with a questioning tone that belied his real understanding of the term "ecological balance."

"Right on, Jeffrey, that's it! You get the cigar! That's our job! That's why we're here, to disturb the ecological balance. But we just refuse to believe it. Refuse to believe that we are the current epoch sent to change the world." Chris stabbed the stick into the sand and pulled deeply from his wine glass.

Jeffrey wanted to ask Chris why he had a bug up his ass but didn't. Instead he said, "Chris, you're giving me a headache with this heavy talk."

"Think about it, Jeffrey, out of all the millions of species that have swum, crawled, walked, and flown on this earth, how many survived?" The wine had kicked in and Chris was enjoying the conversation.

"Don't rightly know, but there seem to be quite a few around right now." A mosquito drilled into Jeffrey's arm. He flinched and slapped at the intruder. "Now if these mosquito bastards were extinct, I could go for that."

Chris took his stick and drew four outlines in the sand. "What are these?" He pointed to what he'd just drawn.

"Well, gee, Chris, I don't know. That looks kinda like a shark, and maybe that's a scorpion, but the other two plumb escape me."

"The shark, the alligator, the scorpion, and the cockroach are the only four species that made it through all the epochs."

Chris added with emphasis, "the four meanest bastards that ever lived."

"A cockroach is a mean bastard?" Jeff asked.

"Put a six-foot cockroach next to you and let's see who runs from whom!"

"So, you're sayin' our job is to get rid of all the species on earth but four?" Jeff said.

"I imagine mankind will be long gone before it comes to that. But, yes, that's our job, to rid the world of almost everything, including us. We have to learn to deal with it."

"Chris, we need to open that other bottle of wine or change the subject. You're not the happiest dinner date I've ever had, by the way!" Jeffrey got up to look for the wine bucket.

The butter pot had melted, and the two began retrieving their reward from the seaweed. Soon the conversation died down as they devoured the baked clams, sweet as nectar simmering in their own juice and free from the grit that sometimes detracts from their enjoyment.

With some heroics, Jeffrey managed to extract some lobster meat from the shell and into his mouth. "Holy shit! How can something this ugly be this good?" The butter- soaked lobster meat was so rich and flavorful the two sighed with pleasure each time they came up for air and a quaff on the second bottle of Le Montrachet.

Sated, they sat for some time staring at the fire they restoked after removing the clambake. "Jeffrey, I don't suppose you're holding?" Chris asked.

"Chris, I hope you're not asking me if I possess controlled substances?"

"Like I say, Jeffrey, are you holding?"

"Chris, I am sworn to uphold the laws of the Great State of Texas."

"So?"

"Actually, someone left a baggie in my truck. It seems this person was not law abiding."

"So can we share a fat one? It's been years."

"Maybe in the interest of science." Jeffrey got up and walked uncertainly to his Bronco.

After their first few tokes, conversation started again and soon almost everything they said was hilarious. Jeffrey stopped laughing long enough to ask, "Chris, why did you build a boat in your downstairs storeroom that's too big to get out the door?"

"How did you know about the boat?" Chris went on guard for a moment, but then broke out laughing again.

"A couple a weeks ago you must've walked up the beach before I came by to see you. I saw the door to your downstairs storeroom was open, so I thought you were in there."

"Was I?" Both laughed aloud.

"Nope, but I went in anyway and saw the boat you built. I mean when you were ordering all that lumber and stuff last year, I knew you were up to something."

"I was building a boat too big for the basement." Both sputtered into laughter.

"Now I know how you feel about people snooping around your place," Jeffrey said, "and I normally wouldn't do anything like that, but, man, that's one beautiful johnboat."

"So you looked it over pretty good?" Chris asked.

"Man, you even carved its name into the bow. *Deliverance*, although I don't know how it will deliver anything if it can't get out of the door."

"Getting it out is not the hard part," Chris said. "It's all those sand dunes between *Deliverance* and the water that's the hard part."

It was soon midnight, and Chris and Jeffrey hugged each other in the way only two stoned guys can, and Jeffrey got in his Bronco and turned back toward Fish Pass Road. Chris picked up the two chairs, and walked over the dune bridge intending to deposit them and return for the remainders of the clambake. A deep weariness came over him when he reached the deck. He stood for a moment considering what to do, and then went inside and up to his bed on the loft. He managed to strip off his sand laden clothes before collapsing into bed and a deep sleep.

About two hours later a car worked its way down the beach between small pools of the incoming tide. The progress was slow, but eventually the car made it to Chris' house, and a female figure emerged. She started up the bridge over the dunes, but, seeing the remnants of the clambake, she stepped back on the sand and moved to stand over the abandoned site, now bathed in moonlight. The tide was encroaching on the residue of the earlier revelry. She tapped the two empty wine bottles with her toe and grimaced. It was obvious Chris had had a visitor for dinner. She shook her head in disapproval.

She entered the house cautiously, and made her way to the loft stairs, climbed halfway, and peered over the edge, afraid of what might be there. Seeing Chris alone, she tiptoed up the remainder of the stairs, walked to the edge of the bed, and stared through the dimness of moonlight at the sleeping man with only a sheet over his mid-torso.

She removed her clothes, crawled under the top sheet, and slid over until her body meshed with his and breathed a heavy sigh of satisfaction. Chris stirred when he felt her warmth on his back, and his hand twitched when she entwined her fingers into his. She kissed him on his shoulder and back, and he rolled over, sleepily wrapping her in his arms. Her lips faintly outlined his before she gently nibbled his bottom lip. He kissed her lower lip, then the other, and then both. They continued exploring each other's lips for a time before they established a union.

A brief twinge passed through Chris when he thought about the guilt that for years had accompanied their lovemaking. Guilt for using her as a surrogate lover. But this time Lottie was a surrogate for a new face.

The Coast Guard morning patrol helicopter hovered momentarily over the dune house as the pilot, Albert Gaines, gave the co-pilot an "Attaboy, Chris!" thumbs up when they recognized the white Jeep Cherokee sparkling with nighttime dew parked in front of Chris's dune bridge. "Old Chris does pretty good for a recluse," crackled over the headset.

The helicopter woke Chris. He rose on one elbow and looked for a long time at the beautiful form of Lottie Langton lying beside him. He always marveled that she survived each of their love trysts and the remaining night's sleep looking as good as if she had just walked in the door. Poodle cut blond hair framed a face that could launch all the boats in Port Aransas. Her breath came in easy whispers as she still slept the easy sleep of a satisfied soul. He shook his head as the pangs of guilt set in again. He eased out of bed, went down to the kitchen, and started a pot of coffee to help clear the remainder of last evening's fun from his clouded brain. A few minutes later he poured himself a mug and walked out to the deck. The sun was well above the horizon, and the sky was blue with only thin wisps of mackerel clouds, which foretold a wind shift back to the north. The surf, undecided as to what exactly to do, rocked gently in the timeless rhythm of salt water.

Something caught his eye just over the dune bridge. He walked to mid span and was assaulted by a view of the previous evening's clambake residue. The tide had moved close enough to the dunes to float the ice chests and to fill the fire hole earlier that morning and now retreated leaving a jumble of picnic equipment and wine bottles. He looked at Lottie's Cherokee and saw the high water mark just below the axle. The whole scene, a monument to overexuberance, procrastination, imperfect tide data, and misdirected passion, would never clear itself without help.

He moved down the dune bridge and was busily cleaning up the mess when he heard, "The recluse gives a shore dinner. For anybody I know?" Lottie stood on the bridge in her bikini briefs and one of his white T-shirts, leaning on the railing as she sipped a mug of coffee.

"You almost lost your car last night." He pointed to the water line on the car just below the axel.

"Don't change the subject. My invitation to this gala is in the mail, right?" Lottie answered.

"Jeffrey and I had a boys' night out, and I guess we overdid it a little."

"So how does a recluse get lobsters and clams for a shore dinner with his really good chum?" She was not smiling.

"I think I can see a cloud on your horizon. You're not going to leave this thing alone, are you?"

"Damn straight! So fess up. What the hell is going on here? I come out here like the midnight skulker and haul your ashes for years, and I'm lucky to get a cup of coffee for my trouble. And here is the shore dinner from hell laid on for God knows who!" Her voice as she spoke assumed the proportions of a fire alarm.

"I told you Jeffrey and I had a little get-together." He looked down and dug his right toes into the sand.

"Old Jeffrey loaded up lobsters and clams and brought them out here for you to enjoy?"

"Not exactly." He didn't look up.

"Well? What exactly?" She was gaining momentum again.

"I helped somebody get their car unstuck, and they gave me a Care package." He was less than convincing.

"And who might that somebody be?" Lottie stood with arms akimbo and no thought to her condition of undress.

"You wouldn't know them." Chris continued to clean up while searching the horizon as if looking for someone to help him out of this jam.

"Try me!" He voice became sharp enough to filet a fish. He spoke so softly it was impossible to hear.

"Louder, please!"

"Trish Lowe." His voice tapered off to inaudible again. "Trish Lowe, the movie actress? You cooked dinner for Trish Lowe, the movie actress?"

"No. She sent the stuff, but she couldn't come. So I asked Jeffrey to join in."

"But she *was* going to come?" Lottie began to regain her composure.

"Yes." He finally looked up to punctuate the remark.

There was a long pause before Lottie replied. "Chris, don't get me wrong, I know my place is somewhere behind a dead girl it seems I can never replace. I know that. And by now you should know that I care very deeply for you. But don't expect me to hang around while you frolic with a movie star. After years of being careful and not compromising your situation, you're willing to cash it all in for a fling? God, Chris, at best you're a curiosity to a girl like that, and she could cost you dearly." Lottie stalked off the dune bridge, retrieved the car keys from under the front seat, started the engine, and circled back toward Fish Pass Road oblivious to her current state of undress.

Chris stood motionless as the Cherokee receded toward the horizon.

Chapter 10: Marin County, 1966

Assistant District Attorney Sid Blevins and Detective Camp Seelig parked their unmarked police car a block from the Marvin Christofferson Art Gallery on the main street of Sausalito and walked to the gallery front door. A sign proclaimed, "Gallery Closed - Paintings can be viewed at the Trident Restaurant."

As the two walked toward the restaurant, their faces reflected expressions radically different about the laid-back hippies milling around the street. Blevins' bemused expression showed curiosity, while Selig looked as if he was walking through a minefield. San Francisco Bay lapped gently at the rocks below the seawall, and the refurbished homes along the main street had become a jumble of artsy-craftsy shops, offering paintings, handmade pottery, macramé, and tie-died fabrics. Restaurants and coffee houses dotted each side of the street and the smell of fresh-baked goods and espresso wafted out each door. Street musicians added verve to what already was a festive scene.

The officers walked across the street. The boardwalk parking deck that led to the Trident Restaurant rested on pilings on the waterside of the seawall. Workmen were building a room addition to the right of the front door. A sign said the room was the future gallery for Marvin's paintings. The Trident foyer held a sampling of them. A For Sale sign asked prospective buyers to contact the manager, Randy Quartz.

In the summer of 1965, Marvin Christofferson had become an artist of some regional renown. His vertical landscapes of the giant sequoia trees in Muir Woods in Tamalpais Valley sold in the mid-four figures. He had a small gallery across from the Trident Restaurant on Sausalito's waterfront to show and sell his paintings, similar to his contemporary, Walter Keene's, in San Francisco's North Beach Area. Though the trademark styles were different, both artists were recognizable even to laymen. Both Keene's whimsical representations of tear-stained, sad faced children and Christofferson's shafts of sunlight piercing through redwoods, igniting the skin of a single male nude, set San Francisco's art enthusiasts atwitter.

DeBotts, the San Francisco Chronicle's fine arts critic, waxed loquacious over Marvin's early works as portraying, "… the innocence of man in harmony with nature, all nurtured by a Greater Good."

DeBotts' critical depth and impeccable artistic taste, if not his prose, warmed Marvin. Critics will be critics, and Marvin accepted their opinions graciously — whether praise or criticism. What really got to Marvin was the pretense of the interior designers and fringe elements, like assistants, agents, and managers sent on pilgrimages to Sausalito by California Greats to purchase the requisite painting "by that Christofferson guy who's paintin' those faggots and big trees." He doubled the price for these phonies. Tripled it for those who wanted "something about this big, right?" Movie stars and their directors were the worst. Much too busy to make the trip, they sent their minions to negotiate for their Christofferson.

Marvin grew tired of painting male nudes. He pinned a notice to Sausalito's Trident Restaurant bulletin board requesting auditions by female figure models. A young Trident waitress named Lesa Tolivar was the first to respond. The previous friendly after-work alcohol and eco-babble sessions with her already had him dreaming about getting her naked.

Lesa's flimsy, braless, batik, flower-child shifts hid something good, he was sure, but until their first trip to the redwoods, he had no idea. The eight years separating their ages disappeared when her shift fluttered to the grass, and she stood nude before him asking for posing instructions. "Art must wait," he thought, aloud. On their fifth field trip, he finally put brush to canvas. Once their passion subsided enough to re-channel Marvin's creativity, his new artistic period blossomed. He was inspired. The gallery's waiting list read like a "Bay Area Who's Who," as all the male art patrons developed lively interests in his work. DeBotts essentially took up residence in Marvin's gallery, because Lesa, the first female ever of interest, had him considering bi-sexuality.

Detective Seelig and Blevins stood pondering the Christofferson paintings in the Trident's foyer. "I'm not sure if he likes trees or naked women more. Me, I could do without so many trees," Seelig said.

"Seelig, there is one thing about you I can count on," Blevins replied.

"Yeah?"

"You're very predictable."

Before Seelig could answer, the hostess approached and asked if they wanted to dine. "Actually, we were wondering if Randy Quartz is available," Blevins said.

"Sure, he's around. Would you like to wait in the bar while I try to find him?" She pointed to a booth.

The two settled into one of the artful booths built in flowing freeform design by wood craftsmen who obeyed neither time restraints nor the laws regarding controlled substances. There could be no question that The Trident, originally owned by the Kingston Trio and named for Neptune's' three-pronged spear, would someday receive a plaque as a state treasure for its hippie deco interior. Wooden wainscoting, banquette booth backs, handrails, roof support columns and beams swirled away in every direction, somehow always ending in exactly the right position, juxtaposed against an adjacent swirl.

"This place makes me dizzy." Seelig rotated for a better look.

Blevins nodded his head, "Yep, you're consistent."

"How can I help you, gentlemen?" Randy Quartz was shorter than average and a bit stocky, a condition caused by his frequent quality control visits in the kitchen.

"Good morning, Mr. Quartz. I'm Assistant District Attorney Sid Blevins, and this is Detective Seelig." Both showed their identification.

Before Blevins could continue, Quartz blurted, "Oh, my God, you're here about the Christofferson thing. What a tragedy, I still get choked up thinking about Lesa."

"You knew Lesa?" asked Seelig.

"Oh, my yes. She was not only an employee but a dear friend."

"Lesa worked here?" It was Blevins this time.

"Oh, no. Not currently. About a year ago." Randy Quartz had a habit of fluttering his wrists to emphasize his statements

"Why did she leave?" Blevins again, but this time with more interest.

"Marvin put a notice on our bulletin board asking for nude figure models, and Lesa responded immediately. She was kind of stuck on Marvin and saw it as an opportunity to develop their relationship. If you know what I mean?" Randy raised his eyebrows for emphasis this time.

"These two were an item?" Detective Seelig asked with his pen poised over his ever-present notebook.

"Oh, my, yes. Thick as peanut butter. I've never known two people more in love." Randy said.

"Did they ever fight?" Blevins asked with even more interest.

"Why do you ask? You're checking out foul play in their accident? Don't even ask! It's preposterous!" Randy's voice elevated into the irate zone, and his wrists beat a counterpoint rhythm.

"Actually we're trying to find Marvin. To ask a few questions." Blevins said.

"The last time I talked to him, he was in the Marin General Hospital." Randy was a little more composed.

"What did you discuss?" Blevins' eyes narrowed.

"He told me he had to get away for awhile, and he asked me to put a notice in his gallery front door." Randy said.

"Why is his gallery moving to your restaurant?" Seelig asked.

"He lost his lease, and we cooked a deal to move him over here. The owners and I felt it would be a big draw for the restaurant. It's a coup!"

"Did he give you any indication when he might return?" Seelig continued writing in his notebook.

"No. But I don't expect him for quite a while." Quartz could not hide his disappointment.

"Why?

"It was the way he sounded, like he didn't care." Randy said.

"He just sounded defeated. Almost suicidal. I tried to get him to let me pick him up and bring him to my home, but he was not interested."

Blevins handed Randy both his and Seelig's cards. "If you talk to him, ask him to call us." Both men stopped to view a Christofferson painting with Lesa in it before leaving the restaurant.

"I wouldn't throw her over a cliff, I can tell you that. What do you think?" Seelig settled in the driver's seat of the county issue vehicle and looked at his partner.

"I think this whole case is a load of crap!" Blevins hunched down in the passenger seat, laid his head back, and closed his eyes for the trip back to the office.

Chapter 11

Jeffrey's cell phone rang twice before he answered it while he poured a cup of coffee at the State Park office. There was no one on the phone, and on the third ring he remembered the phone Trish Lowe gave him for Chris. He rummaged around his desk until he found it. "Hello?"

"Chris?" Trish was relieved. "I'm glad I finally got you."

"No, ma'am, this is Jeffrey."

"Jeff? This is Trish. Listen, didn't you get the cell phone to Chris yesterday?"

"Yes, ma'am. I did."

"Well... What happened?" she asked.

"He wouldn't take it."

"He wouldn't take it? Why not?"

"I'm not sure. He said he hadn't used a phone in ten years and he wasn't going to start now.."

She could tell Jeff was uneasy. "What else did he say?"

"He offered to cook lobster for me."

"You ate my lobster?"

"Yes, ma'am, it was sure good. Those clams were good too," he said, trying to rekindle some composure. "Now that 'Mantershet' wine, now that's some fine stuff too."

"Look, Jeffrey, I'm very glad you enjoyed my dinner, but was Chris upset I wasn't there?"

"No, ma'am, he didn't seem to be. We just sat there eatin' lobster and clams and drinking lots of wine and talking about the end of mankind until about midnight, I guess."

"He didn't watch the Leno show?"

"No, ma'am, we were out in the dunes communin' with nature... kind of a mano-a-mano thing I guess." Jeff cleared his throat, as he understood now that Ms. Trish thought his errand would end differently. "Ma'am, I told you he's a bit unusual."

"I think I'm beginning to believe you, Jeff," she said, about to hang up. After a pause she added, "Jeff, would you take the phone back to him on your lunch break and dial my number and hand it to him?"

"Yes, ma'am, I surely will. By the way, I think he likes you." He heard a click before he finished his sentence.

Chris felt uneasy and adrift as he strolled the beach. There was no poetry in the sand. He had forgotten to submit his latest stanza to the elements the previous evening. He stopped for long periods watching the surf feather out at his toes. He caught himself looking over his shoulder too much, as if something was following him. He remembered the feeling and its absence for years. Now, contrasted against this first stirring of memory, this feeling was disproportionate and painful. Loneliness was a luxury he could not afford. He picked up a stick and wrote in the sand:

Currents of time erode life's miseries
Leaving only voids where once was joy.
Loneliness, like a vacuum, is always hungry.

Chris stood over the verse a moment and then turned back toward his house and saw Jeffrey's Bronco in the distance. They arrived at the dune house at about the same time. They walked over the dune bridge together

"Come on in. What brings you back so soon?' Chris held the door for Jeffrey.

Jeffrey followed Chris to the dining table. "I have something for you. Actually, I need you to do something." As both men sat down, Jeff began dialing a cell phone.

"What's this all about?" Chris asked.

"Just a minute, I have to make a call." Jeff listened for a moment and then said, "He's here." With that he stuck the phone out at Chris.

"What?" Chris, surprised, did not take the cell phone. Jeff said, "For God's sake take it and say, 'Hello'!"

Chris took the phone. "Hello?"

"Chris, this is Trish. Listen, I feel really bad about last night. There was no way to get out of going to Los Angeles yesterday, and we didn't return until early this morning... . Chris, you there?"

"How was your trip?" Chris stammered for words as he tried unsuccessfully to hold the gadget comfortably.

"It was a lousy trip, and I hated it. In fact it sucked, but that's not the point. I called because I'm going to feel terrible if I disappointed you too much. I want to apologize."

"The lobsters were great." Chris held the phone to his head like it was a dead fish.

"Chris, why do I get the idea you're jerking me around here?" Trish said. "If you're upset with me, just say so. I can take it."

"I'm not upset with you. It's been years since I talked on a phone. They were bigger then."

Her voice softened. "God, I'd trade places with you on that one. Chris, you'

re amazing. Why didn't you tell me you are Christopher Maven, my favorite poet and guardian of my soul? You hurt my feelings."

"It wasn't important," Chris said. "You were having fun."

"The most fun I've had in a while. But I told you how much your poetry means to me. I couldn't know who you were. Your book jackets never have a photo on them."

"I'm a recluse, remember?"

"Can I make last night up to you? I mean, can I come out just for a visit?" Her words were tentative.

"I'm not sure. You might get stuck again. But I do need to get your ice chests back to you, or maybe Jeff can return them." He frowned as he talked.

"There you go jerking me around again," she fired back. "What if I rent a bulldozer to come out?"

"I... I'll try to catch another red fish this afternoon."

"What can I bring?" She asked.

"A couple of bottles of wine maybe."

"Yeah! Some of the 'Manterchet' like last night," Jeff interjected.

"I finish shooting about four o'clock this afternoon, and I'll come right out. I won't even clean up. You'll see me at my worst."

"I thought I'd already seen you at your worst." He smiled.

"There you go again!" she said. "Listen, could I speak to Jeff?" Chris handed the phone to Jeff.

"Yes, ma'am?" He listened for a few minutes and answered, "Yes, ma'am I can do that." He pressed the off button and laid the phone on the table. "You are one smooth talking recluse, dude." A grin split his face like a watermelon slice.

Chris picked up the phone and handed it back to Jeff.

Chris landed a good-sized red fish about mid-afternoon, and fifteen minutes later, the hapless fish was two filets in the refrigerator. He crafted New England chowder using the leftover butter, cream, and clams from the previous night's clambake, prepared dirty rice for last-minute warming, put salad in the crisper, and placed the wine bucket at the ready.

He sat sipping a margarita in the late afternoon deck-shade when he saw Jeff's Bronco on the beach. "Not again!" he thought. As the Bronco pulled up to the dune bridge, he leaped up at seeing Trish behind the wheel. He walked over the bridge and greeted her. "I thought I was going to have dinner with Jeff again."

Trish pointed at the gearshift. "Jeff showed me how to use the four-wheel drive, but I didn't need it, thank God. Two bottles of wine, as requested." She jumped down from the Bronco, and presented the wine, one in each hand.

"Corton Charlemagne! I'm impressed. Your Montrachet made a believer out of Jeff last night."

"Don't get used to this. These are the last two bottles in this part of Texas, I think. I came straight from the set. Hope you don't mind." She smiled. She turned and saw the clambake hole. "Is that where you wild and crazy guys did in my lobsters in last night?"

"I'm afraid so. Jeff's going to get spoiled with this high living if you're not careful." Chris took the wine and tote bag and followed her over the dune bridge. There was nothing exaggerated or affected in her walk, only fluid rhythmic movement, gaited to take the inclines and offsets of the dune bridge. Her hip huggers were Capris, and the short blouse left her midriff bare. Loose black hair hung to her tanned waist.

Chris stared, captivated by her hair brushing the small of her back. Trish turned and, failing to make eye contact, wiggled her hips to break his spell.

"Sorry, I didn't mean to stare," he stammered.

"That's the second time you've said that." Her voice lilted into a laugh.

"I guess you're used to people staring."

"I never get used to people staring. I just wish they'd say 'hello' and get on with their lives."

In the kitchen he offered her a glass of the Corton and set about finishing the meal. She watched for a moment and then said, "How about wine and a chat before dinner?"

"Oh... right! A civilized thing to do. I'm a little rusty on the social graces."

They sat in the deck chairs sipping their wine and watching a pod of porpoise in the surf, leaping and writhing around each other. "Playful things, aren't they? Always having fun," she commented. "So carefree."

"They work only about two hours a day feeding themselves. The rest is fun and frolic and freedom." Chris said. "It's a good life if you don't weaken."

She reached out and squeezed his hand, and he slid her hand into his, soaking up its intimacy. He remembered the feeling. Back then, a caressing squeeze always made him feel warm and safe. Now, the vacant feeling of his morning walk on the beach crept in. Anesthetized by time and loneliness, the hollowness in his center began to stir.

Silence fell over the deck. The breeze rustling the wild dune oats and the saltwater lapping the sand masked the sound of their breathing. Even the gulls and pelicans returning to their evening roosts soared noiselessly overhead, leaving their reverie undisturbed. He released her hand and refilled her glass with the Corton, resting in the ice bucket between their deck chairs. She smiled a "thank you" and lifted the glass to her lips, never taking her eyes from his.

Chris stood up and offered his hand. "Come on, I want you to show you something."

"An adventure?"

"We should feed our souls before our bodies. Bring your glass." He pulled her up and held her hand, leading her across the bridge, down onto the beach to where the house no longer masked the setting sun. He steadied her glass as they climbed to the crest of the dunes, where they faced west over Laguna Madre Bay.

"The magic comes just as the sun hits the water." Chris laid his hand, muscular and calloused from beach life, on Trish's shoulder. The sun, so powerful at noon, was a soft scarlet ball festooned with feathery clouds slinking toward the horizon. Then it happened. First an orange-crimson spike of light blazed over the mirror surface of the calm bay. Then a crimson tinge haloed the magenta clouds, followed by indistinguishable shafts of iridescent silver that stabbed cloud holes until, as if making a final statement, every cloud caught fire and the whole sky burned crimson.

"God in heaven!" Trish's eyes glistened with emotion. She drew in a breath, and lifted her glass in a salute to the firmament. "Thank you!"

"It's not Hollywood, but . . ."

She put her finger to his lips and then turned back to soak up the final rays as darkness settled over the island. She was shivering when they returned to the deck.

"Are you shaken," he asked, "or cold?"

Already in the house, he didn't hear her answer. She sat in

the deck chair again, and he returned soon with a light blanket and two large mugs steaming with clam chowder. Handing her a mug, he spread the blanket with one hand, tucking it under her without spilling his cup, and returned to his deck chair. They sipped in silence. A sense of closeness spread over her, and she snuggled deeper into her chair. "I may never leave this chair. Do you treat all your women so tenderly?"

"I'm antisocial, remember?"

"I'm the first ever?" She laughed.

He chose not to answer her rhetorical question, concentrating instead on his chowder. "Why is poetry important to you? At least you led me to believe it is." He had turned on his side to see her better.

"Wow." Her brow furrowed, wondering what kind of guy would ask me this kind of question. "Why is poetry important to me? That's deep." She brushed a few strands of hair out of her face before she continued. "Maybe it's because poetry takes me from where I am to where I want to be?"

"I thought movies did that." He took a sip from his mug.

"Watching — the great ones take us somewhere, not necessarily where you want to be. Making movies just sucks it all out of me."

"How so?"

"Emotionally, physically, mentally I'm drained dry." She sipped from her mug.

"You don't seem dry to me." He gestured toward her with his mug.

She chuckled and nodded in deference to his comment. "Actually, Leah, my personal manager, helps me cope, and I'm better than I used to be, thanks to her. She's like a big sister. She knows when I'm needy," Trish said. "She's the reason you and I met."

"How so?"

"She made the arrangement with Jeff for me to have quiet time at the state park. It was my idea to try a new beach. I wanted to jog and then read your book."

"You were escaping when you got stuck in the sand?"

"And the rest is history!" She smiled.

"Why my poetry?"

"For a recluse you ask a lot of questions, Chris."

"Just interested. I don't get to visit with many of my readers."

"Okay. Why your poetry?" Her brow furrowed, and she settled back into the chaise and pulled the blanket around her. "Can I be frank?"

"Sure."

"I sensed a need in your poetry that parallels mine. It's comforting to know I'm not alone. That someone out there has the same misgivings about life, and where it's going. I felt I could sit on the deck of a beach house snuggled in a cozy blanket sipping warm chowder on a cool fall evening with the person who wrote those words and be totally content." She reached to squeeze his hand again and added, "I was right."

After a time he said, "There's a pretty decent dinner awaiting us."

"You're gonna make me leave my security blanket, aren't you?" She sighed. "Do you smell something burning?" Trish sniffed the air.

Chris had remembered the dish's creator, Chef Paul Prudhomme, of K Paul's in New Orleans, demonstrating this dish on the television the week before. "The secret to preparin' mah Blackened Red Fish, besides usin' mah own" – the rotund chef smiled and held up a commercial bottle of his blackened seasoning – is havin' a really hot skillet." Chris had put his greased skillet on the stove before serving the chowder, determined to make it really hot. His Dirty Rice went into the oven at the same time.

"Jesus Christ!" Chris jumped up, spilling the rest of his chowder. He ran into the house and choked immediately on the smoke billowing from the greased skillet. He grabbed a box of baking soda from the kitchen cabinet, and turned toward the stove just in time to see Trish, who had followed close behind him, douse the smoking skillet with the remainder of her chowder. The resultant steam-fireball produced a mini-mushroom cloud.

Before the steam reached Trish, Chris pulled her into the

corner of the cabinet shielding her with his body. The cloud rose quickly to the high ceiling of the A-frame, and Chris wheeled and turned off the flame under the skillet. With his other hand he opened the window behind the stove, picked up the skillet using a towel, and threw it outside onto the sand dune below.

In an awkward silence they both looked at the kitchen now bespeckled with carbonized clams and other stringy bits hanging from the walls.

Trish drew a deep breath. "Usually the floor show comes after the dinner."

Chris held his protective position, even after the danger had passed. She worked her arms up between his with some difficulty. Her arms slid over his shoulders, and with her hands behind his neck, she stood on tiptoe and lightly kissed him. The kiss was more exploratory than passionate. He responded by caressing her cheek and forehead, repositioning a lock of errant hair while looking at her with an almost pained expression.

She reacted. "I'm sorry, maybe I shouldn't have... "

Before she could finish he lifted her face to his and kissed her so gently, first on the lips, that moisture welled in her eyes as he kissed them. He pulled her into his chest for a long moment. He stepped back, releasing her.

Before he could say anything, she put her finger to his lips and said, "Shhhhh."

Taking his hand, she led him into the living room to the base of the loft stairs where she turned, kissed him again, and said, "May I freshen up? I came straight from the shoot." She picked up her beach bag and disappeared into the bathroom.

Chris was rooted in indecision. He knew he should do something, but he was not sure what. He stepped toward the stereo sound system thinking the moment needed appropriate music, paused, turned, and moved toward the loft stairs wondering if he had put clean linen on the bed. The shower sounds from the bathroom gave him a time frame, and he moved into action.

First he slipped a Vangelus CD into the player and turned the music to an appropriate volume. Then, hurrying up the stairs, he saw the bed in disarray from last night's tryst with Lottie. He ripped the sheets from the bed, wadding and throwing them into a corner of the loft. He opened a window next to his bed to exhaust the vapors that had collected at the top of the A-Frame from the steam explosion. The cool night air moved into the sleeping loft, refreshing him as he scurried around the bed remaking it with clean sheets.

Glad I did the washing yesterday, he thought.

The shower shut off just as he finished making the bed. He slid out of his cutoffs and t-shirt and crawled under the top sheet, still in his Jockey shorts. During the long pause that followed, the enormity of the situation sagged into his psyche.

What do I think I am doing? This is insane. More guilt? More lies? More secrets? An impossible situation with no positive resolution. More pain. More bone-aching loneliness. Nothing good can come of this. Who do I think I am? How could she possibly be interested in me? She could have any man she wants. Why me?

He failed to notice Trish gliding up the loft stairs during this reverie as if she were propelled on a hydraulic lift. Suddenly she was beside the bed, wearing his bathrobe with her freshly washed hair brushed back over the collar. Her fragrance drifted over the bed as she peeled back his top sheet.

Vangelus floated into the loft, masking all but a murmur from the surf. Before he could react, Trish tugged on the bathrobe tie allowing the robe to part and with a shrug, she let it drift to the floor, sliding in slow motion first from her shoulders, then from her arms, and finally crumpling at her feet.

It was a dramatic effect, and Chris was awestruck by the sight of Trish Lowe wearing nothing but Trish Lowe. He felt he was in the presence of near perfection. He stammered, "Why... why, yes, go ahead and slip into something more comfortable."

She pointed to his Jockey shorts. "Are those for your protection or mine?

"Maybe we should just be friends?"

She hooked her thumb in the waistband of his shorts. "You don't get off that easily, mister. These have got to go."

Later she raised her head from his chest and asked, "Chris, why did we make love to funeral music?"

"Funeral Music?" he said. "That was Vangelus. I thought it was romantic."

She nestled back again, closer this time, and said, "Maybe the Beach Boys next time."

Trish awakened well before sunrise and lay in bed listening to Chris's easy breathing. Her eyes dampened at the serenity of the moment, as a slight breeze wafted salt air through the loft windows and the sheer curtains rustled. The heave and sigh of the surf, barely audible, left the rest of the night quiet and restful.

What absolute and complete peace, she thought. She moved her hand and touched Chris. He quivered and skipped a breath before returning to his nocturnal rhythm.

She remembered the tender, almost hesitant lovemaking only hours before, and tried to place it in her life's chronology.

Beauty, fame, wealth – none of it had gelled into cohesive happiness for Trish Lowe. The nagging fear haunted her that she was only a sideshow freak, only a curiosity people gawked at, criticized, and watched with morbid curiosity, waiting for her to self-destruct under the pressure of her good fortune.

But was it possible to live like this, free of demands and at peace with oneself? It was so foreign, it was almost frightening. Could this be what all the songs and poems are about? Being completely fulfilled and totally terrified at the same time, like performing a high wire act over a mountain of cotton candy?

Out of habit she looked at the luminous hands of her wristwatch. "Damn, it's twenty minutes 'til six!" She jumped involuntarily. Her limo would be pulling up to her hotel in ten minutes to take her to a six o'clock cast call for outdoor action sequences. There was no time to get to the hotel.

She pulled back the top sheet, trying to get out of bed without waking Chris. She heard Chris say, "So, that's the shape you're in." He was admiring her nude silhouette against the first morning light.

"I was trying not to wake you."

"I don't have very many people crawling out of my bed this early in the morning."

"I've got a cast call in twenty minutes." She sat back on the edge of the bed.

"Last night was good. How would you like to go for great?" Chris rolled to the middle of the bed.

"Great takes a lot of time, and I have... "

Chris pulled her toward him. "Spontaneity is the soul of joy." He kissed her.

"I guess a little joy couldn't hurt." she smiled.

Later, the two strolled onto the deck in bathrobes, carrying cups of coffee and surveyed a brilliant day in its adolescence. She leaned back against the deck railing completely at ease, inviting a kiss. He responded. "Easy," she said, "or you'll have to give an encore."

"I'm an old man, remember."

Her eyes danced as she looked into his.

He squeezed her hand. "I don't suppose you could no-show today, and spend the day here?"

"Actually, I've already 'no-showed'. Spend the day here? Now that's a joyful thought! She walked inside to get her cell phone. There was a delay before Trish spoke, "Well, good morning to you too, Leah!" Her voice became muffled and Chris could not understand the conversation until she returned to the deck with the phone and snapped, "Fine – yes – I'll be there in thirty minutes."

Chapter 12

Rod Blitzer still smarted fifteen years after failing as an actor. He was too short to be a leading man. He wasn't that handsome either, but his shortness weighed on him like three G's of gravity. He knew Michael J. Fox was the beneficiary of ditches dug for leading ladies to stand and walk in, and that Alan Ladd had stood on boxes to kiss the girls. Nothing about Rod Blitzer moved producers and directors to dig ditches or to provide boxes for that matter.

His last tryout at a casting call for a grade-B flick landed him a speaking part as a gas station attendant who delivered the line, "Fill'er up?" Rod was not unintelligent; in fact he was outright crafty and persuasive in all arenas except representing his own acting career. He felt certain that the three-word speaking part he got after a year of readings and other equally embarrassing attempts at gainful employment was not much on which to build an acting career.

The final dent in his acting ego came from a producer of pornographic movies. Rod was very much economically challenged and a friend told him of some quick money to be had from a porn producer. Reluctantly applying at the address provided, he found after undressing for his interview that shortness again stood between him and success in even this temporary divergence from mainstream acting.

He did, however, make the acquaintance of a beautiful nineteen-year-old girl bent on debuting in a porn flick. He convinced her that, with him as her agent, she would get a better deal than she could get on her own. Rod bargained her to top dollar for her first picture because she was a "fresh face" to the producer, and a face the producer particularly wanted. Rod's new career was launched. He never forgot the lesson learned from his first negotiation: always have what Hollywood wants.

Now he was pushing forty, a bit heavier, and his reputation as a tough negotiator and a good judge of talent had made him a respected Hollywood agent

During his run as agent, he'd moved from the seedier side of filmdom to representing a stable of hunks and starlets whose agent fees provided a living, but nothing fulfilled his dreams. About nine years ago he saw the movie *She,* starring a new actress called Trish Lowe. Trish's star was hovering just below the horizon until she got the break in this piece-of-trash movie. Rod could not take his eyes off her during the film and, even after, his thoughts constantly drifted back to this beautiful girl who could dance in ways that stirred him physically and emotionally.

Even with her one starring role, Rod felt she was not out of reach for him. After all, he was beginning to be noticed as an agent. His initial interest was not so much professional as romantic. He wanted this girl. Bad!

Inquiring through the Screen Actors Guild, Rod located the address and phone number of Trish Lowe, but his telephone messages went unanswered. Finally, out of desperation, he explained that he was an agent and wanted to talk to her about her career. She called back in less than twenty-four hours.

Rod learned several things during his first lunch meeting at Spago's with Trish. She had been romantically involved with her current agent, having fallen for the old line, "I'll make you a star." A promise he kept, but only after moving on to fresher faces and leaving Trish to wonder about the price of fame. She now was actively seeking a new agent. Yes, she was everything Rod hoped she would be. Beautiful, talented, and a genuinely sweet person, albeit a bit wiser and more cynical even at age twenty. She was one of those fortunate or unfortunate women (depending upon your outlook) with whom men who simply passed her on the street would fall in love.

Finally and most importantly, Rod learned that Trish was taller than he. Faced with the lingering obstacles left from her recent agent relationship, her new found cynicism, and his height disadvantage, Rod could feel himself slipping into morass all the more painful because of the constant personal encounters for purely professional reasons. This unhappy lifestyle could lead to bitterness and confrontation, and to his credit, he resisted the urge to get involved, even professionally, through the Crudités of Baby Vegetables and the Watercress Soup courses of their lunch. But when the King Crab Claw with Saffron Scented Low Fat Mayonnaise arrived, he was powerless to resist further, and they agreed to a one-year contract with automatic renewals. Little did they know that this tenuous business relationship would survive their many clashes of will for eight years and more than a dozen starring roles. Through it all, Rod struggled with mixed results to keep his desire from overriding his objectivity.

Rod had called all day and into the evening without success at both Trish's hotel room in Corpus Christi and on her cell phone. He wanted a reading on how the appearance on "The Tonight Show" went. There was no answer; even to ten o'clock West Coast time, which meant Trish was out after midnight. Something was up.

Leah tried to reach Trish by phone but, thinking she might be in the shower, she went to Trish's room and let herself in with her copy of the room key, hoping to share a cup of coffee with Trish before the star's driver arrived.

Trish was not in the shower. Trish was not in the room. In fact Trish had not slept in her bed last night. This revelation sent Leah scurrying back to her own room. The phone rang as she entered her own room and with mercurial speed she lifted the receiver before the second ring. "Trish?" Leah barked into the receiver.

"No, Leah, it's Rod. Were you expecting a call from Trish?"

Leah grimaced at the announcement that Rod Blitzer was on the phone. "Yes, Rod, I left a call for Trish, and I thought this might be her callback."

"You'd be luckier than me if you got a callback. I tried to reach her all day yesterday and last night." Rod sounded perturbed.

There was a noticeable pause before Leah answered as she started spinning the right reply. "Rod, I know they had some problems on the shoot yesterday, and it ran on into the night." Leah waited to see if this fabrication held up.

"Really? I did get Danielle Stokes last night, and she said Trish left the set about four-thirty yesterday. She seemed to be in a hurry." Rod waited for a reaction to his gotcha.

"Jesus, Rod, are you lonesome out there? It sounds like you're running a detective rather than a talent agency."

"I just wanted to know how 'The Tonight Show" gig went. Also I wanted to share some good news."

"What good news? I don't think I can stand any more good news this morning," Leah replied.

"Sounds like we're a little stressed this morning." Rod probed. "I surmise all is not well with our girl."

"Rod, things are absolutely great here," Leah lied.

"There is definitely something wrong," Rod said. "I think I should come out there and give my good news to Trish personally."

"If I listed one-hundred things we don't need here, Rod Blitzer would be at the top of the list. All I need is for you and Trish to get into one of your pissing matches." Leah waved her free hand for emphasis.

"I don't sound welcome there."

"Rod, you're almost always welcome. Just not right now. Right? Stay there, Rod". Leah frowned. "Can I have your word on that?"

"Right! Stay here, right? Not a problem!" Rod hung up the phone and called to his secretary. When she reached his desk, he said, "Get me to Texas tomorrow!"

Chapter 13

The woman's black hair flailed savagely at her face, punctuating her terrified glances over her shoulder. She hunched over the steering wheel of the top-down red convertible, coaxing greater speed. The black van behind her gained steadily as the shoreline of Laguna Madre flashed by. The abbreviated beach of dredged sand lining Padre Island Causeway was a blur in the rearview mirror. Shore birds, fishermen, parked vehicles, clumps of spartina and mounds of drifted seaweed smeared into a colorful collage and then receded as the red car climbed the JFK Bridge.

Her backward glances came faster as the van closed the distance and slammed her bumper. She swerved into the left lane to ward off an attempt to pass her and almost lost control of the convertible. She retreated to the other lane to right her vehicle, and the van made its move, wedging itself between the inside guardrail and the convertible. The mirrored van window rolled down, and the girl screamed as a muscular, tattooed arm tossed a grenade into the passenger seat floorboard of her convertible. She lunged for the grenade, but her left hand hung in the steering wheel, swerving the car toward the outside guardrail as the car approached the waterway under the bridge.

"Cut!" The camera stopped rolling and the car and van slowed to a stop. Director Danielle Stokes once again crackled through the cameraman's earphones as he climbed from the camera rack clamped to the side of the convertible. "Okay! Thanks everybody! Good work and great driving, you guys. I think we have the setup right. Tell Trish we're ready for her?"

After a sort pause, a hesitant voice said, "We can't find Trish. She's not in her dressing room."

The director scowled, "Goddamn it! Not again!" She sat in front of four camera monitors. They were mounted on a table under the bridge that climbed to about seventy-five feet above the Intracoastal Waterway before descending onto Padre Island. A half mile farther south, on Padre Island Drive, Park Road 361 turned onto Mustang Island. Danielle had more to worry about than Trish's absence. The entire bridge stunt was dicier than she and her stunt coordinator liked. She didn't need Trish pulling this crap.

Danielle sighed as she studied the restaurants lining the island side of the Intracoastal Waterway at the bridge. Frenchy's and Snoopy's across the water were both heating up their fryers and readying the shrimp and fish for the onslaught of a lunch crowd tripled in size by the curious coming to watch a movie being made. Sport fishing and commercial shrimping operators inhabited the near side. Somehow her crew had to vault a car over the bridge handrail, catapult a stunt person out of it in a James Bond style ejection seat, and explode the car in midair without debris plummeting onto the commercial operations below, or onto the stunt person riding his seat down into a hidden safety net. They had erected other safety nets over the closest buildings, and they planned for the large expanse of undeveloped tidal flats to catch some of what was left of the car. But the main body of the car was to plummet onto a vacant restaurant on the mainland immediately adjacent to the bridge. The location manager had purchased the partially ruined restaurant and renovated the exterior sufficiently for medium-range shots of diners on the deck bordering the waterway. The stunt was to end with the car, engulfed in flames, crashing onto the restaurant followed by a fireball explosion. The stunt person was to splash down in the waterway from a height of about twenty feet in a later cutaway camera shot. Danielle grimaced as she mentally reviewed the script. The dangerous stunt, its potential aftermath, and the cost of cleaning up the mess, had Danielle contemplating a career change from action flicks to drawing room comedies.

The one good thing about the site was that there was a large area under the bridge for the cranes, generators, grip trucks, dressing trailers, catering and craft services vehicles, all safe and hidden. Traffic considerations were manageable, but required temporarily blocking the southbound lanes of the bridge to traffic.

Danielle removed her headphones as Leah Armour approached the director's table. "Looks like you're making good progress this morning," Leah offered sheepishly, knowing what she had to say next.

"We've made all the goddamn progress we are going to make unless we get a star!" There was nothing cordial in Danielle's voice. "What's wrong! Trish has never treated us – she gestured at the whole crew – like this in the past. Qué pasó, Leah? Trish's been busting our balls around here for days now. We can't do the stunt and blow up the goddamn car until we get Trish's close-ups."

"Actually, that's why I'm here. Trish is having a little trouble getting going this morning. Stomach flu or something, but she will be here as soon she quits vomiting."

"Christ! Not the puking thing! Leah, nobody uses the puking thing anymore. It's so passé."

"Come on, Danielle, you just said yourself that Trish normally would be here unless something was wrong. So give her a break. She'll be here."

Danielle's sigh was audible. "All I know is we have less than two weeks to put this thing in the can, and we're running out of time." Tires sliding in gravel and a truck door slamming interrupted Danielle.

Reese, the stunt coordinator, strode to the table. "What's up, Danielle? The natives are getting restless up top. This is a tough stunt, and it's not good having everybody standing around thinking about it."

"Ask Leah, here, what the hold up is." Danielle pointed to Trish's personal manager.

Leah shrugged. "Trish is a little under the weather this morning, but I think she'll be here soon."

"Real soon, I hope. Or I'll have to put the stunt people on

golden time," Reese replied.

"That's not the half of it. We only have the frigging bridge until four o'clock this afternoon. We have to clear out in time for the evening traffic." Danielle added, "God, am I glad our prick of a leading man is with the second unit today. I couldn't bear to listen to his bitching over this fiasco."

"Is there something else you could shoot while we wait for Trish?" Leah winced.

"Great idea, Leah! We just got the setup right on the bridge, so now let's break it down and go shoot something else, so we can do the setup all over again?" Danielle's voice rose to the pitch of a phone ringer. She turned to Reese. "Is the cast dressed for the restaurant deck shot?"

"I think so. I could see a bunch of people down on the deck when I was up on top."

Danielle keyed her mike. "Dimitri, you there?"

"Here, Boss! We're ready for the close-ups," the director of photography answered.

"We've got a hold up, so pull cameras one and four and set up for the restaurant deck scene."

"You're kidding, right?"

"No. Actually I'm in a hurry, so let's snap to it, pronto! The cast is already on the deck."

"I'm all over it, boss."

Danielle finished checking the camera angles for the restaurant deck scene. Camera number one was mounted on a crane fitted with seats for both a cameraman and the director. Camera number two was dolly-mounted to allow for closer shots after the action started.

The deck had eight umbrella tables scattered about with four director-style chairs at each. The cloudless sky washed the deck with sunlight, so the lighting crew had only to set up a series of reflector panels for additional light under the umbrellas, and the set was camera-ready.

The actors, bored with the tedium of filmmaking, retreated to the shade and lolled about in the chairs waiting for direction.

Danielle made the rounds of the deck for her final inspection, surprised that she didn't recognize any of the actors. They were all quite gregarious in their greetings to her, and she thought, God, I just can't keep up with all these people. I don't know why, but maybe Reese brought in some new stunt people for the action sequences. Walking back out to her camera seat, she keyed her headset mike, "Reese, you have the pick up boats and divers ready for the shot?"

A surprised Reese answered, "Danielle, I'm up on the bridge. What boats and what divers?"

"For the deck shot down here. You're going to have to pick up your stunt people after they go over the side!"

"I don't have any stunt people down there! I thought this was just background filler."

"Who the hell are these people on the deck?" Danielle screamed.

After a slight silence, the voice of the casting assistant crackled over the walky-talky. "They're extras, Danielle."

"Extras? How the hell am I going to shoot an action sequence with extras? They're supposed to dive over the handrail. These people couldn't dive into a bowl of soup!" Danielle's voice had reached the timbre of metal against a grinding wheel.

Another long silence, and then the assistant casting director added, "Actually, Danielle, they are not even paid extras. They're PR extras, you know, the mayor and some city councilmen and their wives, some highway department people. You know, the people who let us use the bridge for this shot."

"Jesus H. Christ! Tell me none of them are lawyers. Have they signed photo releases and liability disclaimers?" The harried producer chimed in over his walkie-talkie.

"You bet! But I didn't tell them they're gonna dive off the deck."

"Reese, how soon can you sign up four stunts for minimum fee and get them down here in blue jeans and t-shirts?" Danielle asked.

"I'll have them down there in fifteen minutes along with the boats and divers."

"You're a can-do guy, Reese." Danielle was over the surprise and well into the problem solving. She climbed into the camera seat and motioned the crane operator to lift her ten feet above the ground. "Could I have your attention, please?" She barked into her bullhorn at the people on the deck, "Thank you. First I want to thank you for helping us out here today and to thank all of you for being so gracious and helpful in the past."

A murmur of appreciation rose from the deck people.

"This scene is quite simple. The waiters are passing among you with plates of food and drinks. Everything is edible to help you give us some realism in the shot. We want you to be eating a nice lunch, but when you hear a gun shot, look up startled and act as though you see a huge explosion above you. Then leap out of your chairs and run to the handrail. Okay, everybody got it? Talk among yourselves, and enjoy lunch, but when you hear a gunshot, move into action. And listen; do not look at the cameras. Got it? Do not look at the cameras! Okay, let's do a run through. Start eating and visiting."

"Roll cameras! Mark! Action!" Danielle signaled to Pyro, the FX man, on the roof of the restaurant, and he fired a blank 357-magnum cartridge. It was loud enough to get the deck people's attention, all but the mayor's wife, a rotund lady, who had found the food on her plate and was not going to give it up easily. For the most part, the group glanced up, and then paused before regaining their composure enough to remember the run to the handrail. The few who got into the scene leaped up from the table and ran to the guardrail and then mugged the cameras as if expecting to receive their Oscars on the spot. Most got up casually and, in grade school fire drill style, they filed out of the tables in an orderly fashion. During the exercise they failed to notice that four strangers had joined the group.

"Okay, well, we did that one." Danielle tried to hide her contempt for what she just witnessed in the camera monitor. "But we need a little more energy, folks! You are about to get killed, so you need to act like it. You looked like you were going through a buffet line. Take your places, and we'll try again." Danielle called Pyro, "You got anything in your bag of tricks that makes a lot of noise but doesn't tear anything up?"

"Boss lady, I could win WW III with what I've got in that bag."

"I think we're gonna have to jar these folks into action, if you know what I mean."

"I can do that."

Back to her bullhorn again Danielle said, "Okay! Now next time let's see a little more animation. Go ahead and keep eating. We have a few things to do before the next run through."

"Let me know when you're ready, Pyro."

But Pyro didn't answer. He was busy resetting the timer on a six-inch diameter aerial bomb to blow at thirty-feet elevation. He then ran detonator wires over the side of the building to get some distance between the bomb and him. "Okay, Boss, I'm ready."

"Reese, you okay with the boats?"

"Ready, Boss."

The delay was long enough for the diners to get back into their lunch and their Margaritas. Their conversation was punctuated by laughter and the clink of glasses. Danielle checked for clouds, for airplanes, and road noise then called softly, "Roll Camera! ... Mark! ...Action!"

Pyro pushed the detonator button, and a thump propelled the aerial bomb skyward. but at thirty feet above the roof a stupefying explosion rent the air. It was loud enough to bring the Second Coming.

It was not apparent to Danielle if the four stunt people were big time into the scene, or if they were as panicked as the rest of the crowd. The first of them leaped up shouting "HOLY SHIT!" and almost knocked over his table as he ran to the handrail and vaulted over it as if it were a gymnastics horse. His was not a ten-point landing as his legs and arms were still flailing as he landed in the water.

Two of the others screamed and followed behind the first stuntman. They jumped flat-footed to the top of the handrail and executed perfect cannonball dives into the water. The backwash of these dives careened over the handrail, dousing the extras who by now were beginning full flight themselves. All had jumped to their feet, except for the mayor's wife, who could not jump on any occasion. She had a large bite in mid-trip to her mouth when the explosion startled her so that she missed her mouth for one of the few times in her life, and her fork flew over her shoulder like a missile and stuck in the wall of the restaurant. She then stood up, toppling the table and umbrella, spilling plates and food onto the deck as, overcoming her sizeable inertia, she headed for the handrail gate at the end of the deck.

Others slipped on the wet deck and executed perfect pratfalls. A few of the more agile had crawled over the rail and jumped. People ran into each other, bumped, and pirouetted trying to escape what must be their certain death.

The fourth stunt man, more for his own protection from the mob than for cinematic kinesis, grabbed the umbrella pole from the toppled table and vaulted over people and handrail and into the water. Madam mayor was by this time in full trot and still gaining speed when she hit the gate with such force she ripped hinges and latch from their moorings. Gate and madam both cleared about eight feet of water before either got wet.

"Cut and print!" Danielle smiled for the first time that day.

Leah waited in Trish's dressing trailer to escape Danielle's wrath and perhaps to hear from her missing ward. She knew Trish must have something going she did not want broadcast, so she fought back the urge to call ranger Jeffrey to see if he knew anything about Trish's whereabouts. Four cigarettes later her cell phone rang. Caller I.D. announced Trish's name. "Trish! Where the hell are you! Danielle's ripping me a new one here."

After a pause Trish said, "Well, good morning to you too, Leah!"

"Babe, this is anything but a good morning. Where are you?"

"I woke up early and drove out to Mustang Island to catch the sunrise. I'm having car trouble?" The lilt at the end of the sentence lacked sincerity.

"No, Trish, you're having stomach flu, and you were vomiting, right?" Leah couldn't help gesturing as she talked.

"Not the puking thing! Nobody believes that anymore."

"Shoot me if that's the most creative excuse I could come up with for somebody that didn't sleep in her own bed last night. I'm not interested in the 'whys' right now. Just the 'when.' How soon can you get here?"

After a pause, Leah said, " Great! But look, if you're really out on the island, traffic over the causeway bridge is stopped dead. We've blocked the southbound lanes, and you'll never get over here to our side. Go to Snoopy's, and I'll pick you up in a boat. Right? Hurry!"

Chapter 14

To clear his head after Trish's hasty departure, Chris went into the workroom under the house. *Deliverance* still sat in dry dock, unattended for over a year. Boats are never finished, he thought; eventually you just quit on them. The fervor he once lavished on building the boat had faded, leaving the craft seaworthy but lacking some niceties like oarlocks, mooring cleats, and an exit from its captivity. They hadn't seemed important, but now he viewed the boat from a new perspective.

His optimism, long a dry abyss, now stirred with renewed expectation. The void Chris felt from Trish's absence was not sadness but rather a hint of loss. Not romantic loss, but the waning of buoyancy her presence brought. Vulnerability gnawed at him like an exposed nerve. There was something he needed — to live once again.

Deliverance was wide enough for two people, about sixteen feet long, and had classic Johnboat lines with her graceful gunnels curving upward to the exaggerated bow point. The hull quickly flared out from the bow to an almost flat bottom with a good keel to hold her line. The teak deck skewed upward toward the stern, attaching to a solid teak transom. The boat was magnificent by any standard. Add the hull with its lap strake boards alternating between dark teak and light cypress, coated in a dozen coats of spar varnish, along with the glistening brass fittings, and the most critical eye could see that *Deliverance* was a work of art.

Chris walked around the boat several times, stopping at the bow and tracing her name, *Deliverance,* with his finger the word feeling the irregularities of hand carving. At one time he had planned the boat to be a centerboard sailboat, but practicality prevailed, and he dropped this idea, opting instead for rowing as propulsion.

The boat had no oarlocks, so he busied himself attaching the oarlock blocks to the gunnels and bracing them back to the hull. He then drilled holes and inserted brass tubes to receive the oar davits. Once the oars were in place, he shipped them astern and crawled into the boat for a dry run. Exhilaration welled in him as he stroked the air with the oars. Long, easy pulls on the oars propelled him toward visions of future possibilities. Eyes closed, he continued the rowing until his arms complained. He shipped the oars astern and sat, eyes still closed, drifting into safe harbor.

The temperature in the workroom rose with the sun on this cloudless day, and Chris finally climbed the stairs leaving *Deliverance* at rest. He sat at his desk and drank a beer while toweling off the sweat from his exertion. His copy of *High Above the Far Below* lay on the desk and he leafed through it, stopping from time to time to read passages, but his thoughts always returned to Trish. He was annoyed at her absence. Trading the book for a notebook and pen, he began composing a verse. Crumpled pages ripped from the notebook ringed the wastebasket before he laid the pen to rest. The completed verse had a different feel to him like someone else had written it. He stood, pondering what should be done and then took the notebook and walked over the bridge.

He ranged barefoot over the beach looking for a suitable driftwood stick and the perfect place to inscribe the verse. He stared at a low mound of sand above the high tide line and felt drawn by a need for this verse to survive. Reading from the notebook, he scratched the verse into the beach sand and stood considering it. It still seemed the work of a different person.

Fatigue settled over him when he returned to the house, and he wrestled with the couch until he finally drank two glasses of Riesling. Slipping into a fitful sleep, dreams flashed and rippled through the hollowness in the center of him. Then the sound came again. Unmistakable. Like the bark of an injured sea lion, then slow grinding. The squeal of overheated brake shoes slipping. Slipping and helpless against the pull of gravity on the steep incline. The apparition appeared through the fog and darkness like a distant harbor light. Fingers of dense fog clung to it like colorless cotton candy. Creeping closer, gaining speed down the cliffside road. The mechanical Cyclops crept past him— brakes howling.

He tried to move, but only slid in the roadway gravel. He screamed, but no sound came. One wheel bumped over the cliff, and then the other, and, as if tilted by an unseen hand, the VW bus pitched forward. Then Lesa's face appeared again as it had a thousand times. The horrified expression plastered against the back door window as the bus disappeared groaning and grinding into nothingness.

The roar of a car engine and whirring tires spinning in sand woke him, and he sat upright sweating, trying to catch his breath.

Chapter 15

Lottie Langton knew her big scene with Chris on the beach was not a positive in their relationship. She wrestled with just how to approach the problem. There was no way to know what's happening out there, she thought. If I just drop in on him, God knows what they might be going on. I don't handle surprises well!

It had been a vexing twenty-four hours for her, finally quieted by the double vodka and orange juice she drank as she considered her future. It seemed unfair that she should be the one to recant. Hell, I'm the one who's being dumped on here, she thought. Loving a recluse really sucks. Talk about your lack of communication. Maybe if I drove out there right now, we could get this thing talked out. Get it resolved. Get back to point 'A'. Or, hell, let's just say it like it is. Get in the sack and work some things out!

By the time the vodka worked its magic in her empty stomach, she was heading out the door to get things right with Chris. Her white Jeep SUV rumbled through Port Aransas past the giant plastic sharks lurking at the entrances to T-shirt shops, their toothy grins filled with tourists and bawling young children. Children smart enough to know a shark's mouth was not a good photo opportunity. She passed The Spaghetti Works, passed Marcel's, passed Sharky's and the beginning of condo row. She gained speed, secure in the knowledge that hers was the path of truth and justice, but her confidence eroded like the dunes in high wind when she reached the turn off to Fish Pass Road. Turning toward the beach, she stopped and sighed when the pavement ended.

She banged her head on the steering wheel, trying to reorder her thoughts. "This is crazy! I'm not going to crawl back to that asshole and apologize. If the bastard wants to see me, he can tell Jeffrey."

She executed a wheel-spinning about-face, spewing sand into the dunes, and returned to the highway where she stopped for a minute considering the direction to turn. Finally she turned toward Corpus Christi. "I'll just go to the spa and get the works. Hair, toenails, fingernails, massage, the works." She thought out loud and smiled at the prospect.

Backed-up traffic trying to turn onto Padre Island Drive forced her to stop several hundred yards before the intersection. Both north and southbound traffic was at a standstill at the Padre Island Drive red light. She pulled onto the shoulder, passing the cars on the right, finally making it into the Circle K at the intersection. A sunburned teenager who would need a wax job if his baggy shorts sagged any lower, walked past her window. "What's the deal here, why all the traffic?" She asked

The kid moved his boogie board to his other hand and stepped closer to Lottie's car for a better look at her cleavage struggling valiantly against her halter-top. "Yeah, man. Like they're makin' a movie! I mean they got cameras and shit all over the bridge. Totally awesome, man. I mean this traffic's goin' nowhere, dude. It's strictly Jam City!"

Lottie translated the information and smiled at the gawking kid. "Thanks, surfer dude." She wondered if Miss Trish Lowe was at the epicenter of this problem, then continued toward the bridge driving on the shoulder. Drivers locked bumper to bumper in the traffic snarl honked furiously in displeasure at her flanking move. Lottie replied to their displeasure by shooting them a reassuring finger. She finally dead-ended against a guard railing at the first culvert. The middle-aged tourist in a minivan blocking her progress frowned when she gestured for him to roll down his window, but he grudgingly complied. Lottie leaned out her window far enough that her halter almost lost control of its cargo, grinned mischievously, and asked, "I wonder if you could back up just a tad?" Mr. Minivan lurched backwards so hard that he slammed into the car behind him and never took his eyes off the impending great escape hanging out of Lottie's window. She seized the day and squeezed inside the guard railing, crossed the culvert, and turned onto the road at the foot of the causeway bridge leading to Snoopy's on the Intracoastal Waterway.

"Hey, Roscoe, too early for a beer?" She strode up to Snoopy's order counter.

"Never too early for you, Miss Lottie."

"Thought I'd check out the action." She tried to pay for the beer.

"Beer's on me, Lottie. I owe you one from the other night."

She smiled a thank you and went out to stand at the guardrail of Snoopy's deck. About fifty yards across the waterway was a blur of activity with people returning to their seats at umbrella tables on the deck of the old vacant restaurant. Waiters moved between the tables serving plates of food and drinks while three authoritarian types in ball caps, tank tops and shorts carrying clip boards and wearing head sets shouted and gestured at each other, occasionally repositioning touristy-looking extras seated at the table. Two people were elevated on some contraption that held what looked like a camera.

From this distance there was no way to tell if one of the people was actually Trish Lowe. Lottie sipped her beer, leaned on the railing, and strained to pick out Trish from all the others on the far side.

The explosion was so loud that she threw her beer into the water and herself onto the deck. When she dared a glimpse, she saw people running in every direction, some falling and others jumping over the railing into the waterway. It was Keystone Cops stuff, and she laughed out loud.

"Cut and print!" echoed from a bullhorn over the water. Boats with wetsuit-clad divers moved in to pick up those in the water, while those still on the deck stood around in an apparent state of shock. After all the swimmers were returned to the deck, a woman got in one of the boats and pointed toward Snoopy's while talking to the driver. He backed out, headed across the channel, and pulled into one of Snoopy's boat slips. The driver moored the boat and helped the woman get out.

"Is she coming over for takeout?" Lottie mused aloud.

As the woman climbed the stairs to the deck, she smiled at Lottie. "Big boom, huh!"

"Damn straight! It scared the hell out of me!" Lottie said. "Actually, you owe me a beer. I tossed mine overboard when you guys set off the atomic bomb."

"Come on in, and I'll buy you one." Leah pointed to the door. Lottie followed her into the restaurant.

"I'm buying this lady a beer." Leah addressed Roscoe.

"Anybody know what in the bejesus all the noise is about?" Roscoe asked. "Some of these shrimp got up and danced around after that boom."

"That's nothing! Wait until you see the stunt this afternoon. It will blow you away." Leah snickered at her pun.

"You're with the movie?" Lottie asked.

"Indirectly."

"Directly enough to know Trish Lowe?"

"Yeah, a little." Leah moved into her protective mode.

Lottie didn't know where to go from there, so she blurted, "I've got a pretty cool bar over in Port Aransas. You guys ever get thirsty, come on over to The Backyard. I'll buy you a drink." The door to Snoopy's flew open before Leah could answer.

A woman strode in and smiled at Leah. She wore a ball cap, sunglasses, a bulky sweater, and Capri pants. Her hair was disheveled, and she wore no makeup.

"God, what a mess out there on the road," she said to Leah. "This was a great idea to pick me up here."

The two locked arms and headed out to the deck. Over her shoulder Leah said in Lottie's direction, "Good to meet you. Maybe we'll see you at your place."

"Yeah, it's The Backyard!" Lottie knew there was something about the second woman. Something she recognized. "My God, that was Trish Lowe!"

"That movie star woman?" Roscoe asked.

Lottie didn't answer, but her mind was whirring. Trish Lowe was on the island side of a bridge that couldn't be crossed from either direction. That meant she was on the island all night. That meant she spent the night with Chris. She spent the night screwing Chris!

"Son-of-a-bitch! That low-life lying bastard spent the night with Trish Lowe last night. I'll kill him!" She shouted and turned on her heel, kicking her way out of the front door.

"Yeah, well, ahh, come back another time, Lottie." Roscoe jumped as the door slammed.

A huge sand rooster tail spewed from under Lottie's tires before they grabbed, and the SUV lurched forward. She was already up to speed, almost going airborne when she hit the pavement shoulder of Padre Island Drive. She again caused some concern and disapproval from the gridlocked drivers on the causeway. As she careened left onto Park Road 361 through the opening in the stalled traffic of the other lane. Trying to regain control of the SUV refocused her mind enough to question her assumption. Maybe Trish was on the island for another reason. Why would she be so eager to leap in the sack with Chris, anyway? Why be so confrontational – why not just have a nice civilized conversation with Chris about their future? That made more sense.

She was back in control again by the time she reached Fish Pass Road. She drove the distance to Chris's at a normal speed and stopped a little way from his walkway to further compose herself. Standing by the car she saw a verse in the sand about thirty feet away and strolled to it, glancing up to make sure Chris was not watching while she read.

> *The silent stirring of renewal*
> *Invades my solitude softly.*
> *On the wings of passion*
> *My soul is borne aloft,*
> *Perhaps to glimpse tomorrow.*

Lottie stared at the verse. She sensed a new beginning. A stirring of hope. A fragment of release. A splinter of light around the door of escape. She had not inspired the verse. She kicked the sand and stomped back to her car. Stopping with her back tires over the verse, she gunned the engine and the rear wheels dug deep ruts through the poem.

Chapter 16

The boat barely cleared Snoopy's dock before Leah dialed Trish's makeup artist. "Gwen? Listen, babe, can you meet Trish in her trailer in five minutes? Yeah, we really are on a tight schedule, so could you round up wardrobe and get Phermona there for Trish's hair?"

Their boat lurched forward, and the engine's roar drowned out all communication until the boat docked again. Leah hoped to avoid Danielle until Trish was safely in her trailer and busy with makeup, hair, and wardrobe. Unfortunately, Danielle had noticed the stunt boat heading for Snoopy's and she followed Leah's movements with interest until she saw the two board the boat for the return trip. Danielle, with arms akimbo, greeted them as Trish and Leah scrambled up the dock ladder.

"Hey, Danielle, sorry I'm late, but I've been a little under the weather this morning." Trish struggled for composure under the withering gaze of her director.

"You didn't want to befoul Corpus Christi's beauty, so you went over to the Island to do your puking, is that it?"

"Actually," Leah chimed in, "the traffic jam is so bad I had her take the ferry across and drive up from Port Aransas to meet me at Snoopy's, so she could even get here at all."

Danielle eyed the two for several seconds. "Ladies, I've heard bullshit from the best. Trust me, you two are not in that league. My advice for you guys? Stick to the truth! Trish, we are dead stopped until we get your chase scene close-ups, and we're running out of time to shoot the stunt. The sun has changed the shadows from the setup, and the traffic noise will pick up soon.

In short, we're screwed if you don't get your butt in gear." Trish looked away and mumbled something about being sorry.

"See how fast you can get ready. We'll send a car." Danielle turned to leave, then pivoted and added, "Trish, you're really on my shit list. We better talk after we wrap up this evening."

"Oops." Leah said under her breath.

Two women lounged about the star's trailer, Gwen on the couch and Phermona in the makeup chair. The trailer was a tribute to star status. Two-thirds of the earth's population would love to live in this traveling palace with its bathroom, bedroom, lounge with bar, dressing area with styling chair, beehive hair dryer, and the ever-present tri-fold makeup mirror rimmed with bare bulbs. All was in readiness for Trish's makeover. Trish and Leah opened the door and clambered inside.

"Lord, help us. Chile, you look more than a little bit used." Phermona greeted Trish as they entered the dressing trailer. Phermona, a strikingly beautiful black girl, always wore skin-tight, black leather pants and a white T-shirt announcing, "Hairdressers do it With Style." Her imitation of a plantation nanny was better than Aunt Jemima herself. She was also the Michelangelo of hair stylists. Trish respected that and enjoyed her ever-present good humor. "How you be smilin' so, when you in such trouble, chile? You must a been into somethin' mighty good last night! Uh Huh!"

Before Trish could answer, Gwen, the makeup artist, moved closer and touched a place on Trish's neck. "Uh Huh is right! Leah, we gonna need another quart of hickey hider before this woman be ready for any close-ups." Gwen's Aunt Jemima suffered some from her being white.

"Okay, guys," Leah, said, "your innuendos are not lost on us, but let's have a little compassion for our wonderful friend here, as she is in a fragile state after a really bad night."

"Gwen, she look fra –` gile to you?" Phermona asked.

"No, fra – gile sounds close, but I don't think it's the ex – act word."

"And I never seen nobody lookin' that way, after a bad night. Uh, Uh! That right, Gwen?"

"All right, you guys have had your fun. I need a hot shower, shampoo and the fastest makeup and 'do in the history of Hollywood. Leah, can you chase down wardrobe and have them here in twenty minutes?"

"Fifty minutes!" Phermona and Gwen said in unison.

"Thirty five minutes," Trish conceded.

Trish sat in the styling chair clad only in bra and panties, trying to stay fresh in the heat of makeup lights and hair dryers. Gwen and Phermona busied themselves resurrecting their charge to star-perfect in record time when the trailer door burst open, and Reese, the stunt coordinator, strode in, script in his hand.

"Jesus, Reese, I'm sitting here with it all hanging out. Maybe you chould knock."

"Yeah, Reese, Trish is fragile today, right, Gwen?" Phermona said without looking up.

"Girls, I've had a year of med school, so I've seen it all. Anyway I'm going to see a lot more of Trish before we wrap this film up." Trish frowned as she remembered her contract for this film contained ambiguous language that might allow a partial nude scene – thanks to her agent, Rod Blitzer. He had pressured her into hastily signing the contract without studying it. When the clause was pointed out to her in a pre-production meeting, Rod's explanation had been, "Simple, you get another two-hundred thousand bucks for showing your breasts." She'd replied something about his questionable ancestry.

Leah returned from wardrobe carrying a pair of hip-hugger blue jeans and an abbreviated t-shirt that was sure to miss the blue jean tops by four inches. "Wardrobe is pretty simple, huh?" Seeing Reese, she asked, "Christ, is this a dressing trailer or a bus station? What are you doing in here, Reese?"

"Boss's orders! Danielle wanted me to go over the scenes with Trish to save some time."

"What's to go over? There isn't any dialogue, right?" Trish asked.

"Correcto! But if you remember from our last production meeting, this is not rear screen projection stuff today. We're shooting in real time. That means you'll be doing your own driving, and since it's a convertible, you have to match the background marks from the stunt driver shots."

"You're kidding, right? Is that even possible?" Trish turned so quickly toward Reese that Gwen's eyeliner drew a dark line across Trish's temple.

"Whoa, there! No quick movements unless you want to wear an eye patch in the close-ups!" Gwen howled.

"It would be a lot more possible if we had more time, but let's not quibble about that." Reese had enough experience not to get into it with the star. "You'll have a walkie-talkie in the car. I'll call out the action as you pass the background marks. Besides, I've seen you drive that little red convertible of yours, kiddo. Speed is no problem, right?"

"It just seems harder than it has to be!"

"You know boss lady as well as I do, and she won't go for fakey stuff in her films. 'Realism, that's our mantra!'" Reese mimicked their director.

"Girls," Trish pointed to Gwen and Phermona, "you better load up your portable kits. We could be up on that bridge a while." Reese plugged a video into Trish's TV. "It might help if you study the stunt run-through to see what you're trying to duplicate, while you finish up here." Reese handed the remote control to Trish. "I've got your car waiting outside. See you on the bridge."

Danielle's table now was stationed on the bridge for a better view of the action. Production assistants, soundmen, cameramen, and assorted technicians swarmed around the table hooking up cables, testing equipment, shouting and generally getting in each other's way. Even from her small standby-tent one half mile down the causeway, Trish could hear Danielle's bullhorn, "Okay! Okay! You guys look like monkeys screwing a football. Get this thing hooked up so we can split screen the stunt run with Trish's takes."

Trish thought, It's the same old hurry up and wait thing. I wonder how much of my life I've spent waiting for somebody to get some damn 'thing hooked up'.

Trish, Leah, wardrobe, and especially Phermona and Gwen had set a record for zero to gorgeous, thrown their respective kits and themselves into the car, and endured the harrowing trip to the standby tent with a driver who sensed emergency in the air. Now she had sat for an hour while the setup was changed three different times. Trish became more irate as the minutes ticked away. Finally the explosion came. "Who the hell is holding things up now? It's damn sure not me!"

Reese and the camera crew rambled about in front of the tent putting the final additions on the stunt convertible and checking the camera cradle for the fifth time to make sure all was safe and in working order.

Danielle's voice on the walkie-talkie said, "Reese, why don't you and Trish do a slow motion drive-through to help her get familiar with the sequence? When you get up here, let's all huddle up before we get going."

The cast and crew closed around the four monitors to watch the simultaneous run-through of the footage shot earlier in the day. "You can see we have good footage from the other three cameras, so if we can cut in some great close-ups of Trish from the car camera, this sequence will really rock," Danielle explained. "Trish, you can't wear a seat belt because your character is supposed to jump from the car, so keep the car's rubber-side down, right?"

"I thought there was some kind of an ejection seat, or something." Trish said.

"Too dangerous, the seat might miss the safety net. We thought about putting a chute on it, but in the end we scrubbed the whole thing," Reese said.

"We bungee hung the car and got some mid-range shots of the stunt person jumping from the convertible." Danielle added sarcastically, "While we were waiting on our star."

"We raise the cutaway splashdown to about thirty feet, and everything's groovy." Reese could not hold back a smile over his creativity.

"Okay, let's do a couple of practice runs to check for problems," Danielle said. "At, 'roll cameras' get the car up to speed before hitting the first mark. I will call 'action' at the first mark, and Reese will prompt your movements by radio."

After three practice runs and six takes, they were no nearer getting the close-up backgrounds to match the final stunt take. The angle of the sun was so different from the final take that morning, even extravagant camera angles could not compensate for the change in the shadows. Frustrations mounted and tempers flared. After each take, Trish needed a remake during which she vented her anger at Gwen and Phermona.

"This whole thing sucks! It's impossible! I'm never going to get out of here today. Christ, Danielle wants to have a heart-to-heart after the wrap this evening. There has to be a better way to make a living!" Trish's new attitude puzzled Gwen and Phermona.

"Now, chile, don't go gettin' yoself all worked up and undone over a thang like missin' a little poontang. It'll still be there when you get back. Beside, if you get feeling all sorry for yoself and bail, why Gwen and I might end up forced to work for some crabby old movie star's always bitchin' an' moanin' 'bout havin' to be rich and famous. That'd be downright unkind, right, Gwen?" In the instant before Trish fired a verbal volley she would regret, the irony seeped in, and she caught herself. Her grin turned to a chuckle, to a laugh, and finally uproar when Gwen and Phermona entered the joviality. "Okay! Okay! I'll quit bitchin' and moanin' about having to be rich and famous. But there is another place I'd rather be."

"Chile I reckon most every woman on earth would want to be there judgin' by all those hickys I covered up this morning." Gwen and the other two dissolved into laughter again.

They were interrupted by Reese's truck sliding to a stop. "Danielle's giving up on the shot," he said, striding into the tent. "You do not want to know her reaction to having to give up on a shot. The big stunt is almost rigged, so we're changing your close-ups to inside the car." He handed a list of the close-up movements they needed to cut into the stunt take. "Here is what we need as quickly as we can get them."

The list included: terrified looks over the shoulder, hunch over the steering wheel, swerve left, swerve right, and diving into the passenger-side floorboard.

Reese, the cameraman, and two best boys reset the car's camera cradle so the shooting angle kept the photo frame totally inside the car. "Trish, get up to speed so your hair is blowing. Then do three or four takes of each movement. We'll do one movement per run, but three or four takes, right?" Reese said. "Gwen, you and Phermona be out at the road to do what little fixing up you have to between runs."

Within thirty minutes they had completed six runs and had all the takes they needed. "Reese, you know if this is it for me today?" Trish asked as she got out of the convertible.

"No, Danielle is going for the splash down shot after the stunt, including your resurfacing close-up. So stay in costume and get ready to get wet." Reese's grin told volumes about the directors' rancor behind this decision.

Danielle's voice broke into Reese's radio. "Reese, the stunt is rigged. All we need is your final inspection. Drive the car up here, and we'll get the camera removed and reset while Pyro loads the explosives in the car."

The stunt was a masterpiece of art and technology. Guide rails were attached to the bridge deck to guide the car up to a pair of ramps. One ramp was high enough only to lift the car over the railing. The second ramp was higher to push the car into a barrel-roll as the car cleared the railing.

The opening shot would be from the rear of the car. The car would then speed toward the front camera rolling over the bridge railing and dropping out of frame as the camera panned left. Cameras two and four were crane mounted on the ground, giving clear vision to the path of the falling car and of the doomed restaurant below.

Danielle surveyed the layout from the bridge with her insides churning over all the things that might go wrong. There were no clouds near the sun that might shadow the shot. She looked both ways for boats running in the waterway or in the bays that might interrupt the sound track. No airplanes were in sight. She flagged the two policemen at each end of the bridge directing them to halt traffic and said to herself, "Well, this is why I get paid the big bucks." She keyed the mike of her headset and announced, "Okay, guys, speak now or forever hold your peace. We are shooting with only four cameras. I wish we had a dozen, but we don't, so you shooters have one chance to get it right. Remember, cameras one and two are real time and cameras three and four are slo-mo. I know you can do it, but remember to keep the subject centered and hold a large enough frame to catch the entire midair explosion. Reese will trigger the bang just as the car completes its first roll on the way down. Pyro will queue the fireball from the ground when the car hits the restaurant. Okay, count off. Camera one?"

"Ready, boss lady."

The director ticked off each responsible person down to the stunt crew who would launch the car. "Security, is the set clear?

"Everybody's clear."

"Here we go! Roll cameras! ... Mark! ... Action!"

The stunt crew launched the car down the tracks. "Go, you mother! Stay in the track!" Reese screamed at the car as it roared past. The car hurtled up the tracks causing even the most experienced in the crew to back-peddle to safety. The cameraman shooting the oncoming view locked down the camera trigger and dove for safety.

The car hit the ramps and headed for the bridge railing. The roll-ramp worked great, starting the car into a slow roll, but the lifting-ramp failed to jump the vehicle completely over the railing, and the tires blew out as they hit the top rail. The railing buckled, slipped from its buttresses, and joined the car in free fall.

"Jesus, God!" Danielle exclaimed scanning her four camera monitors. "What the hell is going on?" The convertible was not rolling gracefully over the railing, but instead was a spiraling missal arcing upward and wobbling out of control.

"Oh, shit!" Reese shouted when he saw the erratic flight of the convertible. Leaning over the bridge railing for a better view, he saw that the car might not reach the restaurant below. "Oh my, God!" he moaned and triggered the car explosion.

The convertible shuddered and with a thunderous report belched a conflagration that blew the seats, doors, and hood from the car, all of which trailed smoke as they began their own separate journeys to the ground. The gas tank exploded, sending up a second orange luminescent cloud that blew off the trunk lid and sent the car somersaulting end over end heading straight for ground zero, the center of the restaurant.

"Incredible! Did we plan this?" Danielle sat bug-eyed staring at her monitors as the scene unfolded. Both cameras two and four were full frame of the explosion and the unscripted somersaulting action.

Pyro queued the fireball when the car careened into the restaurant's roof, and the whole structure erupted. Windows, doors, rafters, roofing all rocketed skyward and the red-orange fireball trimmed in black smoke bellowed upward past the bridge, forming a towering pillar of smoke.

"Boss Lady?" Reese's voice came over Danielle's headset almost a minute later.

"Yes?"

"You gonna cut?"

"Oh ... yeah, cut." It was more awe than authority. "God, am I glad we didn't have a driver in that car." She went limp at the thought. Gathering herself, she shouted, "YES! YES, BY GOD, CUT AND PRINT!" Danielle leaped from her director's chair and hugged the closest person and unbridled excitement broke out on the set with high-fives, dancing, and shouting. In the midst of the celebration, Danielle's bullhorn announced, "Guys, that was great! Congratulations! Now strike this set and bring in the cleanup contractor to get this bridge open again. Reese, we're moving down to shoot Trish's splashdown."

"I'm all over it, boss lady. Okay, cameras two and four are still crane-mounted so move them down to the water. Chop! Chop! Best boys, camera grip, it's an all-hands job, and we're burning daylight."

"Get that bulldozer cleaning up that mess below the bridge." Danielle added, "Anybody know where Trish is?"

Chapter 17

Trish walked up just as Danielle was mounting the director's chair on the camera crane. The second camera was in position, and the construction crane with the stunt platform on its hook awaited the stunt girl before lifting her out and over the channel for the thirty-foot jump.

"How many takes to get it right?" Trish looked up at the director.

"To get a take without the stunt girl's face we will probably need two or three." Danielle counted the takes on her fingers before replying. "Then a couple for your close up."

"Make you a deal. You shoot it in one take, and I'll do the dive and close up shot at one time. We're talking realism here." Trish knew she was speaking Danielle's language.

"You trying to get out of my dog house?" Danielle eyed her suspiciously.

"Yeah, something like that. I cost you some time this morning. Maybe I can make up a little here."

"When did you start doing stunts?"

"Danielle, you know I dived from a cruise liner in my first `movie." Trish mimicked her dive from the ship.

"That's right. She escapes to paradise! I remember that. You sure you're up to it?" Danielle still had a wary look.

"Only if you set up to get it in one take." She held up one finger for emphasis.

Danielle considered all the ramification of the decision and finally ordered into her radio "Bring camera three down to the water for a tripod shot." She looked at Trish still considering if she had made the right decision. "Okay, you're on. You need to hit the water facing the other bank and come up facing the same direction then shake out your hair and turn around facing the close up camera on the tripod then grimace and shield your eyes from the blast you heard during the stunt. Can you get it all in one shot?"

"Piece of cake." Trish made a diving motion. "I didn't see how the stunt girl was moving during her jumps from the car. Should I look at the tape so I'm moving the same way?"

"Great idea." Danielle called into her head set, "Reese, cue up the tape of the jumps from the car so Trish can see them."

"What's up, Boss Lady?" Reese replied.

"You now have the most expensive stunt person in the world."

"Trish is doing the jump?"

"Promises she can get it in one take. The jump, the close-up, the whole deal."

"Sounds like serious suckin' up, Boss Lady." Reese couldn't hide the humor in his voice. "I've got a twenty against her gettin' it in one."

"Twenty for!" The radios sprang to life all over the location. "Twenty against! Forty for! Any takers? I'll take twenty of it. Give me twenty!" From that point there was a garble of unintelligible noise as everyone wanted some of the action.

"Cool it, people!" Danielle's bullhorn warned. "We have a movie to shoot here! Get some poster board down here and somebody post the bets and hold the money. She jumps in thirty minutes."

Trish returned from the director's monitor after viewing the earlier jumps. "What's up?"

"The crew is betting on you getting it in one take." Danielle laughed aloud, and picked up the bullhorn. "Now hear this! As the director, I am the sole judge of whether the first take is a print. So be advised I am open to bribes."

Trish reached for the bullhorn and she and Danielle tussled for it before Trish won. "Okay, here's the deal. If we're ready to go in twenty-five minutes, and I get it in one take, then I'm buying drinks for the house! So don't mess up, right?"

A roar went up from the crew, and things started happening in double time.

Phermona and Gwen wondered about the excitement and came out of the dressing trailer to see what was up. When they heard Trish's announcement, Phermona laughed out loud, "That chile show nuf in a hurry tonight. Uh Huh!"

Reese approached Trish carrying some padded long underwear. "You're going to be landing on your butt, so you better get some padding on under your jeans."

Phermona and Gwen arrived as Reese suggested the padding, and Phermona said, "Gwen, you mind loaning Trish, the stunt lady, a pair of your jeans. Ain't no paddin' goin' in the ones she's wearing!"

"No, I'll get wardrobe to bring over the right rear for her," Reese walked away talking into his microphone.

The clock was winding down to twenty-five minutes when the crane hoisted the platform and swung it out to the prescribed spot, thirty feet above the channel. Trish, the stunt double, and a stunt crewman rode up the distance, all hanging onto the platform.

"God, I've already forgotten which way your arms were wind milling in the car jumps." Trish looked bewildered at the stunt double.

"I'm not sure myself, but I think they were going front to rear." she replied giving a demonstration.

"Anything I should know?" Trish's eyes lids fluttered with excitement.

"Just remember to face the other side when you go in and when you come up. Shake out your hair, then turn around facing the close-up camera and do the "Oh shit!" thing holding your arm up to shield your eyes from the blast. Oh, and remember that bubbles go up, so follow them."

"Let's do it!" Trish gave a thumbs up.

The crewman called to Danielle, "She's ready."

The entire crew gathered around Danielle's crane and a hush fell over them as Danielle's bullhorn blaired, "Roll cameras! ... Mark! ... Action!"

Trish turned to her audience and gave a low bow then turning back to the front of the platform said, "DO IT!" The stunt double gave a mighty shove and Trish launched outward, arms and legs whirling, screaming, and plummeted toward the water. Halfway down she remembered about turning to her back to the camera, but instead turned the opposite direction thinking, Why hide my face? Hell, I'm the real thing!

The water came faster and harder than she anticipated, and when she landed in a sitting position the impact made her eyes bounce like pinballs. A sucking effect caused some air to escape from her lungs as she went under and started them burning. For a minute she felt she was upside down, but seeing the bubbles, she followed them up. She broke the surface exhaled, spewing and coughing, and then remembered to shake out her hair. She looked up toward the now missing restaurant and saw what looked like Rod Blitzer standing on the dock with his arms crossed. She flinched and held up her arm to shield her eyes from the lighting for a better look. It was Rod. Her face showed complete shock, and she yelled, "Oh, shit!" Danielle's bullhorn barked, "Cut and print!

At six o'clock Trish still stood under the shower in her dressing trailer, stalling for time. Danielle, Leah, and now Rod all want a piece of me, she thought. If Rod messes around with Chris, this will be the shortest romance on record.

Trish had a long-term, uneasy feeling that Rod lurked, like Othello's Iago, behind all her past romantic failures. Her love interests seemed almost out of her control. Rod always prowled the area when either party of the romantic entanglement delivered the coup de gras to the relationship.

She stepped from the shower and toweled off, still thinking of a plan that covered all contingencies. Nobody else knows about Chris, but Rod is a bloodhound when he gets the scent. He won't stop until he finds out why I've been distracted. He knows something's up, or he wouldn't be here. What the hell is he doing here anyway? Maybe he's supposed to slap my hand for being a bad girl. Damn! It all adds up to one thing: No Chris while Rod is here.

Trish dialed Leah's hotel room. "What in the hell is Rod doing here?" The long shower had not washed the tenderness in her butt from the dive or her anger at seeing Rod.

"Rod Blitzer is here? Here in Texas?"

"No! Here on location. Right now!"

"That no good, lying bastard! I talked to him yesterday. He asked about you, and wanted to come here and talk to you about something. I told him he would be welcomed like the plague, to stay in Los Angeles. He said he would."

"He's over talking to Danielle right now about God knows what." Trish thought for a second and then added, "Danielle wants to meet with me this evening, and I have something else I want to do."

"Yeah, I need to talk to you about all these things you want to do. Tell me you're not messing around with the Park Ranger." Leah's cigarette hand traced a smoke trail as she spoke.

"Come on, Leah, give me a break! Look, do this for me. I'm going to sneak out of here. You call Danielle and set up a dinner meeting. Include Rod and yourself. Let's get this whole thing out in the open."

Danielle and Rod stopped in mid-conversation as Trish's car flashed by, but before they could comment, Danielle's cell phone rang. "Hey, Danielle, it's Leah. Look, Trish had something to do, but she is offering to buy dinner tonight after she pays off her bet with the crew. How about meeting in the hotel bar about 7:30? Bring Rod with you."

"How did you know Rod was here?"

"I have a real nose for bad news."

Chapter 18

Trish launched the convertible through the loose sand at the end of Fish Pass Road and made it to the hard pan just above the tide line. Her car smoothed over the water-packed sand like she was in the old Daytona 500. She slid to a stop, leaped over the car door, and trotted up the walkway to Chris's house.

Chris was puttering in the kitchen, not exactly sure for whom he was cooking. There were footsteps on the dune bridge. He walked out to the deck just as Trish arrived. She jumped up, hugged his neck, and wrapped her legs around his waist. Laughing, she said, "Hi Honey, I'm home!"

He stumbled backward three steps to recover his balance both mentally and physically. During the struggle he regained his composure enough to reply, "Welcome home, I think?"

She kissed him and dropped to her feet, then hugged him again. "I've got to go!" She frowned. "Something has come up with the filming, and I have to stick close and take care of business."

"What's the problem?" He looked puzzled.

"Nothing I can't handle, but I may not be here for a couple of days. I've decided I need to get away for a few months after the film is over. Maybe longer! I'll be looking for a place to bunk in for a while." She moved closer, kissed him, and turned to retreat over the bridge. "Don't forget me!"

"Wait a minute! What the hell is going on?" Chris waved his arms in desperation.

She blew another kiss over her shoulder, ran to her car and drove away.

There was no time to make herself decent looking after arriving at the hotel, so she went directly to the bar where most of the crew was assembled to collect their reward for the one-take stunt. "Drinks for the house, barkeep!" she shouted as she moved toward the area where the crew made a boisterous presence. A cheer went up as the bartender passed out the drinks. The movie people were bunched in the back of the bar. A few other customers sat in booths near the door and a rustle of excitement went through them when the star entered. One exclaimed, "That's Trish Lowe!" Trish acknowledged the fan with a nod and continued toward the back.

Reese stood, doffed his L.A. Lakers bill cap, lifted his glass, and said, "Here's to One Take Trish!"

Danielle, Leah, and Rod had entered the bar just as Reese began his toast, and they arrived at the group just as a cheer went up for Trish.

Danielle stepped forward, put her arm around Trish, and intoned:

Well hello, Trish Lowe. Welcome home, Trish Lowe.
It's so good to have you back where you belong.

She waved for the whole group to sing.

You're lookin' swell, Trish Lowe.
We can tell, Trish Lowe.
You're still swayin', you're still stayin';
You're still goin' strong.

Everyone swayed in a mock chorus line.

I hear the band playin'; I hear a man sayin';
Golly Gee, follows, Find her a Knee, fellows,
Trish Lowe will never go away again.

The gathering assumed the proportions of a pep rally as the song faded for lack of recalling further lyrics. Shouting erupted along with dancing, hugging, animal grunts, and the flaring of nostrils in the manner of animals in rut.

Rod Blitzer stood at a distance during the merriment, wondering at the adulation the crew had for Trish. He'd never experienced this, even after a lifetime of guileless sucking-up. He could deliver a freshly inked multi-million dollar contract and be less appreciated than Trish was here tonight.

He turned to leave, but Leah caught him and said, "Why don't you walk with me to the restaurant? I've made arrangements for a quiet dinner. Danielle and Trish will be along shortly."

Rod looked at the darkly paneled room. The maroon leather upholstery of the chairs and banquettes under very low lighting created an atmosphere where it seemed a man would feet safe, even if accompanied by the wrong woman. The circle banquette positioned in the far corner from the entrance would insure that even their mothers could not recognize them.

Leah led Rod to this table. "Christ, Leah, I'm following you around this cave like you're a Seeing Eye dog," Rod lamented.

"I could find that table in a blackout, never fear," Leah said.

Once they were seated, leaving room for Trish at the back of the booth, their first martini in hand, Leah said, "So, Rod, you're here. Not in L.A. like you promised. You know this set is closed to agents, right?"

"Come off your high horse, Leah. We both know there's something up with Trish, so fess up. What's the deal?"

"Surely, by now, Rod, you must know I wouldn't share Trish's secrets, even if you tortured me with rap music. Anyway, what makes you think something's up?"

"All the signs are there. No returned phone calls. Late for cast calls. No-showing for cast calls. Missing rehearsals."

"Where did you hear all this?"

"Danielle told me everything. So what gives with our little girl?"

"Trish has not been feeling well lately."

"Come on, Leah, don't give me the puking thing. Unless you're telling me she's pregnant." Rod's expression turned severe. "She's not, right?"

"Get serious!" Leah swung an elbow that scored on the point of Rod's shoulder.

"Geez! You don't have to get violent!" Rod rubbed his shoulder.

"You haven't seen violent until you hang around here and get Trish all worked up as only you can." Leah's eyes told the extent of her maternal instincts.

"Trust me. I'm just here to make sure Trish is okay and to bring her a little good news."

"You keep talking about 'good news'. What good news? What?"

Before Rod could answer Trish and Danielle walked up and seated themselves at the table. Trish squeezed in the back of the booth, flanked by Rod and Leah on one side and Danielle on the other. The two new arrivals glowed a little from their cocktails.

"What wonderful thing are you two discussing that brings you so much joy?" Trish asked.

"I was just telling Rod, here, how thrilled we are that he showed up unannounced," Leah said.

"Ouch!" Danielle winced.

"Yeah, Rod, don't stand outside in the driving rain. Go home!" Trish laughed.

"God, it's great to be so loved and appreciated by the people I work so hard for."

"Ohhhh, now he's going to get all puffed up. Where's Rod's sense of humor gone?" Trish teased – a little tipsy.

"Rod's getting puffed up! Rod's getting puffed up!" Leah voiced.

"Okay, ladies, cut the crap! You all know why I'm here. I'm concerned about Trish and her loss of focus. So why don't we have a decent, normal discussion about what seems to be the problem so we can get it fixed and get this movie in the can? Then we'll get on with the next order of business."

"Here's to getting the picture finished!" Danielle raised her martini, but Trish was the only one whose glass stayed on the table.

"So, Rod, what do you think is my problem?" Trish asked without humor.

Rod fumbled with his cocktail for a moment before answering. "Usually, when you lose your focus on a film it's because there's some guy hanging around. I mean, you even said something about a guy on Jay Leno's show, right?"

Trish averted her eyes. "Well, let's say there is a guy, which there isn't, but if there was, are you saying that I can't have a personal life?" Her voice crackled with tension.

"Hey, listen, guys, maybe you two should take this outside before you start throwing punches." They ignored Leah's attempt at humor.

"That's a philosophical question worthy of discussion, but the short answer is, 'No.' At least if it interferes with filming! Right, Danielle?" His voice was rife with indignation.

"Don't drag me into this. Trish is off my shit list."

"Yeah, Rod, this is between the two of us. Bring it on. What's your real beef? Danielle knows I'll get the picture done on time. So why all the B.S. about loss of focus?" Trish's eyes glowed in the low light.

"Rod, there wouldn't be a little jealousy creeping in here, would there?" Leah twisted the knife a little.

"Jealousy? You think I flew all the way here because Trish is boffing some redneck? I don't think so! I think I came here to tell Trish I have another film for her. The kind she's been waiting years for. Something to show off her dramatic talent."

"You're a little late, Rod, because I decided today I'm not making any more films for a while. Maybe for a very long time," Trish announced.

"Oh, God, it's worse than I thought. You're in love again!" Rod whined. With that he stood up and lunged out of the restaurant tripping several times in the darkness and uttering oaths along the way.

"I think that went well, girls, don't you?" Danielle said as Rod disappeared into the restaurant's semi-darkness.

`His office had booked Rod into the Omni Hotel, but since he was so angry with Leah and Trish an accidental encounter was the last thing he wanted. He explained to the front desk that he had an emergency and could not stay the night. As he left the hotel entrance he saw the Yacht Basin across Shoreline Drive, sparkling with restaurants, bars, and boat lights.

He walked toward the sound and activity livid with anger, crossed Shoreline Drive, and stepped onto the seawall walkway. Behind the decorative concrete railing, the seawall curved gracefully down about twenty feet and out to a base wide enough to buttress against a hurricane surge. The walkway bustled with cyclers, skaters, revelers, strollers, and lovers, all enjoying the cool evening air laced with saltwater spray and the smell of fried seafood. Rod mingled, strolling along the waterfront, trying to reorder his thoughts. Mostly he was upset with himself for once again letting his feelings for Trish surface. And then there was that bitch, Leah, running her loud mouth.

How could someone totally unknown to Trish until just days ago have her thinking about a hiatus from pictures, for God's sake? How could she even consider such a thing? He remembered all the rational discussions and heated arguments over getting her a part other than in another pithy action-based love story. Now, finally, he had scored the movie role of Trish's dreams. It was Academy Award stuff. He was banking on improving his relationship with Trish by scoring this gig for her. Hell, he was fantasizing that Trish might fall lovingly into his arms just hearing about it. There were problems, though. Shooting for the next film started in Russia in three weeks – less that two weeks after the current film was complete. He knew kidnapping her was the only way to get her on a flight to Russia that quickly. Jesus, he thought, I don't set shooting schedules, I just react to them.

Then there were his personal assurances given Meecham and Ivor, the producer-director team. "Put it in the bank! No problems meeting your production schedule in Russia. Actually, Trish is ecstatic over getting to play Anna Karenina. She's dreamed of a part like this for years."

He stopped in the seawall gazebo just past Peoples Street overlooking the L-shaped Peoples Street pier. Sailboats, sport fishing boats and gin palace yachts rocked and swayed, tugging at their moorings on either side of the street that led out to the L-head. The sound of a blues band wailing in the Lighthouse Bar across the harbor drew him in that direction. He stepped from the gazebo, strolled south to Lawrence, and turned down Lawrence Street pier toward the T-Head. The smell of fried seafood intensified, and the blues band was rocking out. He was hungry and out of sorts, and he walked faster, thinking about having some fun for a change.

There was a wait for tables at the Lighthouse, so Rod moved into the lounge and took a seat at the bar. Next to him was a man in his early thirties, trim and decent looking, dressed in a crewneck T-shirt and a pair of Docker kakis. Clean-shaven, his long hair was pulled back into a controlled, short ponytail. Rod surveyed the room for available females and saw a table of four attractive twenty-somethings sitting next to the dance floor.

The Kon Tiki cocktail that Rod had ordered in a moment of self deprecation arrived complete with umbrella. He turned to make pleasantries with the ponytail beside him, but Night Train and the Locomotion blasted into a shuffle rhythm tune, and his neighbor bounded from his bar seat and stood at the four females' table in a flash. He held out his hand, and a Charlize Theron look-alike stood and followed him to the dance floor. Three other guys arrived at the table almost as quickly, and the three new couples moved to the middle of the dance floor and began dancing what Rod remembered as the California Swing. It was a remnant of the late fifties and early sixties when males and females actually touched each other while dancing, rather than standing apart and gyrating their butts while waving their arms. The style and grace, almost elegance, of these dancers had nothing to do with the frenetic jitterbug or boogie-woogie of the forties and early fifties. These dancers moved about the floor like models on a runway, twirling and intertwining their bodies and then miraculously extricating themselves so smoothly that they could balance a book on their heads in the process. When the tune ended, the four men escorted their partners back to their table and disappeared again into the crowd, secure, no doubt, in the knowledge that they had intimidated all the other males in the room.

Rod was thinking his chances with these four women were greatly diminished on the dance floor, particularly since he was shorter than all of them. That only left him the "Hollywood agent ploy," which, of course, was a proven gambit.

He turned to his dancing neighbor. "You're a brave man to walk away from that lady after all the good work you put in on the dance floor."

"Oh, we're just friends," he laughed. "We dance together all the time."

"But you don't sit together?"

"No, it's a game my friends and I play. Every time they play a shuffle tune we grab them and put on a dancing exhibition. Then we see which of all these guys ogling them has nerve enough to ask them to dance."

"Is that more fun than getting laid?"

"We all belong to the Corpus Christi Whip Club. Actually, there normally are a lot more of us here, but the Locomotions don't play a lot of shuffle tunes. Anyway, by now anyone in our club who was going to has already screwed and forgotten about it."

"Whip dance? You guys are into S & M?"

"No, the dance we do, it's the Texas Whip."

"I thought it was the California Swing."

"Or The Dallas Push, The Austin Push, The North Texas Push, and I think they even have an name for it in the Carolinas like 'The Shag' or something like that." He tilted the last of his beer.

"Whatever it's called, I'll buy a beer for anybody who dances like you."

"I guess I should introduce myself to anybody who'll buy me a beer. I'm Buddy St. John."

"Rod Blitzer, here." Rod held out his hand. "Buddy St. John is a very memorable name."

"It's not my real name. It's the name I write under. I didn't think anyone would read anything written by Cleatus Klutzman."

"You may be right. What have you written?" Rod turned his full attention to Buddy St. John.

"I'm a photo journalist." Buddy rummaged around in his wallet for a card. "Sorry, seems I gave my last card away."

"So you're the local paparazzi?" Rod's attention was focusing.

"Except nothing much ever pops in good ol' C.C. Mostly, I make a living doing stuff for South Texas newspapers. Outdoor, Travel, Lifestyle, some reporting when they're short-handed. I even sold a story to *The National Investigator*, but I'm not too proud of that."

"What was that scoop about?"

"A big blob of something nobody could recognize floated onto the beach at Mustang Island State Park, and I drove out and took some pictures. I learned what I could from the Park Rangers and a marine biologist from the UT Marine Science Institute and wrote a piece about it. The Investigator ran it under the headline 'Mystery Blob Threatens Texas Coast.'"

Rod took a pull on his martini. "You haven't gotten anything from the movie that's shooting here now?"

"Man, those people are boring. They make the movie and go to their hotel. That's it. I've asked for interviews and can't get to first base. I thought movie people partied their asses off."

"How would you like an interview with Trish Lowe?" Rod took another pull on his Kon Tiki for emphasis.

"You could have my left arm to the elbow for an interview with Trish Lowe. Why do you ask?"

"I'm Trish Lowe's agent."

Buddy twirled his beer and glanced over twice at Rod before he spoke, "Actually my real name is William Clinton, I'm former President of the United States."

Rod handed him his business card. Buddy turned it over a few times after reading it. "Jesus, you're actually a Hollywood agent?"

"Actually I am, and I think we could be useful to each other. You might get a story People Magazine and every movie magazine and tabloid will bid for." Rod paused for a minute to let that sink in.

"I'm not sure why you'd do this, but you'd be my newest best friend for the rest of my life." Buddy's finger circled the rim of his beer bottle as he tried not to show too much enthusiasm. He'd heard ducks fart under water before.

"Like I say, I think we can be useful to each other." Rod smiled at his new associate. "By the way, is there a hotel near here besides the Omni?"

"There a pretty nice Holiday Inn about a mile south on Shoreline."

"Okay, Buddy St. John, call me about ten o'clock tomorrow morning. Here's my cell number." He pointed to his business card. "We'll get together for lunch and work out details."

Buddy St. John scribbled his name and cell phone number on a bar napkin and handed it to Rod. "Just in case you ever need to call me."

Rod took the napkin. "Okay, now that the business is over, how about introducing me to the shortest of those four ladies, so she can give me a dance lesson."

Rod awoke and sensed he was not alone. He rolled over and saw an attractive brunette lying next to him. As the brain fog from the previous night cleared, he remembered checking into the Holiday Inn at about three in the morning. He felt clammy. An aura of personal odor from sweat and cigarette smoke hung in the room making him queasy and disoriented. His mouth was dry and when he sat up, his head quaked.

The brunette stirred slightly when he stood, but continued sleeping. Rod mentally groped for her name. He remembered dancing. Lots of whip dancing, which he thought must have amused the wallflower spectators in the Lighthouse Lounge, but enough martinis make a man brilliant, tall, handsome and the best damn whip dancer in the State of Texas. He obviously used the "Hollywood agent ploy" at some point during the evening, judging by his bedmate.

After returning from the relief of the bathroom, he sat at the small desk just as the phone rang. Rod's watch showed straight up 10:00 a.m. "Yeah!" he rasped into the receiver. The brunette stirred again but relapsed into sleep.

"Rod, it's Buddy St. John." After a pause the voice again said, "Rod, you there?"

"Yeah, yeah, I'm here …"

"You asked me to call you this morning at ten? To have lunch and talk about the interview with Trish Lowe."

"Oh! Yeah, Buddy. I'm having a little trouble getting it all together this morning." He lowered his voice and asked, "Listen, do you know who this is in my bed?"

"That's Angie. Your dance instructor last night. Sounds like she may have taught you a few extra dance steps." Buddy chuckled.

"Nothing I can really remember."

"So, anyway, are we still on for lunch?" Buddy sounded hopeful.

"Yeah, we need to talk. Say, listen, did I happen to drive my car over here last night?"

"No, I dropped you two off and helped you register. I'll come by and pick you up."

"Yeah, about noon would be great. What do we do with Angie?"

"She's a big girl. She'll figure it out."

"Okay, see you at twelve." Rod hung up and then realized his suitcase was in his car at the Omni. "Shit!" He picked up the phone again and called the front desk. "Listen, the airline lost my bag last night. Could you send up two hospitality kits and a pot of coffee? Yeah, thanks."

Angie was sitting up, wrapped in the covers when he looked back at the bed again. "Good morning, I think." She ran her fingers through her hair as if trying to comb the cobwebs from her brain.

"It'll have to improve some before it qualifies." Rod tried to smile.

"Did you enjoy your dance lesson last night?"

"As much as I can remember." There was an awkward silence interrupted by a knock on the door. "Come in."

A young man wearing a Holiday Inn uniform wheeled in a cart with a coffee pot and two cups. Beside the coffee were two hospitality ditty bags.

Rod signed the room service ticket and tipped the waiter. "Thanks," he added for good measure.

After the attendant closed the door behind him, Angie, bundled up in the sheet, moved to the service cart and picked up a hospitality bag before retreating to the bathroom. "Great smelling coffee. I'll be out in a jiff."

Rod watched her shuffle into the bathroom, trying not to trip on the bed sheets. He poured himself a cup of coffee, added cream, and let it cool while he stirred it. When the bathroom shower started, he drained his cup, slipped out of his shorts, picked up the other hospitality kit, and went into the bathroom for another dance lesson.

After picking up Rod and Angie, Buddy drove to the Lighthouse parking where Angie had left her car the night before. He stopped behind the car Angie pointed out. Rod and Angie both got out, and she asked, "So, Rod, we're on for tonight?"

"Absolutely, I'll call you later to set a time." He kissed her on the cheek and got back in Buddy's front seat.

Buddy pulled away and drove up the T-head Pier, stopping at Shoreline Drive. While he waited at the traffic light he turned to Rod. "Sounds like you and Angie are becoming an item."

"You sound like a Hollywood gossip columnist."

"Two days – two dates, this could be serious." He turned back and laughed.

"There's no question, the girl has talents. She mentioned there's someplace near here, Port 'Arkansaw' or something like that. Out on an island somewhere."

"Port Aransas, on Mustang Island," Rod corrected. "She's right, it's a happenin' place."

"I'm in town a couple of days; maybe we should take a road trip tonight."

Buddy had just parked in front of the Surf Club, and the two got out and walked inside while Buddy thought about his answer. Lunchers crowded the foyer waiting for a table, but the hostess saw Buddy and said, "Hey, Buddy, your table's ready." She whisked the two of them off to a far corner while those on the waiting list looked on helplessly.

"Thanks, Sissy." Buddy kissed the hostess' hand. "I'll do something nice for you sometime."

"I can only hope," she said with a curtsy.

"Very impressive." Rod nodded in appreciation of Buddy's restaurant clout.

"Power of the press," Buddy replied. "Do a few restaurant articles and every hash house in town can't be nice enough to you."

"So about tonight?"

"Great. Angie's got a friend I like a lot. I'll call her, and we'll check out what mysteries the Port Aransas night holds. But I don't think another night with Angie is why we're here."

"You're right." Rod twirled the olive in the martini that had arrived unannounced along with a beer for Buddy. "Tell me what you know about Trish Lowe's love life."

"Nothing, actually. Why?" Buddy looked puzzled.

"That's the point. Seldom is there even any speculation in the press about who she's seeing. Or in the gossip columns for that matter."

"She gets a lot of press, but I don't remember seeing much about her love life." Buddy nodded in agreement.

Rod added, "She's the best there is at keeping her private life out of print. Consider what an article about her new 'Texas true love' might bring, if you could get it with pictures. You could scoop the Hollywood paparazzi."

"Obviously, it would be huge. Does she have a new 'Texas true love'?"

"I think so." Rod twirled the olives again.

"You think so? You're her agent. Don't you know?" Buddy looked confused.

"I know her well enough to say I'm almost positive. I'm saying you can get this story, if you're willing to do some digging for it." Rod leaned forward, giving the feeling of a shared secret.

"I don't get it, you're her agent, and you can't find out who the mystery man is?"

"I'm the last person she would confide in about this. We have a kind of love/hate relationship. She loves my getting her movie roles, but hates being around me."

"So you want me to stalk her until I find out who this guy is and then let the world know, right?" Buddy's voice sounded incredulous.

"If you carry your camera, it wouldn't be stalking. It would be investigative journalism."

"You said we could be useful to each other. What do you get from this?" Buddy ran his thumbnail around the corners his beer bottle's label trying to disguise his interest.

"That's my business, but you have to clear everything through me before it's released." Rod's voice was humorless as he sat back, convinced he had Buddy hooked.

The waitress sidled up to their table, order pad in hand "Our special today is Lump Crabmeat Omelet with Hollandaise served with a Mango Salsa in a basket of Fried Shoestring Potatoes."

Rod decided to have the omelet with an Irish Cream Latté. Buddy ordered a cheeseburger and another beer just to get rid of the waitress.

"So how do we pull this off?" Buddy said when the waitress disappeared toward the kitchen.

Rod's forehead drew into a frown as he considered the options. "I'm sort of working it out as I go, but here is what I'm thinking. Trish will not go near this guy until she thinks I'm gone. She can be really devious when she's this protective."

"So you're going to disappear, and I will take up the chase?" Buddy pursed his lips after the question.

"That's about it. Except I know some of the crew, and I can get a shooting schedule to give you some idea about when and where she'll be." Rod stuck the sword cocktail pick in his mouth and slowly drew it out, leaving the olives as if he had just run his quarry through.

"I need to be there to track her when she leaves the shoots to see where she goes and who she sees, right?"

"Yeah. Eventually she'll meet up with this guy, and you can start finding out all you can about him and reporting back to me."

"She probably won't do this in a limo, so I need to know her car."

"I'll have to get that info for you." Rod's eyes veered to the tray of food arriving. Both men fell silent as they attacked their plates. Rod's cell phone rang about half an omelet later and Caller I.D. showed it was Trish. He hesitated, considered not answering, but instead gave a formal "Hello."

"Tell me you still love me, and you're not still puffed up. I'll be devastated if you're still mad." It was the Trish everyone knew and loved.

"Yeah, I've got a big picture of that." He worked at controlling his voice.

"We had way too much fun at your expense last night, and I am apologizing for everyone. We still friends?"

"Friends to the bitter end. The show must go on, right?" He hesitated and then added, "By the way, say 'hello' to Buddy St John." Rod handed the phone to Buddy.

"Buddy who?" was the question Buddy heard when he put the phone to his ear.

"Buddy St John," Buddy replied.

"Well, hi, Buddy St. John. Who are you?"

"I'm a journalist."

"Buddy, it's good to meet you, but could I talk to Rod?" Buddy handed the phone back to Rod.

Before Rod could speak, Trish asked, "What was that about?"

"We are discussing a possible interview to kick off the pre-publicity for the picture."

"We're on a tight schedule for the rest of the shooting." Trish's voice betrayed her lack of interest. "But I know you wanted to talk some business, and you're probably in a hurry to get back to L.A., right?"

"Not as big a hurry as you guys are to send me back. Anyway, I'll work out the details for the interview with Leah, okay?" Rod sensed the reluctance on the other end of the phone.

Trish hesitated before answering "Okay. Listen, I have an hour between 3:30 and 4:30. Why don't we meet in my trailer? In fact, I'll have the limo pick you up?" Trish sounded a little more upbeat.

"Okay, 3:30, but no need for the limo, I'll drive." Rod flipped his cell phone closed and looked at Buddy. "So, you believe me now?"

Chapter 19

Dark clouds obscure the horizon,
Boding winds of doubt.
Muffled thunder threatens transformation,
And watchful water trembles.

Chris stood over the freshly scribed verse that still seeped water from the wet sand. The previous evening's confusion over the brief encounter with Trish had passed into a night of restlessness. He awakened at dawn, pulled on his cutoffs, and carried a freshly brewed cup of coffee onto the deck. The sun's first rays spotlighted a bank of clouds forming to the southeast. He walked over the dunes to the beach and stood looking at the impending weather. A sense of exhilaration always overlaid the apprehension of a thunderstorm. His index finger still was crusted with sand from writing the verse.

There was little chance of this verse surviving if the threatening storm made shore. That didn't bother him. He yearned for something to wash away his doubts about the sudden changes in his life. In a matter of days a captivating stranger had truncated the routine that had been the foundation of his existence for years.

Years of solitude had left him unprepared for the onslaught of charm and beauty Trish wore as casually as a shawl. Then there was Lottie's disappointment in him and her absence. He had taken her so much for granted; he now felt more than guilt. He missed her. They were lovers, but he also was beginning to understand what a good friend and companion she'd been over the years. His life was so simple that their relationship had never been marred by serious disagreements or lovers' quarrels. Her potential loss now weighed on him.

Chris had met Lottie through Osborn Holmes, the previous owner of the beach house, shortly after Chris had arrived on Mustang Island. Osborn was legendary for his excesses, particularly his zeal to experience everything. He had ventured away from hetero into experimenting with gay sex during a trip to San Francisco, a mistake that had left him HIV positive about six years before Chris' arrival. Osborn was a man possessed and a world-class party guy all of his adult life, but by the time Chris met him, Osborn, in his early fifties, was showing the ravages of AIDS.

Chris learned from Lottie that even in his late forties, young women flocked to Osborn. She also told Chris that Osborn felt no need to discuss his health problem with his friends, since he knew he had the cure for AIDS. According to Lottie, his cure was simple, "Just drink yourself to death, and you won't die of AIDS."

Money was no problem for Osborn as his parents were wealthy, and they agreed that he should take his "embarrassment" somewhere far from Dallas society. Osborn had found this crude A-frame beach house years before and remodeled it into a very pleasant, if rudimentary, pad. The location, about equal distances from both Corpus Christi and Port Aransas, was ideal, as neither Corpus Christi nor Port Aransas police had jurisdiction. Significant political contributions to the Nueces County Sheriff and the Constable helped maintain his anonymity. Constables even handled security at his bigger events. Osborn's reputation for beach parties grew to mythical proportions. When he was in residence, the parties ran day and night for weeks, fueled by new arrivals both from Corpus Christi and Port Aransas. Nothing was out of bounds. "Sandy sex, drugs, and rock-til-you-drop," Osborn always described these marathon parties.

Toward the end of Osborn's odyssey, he knew being bed-ridden was inevitable, so he had the A-frame remodeled into a self-sustaining home with all the things that could help him comfortably practice his cure to its conclusion. Lottie was the only one of Osborn's "friends" who'd stuck with him to the end: daily visits, bringing his medication — scotch mostly – and cooking him meals of which he ate very little.

On one of her Osborn visits in about 1990 she found that Chris had arrived unannounced. He was tanned from outdoor activity, and, in cutoffs and no shirt, Lottie appreciated what a fine looking man he was. His demeanor was reserved, and he seldom laughed; quite the opposite of Osborn who explained only that "Chris is a friend of a friend."

Osborn followed his cure with great diligence, but still managed to survive for over another year, during which time he became fast friends with Chris. Lottie came less frequently after Chris's arrival, but still visited several times a week.

Toward the end of their year's friendship, Osborn was too weak to leave his bed. Chris tended to his needs, as did Lottie when she visited. Osborn knew that Chris wrote poems from time to time. Chris never talked about the poems, and he kept them stashed in an old canvas bag. One day Osborn asked to read some of the poems. The depth of the desire, feeling, and ragged pain in them so impressed Osborn, that after a day's reading, he shouted down to Chris, "Come up here a minute!"

Chris went for the scotch bottle, thinking Osborn needed some medicine. "Yeah, I'll be right up!" Arriving bedside, he set the bottle on the nightstand.

"Pull up a chair, Laddie, I'm going to give you some fatherly advice. In fact, if you never remember anything else about me, you'll remember this. When you're lying in your coffin waiting for them to nail on the lid, you'll rise on one elbow and say, 'I remember when old Osborn told me about life'!" The ragged sheets of paper on which Chris had scribbled his poems over the years rested under Osborn's arms crossed on his chest.

"Is this something I'm going to enjoy hearing?" He pulled up a chair next to the bed.

"Probably not. Probably you won't believe any of it, at least not right now. But someday you will." Osborn propped himself up to an almost sitting position with Chris' help. "Here's the deal." Osborn again adjusted himself with some difficulty, so he could look Chris in the eyes.

"You okay? Chris asked. "Can I help you get more comfortable?"

"I'm as good as can be expected, Laddie. Thank you for letting me read your poetry. I absolutely love it, but it concerns me greatly." Osborn closed his eyes as if in thought before continuing. "The difference between the two of us is," he paused again. "I'm a guy who's living while he's dying. You're a guy who's dying while he's living. Which one of us is the smarter?"

"I don't understand." The squint in his eyes asked for enlightenment.

"Laddie, you're carrying around a load of guilt that would bury any mere mortal. God, man, think about it. You have the soul of a poet and the body of a god, and you're just drifting through life feeling sorry for yourself. Snap out of it! I know you're carrying a lot of baggage from California, but confront your dilemma, come to terms with your grief, and get on with it." Osborn was short of breath.

"I'm afraid it's not that easy, but I appreciate your concern."

"Concern, bullshit, I'm talking about life! I'm talking about your life!" With that Osborn lapsed into a fit of coughing and reached for the bottle of scotch. After a long pull on the bottle, he added, "I'm going to launch you on your next life, just you wait and see. I'm going to get you off this beach and back into life!"

Osborn sent samples of Chris's poetry to an old college roommate, Melvin Ortz, now a New York literary agent. Ortz sold Christopher Maven's first book of poetry, *Surf Sound Soliloquies* to a major publishing house. A recording company bought an option and recorded selections of the poetry recited to original string orchestral music with the sounds of weather and surf in the background. As the sales soared, Lottie commented, "Every guy on the make must have bought one of your LP's."

Osborn's eventual death was difficult for his two friends. The sheriff made sure the death certificate showed the cause of death as pneumonia. This pronouncement led his parents, who had never once visited him, to have Osborn's body shipped back to Dallas for a proper burial. Shortly thereafter, a lawyer contacted Chris through Lottie to tell him that Osborn had left the beach house to him. Along with the legal documents, there was a hand-written note from Osborn, which read, "This is your new vacation house. Get off this beach, and get a life! Come back occasionally and think about your old buddy Osborn and the good times we had."

Lottie and Chris drifted into a relationship while grieving over the loss of their friend. Chris steadfastly refused her request that he move in with her in Port Aransas. On one of her visits to Chris' house she pressed Chris about it. "I really don't see why you want to live out here by yourself. Osborn never spent an hour alone, even when I wasn't here, but you live like a hermit."

"There's a lot about me you don't know..." Chris avoided her eyes.

"That's why people get closer, so they can get to know each other better."

"...things that no one can know. Not even someone like you whom I respect and care about. It's better if I stay away from people."

Lottie searched his face, considering her answer. "Okay, let's say you have to stay out here living the life of a recluse. I still think we're close enough that you owe me an explanation."

Chris sat for several minutes looking a Lottie, feeling his defenses weakening. How long have I wanted to feel safe, telling someone, he thought. He stood and held out a hand to lift Lottie from the couch. He pulled her into a hug. "You're right. Let's go for a walk on the beach."

Lottie was the only one to whom Chris had ever told anything about his past. Their relationship was based on that information and had lasted through the years. At least until now.

Chris lingered so deeply in thought that the approach of a vehicle went unnoticed until it stopped about two hundred yards down the beach from him. It was a white nine-passenger van with no external markings. Two men got out of the van and walked to the water's edge. They alternated looking out into the surf and up and down the beach, gesturing all the time as they talked. Then they walked back to the dune line, one of them pacing as if measuring the distance. They talked for a few more minutes after returning to the van and then drove toward Chris.

He retreated to the dune walkway and stood mid-span when the van passed. The driver glanced at Chris and waved as the van proceeded to a point about two hundred yards up the beach. The two repeated their actions looking, pointing, discussing, pacing, and then moved on up the beach. This time they drove farther before stopping again. Chris watched until they disappeared over the horizon.

He leaned on the railing for several minutes processing this new intrusion into his solitude. *What are these guys up to?* He turned back to the beach and saw their tire track gouged through his verse.

Chris worked at his desk until about noon, then fixed a lunch of ceviche on toast and poured himself a glass of sauvignon blanc. The deck overhang gave some protection from the sun, and he settled onto a lounge chair to enjoy the piquancy of the ceviche with the citric crispness of the wine. The storm still hung well out to sea, causing a cool sea-to-land breeze. He drifted into a deep sleep lulled by his restless night, the food, and the wine.

It was mid-afternoon when he awakened to voices. He sat up, rubbing his eyes, and saw the white van again stopped at the same place about two hundred yards down the beach. This time, there were four people standing and looking out to sea and up and down the beach. They talked and gestured, and one kept looking through some device hung around his neck. Another, wearing shorts, waded out into the surf as if checking the water depth. They piled back into the van and drove to the spot about two hundred yards up the beach. They repeated the process, but with more forceful gestures and dialogue. Finally all four broke into loud laughter. They returned to the van as the wader dried off with a towel. Once in the van, they turned around and headed toward Fish Pass Road.

Chapter 20

Another day, another chase scene, thought Trish. The production equipment had remained in place overnight under the bridge. The boat scenes took very little setup before shooting, but Trish was in her trailer by sunup and ready when Danielle called for her.

By midmorning they had finished shooting the scene of the co-star, driving a boat 007 could only dream about, and swooping in to rescue Trish from the water after the leap from her exploding car.

The boats ripped and roared up and down the channel with the bad guys in hot pursuit, guns blazing and shoulder-fired rockets swooshing and booming like World War III. Security officers held the crowds of gawkers at a safe distance, but the restaurant workers, who had to prepare for the lunch run, found themselves ducking and dodging every time an explosion occurred. At about two o'clock the bad guys scored a hit, and the hero's fire-belching boat disintegrated into a plume of wreckage and water spray.

An hour later, the bad guys, up to no good, fished an unconscious hero from the water. Trish was nowhere to be found, so the malcontents sped off into the horizon to continue perpetrating their nefarious deeds.

Trish stepped from her trailer shower around three o'clock, toweled off, and put on a frayed terrycloth robe that had been her security blanket since her first film eight years ago. She sat on the dressing trailer couch, bundled cocoon-like, her legs folded under her and her hair rolled in a towel. What does Rod want, she wondered?

Phermona and Gwen, tumbling through the trailer door and laughing uncontrollably, broke into her reverie. "It's not nice to have more fun than the movie star, girls." Trish laughed for no reason.

"Lord, Miss Lowe, it's jus' about impossible for good girls like us to remain respectable in this pagan Hollywood environment." Phermona doubled over laughing.

Trish looked puzzled. "So why am I laughing?"

"You know those two camera grip guys that's been hittin' on us since we started shooting?" Gwen asked.

"You know, the black guy and the old guy?" Phermona inserted.

"Yeah, I think so." Trish was not sure.

"These guys just don't give up. I mean it's not they're that bad, really. The black dude is pretty well put together, but he's a little young. The old guy's still holding pretty well too, but he's way old," Gwen said. "They're always joking about Phermona's 'Hairdresser's Do It With Style' T-shirts."

"Yeah, like they're always wantin' to be stylin'." Phermona added.

"They've tried everything in the book to get us to go out. You gotta give 'em 'A' for effort, right? So Pher and I are startin' to weaken a little, and just now they caught up with us outside the trailer," Gwen explained.

Phermona jumped in. "They're wearin' matchin' tee's except one has 'Phermona' on the front and the other has 'Gwen'."

"We tell them the shirt thing is pretty cool, but we gotta get in here an' go to work on you," Gwen said.

"Then these guys smile real big at each other and turn to walk away, and the black grip guy has 'Get a Grip on Yoself!' on his back." Phermona started laughing again.

"And the old guy has 'Experience Old Age Creeping Up On You!'" Gwen said, and Trish lost it again.

When the laughter died a little, Trish asked, "So did they get it done?"

"You gotta go out with somebody can make you laugh like that, right?" Phermona asked as Gwen nodded an agreement.

A car door slammed outside the trailer, and Trish said, "That would be wonderful Rod here for his appointment."

"Well, Gwen, honey, that would be our cue to exit stage left." Phermona made a grand gesture toward the door. The door swung open before they moved, and Rod climbed into the trailer with headroom to spare, banging his briefcase on the door jam. "Rod, Shortie, aah, sweetie, we were just leaving."

"We need to crank up here in an hour, girls. Right?"

"You can count on us, Miss Trish." Phermona purred over her shoulder as they left.

"The troops seem to be in good spirits today." Rod made his way to the other end of the couch from Trish. "The family that laughs together stays together, right?"

"Phermona and Gwen help keep my spirits up as well as keeping me looking better than I really do." Trish gestured Rod to the couch even though he was almost seated. "So how is Rod these days? We don't talk much, except when we need each other."

"Rod is fine. Rod is hard working. Rod is diligent and resourceful in pursuit of financial gain and artistic expression for his clients." Rod plumped up a couch pillow and settled in as if for a long visit. "Rod also is under-appreciated for his efforts."

"Now don't start getting defensive on me." Trish drew herself up in her bathrobe.

"I'm not complaining. I get paid well for what I do. But sometimes it gets lonely at the top." He smiled at his little joke. "Anyway, what was this thing you were saying about not making movies for a while? That came as a surprise."

"I'm exhausted and out of sorts. I mean I've been churning out two, sometimes three a year forever it seems. And it's not like these flicks have been artistically fulfilling. Nothing but pithy romantic comedies and medium-budget action stuff. I'm beat! I need some time to myself. . . get myself together again. Besides, I need to spend time with my folks." She added this almost as an afterthought.

"Your mom? How is she?"

"Not good at all. I tried to talk to her a couple of days

ago, and she didn't know me." Trish's shook her head sadly. "Dad, God bless him, just doesn't get discouraged. He keeps on caring for her even when he should get some help. I need to help out."

"I know it's a trying situation for everyone, and you have my sympathy." Rod seemed uncharacteristically concerned.

"Enough about my troubles. What do we need to talk about?" Trish's tone was more upbeat.

"We've had an incredible stroke of luck. Meecham and Ivor want you to do Anna Karenina in their new production."

"Anna Karenina? Play the lead? Play Anna Karenina?"

"Anna Karenina herself! Can you believe it? Amazingly, you don't even have to read for the part. It's already yours." Rod was smugly excited as well as resigned.

Trish's surprise trailed into disbelief. "Wait a minute. Something's wrong here. This sort of thing doesn't happen. Nobody hands a part like this to an actor like me. What's the catch?"

"No catch. All we need is your agreement."

"Nah, you're not telling me something."

"We're on a pretty tight schedule."

"How tight?"

Rod winced eve before he said it. "Location filming starts in Russia in three weeks."

Trish sat for a long minute staring at Rod. "Meecham and Ivor have scheduled location filming in Russia without a star for their film?"

"Actually, they've been shooting since August."

"Without a star?"

"They had Levin's country house and outdoor summer scenes to do that didn't require Anna's part. They shot the grass cutting and horse race scenes in England before the move to Russia. They'll shoot all the Anna stuff in Russia."

"You waltz in here and tell me I have the part of Anna if I can be in Russia in three weeks? Are you out of your mind? Are they out of their minds? I wasn't their first choice for the part, that's obvious."

"Actually, they had signed Kate Blanchett for the part. But

some major conflicts popped up or something. Anyway they let her out of her contract last month." Rod flinched again.

"Kate Blanchett? A month ago? Why are we just now talking about this?" Trish's eyes flashed in disbelief.

Rod shrugged. "They talked to a couple of other actors in the meantime. This whole thing was kept quiet because Meecham and Ivor didn't want their investors to get spooked."

"They've run out of time and prospects, and now they're offering the part to me?" Trish leaped up and stalked across the room.

"Now before you get your panties in a wedge, let's not forget all these years you've been kicking my butt to get you a part you could sink your teeth into." Rod stood and gestured for emphasis. "Well, here it is, dropped in your lap as if by divine intervention. So don't get too worked up over not being chosen number one."

Trish returned to the couch and plopped down. She could see the elements of her life converging with her personal needs distilling, leaving only the residue of business as usual. Finally she looked up. "It doesn't matter anyway. I'm not doing another picture anytime soon."

Rod slapped his head with both hands in astonishment. "I can't believe what I'm hearing here. You're not doing another picture anytime soon? This is crazy. It's the big break you've dreamed about. This is it! We're talking about Academy Awards here. Nobody can make this picture better than Meecham and Ivor, and they want *you*! Maybe you're not exactly who they wanted, but they're offering it to you now. Come on, babe, seize the day!"

"I can't. I have other commitments." She crossed her arms to emphasize her resolve.

"Other commitments, my ass! You've got a mom who needs the kind of care neither you nor your dad can give, and you have some guy you've known less than a week that you're sweet on. Jesus, hire a full-time doctor and nurse for your mom, pack up your boyfriend, go to Russia, and show all those Hollywood assholes who've stereotyped you for years what you can really do!"

"You make it sound so easy. Just forsake my parents, give

up any hope of a meaningful personal life, and go make movies, right? Make you lots of agent's fees."

"Oh! That's really low! That's beneath you. Don't make me out to be a money grubbing pimp pushing you for the dough. I care for you as a person whether you appreciate it or not." Rod stood as if to go.

"Wait a minute. Don't go storming out again. Give me a break. I mean, this is all really sudden. It's not a decision I can make easily. Besides I do appreciate what you do for me. God, why can't people just give me a break?" She raised her knees and rested her head on them.

"Okay. Okay. You're right. You need a little time. Look, I'm going back to L.A. tonight." He fumbled in his briefcase for a moment and retrieved two weighty documents. "I'll leave the script and the contract for you to look over, and I'll call you tomorrow. We can work out a plan. I can stall these guys a couple of days."

Rod's rental car moved from under the bridge, making its way toward the northbound lane of S.P.I.D. Causeway and Corpus Christi. He flipped open his phone and pressed a speed dial number and waited for an answer. "Hey, Buddy, Rod here. Listen, I would bet a bunch that Trish will head for her true love this evening. She has one last scene to shoot today, so she'll probably hit the road around six o'clock. Right! They're shooting under the causeway at the Intracoastal Waterway. Yeah, she's driving her car, a red Chrysler Sebring convertible. Right, license number BRN - 361. You can't miss it. Yeah, I'll be at the Holiday Inn waiting for your call. Right, I remember we're going to Port Aransas with Angie and your friend. Call me before eight, okay?"

Rod was toweling off from a shower when his cell phone rang. The caller ID showed it was Buddy. "Hey, Buddy, what's happening?"

"You were right. She blasted out of the movie set and headed south. I followed her to a beach cottage about a mile north of Fish Pass Road," Buddy replied. "Funny thing, I know that old beach house."

"You know this place?"

"Yeah, an old guy named Osborn used to live there when I was a teenager. The guy ran a 24/7-beach party. Jesus, as a teenage kid I used to party my ass off there. I mean, you can't believe the women and booze." Buddy sounded wistful.

"So, this Osborn guy still lives there?"

"No, he died. Probably from too much partying. Something."

"Who lives there now?"

"I'm not sure. I think a friend of Osborn's. No more parties, though. I've heard this guy lives a real quiet life."

"So Trish went into the beach house?"

"Yeah. I'm parked down the beach waiting to see if anything happens, but she hasn't come out."

"Jesus, this doesn't make any sense. How would Trish Lowe meet a beach bum? Crazier still, why would she want to hang around him?" Rod was thinking aloud.

"So what do you want me to do?" Buddy asked.

"Angie is picking me up here at the hotel in a little bit, so why don't you just hang around there?"

"We'll pick up your date and meet you at The Backyard on the Island at about nine o'clock."

Chapter 21

Chris watched the white van disappear, leaving the beach empty. Time dragged as the afternoon progressed. Until Trish had entered his life, time had slipped past him, silent and undetected. He now felt an undefined urgency pulling at him, as though he needed something yet unnamed. He knew that seeds of urgency could flourish into discontent, so he struggled to control it. His simple life, designed years ago, now seemed pointless. Loneliness clutched at him, especially in Trish's absence. Loneliness could be his undoing.

He spent the restless afternoon in his favorite chair so disinterested in a novel that he read for over an hour before realizing he'd finished the book last year. Drowsiness set in, and he drifted in and out of consciousness until his dream returned. The numbness in his fingers from clutching the arm of the chair woke him. His mouth was dry, and he went into the kitchen for a drink of water. Rolling the cool glass of ice water across his brow felt good. At the bar, he poured scotch over the cubes, swirled the contents, and drained the liquid in one gulp.

At his desk, he wrote in his notebook, made corrections, rewrote then ripped out the pages and began again. Eventually his pen moved across the page error free and, when it stopped, he stared for a time at his work. He was about to rip out the page again, when he heard someone jogging over the dune bridge. Instinctively, he rose to go to the door but it burst open before he reached it. Smiling, Trish stood silhouetted in the doorway. A shaft of pure sunlight would brighten the room less, he thought.

They moved together, and she threw her arms around his neck, kissing him. He regained his balance and returned the kiss as if it might be their last. Then Trish stepped back. "Did you miss me?"

He looked at her and felt the loneliness melt away. Before he could answer, she moved forward again, snuggled her head to his chest, and held him around the waist. An intrusion like this even by Lottie would have been unacceptable in the past.

Trish must have sensed it, stepped back, and eyed him suspiciously. "Am I not welcome?"

"Oh. Of course you're welcome. It's just that I . . ."

"You...?" She drew him out.

"I just don't know how to react to new situations. I can't process everything. I go into overload."

"Is this the Christopher Maven way of saying, 'back off, baby?'" Her lips turned down in a pout.

"No, it's not that. And it's certainly not you. It's just that I can feel things changing. I'm not used to change."

"Changing for the better?" She looked hopeful.

"I don't know, really."

"I can live with that. Things are moving, but we don't know in which direction." Trish chuckled. "I can tell I have my work cut out for me."

They both laughed, and he stretched out his hand and pulled her to him, holding her close. "I know I like this part," he said.

She told him how she'd spent her day away from him.

"Did you solve the problems you mentioned last night?" he asked.

"Sort of." Her tone was unsure, and she turned slightly away from him, as she answered.

"Sort of?"

"Some things don't have a good solution." She kissed him to change the subject.

"Can you stay for dinner?" Chris asked.

"I thought you'd never ask." She laughed aloud. "Maybe we could order in Chinese."

"You like Chinese?"

"Don't tell me anyone delivers out here. I don't think Chinese restaurants have four-wheel drive delivery trucks." She saw him laugh at the suggestion. "Do you cook Chinese?"

"I have the makin's to do a couple of Chinese dishes, I think. Necessity is the mother of invention out here." He pointed to the kitchen cabinets as he spoke.

"I haven't had good Chinese since I came to Texas. Any man who can solve that problem will go a long way with me."

"We'll need to thaw some scallops and shrimp and chop up some other stuff. How long do you have until you have to leave?" He hoped for the right answer.

"How could I leave a man who's just cooked me Chinese?"

He took the bay scallops from the freezer and placed them in a shallow bowl of Riesling wine to tenderize them. The shrimp went into the sink to thaw. He chopped and sliced an array of leftover vegetables including onions and garlic, then placed a pot of water for rice on the stove to boil.

As he cooked, Trish stood at his desk and saw the open notebook. "It looks like you've been creative." She held up the notebook.

"Yeah, but I'm not too thrilled at the result."

"Maybe it needs the test."

"Could be, 'cause I'm certainly not sure it's ready for immortality. How about a drink?" Chris offered.

"Maybe a brandy and coffee?"

"You got it." He set about making coffee and finding the brandy. A few minutes later, with their drinks in hand, he suggested, "Why don't we go out on the deck and catch the sunset?"

The breeze was cool enough for Trish to snuggle under Chris's arm for warmth. They stood at the railing watching the surf and sun play a sparkling game of tag as the swells broke on the beach and sent the beach-foraging terns retreating toward the dunes.

"God, this is great. Paradise, really." Trish spoke more to herself than to Chris. "The whole world is held at bay by a magic solitude. A life with no demands. No expectations. No pressure. Only peace."

"It *is* peaceful." Chris scanned the horizon as he spoke. He turned to Trish, picked her up, and sat her on the top rail, then stood between her legs and held her in a close embrace.

"I like this view also." Trish smiled at his face. Her expression changed, and she asked, "Do you ever think about a different life?"

"Not really. I've lived this life so long, any other seems too distant and difficult. Why do you ask?"

"I guess I was wondering if there is room in this life for anyone else?"

The look in her eyes was a tug at his soul. The urgency welled almost out of control, but he finally responded, "I think you're right. We should put that poem to the test." He lifted her from the railing and led her across the dune bridge where they looked for a suitable place to write his verse in the sand. He stooped to pick up a stick, and when he stood he looked to the north and saw the storm clouds building.

Chapter 22

Buddy rolled the car windows down, and the salt air flooded his car. The evening was cool but not cold. He had parked away from the water to hide from sight of the beach house, and the breeze rustled the sea oats growing in the dunes near his car. It was altogether a pleasant place to be, and he wondered why he came to the beach so seldom now. Back in his teenage days, he would camp within sight of Osborn's dune house for weeks during the summer. He'd once camped almost in the same spot where he now was parked. Those were magic times for a teenager who'd looked old enough – he'd simply strolled down the beach and merged into Osborn's beach party where both booze and women were free.

On one of these outings a constable, who'd caught him drinking, asked for his I.D., and Buddy explained to no avail that he didn't carry ID in his swim trunks. Osborn's girl friend, Lottie Langton, walked up, hugged the constable, and said he should quit bothering Osborn's guests. The winning smile, the bikini, and the hug won the day for Buddy, and he'd been forever grateful to Lottie.

God, Lottie was a beautiful girl in those days. He never was granted special dispensation to hang around Lottie, but he seldom missed a chance for quality time when it was offered. They'd remained casual friends over the years, and Lottie always bought him a drink when he visited her Backyard Bar. He'd not seen her for several months, and he looked forward to their visit to her bar tonight.

The breeze calmed and changed directions, and he looked past the dunes and saw dark clouds to the north. Lottie always had a good band at The Backyard, the outdoor dance floor was oversized, and he hoped the weather would hold off until much later. He wanted to get in some dancing.

From the corner of his eye, he saw something move, and he focused on the beach house. Trish Lowe and an older guy came out on the deck and looked for a time at the water as they leaned over the railing, sipping from coffee mugs. Trish didn't hold on to him like a casual acquaintance. He helped her sit on the railing and then stood between her legs as she wrapped her arms around his neck. They held this embrace long enough for Buddy to attach his Nikon telephoto lens, to focus, and to frame the couple.

They talked and laughed while holding each other, and Buddy's auto winder whirred as he reeled off a dozen snapshots of their embrace. The sun sank below the dunes and the light faded, but he made out the features of the man Trish was holding. He looked to be in his sixties and ruggedly handsome.

The guy helped Trish down from the railing as Buddy studied him. The two then walked over the dune bridge onto the beach and turned toward him. They studied the sand as if they had lost something. The last of the sun's rays, shining through a notch in the dunes, lighted a spot of the beach where they stopped, and the man picked up a stick and wrote in the sand. Trish stood back a few steps and seemed to admire the sand-writer's work. They both stood and looked at the sand when he stopped writing. She went to him, put her arm around him, and they walked slowly back toward the beach house. At mid-span of the bridge, they stopped and looked in his direction before continuing into the house.

The light was almost gone, so he started his engine and moved up the beach until the car was abreast of the sand writing. The verse was still legible in the fading light, and he studied it for a minute before taking a picture of it. He also took a close-up of the A-frame as he drove past. Continuing down the beach to the next access road, he turned toward the highway and drove to Port Aransas for his evening with Rod and the girls.

He arrived at The Backyard Bar early for his rendezvous with Rod, and he could hear The Blues Project rocking out on the outdoor stage from his car. The girl who was collecting the cover charge recognized Buddy and waved him through with a smile. He was settling at the bar when he felt a warm hug from behind and turned to see Lottie smiling at him. "Hi, stranger, long time no see."

"You know how it is when you're a famous journalist. Never enough time." Buddy laughed at his exaggeration.

"Not even for your old friends, right?"

"I was on assignment here on the island and couldn't pass up a chance to see your smiling face."

"Assignment? On this island?"

"I'm doing some research for a guy. Actually, he's going to be here with a couple of friends in a few minutes. I'll introduce you."

"I hope they get here before the rain." She cast a worried look toward the north.

"Before you go, what do you know about Osborn's old place?"

"Why do you ask?" Lottie became suspicious of this question about Osborn's house.

"I saw it this afternoon for the first time in forever, and it brought back a lot of memories. Like the time you saved me from that constable. I was curious if anyone lives there." Buddy wore a benign expression.

"You looking for a place?" Lottie's antennae were still up Buddy's questions.

"No, just curious."

"I think an old guy lives there. Sort of a hermit type. Doesn't like people. Really wouldn't like journalists, so I hear."

"You know his name?"

"Why would I know his name?" Lottie hid her apprehension behind a puzzled expression.

"I just thought he might be a friend of Osborn's or something."

Lottie again looked quizzical. " Listen, I've got to make a round and make sure the guests are groovin'." With that she turned and waded into the crowd standing around the bar.

The Blues Project cranked up a raucous shuffle tune just as Buddy saw Rod and the two women at the entrance. When a table of four older Lawrence Welk types got up to retreat from the noise, Buddy moved in to claim the table and gestured to Rod, who worked his way through the crowd with the girls in tow. "Hey, guys, welcome to The Backyard." Buddy hugged both Angie and his date, Maggie. "Well, what d'ya say, Maggie." Buddy pointed to the dance floor before anyone was seated. Maggie looked delighted, and the two moved to the dance floor to give one of their exhibitions.

Rod looked a little befuddled and drew out a chair for Angie. "Lost your nerve, Rod?" she chided.

"I do my best imitation of a dancer after a couple of martinis. Besides, we need to get some drinks on the table to anchor it before we wander off." He gestured at the crowd around the seating area.

The shuffle tune lasted longer that any song he could remember, and during the whole time Angie chair-danced, occasionally glancing at him for a dance invitation, but he was busy ordering drinks and surveying the crowd in the manner of an agent working the room at an "in" restaurant in Hollywood. It was a habit he couldn't help. What he saw was a bunch of people whose interest in the two beautiful women he and Buddy had brought was more than casual. He knew they wondered how that short guy hooked up with that hot babe.

The drinks arrived just as Buddy and Maggie returned to the table. "I guess you guys showed the island folks how it's done." Rod lifted his martini glass. "Here's to dance lessons."

"To dance lessons!" They all joined the toast.

Lottie came to their table during the pause between songs and greeted them. "Welcome to The Backyard. So, Buddy, these are the friends you mentioned?"

"Meet Rod, Angie, and Maggie. We've followed the siren song of blues music all the way out here to little ol' Port Aransas, and we're not disappointed."

"You guys are something to see on the dance floor, for sure." She nodded to Buddy and Maggie. "When you're ready,

I'll order another round on me to quench your thirst after all the exercise."

"Rod came all the way from Hollywood to be here tonight." Angie inserted this little bit of puffery. "He's a Hollywood agent."

"So you're auditioning our local talent, are you, Rod?" Lottie smiled at him.

Before he could answer, Maggie added, "He's Trish Lowe's agent." Rod raised his eyebrows at Buddy in disbelief at this line of conversation.

"Wow, you're really Trish Lowe's agent?" Lottie said in mock astonishment, but she still wondered why Buddy showed so much interest in Chris's beach house, and why he was sitting with Trish Lowe's agent in her bar.

"Now don't bust my chops over this. I didn't bring it up, and I would just as well forget it and have a good time," Rod said.

"No, really! You must be here because of the movie she's making over in Corpus, right?" Lottie asked. Before Rod had to answer, the band ripped into another shuffle tune, and Angie grabbed his hand and dragged him to the dance floor. The martini and his previous dance lesson kicked in, and he led into his version of the Texas whip. Buddy and Maggie joined them on the dance floor, and the rest of the crowd hung back in anticipation of another exhibition.

Buddy was amused at Rod trying to keep up with Angie. While he watched them, he noticed two couples that stood in the entrance, stopped in mid-stride. The beautiful black girl wearing a tight-fitting, black leather outfit pointed toward Rod and said something to a younger black man and a white couple. The four laughed aloud and moved to the other side of the gazebo bar from the dance floor.

The band went on break and the dancers returned to their table. Rod made sure he was seated next to Buddy. He leaned over to whisper, "So did anything else happen at that beach house?"

Buddy told him about pictures he'd taken

Rod was so excited he almost spilled his drink. "How soon can you have these developed?"

"I shot in black and white, so I can develop them myself tonight and print them in the morning." Buddy replied. "Why, are you getting a knot in your Jockeys?"

"I'm in a huge hurry! This is Thursday. If I get the prints on Friday." Rod's voice trailed off while his mind worked "Listen, if you can get the prints tomorrow by noon, along with a five-hundred-word piece on 'Who Is This Mystery Man?' I can get you five thousand dollars."

"What are you two talking about? Maggie and I are feeling lonely," Angie blurted out. Buddy waved his hand, dismissing her. "Five grand for five hundred words and some snap shots? Who would pay that?"

"Your old friend, *The National Investigator*. But they close their next issue on Saturday."

"Come on, Maggie, these guys are not paying any attention to us. Let's go to the john." Angie slid her chair back, and the two stalked off to the restroom to the enjoyment of all the male patrons.

"What do you want in the article?" Buddy pulled his chair closer.

"You know, Trish is making a movie in Texas. She's seeing this mystery man on the beach. Some history on the house and that Osborn guy who died there. Conjecture on who the mystery man might be. You know what I'm talking about. Five hundred words of BS and titillation." Rod was annoyed at having to teach the fundamentals.

The storm finally descended on Port Aransas and sent the open-air revelers at The Backyard running to the cover of their cars. Phermona, Gwen, Sam, and Gus, still damp from their Backyard outing, rode home in peals of laughter, especially when Phermona gave a little car seat demonstration of Rod's dancing. "Lord, I just can't wait to tell Trish what a great dancer Rod is." The four dissolved into laughter again.

Lottie sat in the cramped office of The Backyard counting the night's receipts. Although the rain had cut the night short, the early crowd had pushed the revenue to an acceptable level. Wind and rain continued to pelt the office's tin roof as she sat looking out the window at the harbor. The moored boats reared and struggled at their lines like roped mustangs. It was a restless night, and the question of Buddy's sudden interest in Chris nagged at her. Something was not right about Trish Lowe's agent and a local journalist hanging out together and asking questions about Chris. She felt she should warn Chris or do something. She longed to be with Chris, but the beach would be awash with rain and high tide, and she had no hope of making it to his beach house. Besides, who was to say that Trish Lowe had not already beaten her to it?

Chapter 23

The pungency of ginger and sesame oil permeated the house as Chris stir-fried the vegetables, shrimp, and scallops. Trish was hungry from the day's filming, which had not included a lunch break, and the smell of Chinese food made her salivate. She wanted to speed up dinner, so she pitched in and made the hot tea and emptied the rice cooker. Chris poured the stir-fry into a bowl, and she whisked it to the table and plopped down with a beseeching glance at Chris. He brought the Riesling bottle, opened earlier to marinate the scallops, and poured her a glass.

"God, I'm so hungry, and this food smells so good, I'm about to faint." She launched into the stir-fry the second Chris sat and fell completely silent as she scooped up spoonful after spoonful. After a few more bites she looked toward the heavens. "Jesus, this is good! Mr. Maven, you've absolutely won my heart." She stood and leaned over the table to give him a kiss. "I mean, who else in the world is sitting on a deserted beach, in a cozy beach house, and eating fabulous home-cooked Chinese food?"

"A few thousand Chinese, I would think." Chris only sipped his wine and watched the rapture of a hungry Trish Lowe. "You can't spend too much time around me, you know, or you might gain weight."

Trish looked up from her plate. "Now see? There you go again, trying to scare me off. It won't work. I'll be sniffing around your back door looking for my next meal."

With dinner and wash-up complete, Chris led Trish into the living room and sat her on the couch opposite the television. He pointed to the video shelf. "Name your poison."

"A movie? Are you serious?." She pouted a little.

"Out here we look for ways to pass the time."

"Let's see if I can think of any other ways." She laughed, but saw he was not rising to the suggestion. "Okay, okay. How about Anna Karenina."

"Excellent choice. I haven't seen it in more than a year." He pulled a video from the shelf and shoved it into the player. The television blinked twice as the video started, and the opening scene to *She* flashed onto the screen. Trish was seated on a bamboo throne almost nude except for a necklace of flowers covering her breasts and a very short loincloth. Amazon natives, dancing and chanting in some nondescript language, surrounded her. They brandished spears and blowguns in time to the beat of an Amazon drum line that would rival a Grambling College football halftime show.

Trish leaped from the couch, "Oh no you don't! Not a chance! Not possible! Not even possible. Give me the remote control! We're not going to watch this piece of trash!" She moved around the couch as Chris retreated. He leaped over the couch before she could catch him, and she grabbed couch pillows and launched a fusillade at him before storming over the back of the couch herself. She pulled him down into the pillows and rolled on top of him trying to reach the remote he held at arm's length. The full-length body contact felt good, and she stopped her frantic efforts to recover the remote and kissed him. The forgotten remote lay on the floor. They groped at each other's clothes as the drum's volume ascended.

The drumming reached a fever pitch as the chief of the tribe escorted his son, a Latin version of Arnold Schwarzenegger clad only in an Amazon-style Speedo, to the throne of She. The drumming ceased, and all were silent as She inspected her potential prize.

She stepped down from her throne and slowly moved around her husband-to-be, inspecting him as if he were a prize stallion. Looking deeply into his eyes, she nodded once, and the drum line broke out again in full voice with the entire tribe stomping and gyrating in a frenetic dance of approval around the two as they moved to the royal grass hut.

The sounds of the two lovers entwined on the floor continued unabated.

They bundled up on the couch, dozing intermittently to the New Age piano music of George Winston. The first pelting of rain sounded on the roof, gently at first, then building in intensity. A thunderclap awoke them, and they sat on the couch huddled in a blanket against the cold.

"It doesn't look good for your poem," she said.

"I guess the gods have spoken."

They stood looking out the picture window at the storm, both wrapped in the same blanket, silent as they witnessed a greater power needing no commentary.

"Would you think less of me if I said I'm tired?" She tilted her head sheepishly.

"Sleeping to the beating of rain is the best." Chris led her in the direction of the loft stairs. Trish's cell phone rang. Still wrapped in the same blanket they shuffled to her backpack.

She looked at Caller ID and flipped open the phone. "Hey, Leah, what's up?"

"Just checking to see if you're okay. I looked for you to go to dinner, but I couldn't find you."

"Yeah, no problem. I'm just taking care of some personal business."

"How personal?" Leah had a lilt in her voice.

"Very. By the way, I got rid of Rod this afternoon. He said he was flying back to L.A. tonight."

"Great news. Oh, some more semi-great news. It looks like you'll get a couple of days' rest."

"How's that?"

"Danielle said at dinner tonight the weather forecast is for rain and storms through Sunday, and all she has left for you is the one big beach scene. She needs clear skies for that."

"That's more than semi-great news. That's wonderful news." Trish jumped up and down with excitement.

"So when will I see you again?" Leah sounded hopeful.

"Not until the sun shines! If Rod, or anyone else needs me, I'm unavailable." She closed the phone and turned it off.

The next morning Rod sent Angie home early and got on the phone. He called the offices of *The National Investigator* in New York, and told the managing editor's secretary that he had a "Stop Press" piece on Trish Lowe and her new lover. The editor was on the line immediately. "My name is Buddy St. John," Rod lied. "I'm a photo journalist, and I have photos of Trish Lowe loving it up with a mystery man down here in Texas where she's filming a movie. That's right. The guy lives in a crummy little beach house, and he writes poetry in the sand. No one knows who he is. The house has a history, too. I'm asking $10,000 for three photos and five hundred words... . Sure, I'll submit it as a spec piece, but I also want the continuation if you run it. Good! It'll be there Saturday before ten o'clock... . You'll run it next week, right? Good!" He hung up and ordered a huge breakfast to celebrate while he waited for Buddy to show up.

Buddy, suffering from lack of sleep, delivered his photos and "Mystery Man" article to Rod about noon Friday. Buddy explained that he was running late for an assignment, out of town, and didn't know when he'd be back. Rod sat at the room desk, shuffled through the photos several times, and picked three to send to *The National Investigator*. One photo, a long-range shot, showed Trish and the mystery man hugging while she sat on the deck railing. He attached a Post-It with the hand-written caption, "Beach house lovers, Trish Lowe and her mystery man." The sunset's light had produced a dramatic close-up of the front of the beach house to which he penned the caption, "The luckiest man in America lives here – Trish Lowe's mystery lover." He mused for some time over the photo of the sand poem. The inscription in the sand was highlighted by extended shadows, and the lettering indentations oozed water, making the photo very artistic. The poem was so personal it peaked his jealousy, but he had no scruples about including it. His annoyance with the poem showed in his handwriting for the caption, "Mystery man leaves message for the world." He drove to the nearest Kinko and had them create a "Buddy St. John" invoice for $10,000 with Rod's Los Angeles address. He crumpled the transmittal letter Buddy had written, and penned a handwritten note to *The National Investigator* editor. Across the room at the FedEx desk, he clipped his note to Buddy's manuscript and stuffed everything into a FedEx packet marked for Saturday morning delivery.

The next day, Rod called *The National Investigator* and learned from the editor that the article had arrived, and he was running it on the cover of Monday's edition. "Your piece will be on every grocery checkout stand in the country by Monday afternoon."

Rod flipped open his cell phone and pressed Buddy's speed dial button. "Hey, Buddy, you're in like a boy dog . . . That's right. You've got the cover, five thousand bucks, and the continuation . . . That's right, pal. Hey, didn't I tell you we'd be good for each other. Let's have breakfast tomorrow morning and plan the follow-up piece."

Rod had worked his way through the eggs Benedict and was on his third glass of champagne before the article came up. "I don't know how long we can milk this thing, but I think we have at least two more shots at it. The next one should be an expansion of the first with close-ups of the mystery man with Trish, and interviews either with him or with locals who know something about him. The final one should be the interview with Trish where she can do her denial stuff that she's so good at."

Buddy lifted his champagne glass for another sip. "I got the impression that Lottie knows a lot more about this guy than she's letting on. Maybe we can get a picture of her and a statement." Rod lifted his glass in a mock toast. "She's a fine looking babe. A picture of her would spice up the piece. It would boost her business, anyway."

"The rain's stopped, and the beach may be hard enough to get out there this morning. Maybe I should go check out what's happening." Buddy signaled to the waitress for the check.

"Great idea. In fact, I wouldn't mind seeing this place myself. I'll go with you." Rod didn't offer to pay the tab.

The rain and storms continued through Friday and Saturday at Chris's beach house, but even weather-bound, the two barely noticed the passage of time. The days and nights were filled with conversations, reading, eating, and sleeping, liberally accented with lovemaking. Trish slept late Sunday morning and wakened to the smell of coffee and biscuits baking. After a quick shower, she slipped into one of Chris's woolly sweaters, pulling up the sleeves that extended past her fingertips. She found a pair of clean warm-up pants in her backpack, pulled them on, grabbed a headband, and headed for the coffee pot. The smell of the biscuits overwhelmed her, and she lifted the pan from the oven, placing two biscuits on paper napkins. Balancing her coffee cup and biscuits, she wriggled through the screen door onto the deck.

Chris was halfway over the bridge, leaning on the railing, staring intently toward the south. Heavy moisture still hung in the air, even though the rain had moved on. The overcast sky shed an ominous pall on the day, but the surf was calm, and the beach was clean to the dunes. Refreshed by the rain, the Sea Daisies had burst forth, blanketing the dunes in yellow.

Order returns to the world, she thought, and tranquility reigns,.

"If it isn't the Pillsbury Dough Boy." She nuzzled next to him handing him a biscuit. "Life doesn't get better than waking after a night of good lovin' with biscuits in the oven."

He put his arm around her and took the biscuit. "Guess I got preoccupied and forgot the biscuits. Thanks for rescuing them."

She looked up at him. "Is this a poet at work? Am I interrupting the creative process?"

"No, this is a recluse wondering why that same car is parked down there on the beach again." He nodded in the direction of an older model, nondescript sedan parked next to the dunes. "It was there the other evening when we walked on the beach."

"Maybe that's their very favorite place on the beach." She tried to make light of his suspicions.

"You feel up for a walk?" His tone left little choice.

"Let's go for it!" She set her coffee cup on the railing, held her biscuit in one hand, and grasped his hand with her other. They set off down the bridge at a leisurely pace and turned south on the beach toward the parked car.

Rod pointed to Chris and Trish on the dune bridge. "There she is! They're together. Shoot'em." He gestured toward the camera.

Buddy focused the telephoto lens and the winder whirred off six shots. "They're still too far away. This is almost the same shot I got before."

"Wait a minute, they're walking down to the bridge. Great, they're walking in our direction." Rod was excited. The distance between the couple and the car was narrowing. "Jesus Christ, they're coming all the way down here! Shoot 'em and let's get out of here!"

"They're still too far away." Buddy steadied his camera on the steering wheel. "Keep coming," he mumbled

"Keep coming, my ass. Are you crazy? Trish can't see me here! Get the fuck out'a here!" Rod gestured wildly.

"Keep coming." Buddy framed the photo. "Come on. That's right, come on." He saw Chris release Trish's hand and shade his eyes, focusing on the car.

Rod slid under the dashboard screaming, "For God's sake start the car, and let's go." He jerked Buddy's pants leg.

"Cut it out! You're shaking the camera. Okay, there it is." The camera whirred four more times. "I love it. Full frame waist-up. It's a classic." Buddy grinned at himself in the rearview mirror.

"Fuck! I can't believe this. Trish is going to find me wallowing on the floorboard of a 1987 Chevrolet. I'll be ruined. I can never show my face in Hollywood again." Rod squirmed over on his elbows and knees hiding his face in his hands. "I'm begging you, man, start the car. Now!" He heard the starter motor whine, but the motor didn't catch. The starter complained again, but still no engine. Buddy could barely make out the muffled sounds Rod was making as he held his head in his hands on the floor mat.

"You've got to be kidding me." Rod moaned. "This shit bucket won't start? Good God, what a nightmare!"

The engine caught on the third try, and Buddy dropped the gearshift into drive. "Oky, baby, here we go." He stepped on the accelerator and the back tires spun out.

From under the dashboard Buddy heard, "What's happening. WE'RE NOT MOVING!"

"We may be stuck," Buddy said, releasing his foot from the accelerator.

"STUCK! WE MAY BE STUCK? WE ARE NOT FUCKING STUCK!" Rod lunged forward, jamming the accelerator to the floor, and wet sand arced from under the back tires.

Chris and Trish were a few hundred feet from the car when the back tires exploded into action, spewing sand and mud. The car lurched forward, wheels spinning, and swapped ends, still throwing sand halfway to them. The Chevrolet gained momentum and sped off down the beach, fishtailing in the wet sand. They stood watching the retreat of the car, and Trish said, "Professional driver on a closed course. Do not try this at home."

Chris chuckled. "I see some strange things on this beach, but I'm not sure about this one."

"Probably a couple of lovers who didn't want to get caught." Trish squeezed his hand in reassurance as they turned around. "Race you back!" She sprinted back toward the dune bridge. Chris quickly overcame her head start and paced himself beside her with exaggerated movements as if he could barely keep up. When they reached Trish's car, she stopped and leaned against it, panting heavily.

He ran past and stopped at the end of the dune bridge. "The winner!" He raised his arms, acknowledging all of the cheering sports fans. He spoke into an invisible microphone, "I want to dedicate this victory to all the older people of the world."

"You cheated." She wore a mock pout. Rooting around inside the car for a minute, she pulled out a briefcase.

"Is this my prize?" He pointed at the briefcase.

Inside the beach house, Trish set the briefcase on his desk, pulled out the Anna Karenina contract and script. Chris looked over her shoulder. "Pretty ominous documents you've got there."

" 'Ominous' is the right word." She dropped them on his desk with a thud.

He lifted them. "Definitely not light reading."

"My agent wants me to do this movie next. He says I already have the part if I want it." She sighed.

"And what does Trish want?" He laid the two documents down again, looking more carefully at the cover pages. "*Anna Karenina*, That's a long way from *She*."

"I've never been offered a part like this before, but I'm not sure I want to do it. I have other interests now." She flipped through the script lying on the desk.

"I don't know about such things, but this seems like a big opportunity for you, right? What other things could be as interesting?"

"You." She watched him intently for his reaction.

"Me? I'm just an old hippie beach bum who scribbles in the sand." There was genuine surprise in his voice.

"I've been looking for someone like you all my life – you represent a life that's so far removed from mine, and I yearn to share it with you. " He started to object, but she held up her hand. "No. Let me finish. God, I can't believe I started into this. Right . . I met you less than a week ago, so I don't claim to know you, but what I know, I like and enjoy. I think there's so much for us to build a relationship on. I do know that when I touch you, I instantly crave for more, and when we make love I am transported." She held his head in the tips of her fingers caressing gently, then slid her arms around his neck. "I think you're not as happy as you could be, and I think I can help that. I want to be part of your life. There, I've said it." Chris looked at her but said nothing. "It's okay if you want to jump in here anytime and save me, Chris." She searched for something positive in his expression.

"You're right. You really don't know who I am." He looked away. "Not at all."

"Where am I wrong? Who are you, buddy boy?" Her eyes sparkled with good humor.

"I'm a guy with problems he can't deal with, so he lives like a hermit and writes poems in the sand. You're a famous actress, living a glamorous life in the spotlight of celebrity. I'm a guy looking down the back slope of life. You're a young woman with your whole life before you." He held both her hands and cocked his head slightly. "As much as I've loved this past week, I just can't see a future together." He squeezed her hands as he finished.

"But you're what I want. You're what I need." She wrapped her arms around him and held him hoping never to let go.

He paused for a long time and tried to absorb the information. He and Lottie had been lovers for years, and she'd seldom, if ever, talked about a permanent relationship. Now, after a week, Trish was talking about one. His head spun at the magnitude of the idea.

"There's no way you could be happy living my life. You'd grow to hate this place." His speech was hesitant. "To hate me. I mean, it's a perfectly good place to visit, but you wouldn't want to live here." His laugh was filled with uncertainty.

"But that's the point. We could live anywhere we wanted. I have a beach house in Malibu with plenty of sand for writing poems. It was my favorite place in the world until I came here. If I keep making pictures, you could live there when I'm working. You could travel with me when I'm on location, but That's just the thing, I'm not even sure I want to make movies anymore."

"California is a whole lifetime away for me." He frowned at the thought. The urgency he struggled with came over him again. "There are things I can't do."

"Oh, I'm making a mess of this. Why did I bring this up now?" She ran her hand over her face as if to wipe away any emotion.

Chris was about to say something conciliatory when he heard footsteps and a voice from the deck. "Hey, Chris, it's Jeffrey."

"The cavalry again." Chris pointed toward Jeffrey.

He opened the door for the Ranger. "Hi, Miss Lowe, I found you again." He faltered a little when he saw Trish was disturbed. " Miss Armour called and said your cell phone is turned off, and she was pretty desperate to get hold of you. She wanted you to call her." He paused again. "I told her I'd look for you."

Trish took a deep breath. "Thanks, Jeffrey, I'm sorry to put you to the trouble."

"Not a problem, Miss Lowe." Jeffrey smiled broadly at her appreciation.

Trish walked to her backpack and got her phone. "If you two gentlemen will amuse yourselves, I'll see what's bothering Leah." She went out on the deck and pressed Leah's speed dial number. "Hey, Leah, what's happening?"

"Thank God you called. Did the ranger find you?" Leah sounded disturbed.

"No. I haven't seen Jeffrey. I was just calling to see if you had news about when Danielle wants to shoot," Trish lied.

"Yeah, before I forget it, Danielle set a major rehearsal and run-through for ten o'clock tomorrow. She says there will be half a day of clear skies Tuesday morning, and she wants everybody completely plugged in. Apparently, the shoot requires a major equipment move. All the equipment, crew, and players must be on site by first light Tuesday. But there's something else." Leah paused to see if Trish was still on the line.

"What's that?" Trish asked, dreading the answer.

"Rod called me three times trying to get hold of you. He's playing like he's in L.A."

"He is, isn't he?" Her face twisted in confusion.

"No, he's right here in Corpus Christi."

"How do you know?" Trish frowned at the idea.

"I ran into Phermona and Gwen a little while ago in the lobby, and they told me they saw Rod trying to dance at a bar over in Port Aransas Friday night. They said he was with another guy and two women. It seems the other three were great dancers." Leah chuckled remembering Phermona's imitation of Rod.

"Maybe he couldn't get a flight until Saturday morning?" Trish reasoned.

"No, they went to a new place for breakfast this morning, and Rod was there having breakfast with the same guy." Leah was emphatic. "Rod's here in town, and he's up to something."

Trish's mind whirred trying to understand why Rod had lied about going back to L.A. Then she remembered the car on the beach that morning. "Oh, my God! Maybe I know what he's up to."

Chapter 24

Rod undressed for a much-needed nap after Buddy dropped him off at the hotel. Three nights of partying and the morning's excitement on the beach had exhausted him. His cell phone rang as he pulled back the bedcovers, and Caller ID identified Trish. Rod studied the phone while he worked to get his story right, and finally answered on the fourth ring. "Hey, Trish, good to hear from you"

"Where are you, Rod?"

Rod knew this tone of voice from Trish. "At home, why?"

"No, you're not, Rod. You're right here in Corpus Christi." Her voice sparked over the phone.

"Why do you say that? I'm watching the football game in my study." He tried to sound convincing while he picked up the TV remote and punched up CBS. "The Raiders are playing the Jets."

"Let's cut the crap, Rod. Phermona and Gwen saw you Friday night in Port Aransas trying to dance and again this morning at breakfast. I need to know why you're still here in Corpus." She sounded threatening. "You're lying about where you are, and that means you're up to something. Like trying to find out who I'm spending time with."

"Who are you spending time with, Trish?" He could not help smiling at his success at sleuthing.

"That's none of your business, Rod. In fact it's no one's business but mine. That's why I need to know if you've done something we're both going to regret."

"What something?" Rod was getting edgy over the direction the conversation was taking.

"Like getting paparazzi photos of me on the beach this morning."

Rod's pasty smile melted. "Why would I do that?"

Trish switched hands with her cell phone. "I can think of several reasons, but you tell me."

"Have you seen the paparazzi?" He squinted his eyes hoping for the right answer.

"Yes, I think I have." She tried to sound believable.

"Think" was the word Rod wanted to hear. "Sorry to hear that, but all publicity is good publicity. Actually, I don't know anything about it, but I confess, you've caught me. I stopped at a bar on the way back into Corpus after our meeting, Thursday, and met this great looking gal. We've been partying our ass off. I was overdue for a fling." He learned forward anticipating her response.

"If it was anyone but you, Rod, I might believe that. But I know you too well. You're up to something."

"Why would you say that?" Rod crossed his fingers.

"God, because you are perverse, Rod.

"That's what I get paid for, babe. To be perverse. I get people to do what my clients need them to do. I find a way. I get it done"

"But you've never known the difference between what your clients need and what you want." Trish sounded almost resigned. "I'll be at the hotel in about an hour, and I want to meet with you."

"You're driving in from the beach?" Rod cringed as soon as he realized his blunder.

"What did you say? The beach? Why do you think I'm at the beach?" Trish's voice escalated.

Rod's face contorted in pain as he mouthed, "shit!" then said, "Aah, I just thought you might be out at that park you like so much. Leah told me about it. Just a guess."

There was a long pause before Trish answered. "Five-thirty at the hotel!" She slammed the phone closed before Rod could answer.

Chris and Jeffrey remained inside when Trish went to the deck to make her phone call. The two watched as Trish grew more upset the longer the conversation went on. She finally hung up, stamping her foot in anger, and voiced an oath. She opened the phone again, pressed a speed dial number, and began an even more animated conversation.

The two men watched her silently until Jeffrey said, "That's one very upset lady out there. I think I brought some bad news."

"It's hard to say. But you may have helped me this time." Chris shook his head sadly.

"Is there a storm brewing?" Jeffrey watched Chris' reaction. When there was no answer, he added, "Actually, Trish isn't the only lady in our lives who's upset today."

"Why do you say that?" Chris turned from the window to look at Jeffrey.

Jeffrey gestured toward Port Aransas. "I was having a toddy at The Backyard when Leah called me. It wasn't very busy, so I was visiting with Lottie."

"Lottie? How is she?" Chris was apprehensive.

"You're not her favorite person right now, but she seemed concerned about you." Jeffrey had the wistfulness of a man who wished Lottie were worried about him.

"Concerned about what?"

"I'm not sure. Maybe she thinks Trish is using you to get publicity. She was talking about some people who were in the bar last week asking questions about you." Jeffrey shrugged.

"I don't see how I could help Trish get publicity." He shook his head. "A week ago I lived a very simple life, and now – things have changed."

Trish slammed the cell phone shut again and stormed back inside. There was a brief, awkward silence before Jeffrey voiced, "Did I bring bad news?"

"I knew four idyllic days were too good to be true. Leah is very concerned about a problem I thought I'd solved, so I have to go back to Corpus Christi tonight." She headed for her backpack. "I'm sorry to rush off like this, but I have to leave right away." When she finished packing her backpack and briefcase, she asked Jeffrey, "Would you mind following me out in case I have trouble?"

"Not a problem." He brightened at the thought.

"Then could I meet you down at the cars?" She nodded in the direction of the door.

"Oh! Yeah. Okay, Chris I'll be back tomorrow with your provisions." He donned his western hat and disappeared onto the deck.

Trish turned to Chris, standing a step away. She stammered, "I . . ."

Chris moved forward and put his arms around her, holding her close, and kissed her forehead. She raised her head and pulled him into a pensive kiss, running her fingers lightly over his face, then turned and left.

His countenance darkened as if she'd turned off the switch to his soul. He moved to the window and watched her retreat over the bridge and into her car. When the two vehicles turned back toward Fish Pass Road, he stepped onto the deck and continued watching until they were out of sight. Solitude settled in like fog, and he shivered under its chill. When he returned inside, there was no relief. It was suffocating.

He went to his desk considering the verse ricocheting around in his head, but knew he could not sit down. Instead, he went outside and walked over the bridge to the beach. The clouds were breaking up, and sparks of sunshine shone through. The wind still held the chill of the receding cold front, and small waves smoothed out, skittering over the sand. He stood for a minute considering directions, and then turned and walked away from Fish Pass Road. As he walked, the urgency welled in him again, and he moved to a jog. That became a slow run and finally he ran at sprint speed until he fell exhausted and panting in the sand. He lay motionless except for his heavy breathing. Several minutes passed before he finally sat up, knees under his chin and arms around his legs, staring into nothingness.

Chapter 25

Trish threw her briefcase and backpack on the hotel bed. She looked around, and the room was strangely unfamiliar, as if months had passed since she had slept here. Leah's special knock on the door interrupted Trish's dialing her dad's number. She hung up and opened the door.

Leah had an expectant expression as she blurted, "Well? Come on, let's have it. What did you find out?"

Trish motioned Leah in and retreated to sit on the edge of the bed. "It's not a scoop, but Rod is a lying bastard. He finally confessed that he is here in Corpus. Says he met a girl, and they've been carousing since Thursday afternoon."

"That's pretty lame." Leah waved off the idea.

"I accused him of secretly trying to find out who I'm spending time with, but he denied it, of course."

"Who *are* you spending time with?" Leah's eyes arched with the question.

"Geez, not you too!" Trish shook her head in exasperation.

"Now, don't get huffy. You've been more secretive lately than the C.I.A. 'Inquiring minds want to know'." Leah grinned.

"I certainly have my quota of 'inquiring minds,' that's for sure." Trish got up and started pacing.

"So what's your plan?"

"Rod is due here any minute." Trish returned to the bed and smoothed out the bedcover, then glanced up at Leah. "By the way, did you tell Rod about Mustang Island State Park?"

"I don't really remember. I guess it's possible. Why?" Leah looked bewildered.

"He said you told him how much I enjoyed going there."

"We did have a conversation about what you were doing when he first got here, and I might have told him about the park as a cover." Leah shrugged her answer.

The telephone interrupted their conversation, and Trish answered it. "Yeah, come up to room 1602," she said. Her voice sounded like a threat, and Leah rose to leave. Trish motioned her back into her chair. "You need to hear this discussion."

Rod tried to sleep after his conversation with Trish, but his mind kept churning. How could he keep Trish from knowing about his sending Buddy St. John to scout her activities? Finally, he got up and lit a cigarette. He paced around the room worrying about how to handle damage control when *The National Investigator* article hit the newsstands the next afternoon. Maybe he was wrong about Trish having just another fling. It was not something he understood, but maybe she had real feelings for this guy. There would be an absolute shit storm when Trish saw the article if that were true. This could be a lot worse than he bargained for.

Finally, at five o'clock, he dressed and drove the short distance to the Omni. As he drove along Bayshore Drive toward downtown Corpus, the sailboats on the bay caught his eye. The sky was a patchwork of clouds moving south on a spanking breeze that pushed up whitecaps on the bay. The boats seemed to be a regatta, probably from the local yacht club. He once thought of having his own sailboat but had lacked the time and money. This Anna Karinina gig wouldn't make the commission of a good action thriller, but maybe it was time to splurge anyway. He smiled at that thought.

Leah opened the hotel room door. Rod was genuinely surprised to see her. He glanced around the room for Trish as he entered. The bathroom door opened and she emerged. Before anyone else could speak, Rod said, "Oh, boy, a menage a trois, every man's fantasy."

"In your dreams, shorty." Leah snorted.

"Okay, you two, let's get to it." Trish was matter-of-fact. She walked to a high backed chair and motioned the two to the couch. Both Leah and Rod assumed the demeanor of deer in headlights. "It's time for true confessions. Rod, you go first. I need to know exactly what you've been doing since I saw you last. Just cut the bullshit and tell it like it is."

Rod stammered a bit. "I told you, I met this girl and we've been having a great time. She's been showing me the town."

"And?" A frown creased Trish's forehead.

"And nothing!"

"What about the guy you've been seen with? A guy nobody knows."

Rod winced, "I met this local journalist. He seems like a great guy, but he hasn't been able to get any stories from the movie shoot. So we talked a little about a possible interview. I told you about it on the phone, remember?" He heaved an invisible sigh of relief over having had that conversation with Trish.

"Actually, no, I forgot all about that. So you're saying this is the guy you went dancing with?"

"Yeah, why? What's the big deal here, anyway? Do I have to check with you before I talk to anyone?" Rod went on the offensive.

"Settle down, Rod. Leah knows how many times you've meddled in my personal affairs. Always to my regret."

Leah chimed in. "Rod, just tell Trish that you haven't been trying to find out anything about who she's seeing here."

"I'm clean!" Rod held his hands up in surrender.

There was a long pause. Finally Trish said, "Okay, Rod, I'll accept that. And I'm going to tell you what my plans are."

Rod and Leah squirmed in their seats as Trish told them about meeting a man she wanted to spend the rest of her life with. They glanced at each other when Trish started discussing Anna Karenina. She knew it was the chance of a lifetime for an actress like her. It would be difficult for the man she loved to adapt to Hollywood. She was tired of making movies and wanted to settle down to a normal life with fewer demands. She thought this man could give her the life she wanted. She was not sure if she could convince him to join her in a life, but she was going to risk everything to try.

Rod and Leah sat silently for a time, considering the economic implications of Trish's news. Finally Leah said, "*Anna Karenina* is a huge opportunity, that's true. But you're a good person, and you deserve happiness. If this will make you happy, go for it." She got up and walked across the room to Trish's chair and hugged her. "I guess you plan to stay on here after the filming is over?" Trish nodded affirmation.

Rod still sat on the couch, deep in thought. God, this gooey stuff made him sick. Why couldn't they just get on with making movies without all this maudlin horse hockey? The best news he'd heard from Trish was that this guy was not totally sold on Trish's plan. He smiled briefly at the thought of the "Mystery Man" article hitting the newsstand tomorrow. He rose and went to Trish, offering his hand saying, "This is a very big move you're planning. I think I'll stall the *Anna Karenina* people and hang around a few days just in case."

"Thanks for the vote of confidence, Rod." Trish said. She ushered the two of them out the door. Returning to the bed, she picked, up the phone again to call her dad. After two rings he answered. "Dad, it's me."

"Hey, Pumpkin, good to hear from you." His voice brightened. "How are you doing?"

She paused not knowing how to answer. "Pretty good, Dad."

"Only pretty good? What's the matter?" Again the concern she always counted on.

"I met a man, Dad. His name is Chris, and he's a lot like you," she explained.

She waited for his answer. "That's great, Pumpkin. But you don't seem excited."

"It's not all wonderful. I really hoped it would go differently with Chris, but I have a bad feeling about it now."

When she told her dad about the role she had been offered and the dramatic challenge *Anna Karenina* offered, he was genuinely pleased for her.

"I'm confused, dad. I don't know what to do."

"There will always be other movies. The question you have to decide is, will there always be someone you care for as much as Chris?"

"I thought you'd say that." She nodded her head, thankful for his support. After she learned more about her mother's continuing decline, they rang off. Saddened by her mother's condition, but bolstered by her dad, she decided to drive back to Chris' for the night, but when she picked up her backpack and briefcase, the phone rang. She answered thinking it might be Leah.

"Boy, am I glad I found you! We've got a problem." Director Danielle Stokes sounded frantic.

"And how are you, Danielle?"

Catching Trish's sarcasm, Danielle retreated, "Oh, yeah, sorry. How are you, Trish?"

"Fine, Danielle. Do you have a problem?"

"Boy, do we. I went back through the rushes during this weather delay, and the scene where the bad guys rough you up just doesn't work. There are three whiffs where I can see daylight between you and their fists when they punch you. Frankly, I don't know how I missed this during the shooting. In fact the whole scene is stiff and fake, especially when you fight them off and escape. We have to reshoot the whole thing."

"You've got to be kidding. That was five hours of shooting plus, makeup." Trish threw her luggage on the bed.

"I know. I know. Anyway, I've scheduled a meeting and run-through with the fight choreographer this evening, and I'm getting the set staged again to shoot it tomorrow after our meeting on the beach scene. You know about that, right?"

"God, Danielle, I really have something important to do tonight."

"Sorry, babe, but we've got to get this right. It's an important scene. We can't just cut it."

"What time's the meeting?" Trish slumped in resignation.

"I'll have the car there to pick you up in an hour." Danielle hung up.

It was almost midnight before the cold drove Chris over the dune bridge and into the dark beach house. He had hoped for Trish's return, and he wanted to be there if she came back. It was vital to tell her things. To tell her he wanted her – needed her. To tell her that everything would work out. Tell her that he... loved her.

Chapter 26

Lottie awoke just before noon on Monday, a little hung-over from joining in the fun at The Backyard the night before. Inclement weather had produced an unusually bad weekend for business, so she had whiled away last evening over a few martinis with Jeffrey who, unlike his normal self, seemed a little reticent, particularly about Chris. He'd finally told her about the afternoon's trip to Chris' place with the message for Trish Lowe. That news prompted a few more martinis, and she was paying for them today.

The hot shower felt good, and she spent extra time trying to wash away all the fun, even though the bar was supposed to open in less than an hour. The rain was gone, but a chill persisted, so she pulled on a pair of warm-ups over her usual short shorts. She ran a quick hairbrush through her poodle cut and left for the Family Center Grocery on Alister Street to replenish The Backyard's supply of bar garnishes and daiquiri fruit.

She wheeled her basket of lemons, limes, oranges, strawberries, and pineapples to the checkout stand. Two shoppers waited at the only open checkout lane, so she vacantly watched the newspaper distributor, two lanes over, replacing all of the trashy weekly tabloids. The headlines were easy to read from her distance; and she mused over each as it was placed in the rack. "Woman Gives Birth to Martian" seemed especially noteworthy, as was "300-Pound Elvis Sighted in Memphis Homeless Shelter." The newsman bundled up a dozen issues of *The National Investigator* and slipped them into the rack. "Who Is This Mystery Man?" was particularly fascinating, but from her distance she could not make out the photos, except the picture of an A-frame house set amid sand dunes. That looks a little like Chris's place, she thought. Actually, it looks a lot like Chris's place. Lottie left her basket, walked to the news rack, and picked up a copy of the Investigator. In addition to a picture of Chris's house, there was a telephoto shot of Chris and Trish hugging it up on the deck and a photo of a poem written in the sand. She quickly read the article, which gave the location of the beach house. The poem leaped from the page:

> *Magically my soul is thawed*
> *By the warmth of your embrace.*
> *Revived anew,*
> *It soars like a gull*
> *Toward unimagined expectation.*

"THAT ROTTEN BITCH!" Every head pivoted toward Lottie who stomped out of the store.

The newsvendor shouted, "Lady, you didn't pay for the paper!" Employees, customers, and the newsvendor watched in amazement through the plate glass window as the Jeep SUV smoked its wheels out of the parking lot.

Chris lay startled and confused by the loud knock on the door. He new his condition even before he sat up – the almost empty tequila bottle sat on the coffee table. He ran his hands over his forehead and through his hair to erase his confusion. A second wave of pounding on the door moved him to his feet, stumbling toward the door. He grabbed the knob angrily and yanked the door open. The photoflash was so intense it blinded his sleep-bleary eyes. He staggered back two steps shouting, "Jesus Christ! What the ..."

When his eyes focused again he saw an oversized teenage stranger holding a camera and smiling. "Hey, Mystery Dude, is Trish Lowe here?"

By reflex, Chris lunged through the door and buried his fist in the stranger's face. The teenager staggered backward, nose spouting blood, finally catching himself on the deck railing. His camera dropped to the deck. Chris stomped on it and heaved it into the sand dunes. "Get out of here!" He shouted as he grabbed the teenager by the back of the neck and shoved him toward the dune bridge. The stranger accurately assessed his peril and tried to run, but Chris landed a well-placed foot in the center of his ass, sending him sprawling. The boy recovered before Chris reached him and began running, with Chris in pursuit. Halfway over the bridge Chris noticed the people on the beach. There were about two-dozen vehicles parked and others were filing down from the road. People stood around in groups talking and pointing at the dune house.

He pulled up short and looked in amazement at the crowd that was forming. Several were talking on cell phones, and one shouted, "Hey, Mystery Man, where's Trish?"

Camera flashes popped regularly. Another gawker shouted, "How about an autograph?"

Chris backed up like an animal at bay. He heard the teenager shout, "Hey, asshole, you broke my nose!" Chris turned and walked quickly into the house slamming the door and locking it. As he lowered the blinds he saw Lottie's SUV swerving through the crowd and sliding to a stop. Lottie leaped from the car, shoved several people out of the way, and jogged over the dune bridge with a newspaper in her hand. He unlocked and opened the door when she was on the deck, and he could hear people shouting, "Is that Trish Lowe?"

"What the hell is going on?" Chris asked when she was inside.

"This is what's going on!" Lottie slapped the paper into his chest.

Chris opened the paper and saw the pictures of his house, his poem, and him and Trish together. "I don't understand this." He shook his head and walked to the dining table.

"Your little fling with Trish Lowe could change your life. Maybe even end it!"

Ranger Jeffrey had completed Chris' weekly shopping at the HEB Food Store in Flour Bluff on his lunch hour and had just descended from the JFK Causeway bridge when he heard an "any vehicle in the area" call on his radio about an assault and disturbance on the beach just north of Fish Pass Road. "Jesus, that's Chris' place," he said aloud, flipping his siren and light bar on.

The traffic in front of him pulled over as he raced down the beach. He could see cars and people in front of Chris's house. He weaved his way to within a few feet of the dune bridge, stopped, and got out. "What's going on here?" he asked with real bewilderment when he saw Lottie's car.

"That asshole in there broke my nose and ruined my camera." A teenager with Kleenex stuffed into his nostrils shouted at Jeffrey.

"Why would he do that?" Jeffrey asked.

"I don't know. All I did was go up there and take his picture." The teenager shrugged.

"That would certainly do it." Jeffrey said as he turned to cross the bridge.

"Hey, man, I want him arrested." The teenager raised his arms pointing in the direction of the house.

"Forget it, kid. You were trespassing. You're lucky he didn't do worse." Jeffrey stopped and returned to the foot of the bridge. "Hey! Listen up! Let me have your attention!" A group of about fifty stopped milling about the beach and moved in Jeffrey's direction. "Listen, I don't know why you're here, but there's something you need to know. Anyone who sets foot on this dune bridge is trespassing. So my advice is stay away. In fact, why don't you go home before somebody else gets hurt?"

"Man, that sucks! This is a public beach, Ranger Dude." The teenager looked around for support in the crowd.

"You've been warned!" Jeffrey turned on his heel and crossed the dune bridge. He knocked on the door of the A-frame and shouted, "Chris, it's Jeffrey!" He heard the lock release, and Lottie stood in the partially open door. He stepped through and waited for his eyes to adjust to the low lights. "Looks like we've got a situation here," he said looking at Lottie.

"Yeah, it's just what I said would happen." Lottie nodded her head.

"Anybody know what caused this commotion?" Jeffrey saw Chris raise a newspaper over his head from his seat at the dining table. Jeffrey went to the table and took the paper. He looked at it for a minute. "Holy shit! I guess being famous was about the last thing you wanted."

"The very last thing, actually." Chris lowered his head into his hands.

"The question is what happens now? I don't think Chris can stay here any longer. I think you should come into town with me." Lottie said.

"If he leaves with you, they'll just follow you into town. It'll look like a parade." Jeffrey's voice carried the authority born of experience.

After a thoughtful moment, Chris said, "This will blow over. They've got to get tired and go home eventually."

"It's just the first day, for Christ's sake. Wait until all of mankind reads this scandal sheet. Worse still, what if mainstream news picks it up? There could be a remote television truck on the way out here to do a 'Live Eye' telecast on the 'The News at Six.' Christ, it could get on the Internet. I can see it now, www.MysteryMan.com." Lottie chuckled at what she hoped was an exaggeration.

"You laugh, but you might not be far from wrong." Jeffrey took his hat off and ran his fingers through his hair.

"You have any more trysts scheduled with Miss Trish?" Hurt crept into Lottie's tone even though she tried to hide it.

"I don't know." Chris returned his head to his hands.

"How could you not know?" Lottie sounded irritated.

"I just don't know... Trish and I had a misunderstanding yesterday." Chris' voice trailed off.

The conference room was set with a U-shaped table, about ten seats per side. Danielle sat at the head table flanked by Trish and the assistant producer. Reese and the stunt people were there, as were the Best Boy, Driver Captains, and Lead Grip. The camera crews and camera grip sat together.

After Danielle called everyone to order, the location manager stood. "We've scouted every foot of beach in the area and found the best location for the beach rescue scene. We have the permits in place, and the drivers should schedule about forty-five minutes' travel time to get to the location."

The Teamster boss held up maps. "I've redlined the routes for both heavy equipment and personnel vehicles. We've already loaded the trucks for the move. I need all heavy equipment drivers, camera crews, and grip here at five a.m. for transportation to the site. Personnel drivers will pick up at six."

"We need all power, lighting, cameras and equipment set up by seven and shooting will commence no later than eight-thirty." Danielle left no room for argument.

The meeting room lights lowered, and Danielle projected the storyboards on a screen at the front of the room. "I repeat, weather tells us we'll lose our clear sky about noon tomorrow. Location reports there are only about two helicopter flyovers to worry about, and they should be out of the way before we start shooting. So can we get this done before noon?" There was a rustle of affirmation. "I can't hear you people. Can we get this shot by noon?"

A chorus of "BOOYAHS" rang out loud.

"Okay! That's what I want to hear. Just to make sure, we're going over this until everyone can do it in their sleep. Oh, and while I'm thinking about it, we've booked the Remington Room for a one-of-a-kind wrap party tomorrow night– Now, let's get today's work done."

A louder chorus of "BOOYAHS" sounded.

The meeting lasted until afternoon, leaving less than an hour for Trish to grab a sandwich and freshen herself in her room before the limo drove her to her dressing trailer for the re-shoot of the fight sequence Danielle had set up for that afternoon. She used her cell phone to call Jeffrey, hoping to get a message to Chris, but there was no answer. She left a message. "Jeffrey, Trish here, I am completely tied up this afternoon filming, but try to call me when you get this message."

Makeup was barely underway before Phermona began regaling Trish and Gwen with stories of her experiences over the weekend with Sam. "Sam has given me reasons to believe that younger men are the answer to prayer. I mean, younger men really need consideration in the big scheme of things, don't you think, Gwen?" Phermona philosophized.

"How many reasons?" Gwen held up all ten fingers with a questioning look.

"Oh, yeah! I mean lots of reasons, girl." Phermona nodded her head in affirmation.

"Well, now, just how big is Sam's scheme of things?" Gwen raised her eyebrows.

"Think about global proportions." Phermona laughed wiggling her body and waving her arms in the air shouting, "Can I have an amen?"

"Amen!" Trish and Gwen intoned.

"In the beginning there was Sam. In the middle there was Sam! And praise be, at the end there was Sam!" Phermona's voice rose in a crescendo. "I say, praise be! Can I have another amen?"

"Amen!" the three exclaimed in unison.

"Now let's not overlook those men of the older persuasion," Gwen said. "They have their good points too."

"Amen!" Trish shouted.

Gwen and Phermona looked at each other surprised at Trish's enthusiasm. Gwen added, "When it comes to that con-sider-ation you mentioned, you're talkin' 'bout older men."

"That's right, girl, they have to con-sider it first, right?" Phermona slapped her leg laughing.

"No, girl, they show consideration for the lady. You know what I mean?" Gwen made a cuddling motion. "They know how to treat a lady. Right?"

It was Trish again. "Amen!"

Gwen and Phermona looked at each with arched eyebrows. "Now, take Miss Trish here, she seems in with older men." Phermona held the hairbrush up to Trish as a microphone. "Now, Miss Trish, give it up for these older men you know so much about."

Trish took the hairbrush mike and began mimicking a television interview. "Let's see, now. I have reason to know that older men are, yes, considerate." The lilt left her voice, and she turned pensive. "But there's more. Much more. He is wise and kind. He's interested... and interesting. He's a good person, though sometimes I'm not sure he knows that. When we make love I'm taken to another place. A place I've never been before... "

Phermona took back the hairbrush and looked at Gwen in amazement, then back at Trish. "Girl, you got it bad!"

The shoot dragged on for hours while Danielle worked with the stunt people and the fight choreographer trying to perfect the scene. Yesterday's rehearsal didn't seem to work on the set. Tempers flared, especially when a punch actually landed. Danielle knew re-shoots always put cast and crew on edge, and the idea of having to start over from the top after thinking the scene was in the can grated on everyone. She worked at keeping her own demeanor light and professional in the hope it would be infectious, but it was getting more difficult.

The plan was to finish the scene before dinner break, but as the dinner hour approached, it was decision time. To keep shooting meant premium pay for the crew. To stop for dinner meant the cost of the meal. At last she called in an order to the caterer for a meal at the regular time. She broke early to let tempers cool and went to Trish's dressing trailer to explain that they would be running late.

Trish had paced the trailer for most of the afternoon wanting desperately for the shoot to end, so she could return to Chris. Close-up stunts requiring her were interspersed between long waits. She was so restless that Phermona and Gwen spent most of the time hiding on the set. When Danielle entered the trailer, Trish looked hopeful. "Tell me we're about through here."

"I just came over to tell you we're breaking for dinner."

"Jesus, I can't believe this. What do we have left?" Trish scowled at Danielle.

"Most of your stuff, actually. I got a rewrite this afternoon to clean up some of the segments. I brought a copy for you.

There're no major changes, but some things make the scene more believable." Danielle handed the rewrite to Trish.

Trish took the pages reluctantly. "So, when will we wrap it up?

"Some time between eight and nine I expect."

Trish slumped into the makeup chair. "God, this is too much."

"Come on, where's our trooper? It can't be that bad." Danielle tried to smile.

"I told you I had something really important to do."

"What can be so important, anyway?" Danielle was truly concerned. "Is it this guy that Rod was talking about?" Trish nodded her head yes. "What's the problem?"

"We had a disagreement yesterday, and I had to leave before we settled it. I heard Rod was still in town.... Then you called this rehearsal and shoot in addition to the meeting about tomorrow. I can't get back to smooth things out with him." Trish dropped her head. "The whole thing is miserable."

"I don't know too much about men, but I've been told that making them sweat a little is good for them. They want only what they can't have. We'll be through by nine. You bunk in early, get up at dawn, and we'll finish the shoot by noon. You can spend the rest of your life with him." Danielle hugged Trish.

"There's nothing I'd rather do."

As Danielle left the trailer, Phermona and Gwen came in carrying a tray of food for Trish and a newspaper. "Girl you are not gong to believe this!" Phermona handed the paper to Trish.

"Sam and Gus saw some crew guys talking about this paper and grabbed it. They gave it to us for you," Gwen explained.

Trish opened *The National Investigator*, and her mouth fell open. "Good God in heaven! This can't be happening!" She screamed. She looked at the photos and read the article. "Jesus, they even gave the exact location of the beach house." She lingered over the poem. Hurt registered visibly in her eyes, followed by anger. She picked up her phone. Jeffrey's cell phone rang several times. "Come on... Come On... Answer, Jeffrey!"

An operators voice came on the line. "The voice mail box of... 'Jeffrey Randall'...is full and can take no more messages at this time. Please call back later."

"Shit! I just need a little help here. Please. Please. Please!" Trish implored.

She dialed Leah and her phone answered on the first ring. "Trish... "

"Leah! Thank, God, you... "

" ...if this is you, I left this message since I couldn't get hold of you this afternoon. I, being of sound mind, have gone to a movie. It's not like I don't spend enough time around movies, right? Anyway, I'll ride out to the shoot with you in the morning. See you then." The phone clicked off.

"God, will somebody please answer the damn phone!" Trish punched Rod's speed dial number so hard it almost flew out of her hand. "The bastard's not answering... Rod, I just read *The National Investigator* story, and there is no way I will ever believe that you're not involved in it, you miserable piece of shit."

Chapter 27

Chris desperately wanted Jeffrey to call Trish and ask about the article, and if she would be coming back. But with the crowd on the beach and Lottie's presence, he could not bring himself to ask. Jeffrey left to report back to the park, saying he would do what he could to thin the crowd on the beach. Later, Lottie finally left to open her bar, and Chris plunged back into uncertainty.

Car doors slamming, engines starting, dogs barking, people talking – the sounds wafted on the sea breeze, creating an ambience unfamiliar even during the height of tourist season. He partially opened the window blinds and saw a group of gawkers with Frisbees playing on the beach.

Before Jeffrey left, he brought Chris' supplies in. Even though they both felt it might look unusual for a Park Ranger to deliver groceries, Chris was low on provisions. Jeffrey rolled the cart down to his truck and loaded it.

One of the gawkers shouted, "You need some help with that?"

Another cynic shouted, "The state delivers groceries now?"

Jeffrey nodded at the two and without comment rolled the cart over the bridge and into the house.

The cart remained untouched until almost dark, when Chris could barely see the people on the beach. Finally he set about stocking his cabinets. The refrigerated items were still cool. Periodically, he went to the window and checked to see if the crowd was gone. Cars started, headlights flicked on, and he could see a trail of taillights receding toward Fish Pass Road. Only a handful of cars remained with the diehard gawkers scrunched down inside them, hoping for a glimpse of Trish Lowe.

The hunger from not eating since noon the previous day gnawed its way into his consciousness. Too many distractions, he thought, too much to process. He didn't want to cook, but he had to eat. Opening a can of Campbell's Vegetable Beef Stew, he heated it in the microwave. The aroma of the stew ratcheted his hunger to the level of pain. He poured the soup into a mug, sliced some crusty bread from Jeffery's delivery, and opened a bottle of Pinot Noir red wine. He went to the window again to check the beach and saw the gawkers had slipped away like a band of nomads.

Carrying the soup, wine bottle and a glass, he squirmed through the door and onto the deck. Setting his meal on the table beside his deck lounge chair, he went to the railing and took a deep breath, filling his lungs with the salty air he loved so much. The sky was brilliantly clear and a full moon over the horizon cast a warm glow on the water. The north wind had subsided and all was calm and silent. It was the kind of peace he'd not felt for days. The kind of peace he knew before Trish had entered his life. He returned to his lounge chair, dipped the bread into the soup, and held the combination in his mouth for a time, enjoying the simple richness.

A chill woke him. He carried the Pinot Noir bottle and glass up to the loft, setting them on the nightstand table. Both the bottle and glass were still half full when he drifted off. The excitement of the day sent him deep into troubled sleep.

The wine, resting through the night in the bottle and glass, quivered restlessly. A brief shudder sent ripples circling out from the center. Calm returned. Another shudder and tiny waves peaked in the glass. Microscopic vibrations set the glass dancing toward the bottle. The two circled each other across the surface of the table in a vibrating mating dance. The wine glass rim tinkled against the bottle when the two touched. A deep guttural roar built steadily as the dance grew more frenetic. The loft floor trembled as the roar's volume built. The windows rattled uneasily at first, then complained in earnest. The roar continued building.

He rolled to the edge of the bed and sat covering his ears. The vibration in the floor and windows disoriented him. He felt panic as he tried to comprehend what was happening.

He found himself at the stairs, taking them two at a time. Running across the living room he threw open the door, and the noise brought him to a stop. He stepped cautiously onto the deck and looked in bewilderment at a line of vehicles stretching almost to Fish Pass Road. The roar of diesel engines was deafening. Eighteen-wheelers, one hauling a D9 Caterpillar tractor, bobtail trucks, a generator truck, house trailers, hydraulic cranes, vans, a portable latrine, and a catering kitchen rumbled along the beach. The first truck pulled to a stop abreast of the dune bridge, and the others filled in behind, forming a line stretching for a quarter-mile back down the beach. The roar of the engines continued as workers piled from the vans and trucks and started unloading movie equipment.

He surveyed the scene with growing dismay. The gawkers soon would return, reinforced by those lured to the excitement of a movie shoot. The sun edged over the horizon and urgency welled in him along with a sense of being betrayed, and he shook his head in consternation.

By the time the limo had delivered Trish back to the hotel the previous evening, it was past nine o'clock. She was still unable to reach Jeffrey and Leah. A knock on Leah's door confirmed that she was still out. She thought about driving to Chris' beach house, but feared her appearance would embroil them both in more unwanted publicity. After pacing the floor, she finally collapsed into bed and eventually into a sporadic sleep. Most of the restless night was spent in a disturbing dream of an angry mob pursuing her. She awoke with a start, sat on the side of the bed, and poured a glass of water. It was four-thirty, and her wakeup call was scheduled in half an hour. It was too early to call her Dad, she thought, but she wanted to. Putting on her security robe, she moved to the couch and bundled up in fetal position. Then she got up again, went to the phone, and cancelled the wakeup call. As she returned the phone to its cradle she remembered her dad's ritual of rising at six to read the paper and having his coffee. New York was an hour ahead of Texas time, so she dialed his phone number. He would be sitting at the breakfast table, paper in hand, occasionally sipping his strong brew. She smiled at the remembered sight.

"Hi, Dad, it's me," she said hesitantly after he answered.

"Hey, Pumpkin, two calls in three days. This is great!" She heard the warmth she longed for.

"I know, Dad. I should call more often."

"No, no, I'm just pleased to hear from you anytime. But this call doesn't sound like a happy one."

"You're right, things are not working out the way I'd hoped." She paused for several seconds before continuing. "I've turned a man's quiet life into a circus. Instead of becoming part of his peace, I've made him a part of my chaos. I was crazy to think I could keep this from happening."

"That's the problem isn't it? You two could not be more different or lead more different lives. Honey I've seen this morning paper's 'Entertainment Section' gossip column. There's an item about you and your Texas lover." His voice was intense. "You really believe in this guy, Pumpkin?"

"I really do."

"Then don't worry about it. If he's the guy you think he is, this will all work out, but you have to be patient. There are things he may not understand and accept for a while. In the end, if he can't figure out that my Pumpkin is the best thing that's ever happened to him, then he just isn't the one."

Trish was dressed long before the scheduled limo pick-up. She sat considering her dad's comforting advice. It was so true, but so hard to believe and even harder to follow. She jumped when Leah rapped her secret knock on the door. Trish unlocked the door and jerked it open. "I tried to call you all afternoon yesterday." Trish blurted.

"Well, hello, Trish!" Leah looked surprised.

"I'm sorry, but I've been a little upset since I saw the article in *The National Investigator* yesterday afternoon." Trish motioned Leah in.

"An article in *The National Investigator*? Abou... ?"

Trish went to the desk and brought back the paper. "My worst fear is confirmed."

Leah looked at the paper. "Oh, my God, how did this happen?"

"Take a guess."

"Rod?"

"It has to be." Trish sat on the edge of the bed.

"The piece is by Buddy St. John, it says here." Leah pointed to the byline.

"That's the creep Rod was hanging out with." Trish shook her head in resignation.

"Have you talked to Rod?"

"The bastard won't answer his phone." Trish growled just as the front desk called, reporting that the limo had arrived.

The limo was due at six but had arrived fifteen minutes late, and Danielle was already inside fuming over the late departure when Trish and Leah crawled in. "Already late and the day hasn't even started."

Trish was tired from the troubled night's sleep and the early rising. The warm and comfortable limo helped her doze off soon after departing the hotel. Leah and Danielle said little as the limo moved down Bayshore Drive and onto the S.P.I.D. Causeway. A dead calm had left Laguna Madre a mirror on which the sun's rays, just creeping over the horizon, spread a redish-orange cast, glistening like polished marble. The limo rose up the slope of the JFK Causeway Bridge over the Intracoastal Waterway, and the view expanded to miles of glazed saltwater. At the apex of the bridge, Danielle tapped Leah's arm and pointed toward the rising sun.

Migration was under way, and the first arrivals of white pelicans and ducks flocked in the shallows feeding around the spoil banks left by the channel dredging, decades ago. Egrets and heron stalked schools of mullet that darted and leaped to escape. A flock of roseate spoonbills, approximating flamingos with their salmon colored plumage, settled noiselessly into the flat. The sun's first reflection extended from the Gulf horizon, over the bay, all the way to the bridge, interrupted only by Mustang Island, stretching toward the north.

"It's an absolute painting. This scene cries out to be filmed. Where's a cameraman when you need one?" Danielle had turned completely around trying to hold the image as long as possible.

The driver had to brake severely to keep from passing Fish Pass Road, and the force of the stop woke Trish. She rubbed her eyes and looked around, then squinted and looked closer. "Where are we anyway?"

"Almost to the beach, Mum," The driver answered in his British accent.

"Wait a minute. This is Fish Pass Road." Trish's head swung toward both sides of the road.

"That's right, Mum." The driver's voice carried a hint of surprise.

"You know this place?" Danielle asked.

"It's the road to Chris' house." Trish looked around frantically. "What are we doing here?"

"I guess this is where we're shooting the beach scene." Danielle shrugged

"We're headed for the place shown in the *Investigator*?" Leah looked bewildered.

"Good God, is this some kind of conspiracy? We've moved our whole location caravan to Chris' house? Is this the only place on this whole damn coast we can shoot?" Trish was apoplectic. Danielle and Leah looked at each other, speechless.

The driver spoke up. "Bit early to be bike ridin', I'd say." Even in half-light a lone figure could be made out, struggling through the heavy sand at the end of the road. With great effort the bike rose from the sand onto the asphalt, and the rider pumped hard to accelerate. The limo driver slowed, preparing for the end of the road and came abreast of the rider.

Trish leaped from her seat bouncing off the limo roof when the head passed her widow. "Stop! Stop! Turn around! That's Chris!"

"Can't make no U'ee in this beast, Mum," the driver apologized as he watched the bike recede in the rear view mirror.

"Back up! Back up!" Trish screamed at the driver. Leah and Danielle looked at each other still speechless. The driver threw the limo in reverse and spun the tires as it gained speed. "Hurry up! Hurry up!" Trish urged. The driver had turned half way around and was looking out the rear window, retracing the limo's path.

"This must be the 'Mystery Man'," Danielle said to Leah.

"He seems mysterious enough." Leah strained to get a better look at the man coming into view in the side window. His silver hair stood out from his head like a mane and quivered as the air flowed through it. He wore blue jeans and a windbreaker that occasionally blew up revealing a firm abdomen. A beach bag rested in the front-wheel basket. Leah couldn't help thinking that he was good-looking old guy, really fit.

Trish knelt in front of the door and shouted out the lowered window. "Chris! Chris! It's me!" She shouted louder. "Stop, Chris, we need to talk! Chris, look at me!"

He turned a sad face to her for a few seconds, then looked forward again, still pedaling. He turned back once more. "I've got to get out of here."

"I didn't plan any of this. You've got to believe me. Chris, please stop! Let's talk. I need to explain... " She was leaning far enough out of the window to almost touch him.

He continued, looking straight down the road and pedaling.

"Trish, this isn't working, he's ignoring you. Come on, we've got to go, we're running late." Danielle turned to the driver and spoke sternly. "Get us to the location."

Chris receded into the distance as the driver slowed. "Turn around! Chris! Chris!" Trish leaned further out the window and shouted, "Damn it, Chris, come back here!" Realizing the futility, she slumped back on her heels in utter frustration with tears welling in her eyes. The limo labored through the sand until it reached Trish's dressing trailer. Leah and Danielle got out first, quietly, as if trying not to disturb Trish. The star dragged herself out of the limo last and climbed the steps of her trailer. Before entering she turned on the top step and looked over the set. Reese worked with the stunt people. The stand-ins and camera crews worked to get the camera angles and focus lengths set. The raft, designed to look like boat wreckage, sat motionless in the water, tied off to a stunt boat, waiting for Trish's arrival. Everyone but Trish moved with the sense of Danielle's urgency.

Trish turned and looked at the now vacant A-frame a short distance up the beach. Jumping to the sand, she walked purposefully to the dune bridge. She could make out a hand-lettered "No Trespassing" sign through the door window. She was wretched with longing -- longing to make Chris understand.

Three cars had pulled to a stop near the dune bridge and a small group of people stood looking at the house. One of them said, "Yeah, I'm sure that's the house. Hey! I think that's Trish Lowe."

It's endless, she thought; there's no escape.

"How about an autograph, Trish?" One guy took off his T-shirt and handed it to her to sign, another his ball cap, and one of them offered a pen. She walked to them and took the ball cap and pen without speaking. Before she could sign the cap, the tall, skinny teenage cap owner grinned and asked, "Where's the Mystery Man?" She stood motionless for a moment looking at this truly ordinary person, then shook her head sadly, handed him back his cap and pen, and strode away. The tee shirt guy said, "Really great, dude, we had her going until you opened your big yap. Nice work."

The tires on Chris' bike were almost flat from years of inactivity, so the going was slow for the twelve miles into Port Aransas. As he approached the city limits, the town looked unfamiliar. Many buildings he did not recognize had proliferated along the highway. He remembered that he had to turn right at the Cutoff Road traffic light, but a block later he lost his way and stopped in a Circle K to ask directions. "Do you know Lottie Langton?"

"Lottie? Sure, everybody knows Lottie. Why?" The counter clerk was matter-of-fact.

"Would you know where she lives?"

"She lives somewhere around here, 'cause she's in here all the time." He took out a phone book and looked up Lottie's address. "Yeah, I thought so. If you go down that street two blocks, she's the corner house on the right. It's yellow and white, I think." The clerk pointed the direction.

Lottie's SUV was in the driveway, but the house was closed and dark. Chris leaned his bicycle against the porch railing, climbed the steps, and knocked on the door. There was no answer. He knocked harder. Someone stirred inside, and he heard Lottie issue an oath. The door opened. "It's pretty damn early... Then she saw Chris. "Is this a dream?" She opened the screen door and motioned him in.

He stepped through the door. "I guess I've got a problem. I was wondering if I could bunk in for a while."

Lottie sat him at her kitchen table, and made a pot of coffee. He told her of the events leading up to his exodus. Lottie listened cautiously for hints of Chris' true feelings, hoping to hear the right words. To hear he wanted their relationship to resume. When they didn't come, she asked, "So what are your plans now?"

He stared for a time at his coffee cup and didn't look up when he answered. "I guess you've been pretty shabbily treated in this whole thing. I wouldn't blame you for throwing me out right now."

"I doubt you're the first guy to make a fool of himself over Trish Lowe. In fact, most men would jump at the chance." She took a sip of her coffee. "But I've had a lot of time to think about us, about our past relationship. Truthfully, I can compete with a memory only so long." She was too emotionally spent not to honest.

Chris reached across the table and held her hand. "Lottie, you saved my life. You know that. There's no way I could've ever made it this long without you."

She smiled through squinted eyes. "Why do I think there's a 'but' coming?"

He looked away from her and shook his head. "No 'but'. It's the simple truth."

Lottie had tried unsuccessfully to find an employee to open the bar, so she left Chris at home and went to open it herself. She hummed while she went through the chores. She finally had things going her way with Chris, but a strange feeling nagged at her, the feeling that Chris, even with his disappointment, was still enthralled by Trish.

All of Danielle's preparation was paying off. The calm day required a wind machine to beach the boat wreckage on which Trish clung in castaway fashion,. Aside from that delay, everything progressed as planned. Both that scene and the ensuing one of the bad guys swooping in on Trish as she lay on the beach were in the can. The stunt guys rigged the next scene, which involved the good guy's helicopter diving in for the rescue. Satisfaction spread over Danielle's face as she realized the noon deadline was possible.

Leah camped out by the A-frame doing her best to convince gawkers that Trish was not coming back there. Phermona and Gwen hid on the set again from a less-than-cordial movie star. Trish waited alone in her trailer for her call. She started at the knock on the door and shouted, "Come on in."

Jeffrey came in, hat in hand. "Hi, Miss Lowe, I was on my way to see Chris, and I ran into all this." He gestured around the beach. "I'm sorry about missing your call yesterday. But what with all the excitement here on the beach, I forgot to turn on my cell phone."

"How much excitement was there?" She gestured for Jeffrey to sit.

"Quite a bit. Lots of cars and people. I was amazed at how goal-oriented these folks were. They were by God going to see you or bust."

"Welcome to my world." Trish grimaced. "You're too late to see Chris."

"Too late?"

"He left on his bicycle early this morning." Trish told him of the morning's events.

"Chris left? On his bike?"

"He rode off into the sunrise like Shane, without even a word." Sadness – and anger – showed in her eyes.

"He was pretty spooked yesterday. All this stuff today must have put him over the top. I bet I know where he went, though." He nodded affirmation.

Trish brightened. "Where would he go?"

"Probably to Lottie's place." Jeffrey clinched his jaw a bit. He knew what the next question would be.

"Who's Lottie?" Trish straightened in her chair.

"Just an old friend of his." Jeffrey tried to wave the question off.

"How old?"

"They've known each other for quite a while."

"Jeffrey, why do I think there's something about Chris you've never told me?" She sat on the edge of the chair. "Out with it!"

"I guess you could say they'd been really good friends for about ten years." Jeffrey shuffled the toe of his boot as if flicking an unseen object out of the way.

"*We're* good friends?" Trish looked over the bridge of her nose at Jeffrey.

"I think Lottie got a little upset when you came along." Jeffrey shifted from one foot to the other, running his fingers around the brim of his Park Ranger hat.

"So there's another woman! And I don't even know about her? Jesus, I keep waiting for the good news." She threw up her hands in disgust. "Where exactly is this Lottie person?"

"She owns The Backyard in Port Aransas." Jeffrey said.

"Jeffrey, here's what I'd like you to do."

Chapter 28

The euphoria of the final wrap was infectious. The crews shouting, hugging, high fiveing, and general merriment finally died into the sober realization that they had to pack up and haul everything away. The thought of no morning call tomorrow put Trish in a better mood. She lingered in the dressing trailer waiting for a call from Jeffery. Her cell finally rang. "Yeah, what did you find out?"

"Lottie's not saying, but I know her, and I'm positive she knows where Chris is. I tried everything, but she's very tight-lipped. I'll keep trying, though."

"You think she'll be at her bar tonight?"

"That's where I saw her. She said something about working this afternoon and taking off tonight. Why?"

"No reason. Listen, thanks for the help. I'll call you tomorrow." Trish flipped her cell phone closed, and then called Leah. "When are the limos due back?"

"In about an hour. I wanted time for you to get cleaned up from wallowing around in the sand all day. Is that all right?"

"Perfect, actually. Listen, you think you could arrange for me to have a car to myself?"

Leah laughed. "I think right now Danielle would walk back to Corpus on her hands. You okay? You sure you don't want some company? I'm a little worried about you." It was the concern of a true friend.

"I'm fine. I just need to run an errand. Could you round up Pher and Gwen for me?"

"Consider it done. I'll see you back at the hotel for the wrap party tonight, right?" Leah was still a little hesitant.

"I hope not." Trish flipped her phone closed.

Leah stood looking at her phone and said aloud, "What does that mean?"

Trish had finished toweling off and putting on her security robe when Phermona and Gwen bounced into the trailer. Trish greeted them with, "My man has never seen me in full battle gear. I think it's time."

"Oh my, oh my! Ummhuh! This sho nuf sounds serious." Phermona widened her eyes in surprise.

"Out of the way, people! Hide your sons and husbands. Trish Lowe is bringin' her guns to town!" Gwen announced.

"Ladies, I want to be the girl next door. The girl every red-blooded American male dreams about and lusts over. I want a veil of purity and femininity to gently drift over me like first snow, and to, ever so faintly, cloak the sexual inferno below." Trish sat down in the makeup chair with a flourish.

"Why, Miss Trish, how you do carry on. I think I'm blushing." Phermona patted her cheeks.

Lottie stood in the center of her palapa bar and surveyed her regulars. Her lips twitched in a smile when her gaze rested on "the boys." They were fixtures like the stools they sat on. Lottie often sat with them at the bar, but today she was bartending.

Most of "the boys" were fishing guides who had no client that day, or had just returned from an outing. They had been around the island for decades, routinely overcharging tourists for taking them out on the water. Ever since the Guide's Association had decided last year to upgrade their image, they all wore the regulation kaki: shirt and pants with the Association monogram over the shirt pocket. Being a guide meant fishing every day and getting paid a lot for it, while maintaining some degree of status in Port Aransas "It doesn't get better than that," they were fond of saying. The older and heavier ones accepted only half-day fishing trips. This meant every day, from shortly after noon on, they could be found in their designated seat at The Backyard. They chose these seats because of the unobstructed view though the entrance opening in the fence and into the parking lot. They could see everyone who came and went.

The headlights and front grill of a Mercedes-Benz nosed past the entrance opening. As the fourth side window passed the entrance, Wiley Coots, one of the guides, asked, "Lottie are you expecting the President this afternoon?

"No, Wiley, not today. Why?" Lottie glanced up from the bar sink where she was washing glasses.

"Well, there's a limousine been driving past your entrance for the last three or four minutes, and we're not to the end of it yet." He lifted his beer glass and gestured toward the limo.

Lottie turned toward the entrance, drying her hands on her apron. "Whoa! Check this out, guys." They all turned to the entrance just as the limo pulled to a stop and the driver got out to open the passenger door.

"We're definitely havin' a close encounter of some kind." Wiley gestured with his beer.

Even the distance between the onlookers and the limo could not diminish the aura around Trish Lowe emerging from the door. They all sat wide-eyed, and Wiley said, "Lord, Lord, I think I hear a band of heavenly angels."

Trish wore a pale yellow sundress with slender shoulder straps. The dress conformed lightly to her waist but its almost diaphanous material seemed to hover about her, vacillating, first caressing her skin, then rustling in the breeze. Her perfectly manicured toenails were displayed in gold-strapped Gucci Summer Sandals. Coal black hair was perfectly trained into a ponytail as if each hair were layered individually, and at its end a ringlet bounced with every movement, defying gravity. Close inspection would reveal makeup so artfully applied that the effect was of no makeup at all, but instead a sense of scrubbed purity.

"Oh, my God." By reflex, Lottie plumped up her hair, removed her apron, and smoothed her T-shirt and shorts.

Someone at the bar said, "Fellows, I do believe it's what's her name. You know, that Julia Bullock person."

Wiley continued looking intently at Trish who had begun her entrance. "No, it's definitely Sandra Roberts."

"Idiots! It's not either Julia Roberts or Sandra Bullock. It's Trish Lowe," Lottie said with disgust. A chorus of knowing ahhs sounded from the bar sitters.

"You know her?" Someone asked.

"No, but I think I'm fixin' to." Lottie advanced across to the other side of the circular bar anticipating the assault. Before Trish could speak, Lottie fired a salvo. "Sorry, honey, you have to be twenty-one to be in here." Wiley arched his eyebrows and looked at the other bibbers in surprise.

Trish rocked back, and her laughter sounded like tinkling bells. "Thank you, I like that. You must be Lottie Langton." She advanced and scaled a barstool.

"And who might you be?" Lottie stood adamant, arms akimbo. Wiley looked at the others, pursed his lips, shrugged, and shook his head in disbelief.

"I'm Trish Lowe." She smiled her perfect smile at Wiley and the boys, and their Adams apples bobbed in unison.

"Well, Trish Lowe, what can we do for you?" Lottie had not moved.

"This nice lady looks kinda thirsty, Lottie. Maybe you oughta offer her a drink." Wiley interjected.

"Be quiet, Wiley!" Lottie didn't look at him. Wiley ducked like he was dodging a punch.

Trish nodded apologetically toward Wiley and then addressed Lottie. "I wanted to talk to you about Chris."

Lottie knew it was coming, but that did not make hearing it easier. "I'm kinda busy right now."

Years of communing with invisible prey had honed the fishing guides' telepathic senses, and Wiley said, "Ladies, you better take it inside. We don't want things to get broken up out here."

Trish's tinkling laughter rained down again. "Is there somewhere we can talk?"

Lottie pointed toward the office, raised the pass-through, and led the way. Once inside and seated, she asked, "So, what do you have to say about Chris?" She did not offer a seat to Trish.

"First, I never knew anything about you and Chris until this morning." Trish did not blink.

"Jeffery and his big mouth!" Lottie looked out the window toward the bar "I guess it's not surprising either of them would overlook me in all this."

"Jeffery thinks you know where Chris is, and I want very much to talk to him." The stare continued.

"He doesn't want to talk to you. You and your movie company have essentially destroyed the life he's led for years – the life he's had to live. And no one ever gave a thought about how it would affect Chris." Lottie crossed her arms.

"I can understand how he would be upset. Maybe I was dreaming when I thought I could keep these things from happening, but it's important for him to know I didn't plan any of this."

"You certainly got plenty of publicity out of it."

"Look, if after I talk to him, he still doesn't want anything to do with me, that's fine... . Actually, no, it won't be fine. It will hurt a lot, but I can live with it." She choked back her emotion. After a pause she blurted out, "Okay, I love Chris. There! I've said it. There's nothing I want more than having him in my life. That's what I really want to tell him."

Lottie rolled her chair back as if to get a better look at Trish. Trish's face flushed with emotion and she shifted from one foot to the other under Lottie's stare. Lottie finely spoke deliberately. "Well, Lady, that's something you want and might never get." She shook her head as if trying to understand. "I just don't get how you people think you can breeze into town and rifle though our things, take what you want, and then disappear. Chris is not one of those things. Chris is special. He's very special to me, and I don't want him hurt more than you've already hurt him." Lottie's eyes flashed.

"Why don't we let Chris decide what he wants – what's best for him?"

"You've known him less than two weeks, and you think you know what's best for Chris? Lady, you know nothing. I've known him for over a decade. I knew him back when he thought more about death than about life. Have you ever wondered why a man like Chris lives alone on a deserted beach? You think this is a life he picked? You know nothing about him, little missy!"

"I don't understand."

"That's exactly what I'm telling you. Chris had another life a long time before this one. A life that filled him with such guilt he tries constantly to forget, but it still haunts him almost nightly. You think you can haul him off to Hollywood to display like a trophy? He can't go to California.... . Chris is wanted by the police in California. Christopher Maven is not even his real name."

"The police are after Chris? In California?" Trish fell back into the other chair from shock.

Lottie grimaced at having told the truth of Chris's past for the first time. "Look, I'm sorry, I should not have blurted that out. God, I haven't said those words since Chris told me the story over ten years ago." She paused for a moment then plunged ahead. "Chris was involved in a freak accident that killed his fiancé, a girl named Lesa Tolivar, and their unborn baby. Since drugs were involved, the D.A. went after Chris for murder. Chris is still consumed by guilt over it."

"I... I don't know what to say." Trish's expression told her lack of comprehension at what she just heard."

"For God's sake please don't ever say anything about this. I can't believe I let you get to me like this." Lottie lowered her head in shame for what she had just done. There was silence for a moment before she spoke again. "I'm smart enough to know you will find Chris if you want to badly enough. And you can have your conversation. Maybe he'll understand what you're trying to tell him, and maybe he'll fall madly in love with you. Then what? All he has to look forward to is the gut-burning pain of knowing there's nothing he can do about it. Can you imagine how miserable he'd be, wanting desperately to escape from his personal prison to be with you and knowing he can't? No, Miss Lowe, if you truly love Chris, leave him alone. Let him try to regain the numbness that's kept him sane all these years. Let him pour out his soul into the sand, hoping something will wash it clean."

Trish had not known what to expect from Lottie, but this was the last thing she'd anticipated. She'd hoped through celebrity and guile to wrangle Chris' location from Lottie, to limo over, and to confront him with the facts of the situation. In the movies, they would live happily ever after. But this was definitely not Hollywood. Lottie wasn't fighting fairly. Unlike Trish, there was nothing in Lottie's argument about her personal feelings for Chris. Trish was speechless and ashamed of her personal motives. She stood convicted of wanting Chris without considering how that might affect him. She felt she should apologize for even mentioning Chris. She rose, worked her way around Lottie in the cramped office, opened the door, and walked slowly back to the limo.

Wiley lifted his glass to the others who were watching the office door expectantly. "Chalk up round one to Lottie."

After handing off the baton at The Backyard to her manager, Lottie found herself in The Family Center Grocery, wondering what to do about Chris' first meal in her home. Cooking was not something Lottie did well or often, for that matter. She described her only edible dish as "a simple peasant broth." The occasion demanded more than her broth. Eating and drinking well were two of the three sources of comfort in Chris' monastic life. The third was the occasional roll in the hay with her. The hay rolling she had no problem with, but the cooking thing weighed heavily on her. She was comfortable with the idea of grilling some steaks, since she knew Chris would offer to cook them. A consultation with the butcher, and the promise of free drinks on his next visit to her bar produced two noteworthy rib-eyes. A quick tour through the produce department garnered salad ingredients. A red wine three times the price of what she normally bought finished up the shopping, and she headed for the checkout stand.

Chris had spent an uncomfortable day at Lottie's. Unsure how many denizens of Port Aransas might recognize him as the occupant of the house on the cover of *The National Investigator*, he remained indoors. He was a stranger in a strange land. Television was the only thing of Lottie's he allowed himself to use. He seldom watched television and discovered he had not missed anything. Turning off the TV, he paced and thought about Trish and everything leading up to his current condition. He knew that ignoring Trish this morning on Fish Pass Road was a mistake. Why hadn't I just put on the brakes, stopped, and listened? Now, he might never know what she had been clearly desperate to tell him. He banged his forehead at the idea of a thoughtless decision changing his life forever. The urgency that drove him from his home returned, but he had no place to run.

Dinner was over, and Chris and Lottie worked together cleaning up. During the evening he had studied her. She would pass as a good-looking woman even to the most critical eye. She truly was a great friend, loyal to the core, he thought, as he watched her finish loading the dishwasher. He knew her friendship and consideration had made his life bearable.

Remembering their years of lovemaking brought a flicker of a smile, and he moved behind her, kissing the back of her neck. She turned and put her arms around him. Their first kiss was exploratory and hesitant. Then he pulled her to him and their lips met in a union that was passionate but without aggression. She drew back slightly and grabbed his T-shirt. "I thought you'd never ask," she said and towed him down the hall to the bedroom.

There was always a thrill to undressing Lottie. He had marveled for years at her ability to maintain such soft, smooth skin in this hostile environment. She seemed ageless. He ran his fingertips over her breasts and felt a shudder of pleasure go through her body. He kissed her stomach and then her thighs. There was an involuntary gasp from Lottie as he lingered between her legs. Once inside her, their rhythm intensified until they collapsed, completely spent. As their heavy breathing subsided, Lottie rolled over and propped up on her elbows. She looked at him accusingly. "You made love to me with your eyes closed."

Chris awoke well before daylight and sat on the edge of the bed, watching Lottie's absolute calm. He hung his head, running his fingers through his hair, as the guilt inundated him again. It always returned after their lovemaking. She was everything he had any right to hope for, but he didn't love her. He'd taken advantage of her feelings for him and used her as a substitute lover again.

His clothes lay crumpled around his beach bag next to the bed. He carried them into the kitchen and dressed. On the note pad by the telephone he wrote a short note. The sun's first light glowed over the horizon as he loaded his bag into the bike basket and rode toward the highway.

Chapter 29

One by one, as the movie production trucks were loaded, they rumbled off toward Fish Pass Road. The bulldozer had to tow two of the larger trucks stuck in the sand. The portable kitchen left almost immediately after serving lunch. The dressing trailers left with the limos. As each truck disappeared, so did some of the crowd, feeling a little vacant as the excitement ebbed. Those lured to the beach in the hope of a glimpse of the Mystery Man and Trish Lowe had soon blended with the crowd gathered solely to watch movie making. As the movie company faded from the beach, so did the the gawkers' original purpose for coming. The obviously empty beach house held no interest. The remaining contingent of spectators left with the last truck.

The vehicle ruts in the sand dissolved under the advancing tide, and the beach returned to its timeless, beautiful sameness. A patchwork of cumulus scudded along on a southerly breeze that pushed up small swells that vanished without a sound. Hollywood had vanished too and all was quiet.

A limo nosed onto the beach from Fish Pass Road. Probing at first, it finally turned north and accelerated. A short distance from Chris' dune bridge it stopped. Trish stepped out barefoot and walked to the bridge. Her movements were slow and thoughtful as she crossed the dunes to the deck, where she leaned with her back to the railing as if waiting for an invitation. Retracing her steps to the beach, she approached the water and let the calm surf play over her feet as she gazed at the horizon. She strolled for a while at the edge. A driftwood stick washed up at her feet, and she picked it up. Walking back toward the house, she studied the sand. Near the end of the dune bridge she stopped at a rise and wrote with the stick, then stood, head bowed, for a time, considering her inscription. She dropped her stick, wiped her eyes, and ran back to the limo.

Movie wrap parties traditionally serve as pressure release valves. All of the intensity, stress, anxiety, personal conflicts, egomania, and bone-crushing hard work are released into alcohol-laced mayhem. This one would be no different, Leah thought. She was in the final stages of dressing for the party when her room phone rang. Thinking it might be Trish, she answered on a cheery note.

"We need to talk." It was Rod instead.

"This sounds like the amazing, vanishing Rod Blitzer."

"Listen, Leah. Trish thinks I had something to do with *The National Investigator* article. She called me 'a worthless piece of shit'."

"That's how I would put it."

"Leah, I had nothing whatsoever to do with it. I was working on getting this guy St. John set up for an interview with Trish. You know, for a little pre-publicity, and he ups and does this article. Can we at least sit down and talk about it?"

Leah pictured Rod's pleading gestures on the other end of the phone. She had seen his act before. "You need to talk to Trish. She's very upset and hurt by this whole thing. You may have screwed the pooch on this one, Babe."

"Come on Leah, you gotta smooth this thing out so I can talk to her."

Leah thought for a minute and motioned downstairs. "Meet me in the hotel bar in thirty minutes."

"Actually, I'm calling from the hotel bar."

"You bastard. You knew I would give in." Leah slammed down the receiver and stalked out of her room.

Rod stood and waved Leah to his booth near the back. He looked her over and said, "Hey, you really clean up nice, kid. Thanks for coming." He was in his solicitous mode.

She slid in across from him holding her distance "So what's this wonderful thing we have to talk about?"

"What's happening between Trish and her lover boy?"

Leah could feel the intensity of Rod's eyes. "Rod, you know I don't gossip about Trish."

"It's important, Leah. If she's having trouble with him, she'll blame me. I need to know what's happening before I talk to her."

Leah looked silently at him for a while. "I'll tell you this: I was surprised at how much she cares about this guy. It's definitely not a fling. According to Pher and Gwen, she's got it bad. And as the song goes, 'that ain't good'."

"Bad, huh?"

"Bad!" She nodded for emphasis.

Rod knew he was in more trouble than he thought, and he hesitated before responding. "What about him? It didn't seem like he's on board for the long haul when she talked to us. What does he say about all this?"

"Hard to say, but from what I saw this morning, he may have hit the road." Leah shrugged.

Rod felt a flutter of excitement. "Has she said anything more about doing Anna Karenina?"

"I'm going to forget you asked that, Rod." Leah slid out of the booth and walked away.

Frivolity reigned in the Remington Room. Cast always arrived after crew at a wrap party so they could make an entrance. The knowledge they were no longer working together on the film leveled the guests to the same plebeian plane, which many of those anointed with stardom found disagreeable. Trish Lowe was not one of those. She still wore her sun dress as she approached the Remington Room. She paused before her entry. Suck it up, kid, she thought. The show must go on. She pasted a big smile on her face and waded into the room. Her entrance was greeted with a ruffle of applause, animal grunts, and cheers. She raised her arms in a victory gesture as she beamed at the guests and walked through the room, greeting everyone there by name as she clasped their hands and hugged them in celebration.

The low-lit room sparkled with a Mardi Gras theme. Food service stations positioned around the room offered Creole dishes.

Two beverage bars drew crowds on opposite ends of the room. The Locomotions held forth on the bandstand, and a handful of cast and crew gyrated on the dance floor. The attendees had segregated themselves by craft, as often happened at these functions.

Trish walked directly to the Teamster contingent and began hugging each and thanking them individually for their effort on the picture. She moved to the camera/sound tables and then the stunt people. Wardrobe, property, and makeup had positioned themselves near the tables where Danielle, the assistant directors, and the production staff were seated. She sat for a minute with Phermona, Gwen, Sam, and Gus. "So these are the two wild and crazy guys I've heard so much about." She held out her hand to them.

"This is our chaperone, Miss Trish Lowe. She makes sure Gwen and I are not unduly influenced by the likes of you two." Phermona flipped a back-handed gesture at the men

"I think maybe Miss Lowe should be chaperoning Gus and me, where you two are concerned." Sam made a cross of his two index fingers to ward off Phermona and Gwen.

"Listen, why don't you guys go get some drinks?" Gwen stared at them and nodded in the direction of the bar. "I'm guessing Trish will have a shot of tequila."

"Actually, a shot of tequila might help my attitude," she said and nodded a 'thank you' at the two.

As soon as the guys departed, Phermona leaned close to Trish and asked, "Girl, what are you doing here? I thought you'd be rattling the rafters in that beach house right now."

Trish looked at the floor before she answered. "I'm afraid things didn't work out the way I wanted."

"Is this guy nuts, or what?" Gwen was flabbergasted.

"I didn't get to talk to him. His girlfriend told me a lot of things that make it all different." She held up her hands to close the discussion. "Anyway, I'm putting one foot in front of the other and keeping on going." She shook her head sadly.

They stood; Trish hugged them and moved on to Danielle's table, where Leah was seated.

Leah watched Trish with Phermona and Gwen, trying to get a reading on what was happening, and she rose to greet Trish. "I got the impression you might not make it tonight. What happened?"

"Nothing that I wanted to happen. I was hoping to find Chris and set things straight with him." Trish sighed.

"No luck?"

"None. The whole thing completely blew up when I talked to his girlfriend. The whole picture changed, thanks to this Lottie person." Trish's eyes flashed at the thought.

"You're a real trooper to be here after the day you've had." Leah put her arm around Trish and patted her back. "For what it's worth, Rod crawled out from under his rock, and I met with him about an hour ago. He wants to talk to you. Says he didn't have anything to do with that article."

"You believe him?"

"Can you ever believe anything Rod says?"

They bantered around their table, interrupted only by members of cast and crew coming by to congratulate Danielle and plug for a job on her next movie. Danielle eyed the crowd, considering the proper time to give her thank-you speech. The producer hated to speak in public and left it totally up to her. The director asked Trish if she would mind saying a few words also. She declined at first, but then agreed after the third shot of tequila. Danielle moved to the bandstand and signaled for The Locomotions to take a break. She gave her "show of appreciation speech," which included some funny anecdotes from the filming, including a couple of oblique asides about the prodigal, Trish. Grinning broadly at her teasing of Trish, she turned the microphone over to her.

Trish waited for the standing ovation to end. "I've really enjoyed working with all of you, even though, as Danielle pointed out, it may not have appeared so at times. Some films just are not fun to make. Thanks to Danielle, the production staff, and all of you, this one was fun." Trish paused for a minute looking around the room, then continued, faltering a little. "Thanks to all of you, and to everyone who has helped me grow over the years, I've been offered my first chance at a dramatic role. In two weeks I leave for Russia to play Anna Karenina in the Meecham & Ivor remake of that great book."

Danielle leaped to her feet at the surprise announcement and applauded while the others followed, nodding their surprise at each other and adding another standing ovation.

Trish waved for them to be seated and waited for the room to quiet. "I've worked with some of you almost fulltime for years. Others off and on – so I won't see you for a while. But thank you again, and I look forward to our next film together." She replaced the microphone in its stand and hurried out of the room.

Trish rose early and spent two hours reviewing the Anna Karenina contract and script provided by Rod. The contract seemed standard with the usual clauses in place, and the attached letter from her lawyers confirmed this. She checked the "Nudity" clause and saw they had the right to film frontal nudity. She thought for a moment about the ramifications for a Meecham and Ivor production then crossed it out anyway. The pay was low, as was always the case for any actor wanting to work with Meecham and Ivor. The love of art, the thrill of real creativity, and the dramatic challenge were considered "part of the pay, so to speak."

The script was different from those with which she had worked in the past. It was filled with dramatic prompts and page after page of dialogue. The success of each scene hung on her acting ability rather than an action sequence. The thrill of the opportunity this script offered her was blanketed by insecurity that crept over her as the script unfolded. What have I gotten myself into? she thought. The storyline and script writing so absorbed her, they masked for a time the hurt and sorrow propelling her into this project.

The knock on the door was Leah's. Trish let her in and the two sat on the couch.

Leah pointed to the contract and the script. "So you're really going to do it?"

"Yeah, I guess so. What do you think?"

"I think I don't really understand how 'the other woman' scared you off so easily." Leah started to take out a cigarette before she remembered Trish's no smoking rule.

"You'd have had to be there. She never once mentioned her feelings, what she wants. All she cares about is Chris, what is best for him. How do I fight that? I've known him for two weeks, and she's known him for years. She knows things about him I know nothing about. It came to me in a blinding flash, Chris was an answer to my problems. A way out for *me*. It never entered my mind that I might not be good for *him*." Trish's lips quivered with emotion, but she pursed them tight. "Anyway, this Anna thing is a big step. Are we up for it?"

"You're the one that has to do it. All I can do is hold your hand."

"You mind going to Russia in the dead of winter?" Trish wanted Leah to know that she was needed.

"You buy me a big Russian fur coat to keep me warm?" Leah laughed.

"You got it. And one of those funny-looking fur hats they wear." Trish held her fingers together over her head.

Leah looked concerned. "I've talked to Pher and Gwen about making the trip, and frankly, they have some concerns about going to Russia with Christmas coming on." Leah rose and took her clipboard notes from her purse. "And they have these new boyfriends they like so much. I think they plan on getting something going with them when they get back to California."

Trish looked disappointed. "It won't be as much fun without them, but I'll make sure they know it's okay to beg off on this one."

"I have your plane set up for one-thirty departure. That should have you in New York before six, and a limo will whisk you off to your folks." Leah referred to her notes as she spoke. Glancing up she asked, "You mind if Pher, Gwen and I hitch a ride to the airport with you? We have a flight to L.A. at two."

"Of course not. When do you want to leave?"

"Rod's due here anytime now. Will you be through cuffing him around by twelve-thirty?"

Rod approached Trish's room with great misgiving. Leah had set the meeting at ten o'clock according to Trish's instructions. The grapevine had already told him of Trish's announcement at the party last night concerning Anna Karenina, but the distance between that thought and a signed contract was still lined with pitfalls. He knew he would need all of his skills to navigate these treacherous waters and bring the agreement into port. Anticipating the signing, he had contacted the Meecham and Ivor group that morning to announce that Trish was coming to Russia. His requests for perks in Trish's behalf had effectively stalled them. He knew this version of Anna was to have an "R" rating, and the nudity issue would raise its head, so he laid down the law – no nudity, stating it was a deal breaker. They had agreed, but emphatically demanded, "When will she be here?"

The door opened immediately, and Trish met Rod with a reproachful eye. She motioned him in without a word and gestured toward the other end of the couch. He had the look of a sheep-killing dog. "Look, Trish... "

"Don't 'Look Trish' me." She scowled at him for a time before continuing. "There's something I want you to understand." She spoke in a calm, considered voice. His head bobbed up and down in agreement even before he knew what the proposition was. "You've meddled in my personal life for the last time. If I ever get even a random notion that you are back at your old tricks again, I'll exercise the thirty-day cancellation clause in our contract. Is there any part of what I just said that you do not understand?"

"Trish, I... "

"No!" She held up her hand to silence him. "Don't say something we both know is a lie. It's over, and I don't want to talk about it. I'm trying very hard to forgive you."

He wanted desperately to mention Anna Karenina, but he knew it had to come from her. "So where do you go from here?"

"According to the opinion letter from the lawyers, the Anna Karenina contract is in order. I've looked over it and crossed out the frontal nudity. What are your comments?"

"They've already agreed to canceling the tit clause, and I've picked up a few other little perks you'll enjoy. You have the Presidential Suite at the Marriott Aurora Royal Hotel in Moscow and at the Astoria Hotel in Saint Petersburg. Personal servants will staff both suites, and you will have a full-time limo with chauffeur. I impressed on them the need to be warm, and awaiting you in your suite in Moscow will be a full-length sable coat." Rod was obviously pleased with himself.

"Leah needs a fur coat also."

"I can handle that. It won't be sable, but it'll be warm enough."

"So, where do we go from here?"

"Leah said you're heading to New York, so I thought I'd go up with you, and we can sign the contract in Meecham and Ivor's office there. We might even schedule some interviews, maybe catch a few shows while we're there."

"Cut the crap, Rod. You're not going to New York with me. I'm going to New York to spend time with my folks."

"Fine! I'll have the lawyers FedEx an approved copy of the contract to Meecham & Ivor's office, and I'll meet you there Friday. You can get your marching orders so Leah can get to work on the details."

The Lear Jet lifted from Corpus Christi International Airport Runway 17 and climbed gradually. At five hundred feet, it banked to the left, leaving the traffic pattern. At one thousand feet, the pilot dialed in an autopilot course correction to heading thirty degrees. Trish, the lone passenger, looked out a starboard window. They were approaching the JFK Causeway and the Intracoastal Waterway bridge. She saw Snoopy's and the site of the restaurant demolished by Pyro across the canal. The waterfront houses and condos of North Padre Island grew smaller as the altitude increased. Packery Channel bisected Padre from Mustang Island and marked the boundary of Mustang Island State Park. Further down, Fish Pass Road ran off to the beach, and down the beach was the lone beach house where a part of her now resided. It all was so orderly and understandable from up here. Straight lines and manageable curves. Each item where it should be. Everything visible, believable.

Chapter 30

Chris stopped at the Circle K and inflated the tires on the bike, and then went inside and bought a cup of coffee. The counterman recognized him from the previous morning. "You find Lottie's place?"

"Yeah, I found it, thanks."

"That Lottie's quite a lady, right?"

Chris thought for a moment. "Yes, she certainly is."

The breeze had turned from the south and small cumulus clouds floated past like lumps of divinity candy. Low swells, pushed by the wind, rolled onto the beach. Chris stopped at the end of the Fish Pass Road pavement, dismounted, and rolled his bike through the loose sand onto the hard sand at the water's edge. He stood for a moment looking in both directions. The coast is clear, he thought, and began peddling toward his beach house.

As he approached the dune bridge, a car with Minnesota tags pulled abreast of him and the driver asked in a Norwegian accent if this was Trish Lowe's house. Chris stopped peddling, looked at the driver, and asked, "Who's Trish Lowe?" The driver started to answer, thought better of it, and drove on, rolling up his window.

Chris removed the "No Trespassing" sign from the front door and nailed it at the end of the dune bridge. Cars passed on the beach more frequently than normal for this time of year, but a crowd never formed. Mostly they slowed to a crawl as they passed, uncertain what to do now they were there, and then accelerated down the beach seemingly disappointed by their discovery.

He struggled with restlessness. Doors, ever so slightly pried open by Trish, allowed slivers of light into years of darkness. With the light, a pallor of hope dawned that now dimmed again into emptiness.

He finally grabbed the bottle of Don Sergio and a glass and sat at his desk. Two shots later, he pulled out his notebook and began writing furiously. Crumpled pages piled around the wastebasket as the last of the tequila drained from the bottle. Hours had passed, and the page in front of him still was blank. "Shit!" he shouted to the empty room, leaped up, and walked unsteadily toward the front door.

He wandered the beach with no purpose or concept of time, almost to the state park before he turned back north and trudged home. Thoughts ricocheted through his head, trying to link up into cohesive ideas. Poetry was an emotional release in the past, more like therapy than creative expression. His muses – guilt, anguish, loneliness, despair – occasionally forced pen to paper for a catharsis. This was different. It was compelling – irresistible. He had something to say, and he must get it right.

The early morning, the bike ride, and the long walk had him tired and finally relaxed enough for a nap. He approached the dune bridge thinking only of slipping between the cool sheets in the loft, when a rise in the sand left by the morning's receding tide caught his eye. He had missed it earlier. The sand on all sides of the small mound was troweled smooth by last night's tide, leaving it like a tiny rampart above a broad plane. He went to examine it more closely. Written on the mound were the words:

Never Lose Hope

Television weathermen were fond of calling it the mildest winter on record for the Texas coast. The temperature never dipped below freezing, and, except for a few short stints in the forties, it hung around seventy-five degrees during the day. The water temperature remained warm enough for swimming even in February. The downside of a winter like this for Chris was more beach traffic. Word had spread among beach buffs that good times were to be had, but the interest caused by *The National Investigator* article had died out months before, leaving Chris to his monastic existence.

During those months, Chris maintained a structured life. He salved anxiety, loneliness, or memories with the healing balm of this structure. It produced numbness. He needed numbness. Each morning he rose shortly after sunrise and went for a beach walk and an extended swim. Albert Gaines, the Coast Guard helicopter pilot who flew the early morning beach patrol, circled him to make sure he was not in distress the first few times he saw Chris swimming out in the surf with no one else in sight. The helicopter did a wigwag each day after that, and Chris waggled his arm to send it on its way.

The regular exercise paid dividends physically and mentally. He felt better than at anytime in recent history. His dream still visited at night, but not as regularly. Bouts with depression spaced out over weeks rather than days.

He worked regularly on a collection of poems entitled *"Horizons Passed."* After his swim, he showered, dressed, and prepared a nourishing breakfast including one shot of Don Sergio, "for the spirit." The rest of the morning and usually into the afternoon, he spent at his desk. Writing was different and more difficult than in the past. Previous random expression gave way to structured thought, crafted around ideas. It was slow, and always left uneasiness that saw him scratching in the sand regularly. The partition between meaningful personal investment and simple indulgence in writing was always blurred, and he often strayed over the line. He had asked Jeffrey four times, over as many months, to bring him more writing paper and notebooks.

Wednesday and Sunday were reserved for recreation – fishing , reading, or fishing and reading. Monday and Tuesday were Jeffrey's days off from Park Ranger duties, and he brought Chris' weekly provisions and supplies on one day or the other and often stayed for a visit, much to Chris' approval.

Lottie's visits were not at all structured. Several times a month, she would arrive at night after closing The Backyard, as had been her custom in the past. But she also showed up occasionally on recreation days. They enjoyed either lunch or dinner together, and she often sunbathed while he fished. Theirs was a entente born of need. Lottie hated the limited relationship but was resigned to it. She unwittingly mentioned, on one occasion, Trish's visit to her bar. Chris' hostile reaction and the ensuing estrangement left no doubt in Lottie's mind about Chris' love for Trish.

The rest of the time he worked on his poetry and on his new interest, painting. Several months before, on a particularly bad poetry day, when nothing satisfied his obsession about "horizons," he'd stomped down into the storage room below the house and rummaged around in the closet until he resurrected a paint box and easel. "By God, I'll paint a horizon if I can't describe one." There was one old canvas, left mildewed from age and dampness, that he'd brought when he first arrived at Osborn's. He cleaned it with some of the turpentine that had not evaporated since he'd last tried painting back then. He set up the easel on the deck and opened the paint box. The paint tubes were dry to crusty, and the paints needed to be reconstituted with the turpentine.

Shrimp boats trolled along a horizon that was trimmed in purple-tinged cloudbanks. Flocks of white pelicans skimmed over whitecaps that became translucent as they broke on the beach. Dune oats and brilliant yellow sea daisies cast medium shadows from the mid-afternoon sunlight that bleached the sand to a brilliant white.

He was totally absorbed from the time he sketched the horizon line. The smell of the paints, the feel of the brushes, and the canvas slowly blooming with color and life captivated him.

His first few paintings were rough but gave him a reason to try again. On Jeffrey's next visit, Chris had a list of art supplies for him to purchase in Corpus. Lottie knew her exile was over when he sent word by Jeffrey asking if she would like to pose for a painting. He wanted to paint seascapes with a female figure in them.

Paintings began piling up after four months. Though Lottie had misgivings, she suggested selling some paintings in a art gallery. Chris refused at first, but eventually relented, immediately excluding two seascapes with Lottie posing nude, and finally selected four to exhibit. Lottie offered them to Gary's Gallery in Port Aransas, and he accepted them immediately. When he inquired about the artist who only initialed the paintings "MC," she explained the artist wanted to remain anonymous. "Highly irregular," Gary explained. "Buyers want to know about the artist."

"Then you'll have to make up a story," she replied

In March, Chris gave Jeffrey a large, thick envelope addressed to Melvin Ortz, Ortz Literary Agency in New York. Jeffrey bounced it in his hand. "I brought you about twenty five pounds of paper, and this weighs only a couple. Where's the rest?"

"Somewhere under the sand or in the wastebasket."

In the weeks since completing *"Horizons Passed,"* the loss of purpose sent Chris spiraling again into his lethargy and depression. He saw his book as a plea for redemption, but no redemption came. Instead the void of loss returned as the structure in his life crumbled, and his demons returned. Painting no longer interested him, even though his paintings sold. He drank too much and slept most of the day. Beach walks were purposeless rambles on those sporadic occasions he ventured out. Sleep did not relieve him. The ghostly apparition regularly wrenched him awake, gasping for breath in a claustrophobic panic, sending him fleeing to the beach for respite. Often, hours passed before he could return to the house.

Albert Gaines asked Jeffrey one evening at The Backyard if Chris was all right; he'd not seen him lately on the beach patrol flights.

"Chris is really in the shits." Jeffrey pulled on his beer thoughtfully.

"He's sick?" Albert inquired.

"Not so much physically." Jeffrey answered more to Lottie, who was seated between them, than to Albert. "It's like writing that book of poetry kept him together. Kept his mind occupied. Now he just sits or sleeps."

"It's really bad this time, I know. He's gone past anything I can even understand, much less help him with. He needs to see a doctor, somebody who can do something." Lottie was deeply concerned. She'd helped Chris through several self-destructive periods over the years, but this one was different. It scared her.

Chapter 31

Leah had made flawless arrangements for the trip to Moscow, but the first steps out of the terminal into Russian winter were a harbinger of things to come. People wore their breath frozen into their mustaches and scarves. A howling snowstorm blotted out the sun, leaving only a dim glow in the sky. Leah, making the best of it, said, "Now when do we get these fur coats, boss lady?"

Whether real or imagined, Trish felt Meecham and Ivor lacked confidence in her. Maybe it came from three weeks' delay before she arrived and their ensuing extra week's exposure to the brutal Moscow winter. In her mind it was born of their having to work with a substitute actor, and it produced a hypercritical environment that failed to build her self-assurance.

They were in week four after her arrival, with Leah, in Russia. The first week they rehearsed, did run-throughs, held orientation and dialogue coaching in Moscow, then moved to Saint Petersburg. The train station sequences, including close-ups, were finished in week two. The ballroom scenes together with the introductory scenes of Vronsky, Levin and Kitty also were in the can.

Trish contracted a bad case of bronchitis in week three, much to the consternation of Meecham and Ivor. It threatened to go into pneumonia, so she had spent the week in her suite, with Leah nursing her back to health. A middle-aged doctor, whom Leah immediately nicknamed Zhivago because neither of them could pronounce his name, visited Trish daily taking vital signs, administering medication, and topically treating her sinuses, throat and cough. Toward the end of the week both Meecham and Ivor dropped in to assess her recovery. While there, they decided that Trish's pallor, sinus problems, and occasional cough might lend realism to Anna's birthing and near-death scene. As Ivor put it, "She won't even need makeup."

Meecham looked over the suite and announced that setting up the oversized parlor as a bedroom, they could actually shoot the scene here. Meecham's reputation for being tight with a buck was renowned, so he couched this idea in terms of Trish's well-being. He positively glowed while explaining she would not even have to leave her suite to shoot the scene.

This scene would be her first entry into pure drama, all the previous scenes having some element of action in them. She cast a nervous eye toward Leah when she learned the scene was imminent. Leah gave her a reassuring thumbs up, but was very much concerned about the emotional freefall she perceived in Trish.

Trish had carried as much emotional baggage as Gucci luggage on the flight to Moscow. The hurt and disillusionment of her separation from Chris were unrelenting. She desperately had hoped the time with her parents would bring relief, but each day she saw her mother drift farther from reality. Her dad was his usual pillar of support and propped up her sagging self-esteem as best he could. She basked in his overt and unflinching love. But she knew her mom's condition had worsened to the point of requiring full time care. Trish's short sabbatical was consumed with medical counseling and agonizing over the best arrangements to make for her mom. They finally gave in to the doctor's advice and placed her in a home. That guilt, compounded with her guilt for leaving her parents to make another movie, weighed on her like a mantle of lead that shielded her emotions from the camera.

The obvious lack of confidence in Trish that Meecham and Ivor showed gnawed at the self confidence that she would require to function well. Take after take piled up before Ivor was satisfied with a scene. The almost perennial darkness and mind-numbing cold of the Russian winter bored into her psyche. Add the discomfort of her sickness, and she was beginning to think it all too much.

Meecham and Ivor had partnered with Len Film Productions of Saint Petersburg for technical and production support. Len's set-dressing staff moved around the suite, purposefully renovating the parlor into a grand bedroom. Next came the lighting, sound, and camera crews. In the adjacent bedroom, Trish, Leah, and the dialogue coach rehearsed Trish's lines endlessly. Leah could see the hesitancy and lack of confidence in her recitations at first. But over time she marveled at the transformation that took place. The lines no longer were Anna's. They became Trish's own lament.

The bedside scene with Vronsky, and the scene with Anna's husband, Alexy Alexandrovitch Karenin, were filmed and complete. Ivor had finished framing the camera for the last scene and moved to the bedside where Trish lay looking like death itself. "Remember, you are in a delirium from puerperal fever, from which only one in a hundred recover." He patted her arm and moved behind the camera. "Roll camera."

The clapper-loader held the scene marker in front of the camera and snapped it. "Scene 3, Take 1, Mark!"

"Action!" Ivor gestured toward Trish.

INT: ANNA'S BEDROOM – MEDIUM LIGHT
CAMERA: WIDE – HIGH

ANNA, pale, feverish, hair tousled, sitting upright near the right side of the bed. Bedclothes are in disarray. Vronsky, head in hands, sits in a chair against the wall on the right side of the bed. ALEXY, sobbing, kneels beside the bed with his head on Anna's arm. DOCTOR and MIDWIFE stand on the opposite side of the bed watching Anna intently.

CAMERA: TIGHT ON ANNA AND ALEXY

ANNA
That is he. I knew him! Now, forgive me, everyone, forgive me!

(shivers holding herself)

They've come again; why don't they go away?
(tries to undress herself)
Oh, take these cloaks off me!

DOCTOR
Anna, you must rest.
(Lays Anna back on pillow and pulls up covers)

ANNA
Remember one thing, that I needed nothing but forgiveness,
and I want nothing more... Why doesn't he come?
(looks toward the door then Vronsky)
Do come, do come! Give him your hand.

VRONSKY
(moves to the side of bed. Starts to speak, but seeing Anna's
condition hides his face again)

ANNA
Uncover your face – look at him! He's a saint.
(gestures toward Alexy)
Oh! Uncover your face, do uncover it! Alexy Alaxandrovitch,
Do uncover his face! I want to see him.

ALEXY
(Takes Vronsky's hands and removes them from his face
revealing Vronsky's agony)

ANNA
(Takes Alexy's hand and gives it to Vronsky)
Give him your hand. Forgive him... Thank God, thank
God! Now everything is ready.
(moves her legs under the cover)
Only to stretch my legs a little. There, that's capital.

CAMERA – TIGHT ON ANNA PANNING TO MIDWIFE
AND BACK

ANNA
(squints and points at the violet ribbons on MIDWIFE's cap)
Look! How badly these flowers are done – not a bit like a
violet.
(winces in pain)
My God, my God! When will it end? Give me some morphine!
Doctor, give me some morphine! Oh, my God, my God!*

The room was silent. Ivor looked at Meecham. Meecham
looked at Ivor. "CUT AND PRINT!" Everyone in the room,
including Meecham and Ivor, leaped to their feet cheering.

Leah leaped the highest, "Yes! I knew it!"

Sailboat shopping became one of Rod's favorite pastimes as
the agent's fees from Anna Karenina piled up. He thought he
might give himself a nice Christmas present. Something about
forty-five feet long. A phone call from Leah in Saint Petersburg
came in while he was standing below deck of a Southerly 135,
an impressive sloop moored in Marina del Rey and offered for a
bargain price by a Hollywood notable no longer so notable. He
climbed out of the teakwood and leather cabin to the deck for
better reception on his cell phone.

"Merry Christmas, Leah."

"Merry fucking Christmas to you too, Rod." Leah's irritation
crackled over the phone.

"We don't sound happy today, do we, Leah?"

"We just got word that we are going to shoot straight through
Christmas to get back on schedule. So we get no reprieve from
this miserable goddamn weather over here."

Rod looked around at the cloudless sky and the seagulls
gliding on a warm breeze through the forest of white sailing masts
moored in the harbor. "Yeah, it's pretty miserable here too."

*Dialogue from *Anna Karenina* by Leo Tolstoy, Trans. Constance Garnet New York:
Barnes & Noble Classics, 2003

"Poor Rod. Did the sun go behind a cloud?"

"Anyway, how's our girl?" He tried to sound upbeat.

"She's had a very difficult time over here. But I've got to hand it to her. She's making believers out of the Meecham and Ivor bunch. They treated her like shit at first, but they've really come around."

"I knew she could do it!"

"Listen, I need your help?"

"Your wish is my command."

"Since Trish can't be with her parents for Christmas, I've ordered some presents from Bloomingdale's for them. But I need you to follow up and make sure they get delivered. Can you help us?"

"Consider it done! Actually, I am going to New York for the holidays myself, and I'll deliver them personally." Pride welled in his voice over the idea. He knew it would be a great opportunity to suck up to her parents.

"Really? You'd do that? I take back every mean thing I've ever said about you, Rod."

"Tell Trish I'll give them both a big hug for her." Rod was almost gleeful. "When do you think you guys will be back?"

"We're picking up some weather delays. I hate to think about it, but it looks like another month."

"It's drinks for the house when you get back."

"No, it's hot tub for a month when I get back." Leah chortled.

"Listen, when the trade heard Trish was doing a Meecham and Ivor movie, offers began pouring in for some really good scripts."

"Rod, I'm going to hang up on that happy thought." The line went dead.

Rod hung up and dialed Angie in Corpus Christi. "Hey, girl, Rod here. How have you been... Great! I've been working on some things for you out here... Right. Listen, how would you like to meet me in New York for Christmas? There are some important people you need to meet. Wonderful! I'll make the arrangements and get back to you."

He hung up again, and dialed his office. "I need to make some travel plans."

It was not a triumphant return, but Trish brought home the sure knowledge of having accomplished something far better than she had ever done before. In her exit interview, Meecham and Ivor never apologized for their early shabby treatment of her, but fairly gushed about the quality of her work. "There is the smell of Academy Awards in the air," Ivor had said, actually sniffing the air around him. They paid her the ultimate compliment: they wanted to work with her again.

Meecham, who also had the Academy Award feeling, wanted to make sure Trish was on board for the promotional push and run up to the Awards in February next year. He planned a forced march to complete the post-production by June and distribution by July.

She assured them there would be no new movies while she recovered from the emotional catharsis of making Anna, so there would be time available for the promotion. They agreed to meet with Rod and Leah at their New York offices to plot out the prerelease publicity tour that would build to a crescendo before a World Premier in Moscow the last week of June. The advertising campaign would run up to the U.S. premier in Los Angeles, during the second week of July.

"The early movie release will allow DVD sales for Christmas," Meecham explained. "DVD's will be included in the promotional release to Academy members. We'll follow this with another round of publicity interviews just before Academy voting."

Winter blanketed New York, but compared to Moscow it was like spring. Living with her dad let spring back into Trish's spirit also. A warning from Leah about Rod's movie plans had Trish wary of incoming phone calls. She never returned Rod's calls. She didn't want to address the issue at this time.

Her dad let her sleep late and always had her breakfast ready when she awakened. Twice a week since she had arrived three weeks ago, he had prepared his specialty and her favorite breakfast since childhood, French toast. This morning she was on her fourth slice. "You've still got it, Dad. You've made French toast an art form."

"That kind of talk will get you two more pieces." He laughed as he flipped the two slices on the griddle. "The secret is simple. Use buttermilk and add vanilla and brown sugar. Beat in the egg yolks and fold in the beaten egg whites. Of course using pure maple syrup doesn't hurt either."

"Hurt is the operative word. What we're doing here is hurting my figure." She reached for her fifth slice.

"You looked emaciated when you first got back. Didn't those communists feed you over there?" He served her the last piece.

"Russia's not noted for its food, that's for sure."

"You're looking a little better now. At first I was worried you were sick." He sat down across the table from her.

"Thanks for those encouraging words on my looks." She grinned at him.

"Forget how you look. How are you?" He reached across the table and squeezed her hand.

"Careful there, you might squeeze out some tears." Her eyes glistened.

"That bad?"

"I really don't understand it. It's like an emotional runaway horse that I can't rein in. Tears come real easy these days, and most of the time I don't even know why."

"Is it the 'Mystery Man' down in Texas?"

"There you go with the 'Mystery Man' thing again. His name is Chris, and yes, he's part of it. But there are a lot more issues. I just feel so sad and helpless around mom. Filming Anna Karenina was like going through an emotional wringer. And when I think about the rest of my life, I get terrified. Things are really confusing right now." She patted her eyes with her napkin

"A few more French toast breakfasts like this one, and you'll get through this depression thing." He chuckled.

"You're cheaper than a shrink, that's for sure. And I get breakfast thrown in for good measure." She got up and came around the table to hug him. "Anyway, it's a beautiful day. Let's take mom for a walk."

Chapter 32

May in Port Aransas was the usual three weeks of incessant wind that kept any sane fisherman in port. The southeasterly wind had blown all the clouds somewhere north of Kansas, and the blue sky was so intense, it made eyes water. The palm fronds on The Backyard palapa bar voiced their restlessness in the wind, and the truly hardy barstool sitters' chinstraps were all that held their hats in place.

Wiley Coots had not taken anyone fishing for over three weeks, opting instead to sleep late and to arrive at The Backyard as the clock struck noon. "This is a nice service you've started here, Lottie." He held his beer mug up.

"What's that, Wiley?" Lottie looked up from cutting drink garnishes.

"Normally, a man has to blow the head off his beer his own self."

"Wiley, it makes me feel really good when somebody like yourself appreciates all the little things we do for our customers here." She returned to her citrus slicing and didn't notice Jeffrey walking through the entrance from the parking lot.

"To what do we owe this honor, Jeffrey?" Wiley held his mug up as a toast.

"Hey, Wiley. Hi, Lottie, got a beer left?" Jeffrey slumped onto a bar stool and cradled his head in his hands.

"Jeffrey, you look lower than whale shit." Wiley was exercising his fish guides' extrasensory communication skills.

Lottie brought a beer and set it in front of Jeffrey. "Yeah, Jeffrey, what's up?"

"What we've got here's the makin's of a truly shitty day." Jeffrey raised the beer and took a long pull on it.

"Can't say's I'd argue that." Wiley nodded affirmation.

"I got called in for a FEMA meeting this afternoon on my day off. I figure it'll take me at least three beers to make it through that."

"What do the Federal Emergency boys have up their sleeve?" Wiley glanced at Lottie.

"Something about Hurricane Alvin. They're gettin' all law enforcement, public works, utility, highway department and emergency people together for a planning meeting just in case Alvin visits Mustang Island." Jeffrey drained his beer bottle and held up his finger for another. Lottie rolled the beer in a napkin, popped the top, and brought it to Jeffrey. "And just to make the day more thrillin', a guy brought this to me." He took out a fat envelope from his shirt pocket and handed it to Lottie.

Lottie opened the flap and took out the papers inside. "Jesus, Jeffrey, Connie's filed divorce papers on you."

"Isn't that a bitch?" Jeffrey returned his head back to his hands.

"Jeffrey, I don't want to make light of this, but surely this can't be too big a surprise." Lottie slid the papers into the envelope and handed it back to Jeffrey.

"She's been gone a long time up in San Antonio, that's for sure. The last time I went up there to try to get her to come home, she didn't have much to say to me." He shrugged and pulled on his beer again.

Lottie reached across the bar and patted his hand. "I'm really sorry, Jeffrey, it's a bummer for you, I know."

"Maybe another beer would make it better." A wan smile tickled the corners of his mouth.

Wiley pointed toward the television across the bar. "It's not that I don't enjoy watching As the World Fornicates, but maybe we ought to switch over to The Weather Channel and check out this Alvin fellow."

Tropical Storm Watch came on, and John Kope, the Weather Channel's elderly hurricane expert, wasted no time getting into his Hurricane Alvin spiel. He pointed to the satellite map of the

Gulf of Mexico. "This huge swirling cloud is Hurricane Alvin, located about five hundred miles off the Texas coast. It's just been upgraded from a tropical storm to a Category One Hurricane. Alvin is the earliest hurricane to threaten the Texas Coast since 1871 when two consecutive hurricanes hit Texas, one on June 2nd and the other on June 9th. Record high tides inundated Port Aransas, Texas in those storms."

The satellite map expanded to include the whole Atlantic Ocean between the Caribbean and North Africa. Kope pointed to clouds off the coast of Africa. "Since the El Ninó Effect ceased, these clouds continue building all the way across the Atlantic. This year's exceptionally warm Caribbean water temperature from the mild winter provides the fuel to build these storms into early hurricanes. Alvin is currently stationary, which makes it hard to track, but I predict its landfall to be between Brownsville and Houston, Texas. The longer it hangs out there, the stronger it will be on landfall."

Wiley looked at the other bar bibbers. "Boys, we sure enough got a cloud on our horizon."

"Guess I'd better get over to that meeting." Jeffrey climbed off the bar stool and paid his tab.

"Check back and let me know what they say." Lottie handed Jeffrey his change.

After the meeting at the Convention Center, Jeffrey felt uneasy as he drove back to The Backyard. He was more keenly aware of the houses and buildings that were Port Aransas. You never know what you have until you might lose it, he thought. The little town had not been hurricane tested for over twenty years, but that string of good luck might end soon according to FEMA.

Jeffery parked his Bronco and walked into The Backyard. The regulars were uncommonly interested in the TV and barely acknowledged his return. Lottie had a beer waiting for him when he sat down at the bar.

"So what's the big plan?" She pointed to the TV.

Jeffrey took a long draught on his beer. "Total evacuation. If Alvin heads our direction they want every living thing off this island. People, dogs, cats. If they could, I think they'd round up the coyotes and haul them off. All electricity, gas, and water shut off. Coast Guard and law enforcement patrols against looters until just before landfall, then a pullback to Corpus."

"That total evacuation thing is a good idea," Wiley said, "but they're gonna have a hard time gettin' ol' Fuck-Em-All-Ted off this island."

"Has he ever been off the island?" Lottie posed the question.

Wiley thought for a minute. "I reckon the beard that hangs down below his crotch was just a five-o'clock-shadow the last time he went to the mainland."

"Well, ol' Ted isn't our only problem." Jeffrey looked at Lottie.

Lottie nodded knowingly. "You're right about that."

The conversation and the meeting about Alvin left Jeffrey feeling he should discuss the impending hurricane with Chris. Chris seldom watched television news.

It was more ritual than necessity, but once or twice a month Jeffrey checked general delivery for Chris' mail when he went to the post office. A letter postmarked "Sausalito, CA" was the last mail for Chris, almost a year ago. Jeffrey emptied his own post office box and asked the counter lady to check general delivery for Christopher Maven. There was a hand-written note postmarked "New York, NY."

Driving through town, Jeffery saw no signs of preparation for a hurricane. The twenty-year hiatus had produced a population with little hurricane savvy. About halfway to Fish Pass Road, three men on horseback were just completing the roundup of the Santa Gertrudus cattle that normally grazed in the fields between the highway and the bay. Jeffrey stopped next to the loading pen corral and one of the men loped up to the truck showing no sense of urgency. He told Jeffery that a truck would be there tomorrow to load the cattle and haul them inland just in case the hurricane landed.

The surf, turbid and angry, broke on the beach in three-to-four foot swells driven by the May winds. At the dune bridge, Jeffrey saw what looked like Chris, sitting in the sand farther up the beach. He took a chance and drove up to the lone figure.

Chris sat with his arms around his knees just at the edge of the surf's rollout on the beach. He wore only a pair of blue jean cutoffs. His hair was tousled, and he was damp from the wind-driven spray of the breakers.

Jeffrey leaned out the window. "Hey, pardoner, how about a lift?"

Chris absently looked in Jeffrey's direction smiling. "Actually, I'm pretty busy here."

"I can see that." Jeffrey got out of the car and stood beside Chris. "A fellow can get more than a little damp here."

"I reckon that's true." Chris rose. "Maybe we ought to go inside and have a toddy."

They were seated at the dining table, Jeffrey with a beer and Chris with a scotch, before Jeffrey broached the subject. "We have a problem we may have to deal with in the next few days."

"The hurricane?" Chris looked at Jeffrey as he stirred his scotch with his finger.

"You know about it?"

"I happened to see something about it last night as I was clicking through the channels." Chris took a sip of his drink.

"If it heads this way, we're going to evacuate the island. We have to make plans." Jeffrey was hoping for the right response.

"I was thinking about it out there." Chris motioned toward the beach with his glass. "I guess they don't know where it's headed yet."

"That's true. The son-of-a-bitch just sits out there gettin' meaner by the hour. Why don't I come by here after work tomorrow and let's board this place up? We can load some stuff and move you in with Lottie, just in case the bastard heads this way. You can leave with Lottie if we have to evacuate. I'll have to stay until just before landfall."

"I appreciate it, but that's too much trouble for you guys, especially if it lands in Houston or Mexico. I'll have to commune with the waters some more before I know what to do." Chris had a vacant stare as he looked out at the water.

Chris followed Jeffrey out to the deck after they finished their drinks, and Jeffrey was already walking over the dune bridge when he stopped and returned to Chris. He pulled Chris' letter out of his shirt pocket and handed it to him. "I almost forgot about this."

Chapter 33

Lottie sat in her San Antonio Spurs basketball jersey nightgown, watching The Weather Channel with increasing dread. John Kope had narrowed the projected area of landfall of Alvin to somewhere between Port O'Connor and Port Mansfield. Port Aransas stood dead center.

Kope pointed to the satellite map. "Alvin's moved less than one hundred miles in the last three days. The intensity now is at Category Three, and it possibly could build to Category Four with winds of up to 155 miles-per-hour by landfall. The jet stream is way down here below the Texas Coast," he pointed to the Jet Stream Map – "and it's holding this high-pressure cell that's blocking the path of the hurricane. If the Jet Stream shifts rapidly to the north, we can expect Alvin to move onshore fast."

Lottie changed channels to a local Commercial TV station. It was in the middle of an hourly update on Alvin, and a graphic showed guidelines for hurricane preparedness. They cut away to live coverage of the mob scenes at grocery stores and lumber yards in and around Corpus Christi where people clamored to hoard supplies and materials to protect their homes. Home Depot was selling plywood directly off eighteen-wheelers. The customers hauled it off strapped to the tops of their cars, or any other way they could manage, including some who pushed it away on Home Depot rolling carts. The camera showed grocery shelves stripped clean of bottled water, canned goods, and batteries. The local weathermen warned of unusually high tides from the stationary hurricane's huge impeller-like swirl pushing water toward shore.

Lottie dialed Jeffrey's cell phone. "Jeffrey, I just got the latest Weather Channel update, and I'm getting really nervous. What did Chris say the last time you talked to him?"

Jeffrey's voice crackled over the phone line. "I went out there last night and tried to talk to him. He changed the subject every time I tried to make plans for the hurricane. I swear to God, he talks like he welcomes it."

"That's insane! You've got to move him in here so I can get him off the island." Mild panic elevated her voice.

"I took plywood out there yesterday to close up the house, but he wouldn't let me help him put it up." Jeffrey paused. "I tell you what, I'll go out there this afternoon and kick his butt. Make him agree to come to town. You need help at your place?"

"I'm fine. I had storm shutters installed last year, and my insurance is paid up. I might use a little help closing up the bar."

"You got it!" Lottie's phone went dead.

Chris sat at his desk staring at the unopened envelope. It was plain white and handwritten with no return address. He picked it up and looked closely at the writing. It had the neatness and flair of a woman's hand. He held the envelope to his nose hoping for a clue and finally put it down again. Several times he had started to open it over the past three days with the same result. At his center he felt a need so great – one letter could produce unbearable disappointment. He stood and went out on the deck, looking at the hostile surf as he leaned on the railing. After a time, he pulled himself erect and walked purposefully to the desk. He picked up the letter and opener, sliced neatly through the flap, and removed a single-fold note with "TL" engraved at the top:

> Dear Chris,
> Critics here are raving about *Horizons Passed*.
> Each verse fills me with rapture, and I feel
> warm and content as if I were there by your side.

I want so desperately to explain how things got
confused and out of control. I pray one day I
will have that chance.

I still love you,
Trish

He sank into the desk chair, still holding the note. A flood of
release flowed over him as he lowered his head and wept.

Chris was on the deck nailing plywood over the windows when
Jeffrey's Bronco wound its way along the strip of beach left by
the big surf. "I like what I see," Jeffery said as he walked onto to
the deck. He pointed to the plywood that was already installed.
"Does this mean you're going to town with me?"

"I have to apologize, Jeffrey. I haven't been thinking straight
for some time now. So if I've been an asshole, I'm sorry." He held
out his hand to Jeffrey.

Jeffrey took the hand and pulled him into a hug. "Not to
worry, Pardner. The main thing is to get this plywood up and
get out of Dodge."

"You've got too much to do. I can finish this and get things
packed, and you can pick me up sometime tomorrow morning."

"I don't think that's too smart. When this thing is going to
land is anybody's guess." Jeffrey made a questioning gesture.

"I just saw a weather update, and they're saying it's probably
still two to three more days. Really, I need to get a lot of things
stashed." Chris waved his arm indicating the entire house.

"That's cutting it awfully close." Jeffrey's expression showed
his concern, and he paused before he continued, "all right, I'll
head into town and help Lottie board up The Backyard and come
back in the morning to pick you up."

A steady stream of vehicles, most pulling boats or trailers,
made their way toward the JFK Causeway as he pulled onto the
highway. The lane to Port Aransas was empty. People in town
were boarding up windows at almost every house and building
or hauling household furnishings and appliances to waiting

pickups and trailers. Strangely, few cars were in the Family Center Grocery parking lot. He saw the manager out front taping up windows, and pulled in to inquire. "We've just about sold it all," the manager explained. Farther up Alister Street, Gary was loading paintings into his truck that doubled as a billboard for his art gallery.

Wiley's pickup, with his boat trailered behind, sat in front of The Backyard. The sole occupant of the bar saluted Jeffrey with his beer mug from his usual seat. "Thought I'd have one for old time's sake, before I head off to San Antonio."

"Going to stay with your brother?" Jeffrey asked.

"Yeah, hurricanes are good for gettin' families back together." Wiley's words gave the measure of his sibling relationship.

Lottie finished boxing up the liquor. "I don't suppose you two gentlemen could help a damsel in distress and haul these out to my car." She pointed to a pickup load of liquor cases, a computer, cash register, and other electronic equipment and small appliances.

Lottie's car loaded, Wiley hugged her. "I'm old enough to remember the last one. I'll warn you, things'll look pretty shitty when this all blows over." He turned and went to his truck.

Jeffrey nailed plywood over the office windows and doors. Lottie had already closed the umbrellas and carried them into the rest rooms, and now was stacking tables and chairs under the bandstand to be tied down. It was dark by the time they finished the securing everything. They walked down to the harbor railing and looked at the slips left empty by boats evacuated to safer water. The wind had picked up noticeably. There was activity, some of it frantic, and the unctuous flow of island nightlife had vanished.

"There was no way to get Chris to come to town with you?" Lottie looked anxiously at Jeffrey.

"It's impossible to read Chris, as you know, so it's hard to say. All I know is he finally was talking like he'd leave at all." Jeffrey shrugged. "So I went along with him."

"Maybe I should go get him tomorrow morning." Lottie ran her fingers through her wind-blown hair.

"I barely made it out there today with four-wheel drive. There's no way you'll make it. It'll probably be worse tomorrow."

"You'll go get him first thing in the morning?"

"I have a FEMA meeting in the morning. I'll get him after that. Then you both should take the ferry and head out immediately."

"You're really nice to do all this." Lottie gestured around the bar. She felt something different about Jeffrey. She recalled the years of friendship with Jeffrey and his wife, Connie. Lottie constantly laughed and joked around with Jeffrey, but lately she was seeing a new side to him. "I made a pot of soup just in case of emergency. Why don't you come over and share a simple peasant broth?"

Chris worked into the night. Anything of value in the downstairs storeroom he carried up into the house. He piled furniture and paintings in the center of the living room, emptied the refrigerator and freezer, and tied their doors open. He went outside below the deck and turned off the propane. He copied all his files on the computer onto Zip Disks, and placed the television, sound system, and computer by the front door for hauling. Finally, Chris packed some clothing, money, toiletries, the computer disks, some books and the video of *She* into a Navy Seal waterproof duffel. About midnight he finished and went out on the deck to check conditions. The sky was overcast except for occasional broken patches that let a full moon cast an eerie light over the scene. The intense wind blew straight from the east. Breakers rolled up on the beach but left a passable opening in front of the dunes. He climbed the stairs to the loft and collapsed into bed from exhaustion.

Jeffrey tried to hide from the irritating noise by putting his head under the pillow. A couple of bottles of wine with Lottie had sent him home to crumple into bed and into a catatonic state. The noise was pervasive. He turned on the nightstand light and looked at the clock. "Four o'clock!" He half shouted. "Hello, Goddammit!"

"Jeffrey, it's Rick."

Jeffrey tried to clear his head. "Rick?"

"Rick out at the park. Listen, Jeffrey, we've got a problem."

Jeffrey finally realized it was the Ranger on night duty at the park. "Yeah, Rick, What's up?"

"They just called from FEMA and Alvin is roaring toward us. It's gonna hit before noon." Rick's voice sputtered with excitement.

"Wait a minute! I thought they said a day or two." Jeffrey's voice was incredulous.

"It's all changed. Something about the jet stream moving up to Oklahoma or some goddamn place, leavin' a vacuum that could suck the chrome off a trailer hitch. That son-of- bitch is comin' at us over fifty miles an hour and accelerating."

"Jesus Christ! This can't be happening." Jeffrey leaped up from bed.

"That's not all. It's pushed the tide up on the dunes already and water is pouring through the beach access cuts. They're expecting the highway and causeway to go under water within the hour. They're gonna have to evacuate Port Aransas with the ferries."

"Good God! When are you leaving the park?

"You're my last call, man, and I'm outta here. They want you in town helpin' with the evacuation. They're goin' door to door. Traffic'll be totally messed up with everybody trying to get on the ferries."

"Listen, Rick, can you go down and pick up old Chris for me?" There was a pleading quality in his voice.

"No way, man! I'm telling you, there's two, three feet of water on the beach and it's startin' to backfill behind the dunes."

"Shit!" Jeffrey slammed down the phone, pulled on his uniform, and ran out to his Bronco.

Lottie awoke to the pulsating wail of the Fire Department emergency siren. Before she could get out of bed someone was pounding on her front door. Wearing only the Spurs jersey, she opened the door to Jeffrey. "Jesus, what's happening?."

"You need to get dressed and get over to the ferry. The hurricane's going to hit sometime this morning." Jeffrey stepped inside.

"What do you mean? I thought we had a couple of days." Her face contorted into dread. "What about Chris? Where is he?"

Jeffrey looked at the floor and shuffled his boots as he spoke. "I'm afraid Chris is stranded. The tide came up fast and there's no way to get to him by land. Actually, Highway 361 and JFK are probably closed by now."

She screamed. "What the are you telling me? We can't leave Chris out there!" She pushed past him headed out the door. "I'll go get him myself."

Jeffrey grabbed her and pinned her arms against her body. "LOTTIE! LISTEN TO ME! NOBODY CAN GET OUT THERE!" She struggled to get free. "LOTTIE! IT"S NO USE!"

She went limp in his arms, and he sat her on the couch. "I knew this would happen."

"Nobody knew this would happen. But it has. So get dressed, and I'll drive with you over to the ferry." He pulled her to her feet again. "Buck up, kid, we've got a lot to do. After I get you to the ferry, I'm going to the Coast Guard station and get them to send the helicopter out for Chris. It's all gonna work out fine."

Lottie said, "I can make it to the ferry by myself. You go on to the Coast Guard. Hurry."

He looked at her suspiciously. "Can I trust you? You're not going to try something dumb are you?"

"No. I promise. Just go!" She shoved him out the door.

The Coast Guard Station was pandemonium. Phones rang, radio messages blasted over an intercom, guardsmen hustled back and forth delivering messages and plotting locations on a large map. Several minutes passed before anyone acknowledged Jeffrey. "Sir, can we help you?" It was the small female Coastguardsman who normally worked the afternoon shift. She overcompensated for her size and gender with an abrupt manner.

"I need to report a man stranded on the beach about ten miles south. His name is Christopher Maven, and he lives in that A-frame you can see from the highway out by Fish Pass Road."

"He's stranded you say?"

"Yes. I was going to pick him this morning, but the beach and highway are flooded. You'll have to use the helicopter." He glowered at her as he gestured in Chris' direction.

She pulled out a form. "Give me the name, location, and condition of the man."

"Jesus, we don't have time to play twenty questions here. Just get the helicopter headed that way." Jeffrey made circular movements simulating a helicopter.

"Sir, nothing happens until this report is filed." Her expression was adamant.

When the report was finished, Jeffrey demanded, "Now can the helicopter go get him?"

"I'm afraid not, sir." There was finality in her voice.

"What does that mean?"

"There's no reason to get upset, sir." She frowned. "We currently are working four distress calls. The helicopter is out working a tanker that's foundering in high seas eighty miles out. When it gets back and refuels we have two other distress calls in front of this one."

"God. I can't believe this. Can't they just swing by and get him on the way?"

"I'm afraid not, sir."

"What about sending a cutter with a zodiac boat to pick him up?"

"One cutter is on its way out to the tanker. The other is working a pleasure craft that was being ferried to Port Isabel and developed engine trouble and is shipping water."

"Let me talk to the Duty Officer." Jeffrey demanded. The clock on the wall showed five-thirty and the anemometer registered winds gusting to fifty-five knots.

"Sir, he's quite busy right now."

"LOOK GODDAMN IT! I'M AN OFFICER OF THE LAW AND I WANT TO SEE THE DUTY OFFICER!" Jeffrey's voice roared through the room.

A young man of slight build wearing lieutenants bars was bent over a table reading a map. He stood and frowned at Jeffrey, then strode across the room. "I'm Lieutenant Rogers. Can I help you?"

"I've got a friend stranded on the beach about ten miles south. It's flooded out there and I can't get there by land. This lady is giving all the reasons why you can't pick him up. I need you tell me all the reasons why you can."

"Where exactly is he?"

"He lives in the A-frame just north of Fish Pass Road.

"You mean the 'Mystery Man's' place?" A smile flickered across his face.

"That's it exactly." Jeffrey refrained from adding, "Asshole!"

"We currently have all of our assets committed. Hopefully, the helicopter will be freed up before the storm hits, and we can get him. Call and tell him to put on a life vest, and we will be there as quickly as we can." The lieutenant turned to go.

"He doesn't have a phone."

Lieutenant Rogers stopped and turned. "We'll do the best we can, but I'll warn you, conditions could deteriorate below our flight minimums." He went back to the table.

The sky roiled with black clouds releasing huge drops of rain that splattered over Jeffrey's Bronco at first, then it bucketed down. The wipers barely kept up at top speed. Trash blew down the streets, and twice he swerved to miss garbage cans tumbling across his path. He pulled into Lottie's drive and saw her car was gone. Thank, God, he thought. At least she's headed for safety. He backed out, drove to the police station, and asked what was he needed to do. The Chief of Police told him to patrol the residential streets and knock on doors of those who had not vacated. No one would be allowed to stay. He put on a yellow slicker and returned to his car. Signs and trees swung wildly in the wind. The streets were flooding, and his tires threw up a curl of water as he drove toward the beach. Two blocks from the beach, he saw four people carrying suitcases and wading in water half way to their knees.

He pulled beside them. "Hop in, I'll take you to the ferry." Once inside they explained their car had stalled, so they had struck out on foot. Traffic now jammed the streets and the queue for the ferry snaked through Roberts Point Park then stretched to Alister Street. Jeffrey doubled back to Cutoff Road and drove the left-hand lane with his red lights blinking. He dropped them as close to the ferry landing as he could, and returned to his patrol. It was not even seven a.m. and the wind was so vicious it rocked his car. The rain had flooded the streets curb deep, and as he turned onto Alister Street he slammed on the brakes to avoid being hit by two Jet Skis skimming over the water. The riders had sports bags strapped to the Jet Skis. They roared down the left lane past the ferry cue. A police car turned from a side street into their lane forcing a James Bond maneuver of jumping the corner curb and catapulting into the side street where the two roared off in the direction of the ferry, much to the chagrin of the cop.

Jeffrey knew every ferry was pressed into service, and they did not load return passengers. They plied the quarter mile roundtrip across the channel at full throttle. Policemen positioned along the route kept the evacuees calm while urging them to keep moving. They directed side street traffic into the ferry line at intervals. The process was orderly enough to raise hope the evacuation might succeed.

The police, sheriff, constable, and state law enforcement cars patrolling the streets started on the beach and south sides of town, and in cattle-herding fashion worked their way toward the ferry, rousting out those mistakenly thinking they were "going to ride it out." These hard cases became more cooperative as the morning progressed and the wind velocity, rain, and flooding increased. Jeffrey had just put a family of four into their car after offering to cite them for recklessly endangering their children, when his cell phone rang.

"Where are you, Lottie?"

"I just got off the ferry. What about Chris?" Lottie's voice was garbled with static.

"The Coast Guard will send out a helicopter as soon as they can." There wasn't much conviction in Jeffrey's voice.

"Jeffrey, what are you telling me? You telling me they may not get out there?" Lottie sounded panicked.

"Lottie, settle down. Anything that can be done is being done. We just have to keep the faith."

"When will you know if they have him?"

"I'm going over there when we finish the evacuation. I'll call you."

"God, this is horrible." She screamed.

Chapter 34

Conditions worsened by the minute as Jeffrey drove the streets, and radio chatter told of winds gusting to eighty knots. Alvin was coming of age on Mustang Island. Rain came in torrents dancing across streets horizontally like windblown holograms. The sky continued darkening until streetlights popped on, adding ghostlike features to the relentless downpour. Headlights ignited the rain-dimpled surfaces into a fireworks display. Loud reports from advertising signs and tree trunks cracking and crashing to the ground occasionally reverberated above the howling wind. Sheets of corrugated steel roofing, stationary for years, tore free of their bonds and danced over parking lots and plunged into the flooded streets, only to reemerge, driven end over end by the current and wind. The island's electricity still functioned, and downed power lines sparked and whipped in the wind like fire-spitting snakes.

The evacuee-drive was complete and about fifty of the last holdouts were herded into the ferry line. All but three of the ferries had been sent to the Corpus Christi harbor. Two of the remaining ferries loaded the last vehicles, and the third waited for the emergency vehicles still on the Island. Jeffrey pulled up next to an officer directing traffic. "I have time to run an errand before the last ferry?"

"You got about ten minutes. Ferry's gonna blow three long blasts on its horn five minutes before departure."

"Don't leave without me!" Jeffrey moved down Cotter Street toward the Coast Guard Station. Axle deep water made going slow even for the Bronco. Though valiant, the windshield wipers were not up to the task, and visibility was less than half a block. Movement caught Jeffrey's eye as he approached Alister Street. At first he thought it was trash blowing, but looking closer he saw a man wearing garbage sacks for raingear sneaking around the corner of Trout Street Restaurant. "Jesus Christ, it's Fuck-Em-All-Ted!" Jeffrey hit his red lights and siren, but Fuck-Em-All broke into to a run, splashing across Trout Street toward Shorty's. Jeffrey turned toward Shorty's, but the water was too high to get through. He backed up and onto Cotter, and just as he righted the Bronco onto Cotter he saw Ted splash through his headlights and disappear through the Tarpon Inn parking lot heading toward White Avenue. Driving as fast as he dared, Jeffrey turned right onto Station Street and circled the block trying to cut the vagrant off on White Avenue, but he was nowhere to be seen. Jeffrey cruised slowly down White Avenue looking for his hiding place. Just as he approached Beulah's parking lot, someone broke out from behind a huge oleander bush, splashing down White Avenue toward Alister. Jeffrey stopped the Bronco, leaped out, pulled his gun and fired a shot into the air. "FUCK-EM-ALL, IF YOU DON'T STOP RUNNING I'LL SHOOT YOU. SWEAR TO GOD I WILL!"

Ted slid to a stop holding his hands in the air as his garbage sacks quaked and his three-foot beard stood straight out in the wind.

Three long blasts sounded on the ferry horn. "SHIT, TED, DON'T YOU MOVE AN INCH!" Jeffrey waded down and handcuffed him, and led him back to the Bronco. The loaders waved wildly to Jeffrey to load his vehicle when he got to the ferry. Jeffrey released the handcuffs from Ted once they were safely on board. "Ted, you might of gotten us both killed."

Ted looked straight ahead and, as expected, growled, "Fuck 'em all."

Jeffrey got out of the Bronco and stood in the rain, watching Port Aransas recede as the ferry got under way. The vessel immediately began bucking wildly as the waves crashed over the bow, and water flooded the deck, causing Jeffrey to lose his footing. He climbed back into the front seat and tried calling the Coast Guard Station, but could not get through. He tried the emergency radio. "This is Ranger Jeffrey. Does anybody out there know the phone number of the Coast Guard at the Naval Air Station?"

There was a pause before a voice crackled over the radio. "Hey, Jeffrey, I've got it here somewhere. Hang on. Here it is -- 555-961-2070. Got it?"

"Thanks, got it!" Jeffrey had trouble dialing the number on his cell phone as the ferry pitched and plunged on its crossing. "This is Park Ranger Jeffrey, let me speak with operations. Yes, sir, this is the State Park Rangers. We reported a Christopher Maven stranded on the beach at Fish Pass Road. Can you tell me if you've picked him up?"

The voice returned after a minute. "No, Sir, I don't have any record of it here."

"Good God! You haven't picked him up? I can't believe this!" Jeffrey pounded his head on the steering wheel.

A muffled "Fuck 'em all!" came from Jeffrey's passenger.

"Sir, the chopper just returned to base about fifteen minutes ago, and the Captain has suspended all operations until conditions improve."

"Is Lieutenant Albert Gaines, there?" Jeffrey's hands shook so from excitement and chill he could hardly hold the cell phone.

"Just a minute, sir."

Several minutes passed before there was any response. "Lieutenant Gaines, here."

"Jesus, am I glad to get you, Albert. This is Jeffrey."

"Hey, Jeffrey, is it a bitch out there or, what?"

"Listen, Albert, about five-thirty this morning I reported to the Port A station that Chris was stranded on the beach. I'm trying to find out if you picked him up." Jeffrey held his breath.

"God, you're kidding me. Ol' Chris was still on the beach when this thing came in?"

"You haven't picked him up?"

"I worked offshore distress calls all morning. I just got back to refuel. Visibility is almost nil in this rain, and the wind is gusting to eighty-five knots, so Captain's suspended ops until conditions improve. We just hangered the chopper."

"Is there anything you guys can do? When the storm surge hits, it'll blow Chris into the next county."

"It's not far over there, let me talk to Captain and try to get permission."

"Hurry!"

Albert burst into the Captain's office. "Captain, there's a man stranded on Mustang Island beach. We need to go get him."

"Whoa, Lieutenant, what's all this about?" The Captain got up from his desk.

"This old guy that lives on the beach by himself got stranded before they could get to him by land. The Park Rangers reported it this morning, but we never got there."

"I'm afraid it's impossible now, Lieutenant. Conditions are just too risky."

"We could be over here and back in twenty minutes, sir."

"Then we might consider it when the hurricane eye passes, but not before."

Albert Gaines stepped back two paces and hit a brace. "Permission to fly a rescue mission, sir."

Captain remained seated. "Have you ever flown eighty-five knot winds, Lieutenant?"

"No, sir!" Albert still held his brace.

"Well you're not going to start on my watch, and that's final." The Captain's voice left little doubt.

Still in his brace, Albert replied, "Permission to attempt a rescue mission, sir!"

"Dismissed, Lieutenant!" The Captain returned to the papers on his desk.

Chapter 35

The VW bus drifted slowly down – down – settling toward the bottom. A face approached dimly into view through the rear window. Hair hovered and floated about her head. Her eyes showed no panic, only stared questioningly at him. She mouthed a soundless word. The lips moved in exaggerated slow motion as the word formed again. Chris sat upright in bed sucking in a deep breath and held it, tying to clear away the apparition. Gradually he exhaled as things came into focus again. It was dark, and he knew the electricity was off. The house rocked on its pilings as the wind howled and buffeted it. Rain pelted the roof. Shit! I slept too long, he thought; Jeffrey should have picked me up by now.

Still wearing the blue jeans and a T-shirt from last night, he took the flashlight from his nightstand and made his way down into the living room. He couldn't see out the boarded windows. When he turned the knob, the front door exploded open, catapulting him back against the couch. Lying there stunned, he saw a pale greenish glow to the watery landscape outside the door. Wind and rain blasted through the opening while he struggled to close the door. He could see waves crashing on the dunes and water filling in behind them. A panic shuddered through him. I'm totally screwed, he thought. "I'm totally fucked."

He was unable to reach the apex window on the back of the house when he boarded up, so he climbed to the loft again and stood in a chair looking out it now. Rain clouded visibility, but he could make out the highway enough to see there was no traffic. Water threatened to overtop it. Sitting on the bottom stair, he rubbed his head trying to think what he should do. The situation must have changed so fast that Jeffrey was unable to get there. Jeffrey would be working on Plan B, whatever Plan B was. Maybe he'd contacted the Coast Guard. Where was the cavalry when he really need them? He knew this was not the main storm. The weathermen had warned of a possible thirty-foot storm surge. That meant the worst was yet to come.

Maybe he could make it to the highway and walk into town before the surge hits, he thought. Using the flashlight, he looked through the pile of tools and equipment he had brought up from the storeroom below and found the sledgehammer and chain saw. He stuck the flashlight in his pocket, grabbed the sledge and chainsaw in one hand and the waterproof duffel in the other, and inched his way to the front door in the dark. Standing to the side, he turned the doorknob and was almost dragged down when the door exploded open before he could free his hand. He struggled through the door, carrying the bag and equipment. The door was impossible to close, and the plywood sheet left for boarding it up had blown away. He crawled to the stair leading down to the storage room, and threw the hammer and bag down the steps. With the chainsaw in one hand, and his other arm wrapped around the railing, he inched down the stairs as the wind ripped and tore at him. Rain stung his face like wasps.

Once inside the storage room, he turned on the flashlight and made his way to the back wall. Rising water was already ankle deep. He put the chainsaw and sledge on the workbench. The flashlight passed over the johnboat, *Deliverance*, as he inspected it. She sat on the two support horses about two feet above the rising water. He waded around the boat, placed the oars into the oarlocks, and tied a thirty-foot length of rope to the waterproof bag and threw both into the boat. Returning to the workbench, he laid the flashlight down, grabbed the chainsaw, and pulled the starter cord. Nothing. Choking it, he tried it again. Still nothing. Working the throttle trigger and choke again, he cranked it one more time. "Come on, baby, I need a little break here," he whispered. He choked it again and pulled the cord. The saw roared into life.

Water was about mid-calf now and he sloshed to the rear of the room, carrying the saw and the flashlight. He balanced the light on the boat, shining it where he wanted to work. About a foot above his head he punched the saw through the back wall and sawed a ragged gash horizontally almost the width of the room across the studs and siding. Then he tried to cut vertically at the one end of his horizontal cut but the saw was very difficult to hold in this position. After several attempts, he finished the cut and sloshed to the other side of the room. Again he tried a vertical cut with very little more success. Halfway down the makeshift door opening he was cutting, the saw blade jammed, kicked back, and he lost his grasp it. It hung for a second in the siding then slid out, landing in the water. "Shit! You son-of-a bitch." He knew the saw would not start again.

He backed away from the wall as far as he could and sloshed through the knee-deep water and slammed into the partially cut-out section, but it budged only slightly. Backing up, he tried again. It still stood stubbornly in place He grabbed the sledgehammer and swung at the base of the siding, but it only splashed under the water without reaching the wall.

Deliverance sill rested on its supports with the stern about three feet from the back wall. With his back to the boat's transom he rested his weight on his elbows and hopped with all his strength, doubling his legs as he swung them up and gave a mighty kick, landing both feet on the siding. The makeshift opening nudged forward slightly, but the force of the kick sent *Deliverance* rocking forward on its supports and the boat fell, plunging Chris and the flashlight underwater. He came up sputtering, trying to regain his balance in the darkness. The only light now came in through the partial cutout. *Deliverance* was afloat in the waist deep water, and he clung to her as he felt his way to the bow.

"It's time to see what you're made of," he said to the boat as he pulled it as far forward in the room as possible. With every bit of strength left he lunged forward, shoving *Deliverance* toward its possible escape. The mass of the boat hit the cutout section, and the siding yielded with an audible groan to the greater force.

He backed the boat up again and slammed it into the wall, this time continuing to shove with his full strength as the boat's keel ground over the dislodged wall.

The force of the wind surging around the house created a suction and *Deliverance* began accelerating as it came free from the submerged lumber. The wind caught the high johnboat bow, and it spun around. Chris momentarily lost his balance and fell to his knees as the boat yanked itself from his grasp and began pulling away from him. He pushed himself up again and ran up the submerged wall, using it as a springboard trying to catch *Deliverance*. Half stumbling, half swimming, he leaped out as far as he could and got a hand on the boat's stern. The wind and the rain howled and pelted him as he tried to pull himself into the boat. *Deliverance* came to rest momentarily against an Australian pepperbush, and, using it as a crude ladder, Chris swung himself into the boat.

He sat facing the stern, took the oars, and began pulling away from the house, aided by the wind that beat on him incessantly. The water was deep enough to float the boat, but protected by the dunes, it was too shallow for big waves. His oars caught often in the brush that now was underwater, but still he made good progress. Rainwater was several inches deep in the boat, and he realized he had nothing with which to bail. He could not see if the road was totally under water.

Nearing the highway, the sound of the wind changed. Great rushing wind was replaced by a high-pitched swishing/swooshing sound coming from the beach. He stopped rowing, trying to understand the strange noise. He looked past the stern of boat at his house and the dunes, while turning his head from side to side, listening. Finally, he covered his ears as the sound now was painfully loud. His eyes, squinting into the rain, opened in full amazement as he saw a greenish-black monster appear over the dunes as far as he could see in both directions. It came with alarming speed and grew until it towered over the dune house.

The swishing gave way to a roaring crescendo, a monstrous slapping explosion as the surge wave hit the dunes. It erupted into a mountain of white spray and began curling at the top like a giant breaker. The dune house buckled like the knees of a boxer hit with a championship solar plexus punch. It shuddered for a moment, then shouted an agonized groan, trying to right itself. The roof exploded off, and the whole house rocked backward, sighing, and regurgitated itself into the wave. The wave was unrelenting. He recovered from the shock and pulled hard on the starboard oar working desperately to bring the bow around into the wind and onrushing wave. He turned facing the bow and tied the end of the duffle rope to his ankle. "All right you evil bastard! Bring it on!" he screamed

In an instant, the boat catapulted upward. The bow reared, and he lurched forward crashing headfirst into the bow gunnels and slumped unconscious to the deck of the boat with blood streaming down his face. The boat continued its race up the face of the wave. At its crest, the wave's breaking curl flipped *Deliverance* into the air like a matchstick, sending boat, oars, duffel bag and Chris to the points of the compass. He splashed into the water and sank as the storm surge sucked him down. Then the underwater forces loosed their hold on him, and blood traced dark, unintelligible messages around his head as he floated weightless under water.

"Marvin..."

Such a soothing voice, he thought. "My name is... Chris."

"Marvin, wake up."

"Who... who is it?"

"It's Lesa, Marvin... Open your eyes."

"Lesa?... My Lesa?"

"Yes, Marvin."

Lesa smiled at him as he opened his eyes He held out his hand trying to touch the hair floating around her face.

"Lesa... Oh, Lesa, how much I've missed you... "

"I know, Marvin... but now it's time to move on."

"I love you so much, Lesa."

"No one could ever love me as you have, Marvin. But there are things you must do."

"Lesa, can you ever forgive me?"

Lesa's face smiled and began drifting away.

"Wait, don't go. I've waited so long."

"I must go now. There is nothing to forgive, Marvin. It wasn't your fault."

Chapter 36

While Jeffrey was working with the crew assigned to rebuild the RV facilities at Mustang Island State Park after the floodwater had receded, his cell phone rang and Caller I.D. showed "Trish Lowe."

"Hey, Miss Lowe, it's been a while." He was excited by her call.

"Jeffrey, thank God, you're okay. I've been on the promotional tour for Anna Karenina, and, with all the traveling and appearances, I wasn't keeping up with the news. I just heard about the hurricane yesterday."

"It's a mess down here, that's for sure." Knowing she was calling about Chris made Jeffrey uneasy.

"How... Where is Chris?"

Jeffrey didn't know how to answer. "I'm afraid there's a problem."

"What do you mean, Jeffrey?""

"Chris is missing." Jeffrey blurted it out.

"God, no!" Trish's voice broke, and Jeffrey could tell she was crying. "I heard that everyone was evacuated."

"I tried for days to get Chris to move into town and stay with Lottie, but he just wasn't interested. Then, the day before the hurricane hit, he changed completely and started boarding up the beach house. I was going to pick him up the morning Alvin hit, but the beach was flooded, and I couldn't get to him. I tried to get the Coast Guard to him, but apparently they never made it." Jeffrey paused and made shrugged futilely. "The beach house is gone."

He knew Trish was trying to respond. All he heard were gasps of shock and sobs. He added, "Listen, Trish, we haven't given up. We're checking area hospitals, the Red Cross shelters, police reports every day hoping to find him. There are a lot of displaced people all over in Corpus Christi."

Hope for Chris soared shortly after Trish's call when a picture ran on the front page of the Corpus Christi Times showing a johnboat resting in the top of a tree in Corpus Christi Ocean Drive Park. The caption referred to the boat as *Deliverance*. Jeffrey contacted the Corpus Christi Parks and Recreation Department and claimed the boat in the name of its owner. Hope faded as time trudged along with no word about Chris.

Chris's body was not found after three weeks of being listed as "missing." Finally, Christopher Maven was listed as "presumed dead." Jeffrey told Trish of the change in Chris's status during a subsequent phone call, and she became irreconcilably distraught. That finality cast a pall of gloom over them as they worked through the loss of Chris and the guilt they felt.

Jeffrey was returning from Corpus Christi with a pickup load of lumber and other materials for rebuilding The Backyard. He took a side tour around Port Aransas to see what had happened since the hurricane a month before. He knew, from all the old timers that Port Aransas was the most persistent of all the small coast towns. Other villages had simply disappeared after hurricanes, but this eclectic collection of vacation homes turned residence for contemporary squatters on the tip of Mustang Island was so potent it always rose immediately from the muddy tide and debris of successive hurricanes like a finned phoenix. The faithful always returned to rebuild. Everyone knew that nothing was produced in Port Aransas, nothing grown, and nothing caught in commercial quantity. Amazingly, Port A seemed to thrive solely on the joy of living.

Jeffrey could see history repeating itself. A minor miracle had transpired in the four weeks since Hurricane Alvin. The streets were cleared of debris and mud, and utilities were restored. Damaged homes and buildings were stripped of unusable materials or were totally demolished. Rebuilding was underway on many structures. He could see the fires at the city dump billowing smoke signals to the area as Alvin's wreckage was reduced to ash. His neighbors around town were beginning to return their sun-dried household contents, that for weeks made the town look like a giant yard sale, back inside.

Because of the style of construction, The Backyard had been totally demolished; but for the same reason, it was easily rebuilt. That process was proceeding nicely with insurance covering the cost. Jeffrey helped on his days off and in the afternoons after his shift ended.

About six weeks after Alvin, Jeffrey stopped at the post office on his way to help Lottie. He emptied his mailbox and was leaving when the counter clerk hailed him. "Jeffrey, your friend, Christopher Maven, has a package."

He was startled to hear Chris' name spoken. "Right... Yeah, I'll take it for him."

The clerk handed him a smallish package wrapped in brown paper with a handwritten address. "It's sent certified mail, so you'll have to sign for it."

After signing the return receipt, Jeffrey went to his Bronco and sat looking at the package. Finally, he opened it to find a handwritten note enclosed with a red leather-bound book. The book had a traditionally ribbed spine, gold leaf-edged pages, and gold leaf lettering on the cover: *Horizons Passed* by Christopher Maven. Jeffrey opened the note.

> Dear Mr. Maven:
> My father was very fond of telling about the
> mysterious major poet whom he had
> represented for many years, but whom he had never
> seen, and with whom he had never spoken.
> I asked the publisher to traditionally bind the plate
> proofs of *Horizons Passed* in classical fashion for

your library copy and your pleasure. I hope
one day to have the honor of meeting you.

Melvin Ortz Jr.
Melvin Ortz Literary Agency

Jeffrey sat so long holding the book that the clerk, who could see him through the post office front door, came out to ask if he was all right. Jeffrey nodded his affirmation, and started the Bronco. He drove to the liquor store where he bought a bottle of cold champagne, some ice, a plastic ice bucket, and a package of plastic cups. He stopped by Family Center Grocery, bought a beach blanket, flowers, and drove to The Backyard.

Lottie's hair was covered with a bandana, and she wore a cap with its bill backwards. Her face was spotted with paint from the brush she was wielding. Jeffrey stood for a minute admiring her. "I think it's time we launched that wild, passionate love affair we've talked about for so long."

Lottie turned around smiling. "You've talked about so long."

Jeffrey took the paintbrush from her hand and closed the paint bucket. "You've worked enough for today." He took her hand and started for the entrance.

"Whoa, wait a minute! What are you up to?" She couldn't help laughing.

"We have something important to do." Jeffrey's arm swung behind her legs, and he scooped her up and walked out the entrance.

Chapter 37: Marin County, 1999

District Attorney Sid Blevins often thought back to his days with D. A. Romney Anderson, a person who had seriously misjudged the power of "flowers." Anderson's zeal to rid the whole Marin peninsula of hippies and quash Flower Power permanently in a bid for reelection in 1966 was general knowledge. His plan was flawed by the fact that hippies voted. Not only voted, but marched in the streets with placards beseeching other voters to "RID US OF ROMNEY!" Flower Power had morphed nationally into a fledgling political activism, militating against the Vietnam War and anything else that could provide a plausibly good reason for a drug-laced demonstration or sit-in. The ridding of Romney was not a daunting task for them.

The year 1966 ushered in the laissez faire era of Eugene Krantz as Marin County District Attorney. He was sworn in at age twenty-nine, wearing an open collared shirt and bell-bottom trousers, the youngest District Attorney in California history. Krantz moved gracefully through three-plus terms of office while hippies changed to yuppies, molting their tie-dye in favor of Brooks Brothers suits. Along with this came a national awareness of drugs followed by a War on Drugs, which finally snared Krantz himself on a charge of possession of marijuana. Apparently Eugene had never lost his fondness for smoking an occasional "fat one."

Sid Blevins still smiled when he thought of how he had persevered in the trenches as Assistant DA, and how he was elevated to District Attorney in 1985 after the conviction of Krantz. He had flourished in the job, even though some thought he lacked the killer instincts of a true prosecutor. Others knew, much to his discredit in their eyes, that D.A. Blevins always sought justice rather than a conviction.

On July 7, 2000, Blevins sat at his desk reviewing correspondence when his administrative assistant announced, "There's a man named Marvin Christofferson here to see you."

"What about?" Blevins didn't look up

"He didn't say. He just said it's important," she replied.

"Let's hope so. I have plenty to do without Mr. Christofferson."

"Marvin Christofferson." She emphasized the name over her shoulder.

A tall gray-haired man about 60, tanned and fit, wearing blue jeans and a T-shirt was ushered into the office and stood by the clients' chairs.

"What can I do for you, Mr. Christofferson?" Blevins didn't rise to meet the visitor.

"I'm wanted for the murder of Lesa Tolivar." Marvin shuffled his feet as he made the pronouncement.

"In that case, Mr. Christofferson, you'd better sit down." Blevins motioned to the chairs while trying to look as little surprised as possible. "When exactly did this murder take place?"

"It was an accident, actually, but it happened in 1965." Marvin looked directly into the D.A.'s eyes as he spoke.

"Can you fill me in on some of the details? I'm having... "

"A VW bus went over a cliff on the Marin Headland Road with my fiancée, Lesa Tolivar, in it. She was killed." Marvin spoke matter-of-factly.

"Wait a minute. I remember something about that. You were a pretty famous painter in Sausalito when it happened." Blevins looked proud of himself. He punched the intercom button. "Will you get 'Records' to pull up a cold case dating from 1965 on an indictment of Marvin Christofferson for the murder of Lesa Tolivar, and I think... her unborn child?" Blevins looked at Marvin, who nodded agreement. "Now, Marvin, can I call you Marvin? What do you want to tell me?"

"What do you want to hear?" Marvin shifted uncomfortably as he spoke.

"Everything." Blevins learned forward. "Actually, Marvin, I'd like to record your statement, if you don't mind." Marvin nodded agreement. "It will take a few minutes to get set- up, so would you mind waiting in Mary's office?" Blevins punched the intercom again. "While you're at it, please get 'Records' to bring up a camcorder to record a statement, oh, and offer Mr. Christofferson something to drink while he waits."

The camcorder and lights were set up, and Marvin returned to his chair. The preliminaries of establishing Marvin's identity that he was testifying voluntarily, that he did not want a lawyer, and that his statement could be used against him in a court of law were complete. Blevins said, "Okay, Marvin, just tell us in your own words what happened on that day in 1965."

Marvin squirmed in his seat and fumbled uncomfortably with the mike in front him: First, I want to say that this was the most desolate day of my life and still causes me unbearable grief even today. That day began as a grand adventure with much excitement. We loaded Lesa's Volkswagen van for a trip up the Marin Headlands to paint the pines with San Francisco and the Golden Gate Bridge as a background. This was to begin a new era for my painting...

Chris recalled everything with an awful clarity. In the 1960's, the ease of access through Fort Baker to the scenic grandeur of the Marin Headlands guarding the entrance to San Francisco Bay was known only to a few of Sausalito's overripe Beatniks, mostly in the art community. They had convinced Marvin that the Headlands view of San Francisco, framed by the Golden Gate Bridge, was a landscape painter's dream.

A stand of tall pine trees was rumored to be perched on the cliffs overlooking the Pacific Ocean, high above Fort Baker, an army base that supplied the men and the armament of the day to the current installations. As legend had it, the army had planted the grove decades before and made it into a picnic area with thick grass watered nine months a year from barrels hauled up the

Headlands road, which was chiseled from the cliffs overlooking the ocean.

This possible change of painting subject overpowered Marvin. He borrowed a fellow artist's bolt cutter, packed up Lesa's VW bus, and the two lovers headed for an adventure.

"My ears are popping," Lesa said as the VW ground its way up the hill.

Marvin only nodded. Rounding the first outside curve of the narrow graveled road, Lesa shouted. "Great God, we're gonna die!" A shear cliff plummeted hundreds of feet to the Pacific Ocean.

"Easy, girl, we're not the first to do this. Just relax and enjoy the view," Marvin said, but his jaw jutted more at each switchback while Lesa disappeared further into her seat.

Finally Lesa shouted in earnest, "Let's go back before we kill ourselves!"

"Go back? How the hell can we turn around on this road? We're almost there... I think."

"Let me know when we're having fun." She added, "This doesn't bother you?"

A long pause followed before he answered, "I'll admit it. My butt's so puckered you couldn't drive a hatpin in it with a sledgehammer. If you can just hang on a few minutes, I think we'll make it."

The road turned inland for about a quarter mile just before cresting a small knoll, and they saw the pines in an acre of grass, as promised. San Francisco, Golden Gate Bridge, and the pines were perfect for ushering in a new Christofferson period of inspiration.

Blowing a joint settled their nerves a little. The second shared roach set them talking again. Laughing, actually. Laughing and leaping insanely. They danced jigs, rolled in the grass, and churned in circles until they collapsed, exhausted, on the grass beside the picnic basket.

The basket held some bits of cheese and crackers and three bottles of wine. Burgundy sloshed over their chins, spiraling rivulets down their necks, dripping and disappearing into the turf as they lay on their backs swigging from the bottle.

"Did your life flash before your eyes on that cliff?" he asked.

"No, but I almost wet myself."

Marvin outlined her breasts with his finger, and shivers rippled over her skin. They fondled and caressed each other like two people taking inventory. Lesa slid the straps of her shift from her shoulders, and it shed like water from her skin. They thrashed away as if The End was nigh, from the moment they joined until they lay on their backs gasping for breath. When Lesa's breath slowed, she asked, "Well?"

"Well, my dear, I think we blasted through the land of love like it was a cemetery and moved into the maelstrom of deep sex from which only the brave, the true, and the strong ever return."

"Yeah, it was good for me, too." The sun-warmed breeze soothed them, and they drifted to sleep in each other's arms.

The chill of the fog bank spilling over the Headlands woke them. The sun's last glow faded, and fog rang down the curtain on San Francisco.

Marvin crept down the Headlands road, knuckles white on the steering wheel of the Volkswagen van. Fog plugged the entrance to San Francisco Bay, curtaining off the entire world outside the twenty-foot dimness of their one functioning headlight. He and the VW bus were mechanized rock climbers suffocating in opaqueness, feeling their way along this cliff-side trail with no guardrails for protection.

The bus inched forward. Rocks, loosed from under the right front wheel tumbled down the cliff. Lesa moaned. The evil smell of burning brake shoes pervaded the bus. Marvin glanced at Lesa's pained expression and brimming eyes, and he stopped the van, setting the parking brake.

"Why are you stopping?" she asked

"It's hard enough to concentrate without your moaning and whimpering."

Climbing over the seat he moved all his art equipment to one side of the mattress in the back of van. "Hop over and take a nap, we'll be home when you wake," he said, offering his hand. She crawled onto the empty half of the mattress.

"Here, take this. It'll help you rest," he said. She swallowed the Quaalude offered from their stash bag with the dregs from an empty wine bottle.

They hugged; he wadded his coat, laid her head on the makeshift pillow, kissed her lightly on each eye, and said, "Sleep tight."

The fog finally blindfolded the windshield. He stopped, shouting, "Jesus H. Christ! Give me a break!" No break responded in the fog. He set the hand brake, left the engine running, got out of the bus, and looked for a rock to chock a wheel. The smell of the overheated brake shoes hung in the fog. Finding no chock, he felt his way down the bar ditch and around a curve into total darkness.

Something tangled his feet and sent him to his hands and knees. "Shit!" He felt around and found the offending stick. It was long enough to use as a cane, so he stood and tapped his way along the road trying to get his bearings.

He moved faster, scouting the general layout of the road ahead of the bus, and then a sound resembling a seal's bark froze him. The grinding noise that followed was unmistakable. The pitch was rising, and he knew the heat-glazed brakes on the VW van were slipping.

Spinning, he ran, stumbling back up the road. Rounding the last turn he saw the bus's headlight through the fog. Running faster he tripped and fell sprawling again. The bus gained speed. Scrambling up, he ran to the bus and slammed into the grill like a football linebacker. The impact slowed the bus, but his shoes slipped in the gravel inching him toward the cliff. "Lesa! Wake up! Goddammit, Lesa, get out of the van!"

His feet slid from under him, and the front tire grazed him as the bus ground past, brakes howling. He lunged and missed the door handle, and barely rolled away fast enough to save his arm from the back wheel. "LESA! WAKEUPGETOUTATHEBUS! IT'S GOING OVER THE CLIFF!" He grabbed the rear bumper and pulled himself up then dug in his heels trying to slow the runaway vehicle. Furrows plowed into the gravel, and still the bus edged closer toward the cliff.

The right front wheel cleared the cliff and the bus bucked, dropped to its frame, and slowed almost to a stop. The jostling woke Lesa, who sat up and saw Marvin screaming at her through the backdoor windows. She reached for the door handle just as the left front wheel bumped off the cliff, and the back of the bus flipped up throwing Marvin back on the road. Then, as if tilted by an unseen hand, the bus pitched forward and Marvin's last memory of Lesa was her horrified face plastered against the back door window as the bus disappeared, groaning and grinding into nothingness. The silence was dreamlike, but the crash of the bus hitting the water and rocks below was real. The shock and horror frozen on Marvin's face lasted through the night. The MP patrol that found him the next morning, logged "... comatose..." into their notebook, and lifted him into their jeep.

I couldn't face returning to my old life, so I asked a friend to look after my art gallery, and I left town with no particular destination. I wanted only to get away. I read about the criminal charge in a Phoenix newspaper several days later. I was suicidal and couldn't handle the mental anguish of a criminal trial.

I didn't fear the punishment. I feared a trial in some way might exonerate the burden of guilt I felt for allowing Lesa and our child to die. The pain I've felt every day since then is far greater than any sentence or punishment by a trial.

For more than twenty years I drifted around working on my sober days as a house painter. During the good times I would scrounge up some paints and canvas and paint Lesa from memory. My only contact with my former life was with Randy Quartz, who for years was the manager of the Trident Restaurant and later managed my art gallery.

Randy told me of a friend on the Texas Coast who was dying of AIDS, and had no one to see him through his final months. I've lived there since that time.

The room was completely silent for a time. "Were you there during the recent hurricane?" D.A. Blevins asked.

"I got washed away along with my beach house."

"How did you survive?"

"I tried to escape in a boat, but it capsized. I had my things in a Navy Seal bag tied to my leg, and it acted as a buoy and rode the storm waves across Corpus Christi Bay. I hit shore near IH 37 and hitchhiked to San Antonio where I took a bus here to see you."

Blevins said, "Just incredible." He sat for a time staring blankly at Marvin. "The news coverage was amazed that only one person was missing. Was that you?"

"They must think by now that I'm dead." Chris's brow furrowed as he thought of Lottie and Jeffrey and how they must feel over his death.

Blevins could see Chris' discomfort at the thought of his "death." "Is there someone we should notify?"

"I had only two friends who would care." Chris rubbed his forehead thinking of the right thing to do. "I really think they will be better off with things left the way they are."

Blevins nodded as if he comprehended. "Are you staying locally?"

"I spent last night in a motel down the street."

"It will take me some time to get up to speed on this case. I wonder if you'd come back tomorrow about three o'clock?" Blevins stood as he spoke.

"Don't I have to go to jail?" Marvin looked bewildered. "You're not locking me up?"

"Should we?"

Marvin rose to leave, then turned. "Thank you... I appreciate it."

Late that afternoon, Blevins' assistant brought in the case file to him and he looked at the tracking sheet. "God, this case is so cold he could have moved next door to the police station and not gotten caught."

He spent the afternoon and early evening reviewing the file. Most of the time was spent going over his ancient notes to the file about discussions with Romney Anderson regarding prosecuting the case. Blevins had been convinced the charge was unfounded back then. He turned off the desk lamp and sat in the dark for a time before going home.

Marvin arrived promptly at three but still sat silently in the anteroom almost an hour later. Blevins' assistant had acknowledged him, but was totally absorbed in gathering documents and running them in and out of District Attorney Blevins' office. Men in suits came and went carrying sheaves of paper into and out of the DA's office while he waited. A growing uneasiness built inside him. He could sense things were not right. He considered the consequences of his coming here the day before. Of telling his story and having it recorded by the DA. The thought of long term imprisonment or worse loosed a panic in him. This was going terribly wrong, he thought. He rose and went to the door and looked both directions in the hall, then back at the DA's closed office door. He turned and walked out.

"Mr. Christofferson!" The assistant followed him down the hall, and her voice had an edge of urgency. "Mr. Christofferson,

I'm sorry for the delay. There was so much paperwork, but Mr. Blevins will see you now." He stopped for a moment, and she caught up with him. "Please, Mr Christofferson, come back to Mr. Blevins' office." She walked to him and touched him lightly on the elbow, and Marvin moved toward her with uncertainty.

Blevins motioned for him to be seated and stared at Marvin for a time before speaking. "Why did you come in and tell your story after all these years? We both know you could have lived out your life without us ever knowing anything about you."

Marvin moved forward in his chair. "I finally came to terms with myself over Lesa's death. I had to have a new life. I had to do this to completely erase my past."

"It was a very brave thing to do, considering all you could lose." Marvin shifted in his chair but didn't respond. Blevins continued. "I spent a very long night reviewing your case, trying to reconstruct all the events and to get an understanding of motives. Frankly, I didn't get to sleep until very early this morning." He rocked his overstuffed executive chair forward and placed his hands on the desk. "Marvin, I decided the people of the State of California have done you a grave injustice. Charges should never have been filed against you. I am dropping the charges against you, and I personally will see that it is taken off your record."

"What are you telling me?" Marvin looked astounded.

"I'm saying you can go. You're a free man." Blevins smiled broadly as he spoke.

"I can leave? No charges? No trial?" Marvin had a dazed expression

"That's right. What do you plan to do now, Marvin?" Blevins seemed genuinely interested.

Marvin thought for a moment. "I recently had a chance at a different life." He continued as if thinking aloud. "So different it couldn't have worked."

"Maybe it's still worth a try." Blevins asked

"I don't know... I just don't know." Marvin's eyes glistened with emotion.

"Well, good luck at whatever life you choose." A smiling Blevins rose, shook his hand, and called his assistant to escort Marvin out.

Marvin stepped through the front door of the Marin Civic Center and down the steps to the sidewalk. The panorama stretched across the valley bisected by Highway 101. Cars rushed heedlessly in both directions, oblivious to anything but their own destinations. He looked to the left, then to the right, and then stared into the distance trying to decide which direction to take.

Chapter 38

The dim hope of one day rejoining Chris was gone. That thread had, for the months since leaving Corpus Christi and Mustang Island, sustained Trish. Often she had uncontrollable urges to call Jeffrey. To hear something – anything – about Chris would have sent her soaring again, but in the end she could never bring herself to call. The risk of breaking that thread was too great. Only after accidentally finding Chris' new book, on display in Barnes & Noble and reading it, did she get the nerve to write him a note.

For weeks, she'd been on the merry-go-round of pre-release publicity for *Anna Karenina*. Talk shows, press interviews, trade paper interviews, and Internet appearances paraded end-to-end. The whole marathon had to be repeated in Russia because of the Moscow World Premier.

Leah, during a phone call about the impending trip to Moscow, had asked her if she knew about the hurricane in Texas. Trish was unable to speak while she rushed to turn on TV. Fox News was showing live coverage of the devastation in Port Aransas. She had told Leah that she had to call Jeffrey immediately. Then for three weeks she'd called Jeffrey daily, each time hoping to hear the right thing. The weeks dragged by painfully as she realized the horrors the hurricane must have visited on Chris. Personal appearances became serious acting engagements. She cancelled two appearances and secluded herself in a Miami hotel when Jeffrey gave her the news of Chris being "presumed dead."

The room phone rang eight times before she lifted it from its cradle. "Hey, Pumpkin, it's me."

"Hi, Dad."

"Leah tells me you've had some really bad news."

"Yeah... " She was having difficulty forming words. "Yeah... I guess Chris is gone."

Her dad didn't answer immediately. Finally, he spoke softly, "It's rough losing someone special. Someone you really care about. I live with it every day, watching your mom drift away." Her dad's voice carried the immutable weight of Gibraltar. "I grieve for your sadness, Pumpkin."

"It's difficult to understand. Out of everybody, why Chris?" Her voice was barely audible.

"I wish I could tell you, Pumpkin."

"The hard... the terrible thing... it's the selfish thing that's hard to deal with. Being able to separate grief for Chris from grief over my disappointment at knowing that someone who could change my life no longer exists."

"You still exist. That's the important thing. It's okay to feel disappointment over losing your dream and the pain of losing a loved one. There is nothing I wouldn't do to get your mom back, but it's not going to happen. All I can do is try to build back a little each day, hoping someday there will be happiness and hope again."

"It's really hard starting over again this soon. I really loved him, Dad."

"That's why I called. I wanted to make sure you remember who you are. You're that little girl who never gave up on anything. There's no way you will ever forget your love for Chris, but you have to get on with building another life. So get your chin off your chest and get out there and make good decisions."

The Moscow World premier of Anna Karenina was surprisingly tolerable, even uplifting for Trish. She knew Russians were not fabled for their hospitality, but the pre-publicity events, parties, and the premier itself all had an air of cordiality. Most Russian film critics and social commentators felt the Yankees finally got Anna right, after so many attempts in the past. Others still believed that non-Russians lacked the emotional capacity to delve deeply enough into the complicated Russian psyche to portray characters living between the pages of the Motherland's revered authors. They felt only a lifetime of Russian winters could grind away the sensibilities to sufficiently expose the dramatic nerve endings.

Hubris infected the Meecham and Ivor people and the actors attending the premier. They all knew they had a winner, and Academy Awards speculation punctuated every conversation. Trish was not a household name in Russia because most of her past films lacked the budget to warrant Russian language sound tracks, which made her performance in Anna all the more astonishing to the Russians.

The intense media hype in Moscow attracted politicians who came to bask in the visibility of the event. Even Russia's Premier attended the grand after-party.

Trish spent a few days with her dad on the return trip and then flew to Los Angeles to prepare for the Hollywood premier. Leah had preceded her to L.A., and rode in the limo to pick her up at the airport. They drove directly to her Malibu beach house. Once at the house, while the caretakers unloaded the luggage, Trish and Leah settled down with drinks for a visit.

Leah brought out a stack of newspaper film critic reviews from her briefcase. "Here's some light reading for your enjoyment."

"I like the sound of 'enjoyment.'" Trish picked up the top one and scanned it.

"The critics are all amazed by your performance. They love the film, and most say you should be working on your acceptance speech for an Oscar." Trish could hear Leah's pride.

"I should be the happiest girl in the world, right?" She took a sip of her tequila.

"You're on a career track only a handful of people could even dream about. Unfortunately, that just doesn't get it done where happiness is concerned." Leah's eyes betrayed her personal experience.

Trish got up and walked to the windows, absently looking out over the beach. "Truthfully, the good things that happen fade so quickly without someone to share the joy with."

"Speaking of someone to share it with, I have a list of available Hollywood hunks to escort you to the premier on Friday." Leah took some papers from her briefcase. "You can give the tabloids something to gossip about."

"Do I have to pay them?" The first smile Leah had seen in weeks flickered across Trish's face.

"Boy, what a headline that would be, 'Hollywood Love Goddess Pays Male Companions'." Both laughed aloud.

"Actually, Leah, my dear, how about being my date? It's time for you to hit the red carpet. You can save me from some ego-maniac mugging the cameras for the publicity."

Leah blushed slightly. "That's a nice offer, Trish, but I really don't have a thing to wear."

"Tomorrow we'll hit Rodeo Drive and get you decked out. Phermona and Gwen will make us beautiful on Friday and we'll knock 'em dead."

Leah let out a girlish giggle. "Will they think we're gay?" The house phone rang.

"Who the hell would think I'm here? Who even has this number for that matter?" Trish looked at Leah. Leah looked at Trish.

Together they said in unison, "Rod!"

Caller ID confirmed it when Leah picked up the phone. "You have reached the Leah Armour Agency. We manage the stars. Unless you are reporting your demise, then please call back sometime after your departure." Trish laughed aloud.

"Very frigging funny, Leah." Rod's voice had the irascible tenor of someone chafing from months of neglect. "Let me talk to Trish."

"I would, Rod, but she doesn't want to talk to you."

"Dammit, Leah, she's been ignoring me for months. I've got dozens of projects lined up for her. Great stuff. The kind of parts other actors only dream about. I could book her into the next century." Rod almost screamed into the phone.

"That's what she's afraid of, Rod." Leah was all business now. "I can't speak for her, but in my opinion, she'll do only a picture every year or two from now on."

"That's not how the business works, Leah, and both you and Trish know it. You gotta grab it while you're hot, cause when you're not, you're not." Rod sounded like he was reading scripture.

"I think one day Trish will forgive you, Rod. But here is some friendly advice: don't bother her at the premier."

"What the hell does that mean?"

"That means, FUCK OFF, Rod. Don't call her. She'll call you!" Leah hung up.

Over-blown Hollywood premiers had become a little passé through the years, so Meecham and Ivor's people had originally scheduled the Anna Karenina Premier in a smaller venue, but the prerelease publicity had paid off and ticket sales outstripped the theater. Word was out around town that this was going to be the biggest event since the premier of *Gone With the Wind* and requests started to pour in from Hollywood royalty for Red Carpet arrival times, theater tickets, and invitations to the after-party. Finally, the premier was shifted to the Kodak Theater, home of the Academy Awards. The 3,400-seat venue was sold out and The Entertainment Channel booked over ninety-minutes of live Red Carpet arrivals to be televised nationally.

Searchlights blazed into the twilight of the Los Angeles smog, and paparazzi flashes and TV flood lights transformed darkness into daylight as the limos paraded past one by one, spilling their glittering cargo out onto the red carpet. Fans in the grandstands cheered themselves hoarse as the very famous waved regally and glided into the theater.

The EC announcer chortled, "And here she is, Miss Trish Lowe, and her escort . . aah, and a friend. Trish Lowe, star of Anna Karenina."

Trish and Leah waved a Queen Elizabeth style salutation and moved to the microphone where the host said, "A big night, Trish, everybody's expecting really good things from this film."

"We hope everyone enjoys it." Trish offered a big Hollywood smile and wave.

"Rumor had it we might see your new guy tonight." The announcer looked a little peevish over the substitute.

Leah leaned into the mike. "Actually you are. I just like to wear drag."

The announcer laughed an uncertain laugh and added, "Well, it should be a grand night for you, Trish." She started to phrase her next question, but Trish and Leah moved away waving to the crowd.

The audience gave a standing ovation during the curtain call after the screening. Meecham and Ivor took their kudos smiling, laughing, and slapping everyone on the back. Then a chant trickled through the audience building in a crescendo. "Trish! Trish! Trish!"

Finally, Ivor escorted Trish to the microphone and gave an understated introduction, which she did not need: "Here she is, Ms. Trish Lowe."

Trish stood for a moment listening to the chant as it broke out again. "Thank you. Thank you, very much." She tried to quell the applause, and waited until it died down. "You make me feel very welcome. I appreciate it more than you can ever know." The chant and applause turned to murmurs. "I want to thank Meecham and Ivor for their faith in me on this picture." She looked at the floor and shuffled nervously, then looked directly at the audience. "You know, some people seem unrealistically fortunate. It's as if things just fall into place for them... by chance or by good luck. But it's not by chance at all. Each person's good fortune is built with blocks chiseled and placed by other people helping them. By people who love us, and some who don't, but all doing the necessary things that, together, add up to our good fortune. I am one of those unrealistically blessed people. All of you I've worked with on previous films, and the others over the years who helped me grow have added to my good fortune. And because of all your help, I was given this opportunity. I've had a great personal loss in my life recently, and feeling your warmth and acceptance at this time is truly wonderful. Thank you very much."

The press people scribbled furiously in their notebooks, sensing a continuing story in Trish's "personal loss." While the audience stood applauding, the press scurried out of the hall vying for an interview with Trish.

"You were really a good sport to go with me tonight." Trish squeezed Leah's hand as the limo smoothed through Malibu. "I'm sorry about being a party pooper. I just couldn't face all those people at the after party."

"The night was a smashing success for you. You should be very proud of your accomplishment. I know I'm proud for you." Leah patted the back of Trish's hand. "Have I ever told you how wonderful it is working with someone like you? Someone I can love as a friend?"

"Now don't get all soggy on me. You know I get emotional easily these days."

The limo pulled into the driveway, and the two got out. They hugged each other, and Leah asked, "You sure you don't want me to come in and keep you company? I hate for you to be alone on such a special night."

"No, I'll be fine. I just want to collapse and spend a little time with myself. I'll talk to you tomorrow." They hugged again and Leah got back in the limo and waved as it backed down the drive.

Once in her bedroom, Trish took off her evening gown and put on the oversized sweater she'd never returned to Chris, her bedraggled security robe, and a pair of pink fuzzy bunny-slippers that were traditionally part of her Malibu homecoming ritual. She spent some time at her vanity removing her makeup and combing out her hair, then padded in her slippers to the bar and opened a bottle of wine, took the wine glass, and went out on the deck overlooking the beach. She settled on her favorite lounge chair. There were no lights. A full moon danced over the surf, and gave the beach an ethereal glow. Palm fronds rustled like dune oats, and the surf sighed as it rolled out on the beach. She untied the robe, opening it, and the scent of Chris wafted over her from his sweater. So few nights with Chris, she thought. Nights with salt-laden breezes, quietly heaving surf, wrapped in love's ageless embrace as close as surf to sand, cloaked in his warmth. Now a life of regret and memories.

When the wine bottle was almost empty, she set her glass on the table. Gathering Chris' sweater in both hands, she brought it to her nose, and felt his presence again. She drew her security robe around her and drifted off to sleep.

The shadows crept steadily back onto the deck as the sun claimed the morning sky. The ocean was calm, and brilliant sparks splashed from its few ripples. Insects buzzed in the quiet air, and a fly circled the wine glass, considering a liquid brunch. Instead, it established a beachhead on Trish's nose. She swatted it in her sleep and woke herself. Rising to her elbow, she tried to reconstruct her condition. The wine glass and bottle rekindled her memory of the previous night. Sitting on the edge of the chaise, she stretched and straightened her robe. She grinned down at her bunny slippers and wiggled her toes, flopping their ears. Using the chaise arms, she pushed herself up and stood for a moment before walking to the deck railing. The ocean, the sky, the beach – all were pristine. She held the railing and leaned back to look for anything of interest overhead. When she rocked forward she saw something in the sand below the railing. Some kind of writing. Adrenalin set her heart pounding, and she vaulted over the railing, burying her bunnies' ears, deep in the sand on impact. She dropped to her knees, almost suffocated with joy as she read:

Horizons past were filled with dread
That barrier bisecting earth and sky
That stifled all escape.
Then you appeared and filled the void
With touch, and smile, and sacred scent,
And with your eyes you cast a light
And woke my soul
To dream
To love
To Soar
Beyond horizons past.

Acknowledgements

Some of the most enjoyable times of my life were spent in Port Aransas and with its wonderful denizens. But this story is not about any of my Island experiences and is the product of my imagination.

The members of Daedalus Writers Group: Cindy Leal-Massey, Ned Bailey, Linda Schuler, Florence Weinberg, Diana Lopez and Jim Peyton, all accomplished authors, waded through chapter after chapter, applying the polish to *Horizons Past*. I'm fortunate to have friends willing to invest this much in helping me.

My long time friend John Mills, author, artist, and founder of Franklin Scribes Publishers, contributed immeasurably with support, graphic design, and book design. To these and many others who helped along the way I offer my deepest appreciation.

Appreciation

A big hug of appreciation to you for purchasing *Horizons Past*. If you enjoyed the book, you might check out *Vámonos!* and *Woke Up This Morning*. Both are in Kindle and Trade Paperback format, available through all major internet booksellers.

Even more love to you if you write a Customer Review on Amazon or Barnes & Noble. Sharing *Horizons Past* on your Facebook page and on Twitter really helps also. While you're at it, check out www.facebook.com/authorbillstephens, and I really enjoy hearing from readers by email at   stephens.billy @ att.net, so shout out.

9 780988 643352